The Allotment
Lyn Behan

Behan Publishing

Contents

Who's who

Bill Thompson – recently widowed after nearly fifty years of marriage

Brenda Evans – thirty-four, lives with her cantankerous mother

Neil Blakey – forties, ex- army, suffering from PTSD after deployment in Afghanistan

Anna Bridges – Neil's sister and Bill's cleaning lady

Colin Barnes – Brenda's boyfriend

Amanda Harris – the warden at the allotment – single, fifties, recently made redundant

Mary Flynn – young widow. Husband, Peter, had an allotment

Carol Patterson – forties, divorced. Took an allotment to help her Down Syndrome son, **Douglas**, thirteen, going on fourteen

Donald Jenkins – new to allotments, retired naval officer

Daniel Burrows and his daughter, **Jayne**

Clare – Douglas's girlfriend

Angus - Douglas's father

Paddy Murphy – a sad old man

Chapter One
January

The Allotment - I don't go back as far as Anglo-Saxon times - this land was originally part of Sherwood Forest, but I was here during the time of strip farming. We British allotments have been in existence for hundreds of years when peasants had a communal strip of land on which they could grow food and, after the harvest, let their animals, pigs, geese and so on graze on it. The strips were rotated so that each one could rest every third year.

People understood the land in those days, were part of it, and knew that we needed a rest, same as everyone. Not like today with their intensive monocultures, chemical fertilisers and pesticides. Yes, I was one of the lucky ones when I was established as an allotment. I'll tell you more about allotments later, as one of my favourite allotmenteers has just arrived ... I don't know what he intends to do because it's January and cold and miserable, but his wife died recently and he seems to take comfort in just being here ...

***

Bill parked in the small reserved area and groaned as he eased himself out of his car - this cold, damp weather made his joints ache. He grasped the old leather bag containing his lunch and packets of seeds from the passenger seat and made his way to his plot. He studied the other gardens as he went, making mental notes of what they were growing. He frowned at the plot next to his. Poor old Arthur. He'd had a stroke and his plot had become very neglected. Usually, other allotmenteers chipped in and helped when someone was sick, but somehow what with Christmas and the bad weather, Arthur's plot had missed out.

He opened the padlock to his shed, where the damp earthy smell cheered him. Bit silly coming today, he thought, drizzly and cold and too wet to do anything, but it got him out of the house. He felt a fullness in his bladder. *Bugger this benign prostate hyperwhatever the doctor called it!* He went to the bucket he kept for this purpose in his shed ... urine was good for citrus. He had a miniature lime tree on his plot which thrived on his contributions. He smiled as he relieved himself. Hazel had appreciated the limes anyway. His smiled faded.

'What do you think, Hazel?' He addressed the framed photograph hanging on the wall of his shed. He imagined he saw her smiling back at him. She was always smiling. He wished he could join her. Life wasn't worth living without her ... his eyes travelled to the moon planting calendar pinned up next to the photograph.

Have to order a new one. Usually, he did it in November or December, but somehow he hadn't got around to it. He pulled a crumpled handkerchief from his pocket – Hazel used to iron them – he didn't bother – and tied a knot in it to remind him.

He sat on the makeshift bench and gazed out the door. The drizzle was getting heavier. Forecast was for sub-zero temperatures overnight. Not much he could do today. He sighed and took the flask of soup from his satchel.

Checking his watch, he decided he'd have his lunch and go home although it was no pleasure going home to a cold, empty house. When Hazel had been alive home was always bright and welcoming, with the smell of something cooking. He wondered what to have for dinner. Maybe stop at the shop and buy one of those frozen meals. He poured his soup into a mug and sat, slowly sipping it.

***

The Allotment - Poor Bill. I know he misses his wife. I rarely saw her. She only came on odd occasions, like the Winter Solstice in December when all the allotmenteers had a bit of a party. Hazel made mince pies and everyone loved them. Her own special recipe apparently, with lots of alcohol and dried fruit. But not last year. I saw grumpy old Paddy Murphy who never talks to anyone, shake Bill's hand and say "sorry for your troubles" just before Christmas, so I think she must have passed over around that time. She used to collect left-over vegetable scraps from her neighbours for Bill's compost heap. I love his compost, it's the best of all the allotmenteers.

It's getting dark and he's locking up now. Won't be anyone else coming today. Might snow tomorrow … that would be nice, I like being covered with a warm blanket of snow.

***

Brenda shivered as she came out of the house, sorry now that she hadn't parked her car in the garage the night before, but she'd been too tired after finishing her shift.

The row of terraced houses where she lived backed onto an access lane which led to the garages at the rear of each house. On the other side of the lane were the garages from the next street of terraces.

The thought of driving down the access lane, stopping the car, getting out, opening the garage doors, driving in, closing the doors and walking up the garden path to the back door had daunted her. She'd been too exhausted.

She scraped ice off the windscreen with her gloved hand and managed to get the key, which she'd warmed before she left the house, inro the driver's door lock. It would take ages for the car windscreen heater to release the frozen wipers, and there was shopping to do and her mother's lunch to cook before her shift started. She couldn't stop thinking about Colin and what had happened. Anger built up in her as she returned to the house for a kettle of warm water to pour over the windscreen. Yet another late shift at the store ahead of her. Her angry breath a white mist.

***

Bill spread the packets of seeds on the kitchen table and scratched his head. 'Not much I can plant at the moment,' he muttered, 'end of January, maybe just do a bit of digging if it's not too wet. But forecast is for freezing conditions.' He looked up at the photo on the dresser. 'Only broad beans, Hazel,' he muttered. 'One of your favourites. I'll head up to the allotment later, see if I can do anything. It passes the time.' He sighed. 'Mrs Bridges is coming this morning. I'd better tidy up a bit.' He blinked away threatening tears.

The rattle of the letter box and the sound of mail plopping onto the door mat brought him out of his reverie. Hope there were no more letters of condolence and sympathy cards, he thought, as he went to the front door. People meant well, but it was two months since the funeral and there had been so many cards and letters. His beautiful Hazel had been so popular. But he hated the constant reminders.

Good, only a circular from one of Hazel's charities and his Royal Horticultural Society Garden magazine. He opened the front door and bent to pick up the bottle of milk. *Bloody gate left open again!* He didn't know if it was the postman or the milkman. He started towards the gate, but in his haste, slipped on a patch of ice and fell heavily, still holding the circular and the bottle of milk. He lay there for a while then lowered his left arm to rest the milk on the ground. His right arm was under his body but he managed to bring it free - it hurt like the devil - then everything went blurry and dark.

'Bill! What happened?' A voice came through a fog. He tried to focus. It was Mrs Bridges, the lady who came to clean when Hazel fell sick and then had stayed on with him.

Vaguely he faced her. 'I think I must have slipped,' he managed to say.

Mrs Bridges took the bottle of milk still clasped in his hand. 'You're frozen with the cold. I don't know if I should help you up or wait for an ambulance.' Her voice seemed to come from a distance.

'Don't need no ambulance. Just slipped,' Bill managed to say. 'You can help me up.'

'We'll see.'

He drifted off again. The next thing he knew he was being lifted onto a stretcher. 'I'm all right,' he said irritably.

'It's okay, Bill, we'll soon have you sorted.'

Bill closed his eyes and mumbled something about not to worry Hazel.

'Don't fret, Bill, I'll look after everything ...'

It sounded like Mrs Bridges ... what was it she kept telling him to call her? Anna? Annabel? He was too tired to think...

***

Neil crawled out from under the kitchen table. They'd been eating dinner when some idiot had let off a fire cracker right outside the front door. He'd dived under the table, to the annoyance of his brother-in-law.

'For Christ's sake, Neil, you've been out of the army for months now. I reckon you're just putting on this PTSD act.' Tom pushed back his chair, managing to shove Neil in the back with his feet as he did so.

Did people really think I'm putting on an act? Neil wondered if the firecracker had been deliberately lit by one of Tom's mates. There was no love lost between him and Tom.

He went up to his bedroom – actually one of his nephews' bedrooms – and lay on the bed until his shaking subsided. The horror that was Afghanistan – supposed to be a peace keeping mission – Hah! The bad dreams ... seeing his mates blown to pieces. He couldn't go on like this, his excessive drinking, not sleeping and knowing he was causing dissention between his sister and her husband, but the thought of trying to find a place of his own was too daunting. Best to end it all. He'd been over various scenarios in the past. Overdose was the way to go. He'd get more sleeping pills from his doctor ... take the lot with a bottle of whiskey. Wouldn't be nice for Anna to find him ... but better than the alternatives. No, he'd go to a motel. Do it there. He focused on his watch – nine o'clock. He saw the date. Shit, it was Anna's birthday. Shit, shit, shit! Better get up and go to the store. And it looked like Tom had forgotten her birthday as well.

***

Brenda – Nine-thirty. Another half hour before her shift ended and she could close. She looked around the convenience store attached to the petrol station. The shelves would need restocking again in the morning. She hadn't had time; it had been such a busy day.

She sighed. Balancing the till would take a while; there had been more cash takings than usual. Outside she could see one person filling their car with petrol, then the shop door slammed. She raised her head to see one of her regulars – "Twenty Benson" she'd nicknamed him - rush in. She was surprised; he'd been in earlier for cigarettes.

'Sister's birthday – forgot,' he gasped. 'Flowers?'

'Down the back.' Brenda pointed. 'Birthday cards too.' She watched him as he disappeared behind the grocery section. *Strange person, never smiles, but good looking ...*

The door pinged. The petrol customer came in, paid and left.

Twenty-five minutes and I can close and make up the till.

She saw a small car pull up outside – not at the petrol pumps - right outside the door. *Probably someone who'd run out of milk.* She checked her watch again, then looked up to be confronted by a man wearing a black balaclava, and waving a gun in her face. 'Hand over the money or I'll shoot!'

She let out a scream, then blinked and raised her hands, her heart thumping.

'Put yer hands down, hand over the money and all the cigarettes!' She saw his hands shaking as he pushed a large shopping bag through the gap in the perspex window. 'And shut yer mouth!'

Brenda's mouth opened and closed, then she was filled with indignation. 'Don't be ridiculous, that's just a toy gun!' She lowered her hands. Before she could utter another word, a bunch of flowers flew into the air and a shadow launched at the gun man.

There was a loud crack, a thud and a shot rang out. Brenda gulped and her hands flew to her face. 'Oh, my god!' she muttered and leaned over the counter to see the gun-man sprawled on the ground with Twenty Benson on top of him. Twenty Benson rolled away, stared at the body, groaned and curled up on the floor.

She ran around the counter, then her head jerked up at the sound of a car speeding away. Glancing down she saw a trickle of blood coming through the gun-man's sweater. 'Oh, my god,' Brenda said again. She tried to remember her first aid, but could recall nothing about gunshot wounds. She found the fallen man's wrist and felt for a pulse. Nothing. Bile rose in her throat. *What to do? Police!* Twenty Benson lay, his knees up to his chest, protecting his head with his hands.

She hurried back behind the counter; her fingers trembling as she dialled the emergency number.

'Gun man, dead,' she said in reply to the operator. She gave the address details and hardly had time to return from behind the counter when she heard the sirens.

She touched Twenty Benson on the shoulder. 'Get up, the police are coming. You saved my life.'

He was unresponsive, making no effort to stand.

She put out her hand, 'Please get up!'

He ignored her. Brenda didn't know what to do. She went to the door of the store and was about to turn the "Open" sign to "Closed" when a police car drew up outside.

Brenda opened the door. 'In here.' She stood back.

A policewoman nodded at Brenda. 'Highway Patrol. We were just around the corner when we got the call. Did you ring emergency?'

Brenda heaved a shuddering sigh, nodded, then stepped back to allow the two police officers to enter. 'I think he's dead,' she said and burst into tears. Blowing her nose, she heard the other patrol officer speaking on his radio after making a cursory examination of the body.

'Forensics, back up and ambulance.'

Twenty Benson was still on the ground, folded into himself, as the policeman bent over him. 'Sir, what's your name? Can I help you to stand up?'

'He saved my life,' Brenda said through her tears.

The policeman glanced at her. 'We'll have to take you both to the station.'

Brenda stared at him. 'But I must balance the books ... and go home ... my mother.'

'Sorry Miss, you'll have to come to the station and give a statement. Same as,' he indicated Twenty Benson. 'Do you know him?'

Brenda shook her head. 'He comes in regularly to buy cigarettes. Twenty Benson and Hedges.'

The policeman gave her a strange look.

'He saved my life, you know.'

The policewoman took over. 'You'll have to come now to give your statement.'

'What about him?'

'Yes, we'll be bringing him too.'

In a daze, Brenda took her coat and bag from behind the counter.

The policewoman watched her. 'This way.'

'I must lock up the store ...'

'No need,' the officer said. 'It's a crime scene, we'll look after it.' She ushered Brenda out of the store.

***

Neil managed to rouse himself. He hadn't thought. His army training had kicked in as he'd emerged from the back of the shop. He'd heard the woman scream, seen the gun, and launched himself at the man, all in one reflexive motion.

The subsequent crash and explosion had triggered a flashback.

Now, from what seemed a distance he heard a voice asking him his name and if he had any ID. He struggled to stand, and made to put his hand into his jacket to get his wallet. In an instant the policeman ordered, 'Don't move. Put your hands up.'

Neil obeyed and the policeman patted him down. 'Okay. ID?'

Neil took out his wallet. He watched as the policeman went through it.

'You're Captain Neil Blakey?'

Neil nodded.

'Right. Well, we'll have to bring you to the station to take your statement.'

Neil heard him radio through for a check on a Captain Neil Blakey. He sighed.

***

Brenda parked in the street outside her house, too tired to drive around to the garage. She'd given her statement to the police and been released. Apparently, there would have to be an inquest. It was now after midnight. As she unlocked the front door, her heart sank as she saw a light still on in the living room. Her mother's head jerked up as Brenda tip-toed in.

'What do you mean coming home at this time of the night?' Her mother thumped the ground with her stick. 'I've been waiting hours for my Horlicks! And I've got indigestion from that meal you left me.'

Brenda sighed as she went back into the hall and hung up her coat. 'I'll get it now,' she said over her shoulder.

'Hmph. So where have you been all this time, leaving your poor defenseless mother here on her own. I suppose you were with that useless Colin!'

'There was an armed hold-up at the store, a man was shot. I had to go to the police station and give a statement.'

Her mother sniffed. 'Hmph.'

In the kitchen, Brenda made a face as she heated the milk. 'I'll help you into bed, Mum, and bring your Horlicks.'

Later, as she climbed into her own bed, Brenda wondered about Twenty Benson who'd saved her life; she'd started to argue with the gunman, not believing the gun was real, let alone loaded. She trembled and the trembling turned into shakes. She might have been killed or badly injured and then who would care for her mother?

How had she come to this? She missed Colin. He'd been her only real friend. Boyfriend. She'd gradually drifted away from her girl-friends; some went away to university, or married and had babies; she no longer had anything in common with them. Her previous few boyfriends had been put off not only by her mother but by the fact that she worked afternoons and evenings, making dates hard to organise. She'd applied for other work but was unqualified for most jobs and the convenience store was, well, convenient. It meant she could look after her mother and do all the housework and shopping in the mornings. It had been even harder when her grandmother and father were alive and she'd had to care for them as well.

She sighed, thinking about Colin. She'd been going out with him for a couple of years; he was so thoughtful, hadn't seemed to mind that she could only meet him at certain times. That was usually at his bedsit where she would cook a meal and they'd lie on his bed and watch a movie. But then came the night a month ago. They were in his bed, and had made love. With a sigh, Brenda had said she'd better go home to her mother. She'd perched on the edge of the bed, putting on her clothes. Colin sat up and pulled her back on the bed and ruffled her curls. 'When are you ever going to stay the night with me?' he'd murmured, pulling off the bra she'd just fastened.

'You know I have to get back to mum, get her into bed.'

'Does she even know you're here? Here in bed with me?'

Brenda avoided his eyes.

'I bet you tell her some cock and bull story about visiting a friend!'

Brenda couldn't deny it. She'd tried to make a joke of it, saying, 'well, only the bull part.'

Colin ignored it. 'What would happen if we got married? Would she have to come and live with us? I'm fed up with our kind of relationship, Brenda. I want to go to bed with you at night and wake up with you in the morning. But I won't put up with your mother. We're acting like a couple of teenagers!' He sighed and flung himself back on the bed. 'I've applied for a job in Birmingham. If I get it, will you come with me? It's a lot more money. We could get married. Buy a house. Start a family.' He reached up and took one of her hands. 'Please Brenda?'

Brenda leaned over and kissed him. 'I'd like that, but let's wait and see.'

Her eyes filled with tears as she went over in her mind again the night when Colin had told her he'd got the job. 'So will you come with me?' he'd asked.

'What about my mother? I don't think she'd like to move to Birmingham.'

Colin had stared at her. 'Your mother? This is your chance to escape. I don't want her living with us, moaning and groaning and treating you like an unpaid servant.'

'I can't leave her.' Brenda had been close to tears.

Colin's stare had intensified, then he'd stood and said, 'Your mother is a selfish old harridan. I don't believe there's anything much wrong with her. And if she can't live by herself then she should go into an aged care home.' When Brenda hadn't answered he'd taken her hand. 'I love you Brenda,' he said gently, 'but I won't stand seeing you a slave to your mother. I've given in my notice and I'll be moving in a few weeks. Think about it.' Then he'd walked to the door and held it open for her.

Tears of self-pity overwhelmed her. She blew her nose and tried to sleep.

The phone woke her. She struggled into her dressing gown and ran down the stairs to the hall as the ringing stopped and switched to answering.

'Who's ringing at this time of the morning? Woke me up ...'

'Mr Dunning from the store,' she shouted up the stairs. 'Wants me to come in a bit earlier today to talk about improving security. He's worried about what happened last night.'

After taking her mother a cup of tea in bed, she came downstairs and sat at the kitchen table thinking about her life. Here she was, thirty-four years old and a slave to a grumpy old woman – yes

– Colin had been right. She, Brenda had given over her youth to this woman. What would her future hold? Would she end up like her mother? She thought about her father. She'd loved him, he used to take her up to his allotment when she was very young and she'd been happy pottering around the small plot, sowing seeds. Her mother used to grumble at him, spending so much time at his plot. Her father merely replied that she was happy to eat the fresh vegetables that he grew. Vegetables that Brenda had to cook as she got older.

A sudden thought came to her: what was really wrong with her mother? According to her father she'd taken to her bed after Brenda was born; apparently convinced Brenda would be a baby boy. She'd sunk into a deep depression when she was delivered of a girl.

'Can't think why,' her father had said, 'you were a delightful baby and little girl, but my mother, your Granny had to do everything after you were born.'

Her paternal grandmother, Granny Evans, had been the main-stay of the family until she suffered a stroke when Brenda was in her last year at school. Brenda's dreams of becoming a teacher were shattered when she was called upon to run the Evans house-hold. Her father had been contrite. 'Sorry, love,' he'd said, 'but now that Granny's not able to do anything, I'm afraid you'll have to leave school and take up the reins ...'

A faint, querulous voice, interrupted Brenda's thoughts. 'Bren-da! Where's my breakfast? Do I have to wait all day for it?'

Brenda sighed and got up from the kitchen table.

'Coming, Mum,' she shouted.

***

Neil came downstairs to the kitchen where his sister was preparing dinner.

'Sorry, about your birthday, Sis,' he said. 'I went to the store to get flowers for you but there was a gunman threatening the cashier.'

'Oh, right.' She kept peeling potatoes.

'Really.' He frowned. 'I jumped him and he shot himself. And then I had to go to the police station to give a statement.'

She turned to him. 'Are you sure?'

Neil Blakey straightened. 'Sorry, if you don't believe me.' He grabbed his coat from the back of the chair where he'd left it the previous night, turned and had his hand on the back door handle when it opened and his brother-in-law came in. Neil grunted and pushed past.

'Neil! Don't be like that!' Anna hurried to the door after her brother.

'What's up now?' Her husband sneered. 'Neil acting the ninny?'

Neil heard his brother-in-law's words and slammed the door. Then he waited outside to listen to his sister's reply.

'He said something about a gunman at the store. I think he might be having flashbacks.'

'Well, this one's for real, see this.' He showed her the local paper.

'Oh, my god, Tom.' Neil heard the rustle of a newspaper. 'He could have been killed.'

Neil thought he heard Tom mumble, 'No such luck'.

'What did you say?'

'You're too soft on that brother of yours.'

Then he heard Anna's voice, 'Guess what happened to poor old Bill when I went round this morning?'

'Dunno.'

'He slipped on some ice on the path when he was bringing in his milk. I had to call the ambulance. They said it might be a broken wrist and maybe concussion. Anyway, they said he'd probably have to stay in hospital overnight. Wanted to know if he had anyone to care for him. I said, no, his wife died a couple of months ago and I only go in twice a week to help out.'

'Hope you're not thinking of going round every day and looking after him? You've got enough to do with your other cleaning jobs and here as well.'

Neil turned away from the door. He tossed up whether to go to the pub and get drunk or go for a walk.

He went to the park, but his usual bench had a coating of frost. He brushed it off with a gloved hand and sat down. Well, it was winter. Cold and miserable. The trees were skeletons, with blobs of crow's nests at their tops. He could never work out how those nests stayed put in the gales.

When it started to sleet, he sighed and got up. Better call into the convenience store and get a packet of fags. The episode last night had shaken him, taken all morning for him to calm down. Brought back all those memories. Blood ... the noise of the gun shot. He shook his head and stumbled out of the park. He'd make an appointment with his doctor and get more sleeping tablets ...

He didn't expect to see the woman behind the counter at the store. She smiled when she saw him. 'Hello Neil. How are you? I have you to thank for saving my life last night.'

He stared at her, trying to remember her name.

'It's Brenda,' she said. 'The usual cigarettes?'

'Yes please, er, Brenda,' he managed to stammer.

'How are you feeling?'

Neil turned around, hoping there was someone else in the store and he could just pay and go. But the store was empty. He turned back to face her. 'I'm okay. How about you?'

'Well,' Brenda hesitated, 'it gave me a bit of a shakeup actually.' She studied her hands. 'Only for you, I'd be dead now. Made me think.'

'Oh?'

'Yes, you see ... I ...'

The door of the store opened, and a woman came in. Relieved, Neil handed over the money and took the packet of cigarettes. 'Thank you, um, Brenda.'

He heard her calling after him, 'Your change, Neil!'

He kept going. Better get back and make his peace with Anna. And make that doctor's appointment for sleeping tablets.

***

Bill looked up from his hospital bed when the door to his ward opened. He thought he recognized the woman coming in.

'How are you, Bill?'

It was Mrs Bridges – he knew her voice. 'Oh, I'm so pleased you're here, Mrs Bridges. They said I could go home but I didn't know what to do. They said they'd ring for a taxi for me, but I haven't got my keys or any money. I don't know what happened ... and I wouldn't be able to get in.'

'It's okay, Bill. After the ambulance left, I went in and did my usual cleaning and locked the door after me. I guess your keys are still inside the house. But I have mine and I can drive you home; my car's outside.'

'Really?' Bill sighed with relief. 'Nurse!' He called to a nurse who had come in to take the temperature of the patient in the bed opposite Bill's.

'Nurse, Mrs Bridges here is going to take me home.'

The nurse nodded. 'Give me a moment, Mr Thompson, and I'll get your discharge papers.'

Bill beamed. 'Can't wait to get home. Thank you so much for coming in, Mrs Bridges.'

'Anna.'

'Yes, well, Anna.'

The nurse returned. 'Now Mr Thompson, the almoner who visited you this morning said you live on your own. Are you sure you can manage? You won't be able to use that arm for several weeks, you know. A nasty fracture of the wrist and a broken arm.'

'I'll be fine. I'm used to looking after myself.'

The nurse looked at Anna. 'Are you a relative?'

'No, but I can pop in everyday and check on Bill.'

'That would be splendid.' The nurse handed him a small package. 'Now here are some strong pain killers, and you're to come back in a week for an x-ray to check your progress. If you get a headache or any swelling you're to ring for an ambulance and come straight in.' She smiled at him.

He was up and ready to leave, his dressing gown wrapped around him.

'It's very cold out,' Anna said, 'I should go and get one of your coats ...'

'No, no! I'm fine.'

The nurse shook her head and smiled at Anna, who took Bill's good arm.

At the exit doors, Anna turned to him. 'Wait here Bill, I'll go and fetch the car so you don't have to walk in the cold. The ground is slippery and you've still got your slippers on. And here's my scarf. Don't want you to get a chill.' She wound the scarf around his neck.

Bill stood at the entrance doors. All this fuss! As soon as the car drew up, he opened the passenger door and got in.

'Thank you, Mrs Bridges, but you really don't need to come and see me every day.'

'We'll see.'

Back at his house, Anna parked, then walked to the front door and unlocked it. 'I'll put your central heating on, Bill, then make you a cup of tea. What about something to eat tonight?'

'Oh, I had lunch at the hospital. I can just have a sandwich.' He was so thankful to be in his own home again.

'I'll make you one before I go, and a cup of tea.'

'I'll manage, really Mrs Bridges, there's no need to fuss.'

'Bill. I think you're right-handed, and that's the wrist you've broken.' He frowned as she indicated the plaster cast. 'I think you might have a problem preparing food. Let me make you a sandwich for later and a cup of tea now.'

He studied the plaster cast on his arm. 'Hmph'

'I'll put the kettle on. It's five o'clock, so I'll pop upstairs and turn on your electric blanket, I expect you're feeling a bit tired and want an early night.'

He nodded and sighed. 'Thank you, Mrs Bridges.'

***

Brenda couldn't stop thinking about her mother. *Was there really anything physically wrong with her?* Perhaps she should go and see their doctor and find out; she'd ring and make an appointment. Then she would find out about things she could do – a hobby – something other than just working and caring for her mother.

In the doctor's waiting room, she sat and glanced around. There was the usual coughing and sniffling patients and a harassed looking woman with a screaming baby. She felt like putting her fingers in her ears but didn't want to seem unsympathetic. At last, it was her turn.

Dr Morley beckoned her. 'Come in, Miss Evans. Sit down.' He indicated a chair. 'Now, how may I help you?'

'It's not me, it's my mother,' Brenda shifted on the hard seat. She clasped her handbag on her lap.

'Your mother? What's the problem?'

'That's exactly it, I'd like to find out what's really wrong with her. I thought you might be able to look at her records.'

Dr Morley sat back in his swivel chair. 'I'm afraid I can't do that without her permission.'

Brenda hesitated. 'I don't think she'd give me written permission.'

'Well, she'll have to come in herself. What's her name? I'll try and find her details.'

'Evelyn Evans.'

The doctor scrolled through lists of patients. 'Date of birth?'

She told him.

'Hmm, it seems she hasn't visited the surgery in the past five years. You'll have to bring her in.' He half made to stand.

Brenda moved forward on the chair. 'You see, doctor, my father used to bring her, but since he died several years ago, I can't get her to leave the house. Dr Dwyer has been doing repeats on her prescriptions as she needs them ... and, well, I was wondering ... my dad said she kind of went into a decline after I was born, couldn't get out of bed, or anything ...' Her voice trailed off,

Dr Morley stared at her. 'Doctor Dwyer retired last year. I'll have to see her before I prescribe any more medication.' He frowned at the computer screen then looked up. 'And the medication she's on is pretty heavy duty.' He stretched back in his chair. 'I'm not prepared to renew her prescription until I see her. So, if you make an appointment for her on your way out, I can get her assessed.' His tone was dismissive. He stood and moved towards the door,

Brenda's heart sank. Getting her mother out of the house would be a problem. She nodded. 'Thank you.'

What did you expect Brenda? Patient confidentiality and all that. She shrugged and tried to stay positive. She wandered along the High Street until she reached the library.

The welcome warmth inside had a calming effect. The librarian smiled as Brenda approached the main counter. 'It's freezing out,' Brenda said, taking off her gloves and stuffing them in her coat pockets. 'I was thinking about taking up a new hobby. Have you any suggestions?'

The librarian nodded. 'Maybe check out the notice board. There are evening classes and other social events, line dancing, the garden club ...'

'Thanks,' Brenda said, moving towards the notice board. Evening classes were out, she had to work evenings. The garden club? But there was no garden at their little terraced house. Just a bit of lawn front and back. She thought about her father and his allotment ... she scanned the notice board where an amazing range of activities was displayed. But the notion of an allotment took hold. She went back to the librarian. 'Do you know how I can find out about getting an allotment?' she asked.

The librarian raised her eyes. 'I think you have to contact the council.'

'Thanks,' Brenda beamed. 'I'll do that, and now I'll go and look at some gardening books.'

Brenda drove home feeling inspired. She had four gardening books to read plus one written by the man who spoke on the radio about his allotment in Wales. As soon as she was home, she'd ring the council and find out about getting an allotment.

Her mood darkened as she neared their terrace house. Between the doctor and the library, she'd lost track of time. It was after one o'clock, she hadn't prepared their main meal of the day and her shift started at two.

She parked her little car outside the house, grabbed her library books and hurried indoors.

'So where have you been and where's my dinner? I could be dead for all you care!'

Her mother was in her usual "good" form. 'I went to the doctors and then the library,' Brenda said.

'The doctor! For what?'

'To get your medication.' Brenda ran into the kitchen, wondering what on earth she could cook quickly.

'Hmph.'

'But the new doctor won't give me a prescription for you until you go in to see him,' Brenda shouted from the kitchen as she rummaged in the pantry. She found a tin of chicken soup and some frozen vegetables. She opened the tin of soup and threw in a handful of the frozen vegetables. Quickly she made cheese sandwiches with pickles for her mother's tea. She cut off the crusts and stuck them under the grill.

Ten minutes later she placed a tray with the soup on her mother's lap.

'What are these bits of toast floating in the soup?' her mother demanded.

'Croutons ...'

'Fancy name for stale bread!'

'I'll have mine in the kitchen,' Brenda said. 'I must be quick or I'll be late for work. I've prepared some sandwiches for your tea.'

'I'm not going to the doctor. He can come here.' Her mother picked the bits of toast out of the soup and flicked them onto the tray.

'Mum, those days are gone. I've made an appointment for you for next week. If you want your medication you'll have to go.'

There was silence.

Brenda felt cheered. It was the first time she'd taken a stand against her mother.

'When I die from lack of medical attention, you'll both be sorry!'

Brenda sighed and rolled her eyes as the doorbell rang. She looked at her mother. 'This must be Edith Milson to see you. I've left a packet of biscuits in the kitchen.'

Her mother had few friends, but Edith Milson had been her mother's bridesmaid and came regularly to visit, competing with Evelyn as to who suffered the most from their ailments.

***

Neil stayed in his bedroom, away from Tom. He heard his sister come in. There was the sound of a chair being scraped back and then his brother-in-law's voice. He moved to the top of the stairs to listen.

'Where've you been? It's after six!'

'I went to the hospital to see Bill and ended up driving him back home and getting his tea ...'

'I knew it! You'll be at his beck and call while your husband is left all on his own.'

'Neil's here.'

'Hmph, fat lot of use he is.'

Neil pretended not to hear. He clumped noisily down the stairs to indicate his presence.

'Anyway, dinner's all prepared. Won't take a jiffy.'

Neil heard the fridge door open and close.

'Poor Bill's fractured his wrist, he's in a plaster cast. It's his right hand too. Don't know how the poor old devil will manage. He was worrying about not being able to work at his allotment.'

'Send your brother to help him. He's only hanging around all day doing nothing ...'

Neil thought the same could be said of his brother-in-law.

'Any work available?' Anna asked.

'Of course not. Those idiots at the employment agency don't know their ass from their elbow.'

Neil shuffled into the kitchen.

***

Bill woke early next morning - his bladder seemed to be bursting and his arm hurt like buggery. He managed to get out of bed, trying to undo his pajama button with his left hand as he made his way to the bathroom.

Too late! A steady stream of warm urine trickled down his inner thigh.

The doorbell rang. *Bugger! It would be Mrs Bridges*. He heard the front door open.

'Are you okay, Bill?'

'Don't come up! I'm not decent!'

'What's wrong, Bill?' There was a pause and then, 'Bill, what's wrong? Can I come up?'

He heard her coming up the stairs. 'No, no, I've had an accident, don't come in.'

'What kind of accident?'

'I couldn't make it to the bathroom ...'

'Bill, I'll go and get my brother, he'll help you. Now you just wrap yourself in your dressing gown and wait for me. Right?'

'Okay.' What else could he say? He stared at the damp patch on the carpet.

He heard the front door slam, wrapped his dressing gown around him and sank back onto the bed. 'Hazel!'

***

Neil had only just managed to get to sleep in the early hours of the morning when he heard his sister calling him in a loud whisper. 'Neil? Neil, are you awake?'

Neil sighed. 'I am now.'

'Can you help me please? It's urgent. I'll wait out the front in the car.'

Neil groaned but five minutes later he emerged from the house, fastening his overcoat. He ran his fingers through his uncombed hair and opened the passenger door.

'What's up, Sis?'

'Get in, Neil. You know the man I clean for twice a week, Bill? Well, his wife died just before Christmas, and he's broken his wrist and it's his right hand and the poor old fellow can't manage. It seems he's dirtied himself and won't let me in to help him, and anyway I have to be at another job at nine o'clock.' Her words came out in a rush.

Neil's brows drew together as he got in beside her.

'It's okay, Neil, I'll do the cleaning up, but he needs a man to help him into clean clothes.'

He grunted.

At Bill's, Anna opened the front door and ran up the stairs. Neil hesitated at the bottom until he heard her calling out. 'My brother, Neil, is here now Bill. Can he come in?'

'Only him.'

Anna leaned over the banisters. 'Please help him Neil, I'll have to leave you now.'

Neil sighed as she came down the stairs. 'Okay, Sis.'

He paused at the bedroom door, and gave a slight cough. 'I'm Neil.' He could see the old man huddled in his dressing gown on the bed. 'What's the problem, Bill?'

Bill was flustered. 'Sorry, Neil, it's this benign prostate thingy, apparently most old men get it, and I can't manage with just my left hand ... I couldn't make it to the bathroom.'

'We'll soon have you clean and dry. Are you allowed to have a shower with that cast?'

Bill frowned. 'Dunno.'

'Well, how about I find a plastic bag to cover the cast and help you have a shower and into clean clothes? Maybe a shave? Or is that designer stubble?' Neil forced a smile. 'I expect it would be difficult to shave with your left hand?'

Bill sniffed and fumbled for a handkerchief. 'You're very kind, Neil.'

Neil managed to get Bill into the shower. 'Promise I won't look.'

Bill gave a little snigger. 'Not much to look at, Neil!'

Ten minutes later and Bill was clean, dressed and smiling. 'Thank you, Neil. I feel so much better now.'

Neil nodded. 'How about we go downstairs and I get you a cup of tea and make some breakfast for you.'

'Thank you, Neil, you're so kind. Like your sister, Mrs Bridges.' He followed him down the stairs to the kitchen.

'You sit down and I'll put the kettle on. Do you mind if I poke around and see what you have in the pantry?'

Bill waved his left hand. 'Your sister got a few things in for me. And there's probably milk from yesterday.' He sighed, 'I thought I could manage but I'm not used to using only my left hand.'

Neil found a loaf of bread and the toaster, and butter in the fridge. 'Mind if I join you? I didn't have time for breakfast, Anna got me out of bed in a rush.'

'Please do. I'm glad of the company. There should be marmalade in the larder.'

Neil pushed away the packets of seeds on the table to make room for their plates.

'They're seeds for my allotment, Neil.'

'Oh, right.' Neil gathered the packets into a pile.

'Don't know how I'll manage with the allotment now.' Bill pulled a face.

Neil made no comment, just buttered some toast. 'Can you manage with the knife, Bill?'

With his left hand, Bill was trying in vain to spread butter on a piece of toast which kept sliding away from him,

'I'll do it for you.'

'Ta. Didn't realise what a handicap a broken wrist could be.' He gave a small laugh. 'Handicap, not at all handy, Neil.'

Neil tried to smile, making an effort to humour the old man.

The two men sat drinking tea and eating their toast.

'Thank you, Neil. I don't want to keep you if you have to go to work.'

Neil grimaced. 'Not working at the moment.'

'Oh?' The old man looked up.

'I was in the army.' Neil lowered his eyes and studied his plate. He licked a finger and caught a few stray crumbs of toast. 'Invalided out. PTSD.'

'PTSD?' Bill echoed.

'Yeah, Post Traumatic Stress Disorder.'

'Think I've heard of that. Like Shell Shock?'

'A bit.' Neil picked up the packets of seeds and started to shuffle them.

Bill sighed. 'I was too young for the war; I was five when it started but my Da was called up and he wasn't the same man when he came back.' He lapsed into silence.

After a while Neil focused on the packets of seeds. 'Have you got a garden, Bill?'

'Only a small patch of grass here, but I've got an allotment the other side of town.' He looked hopefully at Neil. 'Don't suppose you'd drive me over there to check on it, would you?'

Neil frowned. 'I don't have a car.'

'You could drive mine.'

Neil was silent, conscious of the old man watching him. Then he nodded. 'All right. Tomorrow?'

Bill smiled.

***

The Allotment

No snow, but a hard frost last night. Wasn't expecting any allotmenteers but lo and behold here comes The Warden!

She's struggling to get out of her car – it's a red mini. She's rather large – buxom is a better word – and reminds me of a big woolly animal, with her brown parka and fur lined hood and furry boots.

Her plot's right at the entrance. I expect she's come to check nothing untoward is happening.

She's only been on this allotment for the last five years. She started on the furthest plot from the entrance and moved to the one by the gate when it became vacant, then she took over the warden's duties. No-one else wanted the job. She seems a bit bossy. I overheard her telling old Bill that she'd been a Personal Assistant to a high-powered business man ... Bill just blinked and said 'Oh, right.'

***

Brenda rang the council to enquire about an allotment. To her joy there was a vacant plot available.

She rushed upstairs to her mother. 'Guess what Mum? I've got an allotment!'

'An allotment of what?' Her mother was in a bad mood, still upset about the need to visit the doctor. 'I didn't sleep a wink last night,' she grumbled. 'You'll have to go back to that doctor and get me more sleeping pills.'

'I told you; he won't prescribe anything until he sees you!' Brenda tried to stay patient. 'And I've got a garden allotment, I rang the council and they had just one available.'

'An allotment? Like what your father had?'

'Yes!' Brenda beamed. 'I'll be able to grow nice fresh vegetables for us.'

'You know I can't digest many vegetables.' Her mother scowled. 'And you? Growing vegetables? You couldn't even sprout seeds on the kitchen window sill.'

Brenda frowned, thinking back on her abortive attempts with seeds and jam jars covered in muslin and the slimy mess she'd managed to create.

'Yes, well, this'll be different.'

'I suppose this'll be another excuse to leave me on my own. Just like your father, he disappeared for hours to his so-called allotment, leaving me to cope with everything.'

Brenda thought about her father. He'd been over fifty when she'd been born, her parents' first and only child. When they'd married, he and her mother had moved into his widowed mother's house while they saved enough to buy their own place. Somehow that never happened; her father was an only child too and it had seemed sensible to stay, especially when Brenda's mother became pregnant after many years of marriage.

Brenda sighed, she'd been sixteen when her Granny had had a stroke and was unable to walk. That was when she'd had to leave school to take care of the household. Her dreams of going to university were dashed. Her eyes focused back on her mother. 'Well, this new doctor might be able to help you get back to living a normal life.'

'Normal life! I haven't lived a normal life since the day you were born!'

Brenda sighed. 'Yes, Mum, I know it's all my fault but we must look on the bright side and this new doctor may be able to help you.'

'I'm telling you, I'm too weak to go outside.'

Brenda went to the kitchen to prepare the midday meal, excited at the prospect of getting an allotment. Her plot was five rods; she'd checked what five rods was and discovered it was a plot about five metres by twenty-five metres long – about the size of a singles tennis court, apparently. That seemed a lot of ground.

She'd take one of the gardening books into work and study it during her break.

She'd have to pay for a key to be cut to the main gate of the allotment. That was all right. Of course there would be initial expenses, then she'd have to buy tools ... but first she'd look in the shed and see if any of her father's tools were still usable.

'Here you go, Mum, plaice in a mornay sauce with vegetables...' she put the tray in front of her mother, who sniffed disapprovingly.

'Looks like one of those frozen meals.'

'It's winter, Mum! Not much fresh stuff available. Now, eat up and I'll bring you some custard and stewed apple when you've finished.'

Brenda ran down the stairs; she was due at work in twenty minutes.

***

Neil thought about Bill. He'd seen guys like him, only they were young; missing limbs, couldn't pull up their pants with one hand, missing legs ... guess he'd been lucky, but at least theirs was a physical manifestation ... people could see and sympathise ... but with mental problems ... well, people see you with no visible injuries and wonder what's the problem with you? *Why aren't you working? Pull yourself together! Think how lucky you are, all in one piece.*

Neil had finished clearing the breakfast table when the doorbell rang. He went into the hall and heard a key opening the door as his sister came in.

'Hello, Neil, just thought I'd see if you and Bill were okay.'

'All good, you came at the right time, I've put Bill's wet pyjamas in the bath.'

'That's fine. I'll put them in the laundry basket and wash them later. How is he?'

'He's in the kitchen, but he can't manage dressing and undressing with his arm and wrist in plaster. I helped him put his good arm into a cardigan and found a safety pin in the dressing table.' Seeing her frown, Neil added hastily, 'I didn't go poking around, Bill told me to look there.'

Anna went past him and into the kitchen. 'How are you, Bill?'

Bill gave a weak smile, 'Much better, thank you, Mrs Bridges. Your brother has been most helpful.' He paused. 'I'll miss him.'

Neil followed his sister. 'Perhaps you could bring me over this evening, Anna, and I can help Bill get undressed.'

Anna smiled. 'What do you think, Bill.'

'I hate to be a nuisance.'

'I've brought you a sandwich for your lunch,' Anna said. 'I can bring Neil back this evening.' She appeared to think. 'Now, why don't I bring dinner for both of you and Neil can eat with you and get you ready for bed. I can pick him up later.'

Neil appealed to Bill. 'You'd be doing me a favour, Bill. It'll keep me out from under Anna's feet for a few hours. And I can walk back, Anna, it's not far.'

Anna nodded. 'Good. Now, Neil, would you put the heater on in the lounge and Bill might like to watch a bit of TV. That okay, Bill? I'll just pop upstairs and tidy your bedroom.'

In the car going back, Anna turned to her brother. 'Thanks Neil, Bill's a lovely man, and completely lost without his Hazel. It really knocked him for six when she died.'

'Yeah, I remember you saying how devoted they were.'

'They had no children, and their only nephew was killed in a car accident. So poor Bill's all alone now.'

'I can easily walk over in the morning and see to him, Sis.'

Anna parked outside the house. 'He could probably get some kind of help to come round every day,' she said thoughtfully, 'I'll look into it. But it will take a while to organise.'

'I don't mind going over, Sis. It's good to feel useful.'

Later that afternoon, Neil paused at the top of the stairs when he heard his brother-in-law speaking.

'What's all this, taking meals to Bill? And where's that miserable brother of yours?'

'He's upstairs, getting ready to go to Bill's and help him.'

Neil heard the sound of crockery, then Tom's voice.

'I don't know why he has to live with us. I'm fed up with him hanging around the place all day, like a week of wet Sundays.'

'You know very well he has PTSD and suffering from depression. I can't let him live on his own until he gets a bit better, and anyway, he's got nowhere to go since the divorce.'

'He could rent somewhere. How do other people manage?'

Anna's voice was soft. 'Tom, you know he's been suicidal, I couldn't let him live on his own. At least when he's here I can make sure he's eating properly and taking his medication. And anyway, the rent he pays helps out ...'

There was a sudden silence. Fuck! Neil thought. The unemployed Tom wouldn't like that innuendo.

'I'm going out!'

'Tom!'

Neil heard the hall stand rattle and the front door slam. He thought he heard his sister stifle a sob.

'You ready, Neil? I've got yours and Bill's dinner ready.'

'Coming, Sis.' He clattered down the stairs.

'You just have to warm it up,' she told him as he came into the kitchen. 'Stew.'

'Great.' He carried the pot out to her car.

She stopped outside Bill's house.

'No need to come in. I can manage,' he told his sister.

'Okay. Thanks, Neil. Are you sure you're all right to walk back?'

'Yup.' He carried the pot to the front door.

'Hold on, I'll open the door for you.'

'Thanks.'

Neil walked into the kitchen, placed the pot on the stove and lit the gas.

'You there, Bill?' He opened the lounge room door and peered in.

'Didn't hear you come in, must have dozed off.' Bill blinked and reached for his glasses.

'Anna made a big pot of stew. It's on the stove, heating up. Won't be long.'

At the table, Neil noticed Bill fumbling with his left hand trying to cut a piece of meat.

'Hold on Bill. Let me cut that up for you. I should have thought of it.'

'I feel like a child,' Bill muttered. 'Your sister's a good cook. She made a few nice meals for Hazel, coaxing her to eat when she had no appetite.' He sighed. 'She only came to clean twice a week in the beginning when Hazel came out of hospital and was having chemotherapy, then she came round more often, just doing little things to help. Hazel had a lot of friends, but most of them were elderly, like us I suppose. Well, like me and Hazel, not you. They weren't able to do much. Mrs Bridges was wonderful.'

Neil could see Bill getting teary. 'Yes, Anna's a good person. She's been marvellous to me.'

'Oh?'

Neil shifted on his chair. 'When I came out of the ...' he was going to say psych ward, but thought Bill might think he was a lunatic ... well, maybe he was ...

Bill was looking at him.

'Well, when I came out of hospital, Anna took me in. I was a bit of a mess. But I think I'll have to find somewhere else to go now. I can tell things are getting difficult for her with her husband.' *Shit, why did I blab all that out?*

He could see Bill studying him. 'You're not married then.' It was a statement rather than a question.

Neil shook his head. 'Divorced.' He indicated Bill's plate. 'Finished?'

'Yes, it was lovely, thank you.'

Neil took the plates to the kitchen sink. 'Cup of tea? I'll put the kettle on then, if you don't mind, I'll go outside for a smoke while it boils.'

Bill nodded. 'Okay.'

Outside, Neil lit a cigarette and leaned against a wall. He hated having to explain his life, hated having to say he couldn't work. He thought it was unlikely he'd be allowed back in the army and he'd like to get a job, but what could he do? He only knew warfare and how to kill ... He shivered; he never knew when something would send him into a quivering jelly - a car exhaust back firing, Guy Fawkes night, or New Year's Eve with the fireworks. Or a gun shot, like that man in the store ... he took a deep breath, closed his eyes and practiced the technique the hospital had taught him.

'Kettle's boiled, Neil.' Bill's voice broke through his meditation, as the kitchen door opened. 'It's freezing out here, Neil. Come in. No wonder you're shivering.'

***

Brenda studied her gardening book. "Bastard trenching", she read. "Dig (ground) by digging over the lower soil with the topsoil temporarily removed". She tried to visualise it. Okay, you dig a trench two spades deep and put the soil aside. Then you dig another trench alongside the first one, turning the top soil over into the bottom of the first trench. And the next spade depth on top. You keep going until you reach the end of the plot then fetch the first lot of soil and fill in the last trench. It sounded like a lot of work …

Ah hah! No dig gardening! That sounded more her style … flatten the weeds with your spade and then lay several layers of newspaper on top. Cover the newspaper with about four inches of mulch …*hmm better start saving newspapers!* But she didn't get a daily paper, her mother wasn't interested in reading the news and she, Brenda, could read any of the newspapers in the convenience store before they were sold. That was if she had time which rarely happened. Unsold papers had to be returned.

Perhaps she could ask this warden person. She had an appointment to meet her the day after tomorrow. That was when she would get a key to the gate and claim her plot.

***

Bill was thankful to get into bed. He hadn't realised how tired he was. Neil was very kind. Like his sister, Mrs Bridges. He wondered about Neil. It sounded like he and his brother-in-law didn't hit it off. From what he could gather Neil would be happier moving out from his sister's house. And he was suffering from this modern name for shell shock.

'What do you think, Hazel? Should I ask him if he'd like to move in here until I'm out of this plaster cast? He might help out on the allotment ...' He looked at the scatter urn containing Hazel's ashes which sat next to her photo on the bedside table on her side of the bed. The funeral director had shown him a range of urns. He'd seen one with flowers on it and pointed. 'Hazel'd like that,' he'd mumbled.

'Ah! A scatter tube, good choice.' The Funeral Director had made some notes.

He wondered should he go downstairs and make a drink of something hot, help him to sleep ... then decided he was too tired ... *should have asked Neil.*

Next morning, he woke to the sound of the doorbell and the front door being unlocked.

'Only me, Neil,' a voice said.

'Okay,' Bill yawned. He heard Neil coming up the stairs, then he felt a tingling; *better get to the bathroom quick.*

He was out of bed and at the door as Neil said 'Okay if I come in?'

'Yes, yes. I'm just on my way to the bathroom.'

Neil opened the bedroom door. 'Can you manage?'

Bill nodded.

'Right, I'll get your clothes ready.'

At the breakfast table, Bill studied Neil. 'I was wondering if you'd like to stay here for a few weeks until my cast comes off.'

'Stay here?' Neil frowned.

'Well, I thought it might be easier for you instead of having to walk back and forth all the time, especially in this nasty weather. Of course, I wouldn't expect you to do it for nothing. I've really appreciated your help the last few days.' He watched Neil who'd stopped eating and was frowning at his plate. 'You can see I can't manage on my own. And maybe if you wouldn't mind cooking a bit of dinner, simple things ...'

'Well, it would give Anna a break,' Neil said. 'But there's no way I could take anything. It should be me paying you.'

Bill grinned. 'Well, that's settled then. After breakfast you can have a look at the spare bedroom. I think it's very comfy.' He dipped a crust of toast in his tea. 'Hazel didn't like me doing this,' he murmured with a cheeky grin.

'Did you still want to go to your allotment today?' Neil asked.

Bill peered out the window. 'Looks like it might snow. How about you get your stuff and settle in here today and we go to the allotment tomorrow. Why don't you take my car?'

Neil seemed surprised. 'Thanks, Bill.'

***

Neil parked outside his sister's house. He saw her open the front door and bend to pick up the milk bottles. She raised her head at the sound of the car.

'Oh!' Anna stared at the car as Neil opened the driver's door. 'Have you bought a car?'

'No, it's Bill's. He's asked me to move in until he gets the cast off his arm, and he told me to take his car to pick up my stuff.'

'Oh, well come in out of the cold.' She led the way inside.

'Yeah, it'll give you a break from having me around all the time. I'll still pay for my board.'

'Absolutely not! With Andy finishing uni in a few months and Brett in his second year and working in his holidays, well, we can manage okay.' Anna stared at her brother. 'Really, Neil.'

'It'll only be for a few weeks anyway, so we'll keep things the way they are.'

She nodded. 'Thanks, Neil.'

'And don't worry about getting dinner for Bill and me tonight. I'll stop at the shops and get some chops and potatoes and a few other things.'

Anna smiled. 'I know you're a good cook. Deirdre told me.' Her smiled faded. 'Sorry Neil, didn't want to remind you.'

'It's okay, Sis, I'm over Deirdre. I don't blame her, it's not easy being a soldier's wife. So many of my mates went through the same thing.' Neil sighed as he sat on a kitchen chair. 'What do you talk about when you come home on leave? And the phone calls when you're out there. Your wife asks "what's new?" and what do you say? "Oh, my best mate was shot to pieces by an RPG[1] " and they have no idea what an RPG is ... and you can't explain without choking up ...'

Neil put his head in his hands. 'Sorry, Sis.'

'It's okay, Neil. I don't really understand, but I want to help whichever way I can.'

The back door slammed.

Anna started and looked at the door. 'Oh, it's Tom!'

'Just going,' Neil stood. 'I only came to collect a few things.'

Tom glared at his brother-in-law. 'Moving out, are you?'

'Yes.'

As he went out of the kitchen he heard Tom remark, 'About time.'

***

Bill gazed out the kitchen window. 'No point in going to the allotment today, look ...'

---

1. Rocket Propelled Grenade

Neil joined him. The sky was heavy and grey; flakes of snow drifting down and melting into the ground as they fell. 'Not pitching,' he said. 'Won't last. Maybe tomorrow.'

'Hmm. Not much to be done up there, anyway. In this weather I usually just oil my tools, clean flowerpots, sharpen secateurs, that kind of thing.' He studied Neil. 'Anything special you have to do?'

'I've got an appointment with my psychologist this afternoon.'

'Take the car, Neil.'

'Thanks, Bill. I'll get a few groceries on my way back.'

Bill tried to think how to suggest paying Neil. He straightened his shoulders. 'Now, Neil, I have to give you money for groceries. I don't expect you to be here doing everything and helping me for nothing and then paying for food.'

Neil shook his head. 'It's okay, Bill. We'll talk about it later. Not now.'

Bill turned from the window. 'Where did I put the car keys, Neil?'

'On the hook by the back door.'

'Oh.'

Chapter Two
February

The Allotment

"Good morrow, Benedick. Why, what's the matter? That you have such a February face so full of frost, of storm and cloudiness?" – William Shakespeare

Some people think allotments are like community gardens. No! Absolutely not. Each plot on an allotment is allocated to an individual. The allotmenteer can plant and harvest whatever he likes – within the allotment rules, of course! When I look around my allotment, no two plots are the same; some have raised beds, some have green houses or poly tubes, grass paths, fancy sheds or makeshift sheds – endless variety. I sometimes think I can tell what kind of person an allotmenteer is from their plot.

***

Brenda's mother was a problem. She kept repeating that she wasn't going to visit the doctor and the doctor would have to come and see her.

'Well, Mum, you'll just have to make do without your medications.'

Eventually, Brenda managed to get her mother out of the house and into the car for the doctor's appointment. She complained all the way, huffing and puffing and generally making a fuss, hobbling up the path to the surgery, stabbing her walking stick on the ground as she went.

'I could slip on this ice and break every bone in my body,' she grumbled.

Brenda made sympathetic noises and directed her mother to a chair in the waiting room. She sat beside her. 'Not long to wait, Mum.'

'Hmph. I could catch all sorts of diseases here.' She glowered at the other patients who were coughing and sneezing.

Brenda studied her mother. For the first time in her life, she thought her mother appeared quite nervous. Her heart went out to her.

'Mrs Evans?' Doctor Morley had come out of his consulting room.

Brenda stood and took her mother's elbow. 'Come on, Mum.'

The doctor held the door open for them. 'Now, Mrs Evans, sit down here and tell me what the problem is.' He sat in front of his computer and turned to them.

Brenda took a seat beside her mother. She was about to speak when her mother said, 'I just want my usual sleeping pills and other pills, that's all! No need to come in and see you, wasting everyone's time.'

'It's no problem, Mrs Evans. Now take off your coat and roll up your sleeve and I'll take your blood pressure.'

Ignoring her mother's grumbling, Brenda said 'Come, Mum, let me help you off with your coat.'

The doctor nodded. 'Now please stand on those scales and I'll check your weight.

Evelyn Evans was outraged when the doctor told her she was overweight. 'Well, if I am, it's the fault of my daughter, feeding me all those frozen meals.'

Dr Morley glanced at Brenda and raised his eyebrows.

She shrugged, 'No Mum, it might be all those chocolates you ask me to buy.'

Her mother glared at her.

'Now, Mrs Evans, why are you using that walking stick?'

Her mother switched her glare to the doctor. 'Because I can't walk without it,' she barked.

'Right. Well, I think we'll take some X-rays of your hips and knees and I'd like you to see a physiotherapist to give you an exercise program. And a dietitian. Also, I'll need to do some blood tests.' He tapped away at his computer, then stood and handed several printouts to Brenda.

'Here you go, Miss Evans. A referral for X-rays for your mother and blood tests. Come and see me in a week and we'll take it from there.' He turned to Brenda's mother. 'Thirty-four years is a long time to suffer from post-natal depression,' he said dryly.

Brenda thought her mother would explode as she snatched up her stick and turned to her daughter. 'Home!' she ordered.

'Thank you, Doctor,' Brenda said over her shoulder as she led her mother away.

***

Bill went to the window. The sky was grey and low. 'Sleet's easing. How about we pop up to the allotment this afternoon, Neil?'

Neil came up behind him. 'No probs, Bill. I'll bring the car round after lunch.'

Bill beamed. Having Neil living with him was a bonus. He didn't feel so lonely now. And Neil was nice. Bit strange in some ways, not very talkative, and he didn't like his smoking, but then, if he had this shell shock bizzo, well, it explained a lot. And it was nice to have someone with whom to watch the sport on TV.

At the allotment, Bill handed Neil the key to the entrance. 'Here you go, lad.' He turned to Neil. 'I feel like royalty, having a chauffeur!'

The corners of Neil's mouth lifted in a half smile. 'Makes a change from driving a tank ...' His smile faded.

Bill saw Neil's black look, and changed the subject. 'It'll be great to see my plot again. Hope you're good at digging, Neil?'

Neil opened the gate and drove through, then stopped and walked back to shut the gate. He went to the car and spoke to Bill, 'Do I need to lock it?'

'Yes, please.'

Bill watched Neil come back to the car. 'Right, now you park just here and we'll walk up to my plot. Not far.'

Bill handed Neil the keys to the padlock on his gate and the door to his shed. 'Easier for you to unlock it, Neil, boy.'

'Ah, great to be back here.' Bill took a deep breath of the musty air inside the shed. He dumped his leather satchel on the small table. 'Like I said, not much that can be planted. But I was hoping to do a bit of digging ...' He gave Neil a piercing look from under his brows.

Neil gave a small smile. 'No probs, I can do that, Bill.'

***

Brenda parked at the entrance to the allotment. The warden had said to meet her at the gate. She glanced at her watch. Plenty of time. She went to the gate and surveyed the plots within range. A motley collection of gardens – some with rusty old iron sheds, others with greenhouses and one with a picket fence and a shade cloth house. Like a patchwork quilt, she thought. It was not how she recalled the place when she'd come with her father. But that had been over twenty years ago. Things change, she reminded herself.

A voice broke into her thoughts.

'Miss Evans?'

Brenda turned around. 'Yes. You must be the warden?'

'Indeed. Nice to meet you. Welcome to our allotment. Amanda Harris.' The warden held out her hand. 'This way. We have forty-nine plots on this allotment, a nice size, people soon get to know each other and help. This here,' she indicated a small doorless shed, 'is our exchange shed, where you can leave surplus produce, seedlings or cuttings.'

She put her head inside. 'Nothing there today. Not surprising. February.' She shrugged. 'Right' Let's get you up to your plot. It's next to Bill Thompson. I see his car is here, so I can introduce you.' She turned and led the way.

***

The Allotment – all go this morning. Bill's got his arm in a sling and has brought another man – tall, fair haired with a military bearing – haven't seen him before. Now the warden's arrived. She seems to be inducting a new allotmenteer – a woman. The warden called her Miss Evans. She looks young – small with brown curly hair. They're going to Arthur's plot by the look of it. The new woman seems a bit intimidated by the warden.

***

Bill indicated the garden spade and fork. 'There you go, Neil. Doesn't need digging, just needs a forking over really.'

Neil took the fork and nodded.

'Right, Bill.'

The sound of voices made them turn.

'Oh, it's the warden,' Bill said.

Neil raised his eyebrows. 'Warden?'

'Yes, she looks after the place, checks that everyone is doing the right thing. Introduces new people.'

The voices grew louder as two women approached.

The older woman smiled at Bill. 'Well, hello Bill, nice to see you. Just want to introduce a new member of our group. She's taking over Arthur's plot.' She indicated her companion. 'Brenda Evans.'

Bill nodded. 'Nice to meet you, Miss Evans. This is my friend Neil Blakey; he's giving me a hand until I can get this plaster cast off.'

'Oh, Bill! What happened?' The warden peered at Bill's arm.

While Bill explained how he had slipped and fractured his wrist and arm, Brenda looked at Neil and smiled.

'Hello Neil. How are you?'

Neil blinked. 'Um, okay, and you?'

'I'm Brenda from the convenience store. You saved my life, remember?'

Hearing this, the warden halted her conversation with Bill and turned to Brenda. 'You know each other?'

Brenda nodded. 'Neil here saved my life when the store where I work was held up by a gunman.'

Neil lowered his head and kicked at a stone.

Bill stared at Neil. 'You didn't tell me this, Neil.'

Neil shrugged. 'Nothing to tell.'

The warden gave Neil a keen look. 'Well,' she said. 'I'm the warden for this allotment, Neil. Amanda Harris.' She held out her hand.

Neil nodded, took her hand and shook it.

Bill studied Brenda. 'You've got your work cut out with Arthur's plot, Miss Evans. Poor chap couldn't do much for the past few months. He's gone into a nursing home now.'

Amanda Harris frowned. 'Well, I'd better get a move on, I've explained the rules and so on.' She took Brenda's elbow, then had a sudden thought. 'Do you know if Arthur kept a spare key to his shed, Bill?'

'Why yes, should be under the flower pot by his compost bin.'

'Thank you.' The two women moved off.

'Dunno how that little girl will manage that plot,' Bill remarked to Neil. 'It's all weeds. Needs a good digging over.'

***

Brenda had been surprised to see Neil on the plot next to hers, accompanied by an old man with his arm in a sling.

Amanda led the way to Arthur's small shed, retrieved the key and handed it to Brenda. 'Here you go, Miss Evans. All yours. You know how to contact me if you have any problems.' She nodded at Brenda and strode away.

Brenda stared at the key in her hand. It felt strange to unlock the padlock, almost as if she was trespassing. The key turned easily in the lock and she pushed open the door to be greeted by a mouldy smell. A tray of potatoes sprouting pale tendrils sat on a bench. Various tools stood around the walls, and a shelf held a row of labelled glass jars containing various seeds. "Money Maker Toms," read one label.

'Hello? Miss Evans?' A voice broke through her thoughts.

She turned, 'Oh, it's you, Mr Thompson. I was just having a look around.'

'Call me Bill,' he said. 'And you already know Neil. I just thought I'd pop over and see if there's anything you need.'

'Thank you, Bill, and please call me Brenda.' She didn't know what to say. She'd been daunted at the sight of her plot covered in weeds.

'Poor Arthur didn't get to do much over the last few months. His knees were playing up and then he had a stroke. Now he's in an aged care place. I went to see him a couple of weeks ago. I don't think he gets many visitors. Next time I go, I can tell him that his plot is in good hands.'

Brenda stared at her hands. 'Well, I don't know about that. I'm a novice gardener, but I've been reading a lot about it.'

Bill peered around the shed. 'Arthur kept his tools in good condition.'

'Should I pay him for them?'

'Dunno, but maybe if you went to see him, you could ask him. Tell you what. Next time I go, how about you come with me?'

She hesitated. 'Yes, perhaps.'

'Anyway, anything you want to know, give me a shout,' Bill smiled at her. 'Not much to do this time of the year, except digging, but the ground's too wet at the moment.' He looked at her shoes.

Brenda followed his glance. Her good leather boots were covered in mud. 'I'll have to get some work boots.'

'Right. Well, like I said, not much we can do today; and it's starting to drizzle.' Bill turned around. 'You right, Neil?'

Neil, who had been standing behind Bill, nodded.

'Bye for now,' Bill said and the two men walked away.

'Bye,' Brenda echoed. She took a last look around the shed. It was very neat. Then she turned to stare at her plot and her heart sank.

Today was her day off. She wouldn't be able to do anything here until her next day off the following week.

She locked the shed and returned to her car. She hoped she'd be able to make a go of it.

***

Neil drove back to Bill's house.

'I feel sorry for that little girl,' said Bill, on the way. 'That's a lot of ground for her when it's not been cultivated for so long.'

'Little girl?'

'Well, she puts me in mind of those old-fashioned little girls with rosy cheeks and curly hair.'

Neil could sense Bill giving him a sideways look. He sighed.

'Is that a hint, Bill?'

Bill laughed. 'Well, I just thought, if I didn't have my arm in plaster, I would have done a bit of digging for her.'

Neil smiled. 'Well, I'm not much of a gardener, Bill. You could give me some coaching. Don't forget that I need to do some digging for you.'

'Well, there's not much to do on my plot. Just get the potatoes planted next month, St Patrick's day is the time for that according to Paddy Murphy. And it's only another week until March.'

'Okay, Bill. Your wish is my command!'

Bill burst out laughing. 'Thanks, Neil. You're a champion.'

Neil felt a glow of optimism. 'What will I cook for dinner tonight, Bill?'

***

Brenda made the medical appointments for her mother. 'Right Mum, tomorrow morning at half past eight you have a fasting blood test. Nothing to eat from 9 o'clock tonight.'

'Not going.'

'Now, Mum, if you want to get your sleeping tablets and other medication you must go.'

'I'll go after breakfast.'

'No, it's a fasting blood test. You can't have anything to eat beforehand.' Brenda sighed. She could foresee difficulties with the other appointments.

To her surprise her mother didn't kick up a fuss the next morning. Then Brenda discovered why. Her mother now had the lead on her friend Edith.

Brenda smiled to herself at the revelation. It seemed her mother was keen to discover she suffered from some obscure medical complaint.

'That Edith said she's got high cholesterol and a Vitamin B12 deficiency,' Mrs Evans remarked as she sat in the car after her tests. 'She said she has to have blood tests every three months for sugar in her pee, or something like that.'

'Uh huh?' Brenda smiled to herself. 'So, tomorrow is the X-rays of your knees and hips. Ten o'clock, that all right?'

'Can I have my breakfast first?'

'Of course.'

The next day was Brenda's day off. She planned to go and see her allotment after lunch. Hopefully her mother would be tired after the morning outing for her x-rays and would be happy to have a nap after lunch.

***

Amanda struggled into her Mini. All these layers of winter clothes made it difficult to manoeuvre in and out of her little car. *I should really go on a diet.* She'd always been slim. It was only in the past year that she'd put on a bit of weight. She knew she was drinking a few more glasses of wine than recommended, but still. One had to have some little pleasures in life …

The few friends she had also liked the odd drink or two … when they met up for their monthly lunch, she was always careful to restrict herself to just two glasses. A nice cold white to start and a mellow red after the meal … but it was so cold today perhaps something a little stronger and warmer when she got home. A whisky? The thought cheered her.

***

The Allotment – how many people remember this old verse?
  'The north wind doth blow,
  And we shall have snow,
  And what will the robin do then, Poor thing?
  He'll sit in a barn,
  And keep himself warm,
  And hide his head under his wing, Poor thing!
  Gardeners don't like strong winds, young shoots and leaves get shredded and dried.

***

Brenda sighed. It seemed to take longer and longer every day to get her mother out of bed and dressed. It was her second appointment with the doctor this morning.

'Ah, Mrs and Miss Evans, come in.' Dr Morley beckoned them into his surgery. 'Take a seat.' He scanned his computer screen. 'Well, there's good news. Seems there's nothing physically wrong with you, Mrs Evans.'

Brenda's mother bridled. 'I'm a sick woman, doctor.'

Dr Morley surveyed her over his glasses. 'Indeed. Well, your cholesterol is high and triglycerols problematic. I'll just check your blood pressure again, if you'll take off your coat and roll up your sleeve.'

'See, I told you I was a sick woman,' Mrs Evans said triumphantly.

'Hmm. Well, I'll give you a prescription for some medication to treat those symptoms and I'd like you to see a physiotherapist, who will put you on an exercise program to build up those muscles and get those joints moving again.'

'What about my sleeping tablets?'

'I think once you get exercising, you'll find you sleep better. So, we'll hold off on those for the moment. Come back and see me in a month and we can review things.' He turned back to his computer, the printer whirred and he took two sheets of paper from it. 'Here you go, referral to a physiotherapist and a dietician.' He stood up.

Brenda helped her mother with her coat. 'Thank you doctor,' she said as he held the door open for them.

'Oh, Miss Evans. A word.' He gestured for her to come back into his surgery.

'Won't be a minute, Mum.' She turned to face Dr Morley.

'Don't let your mother bully you. You have to make her do things for herself. You must take care of yourself, you know.' He smiled at her.

She nodded. 'Thank you, Doctor.'

Walking out to the car, she felt anger building. The doctor had said there was nothing physically wrong with her mother.

She recalled the image of Colin's face, the last time she'd seen him, when he had called around to ask if she'd changed her mind and decided to come to Birmingham.

She'd avoided his eyes and muttered, 'I told mum I was thinking of moving to Birmingham and she clutched her chest and said she was having a heart attack. I had to call an ambulance ...' She'd pulled out a handkerchief and wiped the tears from her eyes. 'I can't leave her. She has no-one else.'

'I'm sorry, Brenda. I was hoping you'd reconsidered. We could have been so happy, perhaps had a family ...' He'd studied her for a few seconds, then bent down and kissed her. 'Keep in touch, Brenda, stay safe.'

Now Brenda wanted to punch this mother who had destroyed her chance of marriage and a family. Putting on a fake heart attack ...

She walked ahead and got in the car, leaving her mother to open the car door herself and get in. They drove home in silence.

The day of her mother's appointment with the physiotherapist arrived. Her mother fussed and grumbled and wondered what she should wear.

'I'm not going to do any exercises if that's what they tell me. Will I have to get undressed? I'd better put my blue petticoat on ... and my good dress.'

'It might be easier to wear that track suit I bought you. You might feel more relaxed.'

'Track suit! That baggy outfit! Wouldn't be seen dead in it.' Her mother glowered at her daughter.

By the time they reached the physiotherapist, Brenda had had enough of her mother's whining and carping.

'There you go Mum,' she said as she helped her mother into the waiting room. 'I'll be back in an hour.' She set off to buy a pair of work boots.

***

Bill gazed out the window. 'Bit of sunshine peeping through this morning, Neil.'

Neil looked up from preparing breakfast. 'So, we're off to the allotment and I'm to do some secret digging for that "little girl"'.

'Well, she's not very big and she does have a girlish face.'

'True. Now come and have breakfast. I'll bring the car around later.'

'Thank you, sir!' Bill gave a mock salute, and then felt bad. He hoped Neil wouldn't think he was mocking his army training. But Neil had been busy buttering the toast and hadn't seen the gesture.

Bill did his best not to make any sudden loud noises or anything that might startle Neil. He'd seen Neil's reaction when an open door had slammed shut with the wind. He didn't know whether to talk about it or not. He could ask Neil's sister, when she came next. But on those occasions, he and Neil went shopping, or to the allotment. An excuse not to get in her way.

'A lot of people here today,' Bill remarked as Neil parked in the small car park. 'That's nice.'

'Right, so show me what to do and where,' Neil said as they walked towards Bill's plot.

Bill pointed to a garden fork inside his shed. 'Mine only needs a forking over, it's pretty friable, but would you make a start on the little girl's place?'

Neil nodded.

'I'll just potter around and see who else is here. They'll want to know who you are and what happened to my arm.' He walked off, a smile on his face.

***

Brenda was thrilled with her new work boots. She'd been unsure whether to get the ones with steel toe caps ...

'Will you be lifting heavy weights that might fall on your feet, madam?' The assistant in the shop enquired.

Brenda tried to envisage what she'd be doing on the allotment. 'I don't think so, just digging and so on.'

'Then the ordinary ones should be fine.'

She had toyed with the idea of wearing them out of the shop, but then thought her mother would probably make some disparaging remark. No, she'd take them to wear at the allotment. She looked at her watch, hmm, better get going to the physiotherapist.

'What kept you, Brenda?' Her mother complained when Brenda pushed open the door. 'I've been waiting ages ...'

'Well, I'm here now, are you ready?' Brenda was delighted with herself at not answering her mother's question. 'How did you go?' She took her mother's elbow and shepherded her out to the carpark.

'It was a nightmare! The woman made me do all these stretches and bends, wants me back in another week and gave me a sheet of exercises to do at home!' She thrust the papers towards Brenda.

'That's great,' Brenda smiled. 'She'll soon have you mobile, and you'll be able to show Edith Milson when she comes to see you tomorrow.'

Her mother made a hmph sound and subsided into the car.

'Do up your seat belt, Mum.' Brenda usually did up the seat belt for her mother; now she sat and waited while her mother fumbled and grumbled. She leaned over. 'Mum, take this and slot it there.'

Eventually Brenda released the clutch and drove off. Every time she felt herself weaken and start to feel sorry for her mother, she recalled the doctor's words – there is nothing physically wrong with you, Mrs Evans ...

***

The Allotment

Great activity here today, at least five allotmenteers so far. And it's good to see Bill. Apparently, he slipped and broke his wrist and arm ... but he seems happier than he's been of late ... and the same man that he brought before is here too. Heard Bill call him Neil. Hullo, that person is going over to the new woman's plot. It's a real mess, poor old Arthur had neglected it.

***

Neil took the spade Bill had indicated and walked over to the next plot and started to dig. Bill had given him his spare key to Arthur's plot and pointed out the area to dig. 'Lucky, Arthur left me a key to his gate,' he'd said, then told him to only dig a single spade depth. 'Next frost will break down the soil and freeze any weed roots that you turn over, then the little girl can plant Arthur's seed potatoes."

Neil surveyed the plot. It was divided into several beds separated with grass paths. He soon got into a rhythm, feeling his muscles working.

'You're doing great, lad!'

Neil stopped digging and eyed Bill. 'Yes, it's coming on.' He appraised the work he'd done so far. 'Is it "friable", Bill?'

Bill nodded; his eyes filling with amusement. 'Do you know what "friable" means?'

Neil shook his head.

'Look it up.' Bill grinned. 'Now, I'm making a cuppa. Take a break.'

Neil nodded. 'Right.' He stabbed the spade into the ground and wiped his hands on the back of his trousers. He'd enjoyed the exercise. He saw a robin fly down and perch on the handle of the spade. It turned its head to one side, watching Neil.

'Okay, little bird, I'm taking a break. You can search for worms now.'

As if it understood, the robin flew down and plucked a worm from the soil.

Neil smiled.

***

Bill lit the kettle under the camping gas ring in his shed and watched Neil. He'd seen him talk to the robin; the first time he'd seen him smile. *This allotment was going to be good for Neil.*

'Been catching up with a few of the other allotment holders,' he said as Neil approached the shed.

'Saw you,' Neil said.

'Had to explain about my broken wrist and that you were helping me.'

The little kettle on the gas ring started to hiss.

'I'll make the tea.' Neil frowned. 'Don't want you having an accident with boiling water. Er, what did you say about me?'

'Only that you were a friend, helping me out.'

Neil nodded. 'Okay.'

Chapter Three
March

The Allotment

March winds and April showers bring forth May flowers ... so they say.

Bill's daffodils are making a show. Sunny today and several allotmenteers working on their plots. Hello! Here's Peter's wife! Poor Peter, the last time he was here his wife brought him in a wheelchair. Peter loved his roses; he had a beautiful David Austin rose called Mary Rose. He grew it for his wife, Mary. Delightful lady. She's got a big bag with her. She's unlocked Peter's shed and gone in ...

***

Bill watched Mary Flynn make her way to her husband's plot. 'Must go and see Peter's wife,' he said to Neil. 'Haven't seen her since she brought Peter last year, pushing him in a wheelchair. So sad. He was very ill. A couple of men helped her push the wheelchair, and we all did a bit on his plot. Just to keep it maintained, you know.' He stopped and stroked his chin. 'Poor Peter. He loved his plot. Spent every spare moment here. Used to grow this lovely rose, just so he could give his wife a bouquet on her birthday.' He sighed. 'Very romantic, was Peter. Heard he'd passed away. I'd better go and see how she's coping.'

Neil nodded. 'Okay, Bill. Here's your tea.'

'Thanks.' Bill took a few sips, his eyes still on the retreating figure of Peter's wife. He finished drinking and put the cup on the bench.

'Thanks, Neil. That's just how I like it.' He stood and walked out of the shed and towards his friend's plot.

He tapped on the open shed door. 'Hello, Mrs Flynn?'

She turned quickly. 'Oh, hello. Come in. I think you're Bill?'

Bill nodded. 'Yes, Peter was one of our best allotmenteers. I was sorry to hear he'd passed away.'

Tears came to her eyes. 'Thank you.' She turned and indicated an urn on the bench. 'I have Peter's ashes here, he asked that they be scattered over his plot.' She sighed. 'It's six months now since he passed but I haven't had the courage to do it.'

'My wife died just before Christmas.' Bill hesitated. 'I still have her ashes. I don't quite know where to put them.'

'I'm sorry to hear about your wife.' She paused and seemed to become aware of his plaster cast and arm sling. 'What happened to your arm?'

Bill recounted his story.

Mary listened, her eyes full of concern. 'How are you managing with your plot now?'

'Well, I was lucky that the lady who comes to clean for me every week has a brother who offered to come and help me.' Bill pointed out the door. 'You can see him over there, but that's not my plot he's digging, that's a new little lady's ground. She's just taken it over from poor Arthur Brown – Peter may have mentioned him – he's had a stroke and gone to a nursing home.'

'Oh, dear, such a lot of troubles,' Mary murmured.

'Well, most of us are getting on a bit. I suppose it's to be expected.' Bill sighed. 'Well, this new little lady is young and Arthur's plot was overrun with weeds and Neil said he'd dig it for her. She doesn't know yet.'

'That's kind of him.' Mary studied her husband's ground. It was divided into garden beds separated by grass paths. 'I think you must have all been helping to keep Peter's place neat and tidy. Thank you.'

'Peter always helped others if they needed it.'

Mary nodded. 'He was like that.'

'What will you do with it?' Bill couldn't help asking. He'd had the sudden idea that Neil might take it over once he, Bill, was fit again. It might help Neil with the shell shock.

'I don't know. Somehow, I hate the thought of letting it go. Peter loved coming here. He planted a rose for me, you know. Gave me a lovely bouquet each year on my birthday.' She sniffed and blew her nose. 'And then if I scatter his ashes here …'

Bill nodded and shuffled his feet.

'Do you think if I kept it on, that I'd be able to manage?' Mary turned to him. 'I don't know much about gardening.'

Bill smiled. 'Of course, you'd manage and everyone here would help you. And it would be nice for that new little woman, Brenda, to have another woman to chat with. And she said she knows nothing about gardening either!'

Mary gave a weak smile. 'I can give it a try, and I'd feel closer to Peter. How would I go about it?'

'I think you have to contact the council, but I can't see any problem.'

'Thank you, Bill. I think I'll leave Peter's urn here and maybe go to the council now before I lose my nerve.'

Bill walked away feeling a slight sense of achievement. Perhaps he'd helped Peter's widow.

***

Mary spoke aloud to her late husband as she drove. 'Peter, I hope you'll be happy if I keep your allotment. As soon as I get home, I'm going to ring the council and see if I can take over your plot. You'll be pleased, darling, I'm sure.' She was certain she heard Peter say "That would be lovely, but really, whatever you think, dearest."

After ringing the council and putting in her application, she went to her husband's study and found his gardening diaries. He'd kept meticulous records of when and where he'd sown or planted things, and what the results were. She put on a CD of his favourite classical music then took out the previous year's diary and started at March. That was when he'd first got sick with the cancer that eventually killed him. She turned the pages and realised that he'd actually done very little that year. The other allotmenteers must have gradually taken over to keep the plot tidy. Better to take the year before.

Right, here we are. *March 4th. Prepared ground for potatoes. Home Guard sprouting nicely.* Home Guard? Must be a potato variety. She'd go to the garden centre in the morning and find out.

She heaved a sigh. She had a new motive for living; keeping Peter's beloved garden flourishing.

***

Neil took out his phone to check the meaning of friable – hmm, easily crumbled. Okay, so Bill's soil was easily crumbled therefore perfect for planting. He nodded. Right Bill. Got it.

He kept digging. He was half way through Brenda's plot when he saw Bill approaching.

'That looks great, lad,'

Neil stretched and surveyed the plot. 'Hmm.'

'Time to go now, lad. I'll tell you all about Peter's wife on the way home. What do you think about dinner tonight? How about an Indian takeaway?

Neil felt relieved, his back had started to ache, and it looked as if he had a few blisters on his hands. Not used to so much physical exercise lately! He'd got soft. But it felt good. And the dark, freshly dug earth was pleasing.

'Sounds perfect, Bill.'

***

The Allotment

Pasteur said "A day without wine, is like a day without sunshine ..."

***

Amanda knew she was drinking a bit too much. *Don't care, what else have I got in life?* She asked herself. *Apart from you, Cato.* She nodded at her Persian cat who had come and curled up on her lap.

She wondered sometimes if her friends really cared about her. *Do I really care about them?* A little voice inside her said. They were women she'd worked with, women who'd seen her replaced by a younger, more attractive personal assistant. They'd tutted and sympathised and murmured consolingly, things like "bastard men, they're all the same; bit of attractive skirt and never mind if they can't type and field awkward customers ..." She'd lapped it up, it helped her regain her confidence. *But was it just schadenfreude on their part?* Were they secretly pleased she'd had her comeuppance? And now, this young piece, Brenda something, had arrived at the allotment, and all the old men were falling over themselves to help her! No-one had helped her, Amanda Harris, when she first got her plot!

Tears of self-pity threatened. *Get a grip, Amanda!* 'Okay Cato, shift your bum, I must top up my glass!' But Cato merely dug his claws into her lap and refused to budge.

She sighed. *Even Cato is against me.*

She pushed the cat off her lap and stood. *Right! I'll make myself a nice meal and start reading my new library book and stop all these negative thoughts!*

***

Brenda had been anticipating her next day off. She'd planned what she would do. First, get going with digging the plot. Then, according to her gardening books, she could plant the potatoes she'd found sprouting in Arthur's shed. Maybe she'd start small, just a couple of rows to begin with ...

She opened the front door, then called up the stairs to her mother, 'Mum, I'm off to the allotment. I've left your breakfast on the table. You just have to boil the kettle to make your coffee.' She took a deep breath, 'And don't forget, the physio said you have to make an effort, up and down the stairs a few times a day and be more active ...' She went out the door not waiting for her mother's reply, closing it behind her. *Phew, I did it!*

She hurried out to her car where she'd already stowed her new boots and a flask of coffee - elated at escaping her mother. She looked up at the sky. The forecast was good, chilly but no wind and a glimmer of sunshine.

At the allotment she parked and changed her shoes for the new boots. There were already a few people who waved to her as she passed by. As she approached her plot, she saw the freshly-dug earth. *Have I made a mistake? Is this my plot?*

She took out her key and tried the padlock. It worked! *Where should I start? More digging, or plant the potatoes?* She saw a woman approaching.

She looked at Brenda as she came near. 'Hello, you must be the new lady. I'm Mary Flynn.'

Brenda smiled. 'Yes, I'm Brenda Evans and this is my first day. I thought there must be some mistake as it looks like someone has been digging here.' She indicated the section of her plot.

'I'm kind of new too. I've taken over my late husband's plot.' Mary's eyes clouded, and she paused. 'Well, he loved his allotment, so I thought I'd keep it going. Peter kept a gardening diary so I'm going to try to follow what he did.'

'That's nice.' Brenda didn't know quite what to say. 'Um, my gardening book says now is a good time to plant potatoes. The previous tenant, Arthur, left a tray of seed potatoes so I was going to plant them today. But there seems to be a lot. Perhaps you'd like some?'

'Thanks, I would. I went to the garden centre yesterday to buy Home Guard seed potatoes but they'd sold out.' She paused and regarded the freshly-dug earth. 'I was talking to one of the men here last week, Bill. He's broken his arm and had a man helping him. I think that's who's been digging your plot.'

'Oh! That must be Neil. Tall, fair curly hair, nice looking?'

Mary nodded. 'So, you know him?'

'Not really, but he saved my life a few weeks ago.'

Mary started. 'Really? How?'

Brenda related the story of the armed hold up at the convenience store.

Mary shook her head. 'You were so lucky!'

'Yes.'

'Well, I suppose we'd better make a start. Peter sowed potatoes at this time, so I'd be grateful for a few.'

'Come in.' Brenda went into her shed and showed Mary the trays with the potatoes. 'There's an empty tray under the bench, I'll put some in there for you. My gardening book says you dig a small trench about four inches deep and put the potatoes in ten inches apart. And then rake soil over them. Oh, and make the rows about two feet apart.' She looked up at Mary, who nodded.

'I'll try and remember that. Oh, that's plenty, thank you, Brenda.'

Brenda laughed. 'You're doing me a favour! Less work for me today!'

'Well, we'll see how we both go!'

Brenda watched Mary walking up the path to her plot. She felt good meeting another newbie. And fancy Neil doing all that digging for her.

She found a hoe and started dragging it in a line along the ground to make a furrow. It didn't look very straight. Absorbed in her work she didn't hear Bill come up behind her.

'Hello Miss Evans, looks like you're making a start.'

Brenda jumped. 'Oh, Bill, Mary um Flynn said that Neil has been doing some digging for me. That was so nice of him. How can I thank him?'

'Well, he's just over in my shed, he's going to put in potatoes today.' He frowned at her furrow. 'You need a string line for that. I've got a couple of sticks and some string in my shed; I'll go and fetch them.'

'Thanks, Bill. Please call me Brenda.'

He smiled. 'Right, Brenda.'

A few minutes later, she saw Neil coming up the path.

'Bill said to make you up a string line.'

'Thank you, Neil, and for doing all this digging.'

He nodded. 'No problem, any time.' He tied the string to one stick and put it in the ground at the start of Brenda's furrow. Then laid the string in a line, tied it to the other stick, wound it around a few times, pulled it taut and stuck it in the ground at the end of the furrow.

Brenda smiled. 'Yes, that's much better. Thanks again.'

'Hmm. Better get back and plant Bill's spuds now.' He turned and walked away.

Brenda watched him. She wondered how he could spend so much time with Bill.

***

The Allotment - After a lifetime of blaming most sickness on bacteria, on his death bed Louis Pasteur apparently said to Professor Rénon who looked after him: "Le germe n'est rien, c'est le terrain qui est tout." ("The bacteria are nothing. The soil is everything.")

But did anyone pay attention?

***

Bill worried about Neil. 'You don't need to spend all day with me, you know,' he'd told Neil the first day Neil moved in. 'And feel free to watch telly any time you want ...'

'Thanks, Bill.'

'And take the car any time you need to.'

'You're too good, Bill.'

Bill thought he saw Neil's eyes moisten. 'No, you're a godsend for me. I couldn't manage without you.' He stood and patted Neil's shoulders. 'Now, why don't you go and see how your sister is?'

'Okay. I'll walk over.'

'Take the car.'

'No. The walk will do me good. I'll be back in time to get dinner.'

After Neil had left, Bill stared at Hazel's photo and sighed. 'Dunno, Hazel my love. Poor Neil, he's just so sad all the time. Depressed, I suppose. Like me after you left.'

***

Neil walked over to Anna's house. He knew she wouldn't be working that afternoon.

He knocked on the front door; he didn't like to just walk in as if he had a right to be there.

'Neil! Why didn't you just come round the back and walk in!'

Neil shrugged. 'Didn't feel right.'

Anna held open the front door. 'Well, come on in. Good to see you. How's Bill?'

'He's good.' Neil walked through to the kitchen.

'What's been happening?'

Neil looked around. 'Where's Tom?'

Anna shrugged. 'Dunno.'

Neil frowned. 'Is everything okay with you two?'

Anna slumped into a kitchen chair and put her head in her hands. 'I don't know, Neil. He's just so moody and miserable these days. Depressed, I suppose, ever since he was made redundant at the factory.'

'Hmm.' Neil could identify with that feeling. 'So, no prospect of any other work?'

Anna shook her head. 'And he feels it when he thinks I have to work at menial jobs to keep us afloat.' She looked up at her brother. 'How've you been, Neil?'

He got up and paced around the kitchen, then came back and sat opposite her. 'Okay, I 'spose. I've been up at Bill's allotment, digging his ground and another plot. A new woman. She works at the convenience store.'

Anna brightened. 'Is that the woman whose life you saved?'

Neil grimaced. 'The very same. But don't get any ideas, Sis. She's not my type.'

Anna nodded. 'Well, that's good news. Your type hasn't been much of a success ...'

'Don't be bitchy, Sis.'

'Sorry Neil. Didn't mean it like that.'

Neil stood. 'It's all right, Sis.' He walked around the table and patted her shoulder. 'I'm fine.. But I worry about you and Tom.' He glanced at his watch. 'If there's anything I can do ...' He stared at her for a moment. 'Well, I'd better go, Bill'll be worrying about me. He's such a nice guy.' He sighed.

***

Brenda finished making a narrow trench along the string line and had started placing the seed potatoes when a voice startled her.

'You're not doing that right.'

She raised her head and saw a young boy frowning at her. 'Oh?' She straightened.

'No. The eyes have to point upwards.'

'The eyes?'

'Yes, the sprouting bits.'

'Oh. I thought they were roots.' Brenda studied the neat row of potatoes she'd carefully placed in the furrow. She looked more closely at the boy.

He smiled. 'I'm Douglas Patterson. I've got Down Syndrome,' he recited proudly. 'That means I'm special.'

'Oh.' Brenda didn't know what to say.

'Yes. Most people have only forty-six chromosomes, but Downs people have forty-seven.'

'I see.'

Just then she heard a voice calling, 'Dougie, where are you?'

'That's my mum,' Dougie said turning round.

A woman appeared at Brenda's plot, somewhat out of breath. 'Sorry,' she said, 'is Dougie annoying you?'

'No,' Brenda smiled. 'He told me I was planting my potatoes upside down. I'm very grateful for his advice.'

Dougie beamed.

The woman smiled at Brenda. 'I'm Carol, Dougie's mum. We have a plot further up the allotment.' She waved her hand in the direction from which she had come. 'Dougie's a great gardener.'

'That's good to hear, because I'm very new and don't know much about gardening. Oh, and I'm Brenda.'

'Nice to meet you, Brenda. Now, come on Dougie, we've got a lot to do today.' Carol took her son's hand and guided him away.

'Nice to meet you, Miss Brenda,' Dougie sang out, looking back over his shoulder at her.

Brenda turned back to her potatoes. *I'm learning something every day.* She turned each potato over and used her hoe to backfill the furrow.

***

The Allotment – The new woman, I heard Bill call her Brenda, doesn't seem to have much of an idea about gardening … even young Dougie knows more. He's really blossomed since he and his mother started their allotment. Maybe blossomed isn't the right word for a boy – flourished? Developed? And Brenda was good with Dougie. I think she'll fit in …

***

Bill peered over his glasses at Neil. 'Have to go to the hospital today to get my cast off. Can't wait, the itch is driving me mad.' He pushed a knitting needle he'd found in Hazel's sewing box up into the plaster cast and twisted it around.

Neil smiled. 'What time?'

'Ten.'

'Right so, I'll bring the car round.' He frowned down at the breakfast table. 'I guess you won't be needing me to drive you anymore.'

'I think my arm will be a bit weak for a while. Have to go to physiotherapy apparently, so I'd appreciate it if you stayed here a bit longer … that's if you don't mind?'

Neil looked up. 'You're not just saying that?'

Bill's eyes turned towards the photo of Hazel. 'You know something, Neil?'

Neil shook his head.

'I really enjoy having you here. I was so lonely after Hazel passed away.' He wiped his eyes. 'I know it's not very exciting for a young fellow like you, being here with an old bloke like me … I've always been a bit of a boring old fart. I don't know what Hazel ever saw in me. She was the love of my life, you know.' He sniffed and blew his nose.

Neil was silent for a while, then said, 'Bill, you're definitely not a boring old fart!' He scratched his head. 'And, well ... I like being here too. And I'm beginning to enjoy the allotment.'

'So does that mean you'll stay a bit longer?' Bill leaned forward eagerly.

Neil smiled. 'Love to! Now, I'll get the car.'

***

'All done,' Bill said, emerging from the treatment room and entering the hospital waiting room. 'Look at this puny arm!' He held out a skinny, pallid arm. 'I have to go to physiotherapy twice a week and do all the exercises the physiotherapist gives me. They made an appointment for me for tomorrow morning.' His brows met in a frown. 'It's so painful to move it, Neil.'

Neil nodded. 'That was a nasty fracture, Bill. Wrist and arm. Not good.'

Bill sighed. 'So good to have you, son.' Then he realised what he'd said. He wished he'd had a son like Neil. He and Hazel had never been blessed with children, but if they'd had a son, he would have liked him to be like Neil.

'What about dinner, Neil? Indian takeaway?'

'Sounds good to me.'

***

Neil let in the clutch of Bill's car. It was a relief to know that Bill needed him for a bit longer. But he really had to get his act together. He couldn't stay forever at Bill's. And it appeared Anna was happier with him not being at her place ... He came out of his reverie to hear Bill chatting away about the gorgeous nurses and doctors at the hospital …

'I told them I had this lovely young bloke helping me,' Bill was saying. 'Told this young nurse about you, said you were a treasure. Think she's interested, Neil.' He nudged Neil's thigh with his knee. 'What do you think, eh?'

Neil made a snorting sound. 'Oh, Bill, I'm not exactly a great catch for any woman!'

'Now, now, you're a handsome young fella, Neil, just what a modern young lady needs!'

Neil burst out laughing. 'Bill, you're a tonic!'

'Do my best, Neil.' Bill gave him a sidelong look. 'You'd like a new lady in your life, Neil, wouldn't you?'

Neil shrugged. 'Too much baggage, Bill.'

'Baggage?'

'Yeah, that's the technical term for all that's happened in my life that stops me from forming a new relationship.'

Bill was silent. They drove for a bit, then Neil said, 'But thanks for trying, Bill.'

The next day, Neil parked the car outside the physiotherapist. 'Here we go, Bill, if you find out how long you'll be, then I'll go for a walk and come back for you.' He held the door open for Bill and waited for him to talk to the receptionist.

'About an hour,' Bill said.

'Great.' Neil turned to go out the door as it opened and an old woman came in.

'There you go, Mum, I'll see you in an hour.' The voiced sounded familiar.

'Oh, hello Neil, fancy meeting you here.' It was Bill's "little allotment woman".

'Um, yes, just bringing Bill for physio on his arm. He had the cast off yesterday.'

He saw her hesitate.

'Er, I was going to go for a coffee while I wait for mum. Don't suppose you'd like to join me? I want to thank you for doing all that digging at my allotment.'

The last thing Neil wanted was to have to sit and talk to this woman whose name he kept forgetting, but then she looked up at him and he couldn't refuse.

'I'm Brenda, you saved my life.'

He sighed. 'Thanks, Brenda, coffee's a good idea.' He wished she wouldn't keep banging on about him saving her life.

She led the way to the other side of the car park. 'I usually have a coffee here while I wait for mum. Your dad will probably finish around the same time.'

'My dad?' Inside the café, Neil pulled out a chair from a free table and gestured to Brenda to sit down.

'Oh!' Brenda appeared confused. 'I thought Bill must be your father.'

'No. My sister knows Bill and when he fell and broke his arm, she suggested I stay with him for a while to help him.' He waited for her to ask was he married and how did he get time off to take Bill around.

'That's nice for you both,' she said and stood. 'Now, what would you like?'

'Please, let me,' Neil also stood.

'No, it was my suggestion.' She smiled. 'I'm having a flat white, how about you?'

'Long black, please. Thanks.' He sat down and wished he could have a cigarette. He watched her at the counter. She seemed quite nice. Single by the look of it.

She came back and sat opposite him, putting her handbag on the empty chair beside her. 'I can only get to the allotment on my days off, so it was lovely to find a freshly dug patch. I don't know much about gardening, but the other people there are so helpful.'

Neil nodded. He didn't know what to talk about. Again, he waited for her to start questioning him, but she was gazing out the window.

Their coffee arrived and they sat in silence until Neil remembered her mother. He grasped at the thought.

'How long has your mother been going to the physiotherapist?'

She seemed relieved to be able to talk. 'This is her third time.'

He racked his brains to think of something else to say. 'Did she break something?' *Stupid question Neil.*

'No, she's been an invalid for a long time and her muscles have wasted a bit.'

'So, she's getting stronger?'

'Slowly.' Brenda took a sip of coffee and waved a hand at the window. 'Looks like it's turning into a nice day. That usually happens when I have to work, and then it rains on my day off and I can't get up to the allotment.'

Ah ha! Talk about her job, Neil.

'Have you been working in the convenience store for long?'

'Too long, probably,' Brenda sighed. 'But it's convenient, so to speak. It allows me to take care of mum in the mornings, get her meals and so on.' She grimaced. 'And I'm not qualified for anything else really.'

He could think of nothing more to say.

She glanced at her watch. 'I'd better be getting back to the physio for mum.'

'I'll come with you. Bill will probably be ready.'

She smiled.

As they walked out the door, Neil turned to her. 'Do you mind if I smoke?'

'Not at all.'

***

Brenda was surprised to get a message from Colin:

Hi Brenda. Job's going well, and I've found a nice little town house to rent. I'll be back next weekend to collect some of my stuff. Can we meet? Have you thought any more about joining me?

What about coming down to Birmingham and spending a week here? See if you like it.

I've been doing some research into Aged Care homes in Birmingham and found two really lovely places. You could come and check them out.

Love

Col xxx

She blinked away tears. She'd thought it was all over once Colin moved. And she missed him. Why was life so difficult? She resolved to tackle her mother in the morning - she didn't know how to reply to Colin.

Next morning after her mother had eaten her breakfast – at least now she came downstairs for it – Brenda sat at the table opposite.

'Mum, you know Colin has moved to Birmingham?'

'So, you said. Wanted me to go too! As if I would! I suppose he's found a new girl-friend there. Never liked him. Still. Beggars can't be choosers, you're not exactly a great catch, are you?' She dug a spoon into the marmalade jar.

Brenda took a deep breath. 'Colin wants us to get married.'

Mrs Evan's head jerked up. 'Married? You? And what about me? I don't want him coming here to live, drinking beer and hogging the telly with his sport.'

'Well, no, it would mean moving to Birmingham.'

'I told you, I've no intention of moving anywhere!'

Brenda struggled on. 'Apparently there are some lovely aged care places around that would suit you perfectly.'

Her mother banged her spoon on her plate. 'Aged care? AGED CARE! So that's your little plan, is it? Stick me in a home, sell this house and take off with the proceeds!'

'No, Mum! It's not like that! But I need to live my own life! I could marry Colin and have a family. You could have grandchildren.'

'Phut! What would I want with grandchildren? You were bad enough, always whining and crying. Anyway. What about your allotment you're always going on about? You'd have to leave it AND your poor old mother!' She groaned and grasped her chest. 'Oh, oh! That pain is coming on again!'

Brenda tried to harden her heart. 'The last time that happened, do you remember, Mum? The hospital said there was nothing wrong with your heart. It's all in your mind.'

Her mother took out a handkerchief and blew her nose. 'You're so hard, Brenda!' she snuffled. 'How did I ever give birth to such a thankless child? After everything I've done for you!'

'Anyway, Mum. Think about it. You'd like it in an aged care place. They have lots of activities and outings for the residents. And I'd be able to come and see you often.'

Her mother wiped her eyes.

'Well, he's asked me to go and stay for a week ... have a break.'

Her mother sniffed.

Brenda stood and cleared the table.

***

Neil took Bill to his next physiotherapy appointment. He held an umbrella over Bill as they walked from the car park. The rain was heavier.

'Don't need to mollycoddle me, Neil!' Bill grinned. 'Oh, look, there's that nice little girl, Brenda, with her mother.' He eyed Neil. 'You could take her for a coffee.'

Neil pretended not to hear him.

They drew near. 'Hello, Brenda,' Bill called out. 'Neil was just wondering if you'd like to go for a coffee.'

Brenda turned. 'Oh! Bill! Right! Yes, Neil, that would be nice.' She smiled. 'There you go, Mum.' She pushed her mother into the physiotherapist's rooms.

Neil held the umbrella over Brenda as they walked across the car park to the café. 'My turn,' he said, as he shook his umbrella and opened the café door.

'Thanks, Neil.'

The coffee shop was warm and fuggy. 'Phew,' said Brenda, loosening her scarf. 'Bit steamy in here.' She scanned the room. 'I don't think there're any empty tables.'

Neil's hopes started to rise. He didn't like the noisy atmosphere.

'Oh, those people are just leaving.' Brenda indicated a table.

Neil nodded. 'Flat white?' he asked.

'You remembered ...'

He went to the counter and ordered, then returned to her table and sat opposite her.

She seemed far away, a slight frown on her face.

'Won't be long.'

'Hmm?' She raised her eyebrows.

'Just saying, coffee won't be long.'

'Thanks.'

'Um, is everything all right? You seem a bit ...' he didn't know how to continue.

Brenda blinked. She looked down at her hands. 'No, I'm fine,' she mumbled. 'It's just ... well, my boyfriend has moved to Birmingham and wants me to go and stay for a week ...' She raised her eyes. 'But I don't know how I can leave Mum.'

'Oh, right.' He surveyed the crowded room, wondering what to say. 'Hasn't she got any friends that could stay with her for a week?'

Brenda stared at him. Then her face brightened. 'Edith Milson! Of course! Thank you, Neil! You really are a life saver, you know.'

He frowned, unsure what she meant.

Brenda beamed. 'Well now, how's Bill going?

'He seems to be doing well, arm's getting stronger all the time.'

'What does that mean for you, Neil?'

He scowled. *She sounds like a bloody psychologist!*

'What do you mean?' He stalled.

'Oh, it's just that I thought you were only staying with Bill until he was strong enough to manage on his own.'

He stared at her.

'Oh, I'm sorry, I didn't mean to be intrusive. It's none of my business.' She fidgeted with her watch.

Their coffee arrived.

'No, it's okay,' Neil said. 'Bill would like me to stay a bit longer. He seems lonely on his own since his wife died.'

Brenda nodded. 'Yes, it must be hard when you've lived with one person all those years and then suddenly they're no longer there.'

'Hmm.' He didn't know what to say.

'My mother's getting stronger.'

'Good. Um. How is your allotment going?'

'Haven't been up there for a while. It's been too wet and windy on my days off.' Brenda sighed and looked at her watch. 'Sorry, Neil, I've got to fly, have to do some shopping before I get Mum from the physio.'

He nodded and stood. 'No probs, Brenda. Might see you next week or at the allotment.'

'Yes. Thanks for the coffee.' Her smile spread across her face. 'And thanks for the idea about Edith Milson! Bye Neil.'

He watched her walk out of the café. He had no idea what Edith Milson had to do with anything. He finished his coffee, collected his jacket and scarf from the back of his chair. Mustn't forget his umbrella. He was gasping for a cigarette.

***

Brenda felt elated walking back to the physiotherapist. She'd ring Edith Milson as soon as she got home. What a great idea of Neil's! Well, that was if Edith would do it.

Back home, she waited until her mother was eating her lunch then she went to the telephone in the hall, shut the doors and dialled.

'Oh, hello, Mrs Milson.'

'Edith, dear, call me Edith. It's Brenda, isn't it? I recognized your voice.'

'Yes, it is. Well, Edith, I was wondering if you'd come and stay with Mum for a few days while I had a break ...' Brenda didn't quite know how to say the words.

'You mean, come and stay and look after your mother?'

'Well, yes ...'

'I'd love to!'

'Oh, Mrs Milson, I mean, Edith, that would be fantastic! I'm not sure of the dates yet, just wanted to check with you.'

'That's all right, dear, I don't have anything planned for the next few weeks.'

Brenda felt pretty sure that the "few weeks" were actually a few months.

'Thank you so much, Edith. I'll firm up the arrangements and get back to you.' She hesitated. 'Don't say anything to Mum at this stage until I finalise things.'

'Of course, dear! Mum's the word!'

Brenda heard her chuckling.

***

The Allotment – Strong winds this March. A lot of plots suffered damage. One shed had the galvanized roof blown off. It was a pretty shabby job anyway. That plot is a rag tag affair... Stuff coming up all over the place, no paths or proper beds. I heard the warden admonish the plot holder - think he's what they call a Hippie, he's got a pony-tail - about it letting down the tone of the allotment. But he replied "Fukuoka". The warden frowned and went red. 'That kind of language is inappropriate,' she said, straightening her shoulders and frowning. Then he laughed and explained he's basing his allotment on Masanobu Fukuoka's book *The One Straw Revolution.*

'I'm sure you must have read it,' he said and she looked all confused and stalked off.

***

Bill tut-tutted when he saw the broad beans bent over from the wind.

'We'll soon get them upright,' Neil said. 'I'll put a few more stakes in and tie them up.'

Bill looked up at the sky. 'Bugger, the rain's getting heavier, we'd better head back home. Good match on the telly tonight.' He loved having Neil watch the matches with him. Hazel had never been interested in football or cricket, so he'd always watched the games on his own while she did things with her friends. It made such a difference having Neil.

Neil nodded 'Okay, Bill, should be a good game.'

***

Neil was happy to watch the matches with Bill, but sometimes the noise bothered him. He probably needed to go back to his group meetings. Hadn't been for a few weeks. He was trying a new, well, new to him anyway, technique, EFT, no, not Electronic Funds Transfer, ha ha! Emotional Freedom Technique. Tapping on the meridians. He felt a bit silly doing it, but at this stage he'd try anything to get back to normal. Whatever normal was. He'd been practicing it in the kitchen one morning when Bill walked in. Bill seemed a bit bemused, but you had to hand it to old Bill, he took everything in his stride – didn't question what he, Neil, did.

***

Amanda was annoyed with herself and with that Mr Saraswati as he called himself. Put her on the back foot. But she'd better get that book he was talking about. If she could remember the name.

Something about Straw. She'd ask at the library. Even so, surely, he could keep his allotment tidy.

***

Brenda sent a message to Colin:

Hello Colin, well, I've arranged for one of Mum's friends to come and stay for a few days so I'll be able to take time off and visit you whenever it's convenient.

Xxx Brenda

She pushed the send button and sat back. *Phew! I've done it.*

Later that afternoon her phone rang.

'Hi Brenda, it's me, Colin. I got your message.'

'Oh right. What do you think?'

'I could take next Friday off and drive up and fetch you.'

'I could drive myself ...'

'Dunno, love. You're not used to driving in city traffic and my place is a bit tricky to find.'

Brenda sighed with pleasure. *Colin was so considerate!* 'Okay, then, that sounds good. Let me know what time to expect you.'

'Can't wait to see you, Bren. But I've got to dash now. Got a darts tournament at the local pub.'

'Oh! Right. Well, bye for now. Love you!'

'Love you too.'

'Who was that on the phone, Brenda?' It was her mother calling from the dining room.

'Um, it was Colin, Mum.' She hesitated, 'He's coming up next Friday and I'm going back to Birmingham with him for a few days. Edith Milson is going to come and stay with you while I'm away.'

There was silence. Dreading the worst, Brenda held her head high and marched into the dining room.

'So!' thundered her mother. 'You're going off for a sleazy week-end with that no-good Colin, leaving your mother to the mercies of that hopeless Edith Milson!'

'I thought you liked her,' Brenda muttered.

'Hmph! Couldn't care less if I never saw her again, but she seems to like coming round here, so, out of the goodness of my heart, I humour her.'

'Well, she's all excited about coming to stay ...'

'So, you two cooked up this plan between you, without consulting me?'

'Well, there would have been no point in consulting you, would there?' Brenda had suddenly had enough of pandering to her mother. 'You wouldn't have agreed, would you?'

Her mother's mouth fell open, and she stared at Brenda.

'So, it's your choice. I've got time off work and I'm going. You can either stay here on your own and look after yourself or have Edith come and stay with you.'

'What about my physiotherapy treatment?' her mother's voice quavered.

'I can book a taxi to pick you up.' Brenda turned and walked out of the room, her heart thumping. It was the first time she'd had the courage to answer her mother back. She felt quite shaky. Maybe she'd pop up to the allotment to calm herself. It would be another hour or so before it got dark.

'I'm going to the allotment,' she called out.

***

The Allotment - been drizzling all day, only old Paddy Murphy showed up. Poor Paddy, very sad what happened to him. Oh! Hello! Here's Peter's wife ... what's she doing here in this bad weather? And now I can see the new little woman parking her car. They say misery loves company ...

***

Mary had been steeling herself to scatter Peter's ashes on the plot. Every time she went to the allotment, there were people around. She wanted to do it with no spectators, no-one to pass by and stop and chat. She wanted a private moment, where she could shed tears and not have anyone come and sympathise or tell her time was a great healer. She wanted to scream – shout out to Peter – he should not have left her, not got cancer ...

Now it was late afternoon. It had been raining so probably no-one would be at the allotments. A watery sun tried to burst through the clouds. *Anyway, it didn't matter if it rained – it suited her mood.*

She parked at the allotments. *Good, no other cars ...*

She hurried up to her plot, noticing that the potatoes she'd got from that little woman had started to show through the ground. *What had Peter's diary said? Earth up the new growth. Whatever earthing up meant! Right, I'll do that the next time. Right now, my mission is the urn.*

She unlocked the shed, went in and took Peter's urn in her arms.

'Okay Peter ... your last wish ...'

She walked out carrying the urn. Tears rolled down her cheeks. 'Peter, I love you!' she screamed. 'Why did you leave me?'

She felt like dashing the urn to the ground and letting the ash fall in a clump. She made her way down the grass path to the end of the plot and taking a deep breath, up ended the urn, letting the contents trickle out onto the ground. Tears obscured her vision.

'Why did you have to go, Peter?' she yelled and walked backwards shaking the urn as she went.

She'd reached the shed, still clutching the now empty urn, when she heard a voice.

'Are you okay?'

'What do you think? No, no, no!' Then she noticed that little woman.

'Um, I heard shouting and thought I'd better see if you were all right ...'

Mary took a deep breath and closed her eyes. 'I was scattering my husband's ashes.'

'Oh! I'm sorry. I didn't mean to intrude ... as long as you're all right.'

'I'll never be ALL RIGHT again!'

'Sorry ... well I'll go then.' Brenda turned.

Mary took a deep breath. 'Sorry, um, forget your name, but I'm okay, just ... um, well thanks for checking on me.'

'It's Brenda. Sorry. I'll leave you in peace.'

Mary took another breath. 'No. Don't go just yet. Come into my shed ... my late husband's shed, please?'

Brenda frowned. 'I only came up here to get away from my mother. I'd better get back to her now.'

'No, please. Just stay and talk normal things.'

'Normal things?'

'Well, you know. Stuff that normal people talk about.'

Brenda grimaced. 'Sorry,' she hesitated. 'It's Mary, isn't it?'

Mary nodded.

'Well, I don't know what normal is.'

Mary's interest was piqued. She carefully placed the urn on the bench in the shed and turned to Brenda. 'What do you mean?'

Brenda shrugged. 'Well, here I am, thirty something years old, living with my mother, a miserable job, boyfriend moved to Birmingham, just shouted at my mother ...' She rubbed her eyes. 'Right. As long as you're okay, I'd better get back. To my mother. Just thought, well, I didn't see any one else here ...'

Mary patted Brenda's shoulder. 'Thank you, Brenda. That was very nice of you.' She paused. 'Um, how about we go for a drink? Relax, have a little chat.'

Brenda stared at her. 'My mother ...'

Mary turned away, 'Of course. Yes, your mother. Sorry.'

'Maybe another time?'

'Yes, of course.' Mary started to gather her things. She glared at the urn. 'What does one do with an empty funeral urn?'

Brenda stared at the ceramic urn which was decorated with blue mosaic. 'It's very attractive. Well, I suppose you could make a lampstand?'

'With a pretty lampshade? What a great idea!' Mary suddenly burst into a raucous laugh. 'A great idea, Brenda! A permanent memento! The lampshade could be a collage of photos of my husband! Shed a little light on my misery!'

Brenda blinked. 'Er, well, I'd better go.'

Mary stopped laughing. 'Sorry Brenda. I didn't mean ... please excuse me, I'm a bit upset at the moment. Yes, get back to your mother.'

Brenda started to walk out of the shed, then she turned back. 'I suppose we could go for a quick drink, Mary.'

***

Brenda smiled at Mary, who now seemed reluctant to go for a drink.

'No, no. you get back to your mum.'

Brenda took Mary's arm. 'My mother needs to realise I'm a grown woman with a life of my own.' She tried to convince herself.

'Right, come on then. I know a nice little pub near here, The Water Mark. Peter and I used to go there a bit.' Mary swallowed hard. 'Do you know the way?'

Brenda shook her head. 'No.'

'Right, well I'll drive ahead and you can follow me.'

Brenda parked and followed Mary into the pub. She noticed the sudden silence as they entered. Men's heads turned to look at Mary. Not surprising, Brenda thought. Mary was beautiful; her long, wavy dark hair framed an elfin face, blue eyes with long lashes and that rosebud mouth. Brenda felt a twinge of envy.

'This okay?' Mary's voice broke through Brenda's thoughts. She was indicating a corner seat in the snug.

'Yes. Fine,' she hesitated, 'Mary, what would you like to drink?'

'Brandy, please.' Mary slumped onto the corner seat. 'A double.'

'Right.' Brenda went to the bar. 'Double brandy and a bitter lemon please.'

The barman smirked at Brenda. 'Right, love. Bitter lemon's for you?'

Brenda nodded.

'Here we go, brandy for your friend.'

Brenda carried the drinks back to the table where Mary sat. Already there were two men there. 'Excuse me,' she said, placing the brandy in front of Mary. 'Excuse me,' she repeated in a louder voice. 'We're having a private conversation here.' She stared at them until they got up and left. Mary scarcely noticed.

'Thanks, Brenda.' She downed her drink in one gulp.

'Um, would you like another?' Brenda felt dismay at Mary's swift emptying of her glass.

'Yes, please, but it's my turn.'

'No, it's okay. Stay where you are.' Brenda looked up to see the barman watching them. She indicated Mary's empty glass and he nodded. Brenda went to the bar.

'Here you go, Mary.' Brenda placed the full glass on the table in front of Mary.

'Thanks, Brenda.'

Mary's eyes clouded as she focused on Brenda, who was relieved to see Mary take just a sip of her second drink.

'He was the love of my life, you see.'

'You were lucky.'

'Lucky? What do you mean?' Mary stared at Brenda.

'Well, to know such love.'

'Hadn't thought of it that way.' She heaved a sigh and drank more of her brandy. 'I was eighteen when I met him. He was forty-two, married with a son. His son never forgave me for breaking up his parents' marriage. Never forgave his father either.'

She stared at Brenda. 'What am I to do, Brenda? How can I keep on living?'

Brenda looked around the crowded pub, as if seeking an answer. 'No idea, Mary, look after his allotment perhaps. Just keep going, I suppose. One day at a time.'

'Is that what you do?'

Brenda shuffled on the hard bench. 'Well, I guess it is.'

'You said you have a boyfriend.' Mary's voice trailed away.

'Yes, but he's moved to Birmingham.'

'Will you go after him?'

Brenda swirled her drink and studied the bubbles. 'I'm going to stay with him for a week soon. It's just been a bit hard organizing someone to stay with my mother. She's never been left on her own before.'

'If you really loved him, you'd have just up and gone.'

'Hmm.' Brenda turned her watch on her wrist.

'You want to go?'

'Well, it's just I have to get my mother to bed.'

Mary snorted. 'Go then.'

'Mary, I can't just leave you here. And I think perhaps I should drive you home.'

'I'll have another drink first.' Mary opened her bag and took out her purse. 'Here, get me another, please. And one for yourself.' She thrust a twenty-pound note at Brenda.

Brenda took the note and went to the bar. 'Same again, please.'

'You want to keep an eye on your friend, love, can't serve her anymore drinks tonight. Not after this one.'

'Okay, thanks.'

Brenda returned to Mary. She didn't know what to say. She took another surreptitious look at her watch.

Mary stood. 'It's okay, I'll leave now. Don't need you to drive me.' She drained her glass and placed it unsteadily on the table.

Brenda followed her out of the pub. 'Please let me drive you home, Mary.'

Mary stumbled to her car, a racy, red sports model and fumbled for her keys.

Brenda took her arm. 'Please, Mary? I'll worry all night otherwise.'

Mary gave a harsh laugh. 'Poor little worry-wart Brenda.' After struggling unsuccessfully to get her car key in the lock, she turned to Brenda, her bravado suddenly gone 'All right, you win.' She turned to the car parked next to her. 'This yours?'

Brenda nodded.

'It suits you.'

Brenda opened the passenger door of the small grey hatchback. She didn't ask in what way it suited her.

She started the engine. 'Where do you live, Mary?'

Brenda was thankful that the address was on her way home. She stopped outside the house and turned to Mary, whose chin had sunk onto her chest. 'Wake up, Mary. You're home.'

Brenda managed to get Mary out of the car and to the front door.

'I all right now,' Mary slurred, as she rummaged in her bag. She found the front door key, tried and failed to get it in the lock.

'Here, let me.' Brenda opened the door.

'Come in and talk to me, Bren.' Mary staggered to a couch in the living room and collapsed onto it.

'I'll just lock my car.' Brenda didn't want to stay and talk but neither did she like to leave Mary. But when she returned, she found Mary fast asleep on the couch. A throw blanket was on the back of the couch. She took off Mary's boots, lifted her feet onto the couch and tucked the throw around her.

She studied Mary for a few minutes, then, thinking it safe to leave her, she put the key on a hook beside the front door and went out, closing the door behind her.

She checked the time. Ten thirty. Her mother would be spitting chips. And so much for her day off.

***

Neil had to get out and walk sometimes. 'Just going for a walk, Bill,' he called out. Ten o'clock. He needed to walk in order to get to sleep tonight. The last few nights he'd hardly slept.

'Okay, I'll just watch a bit of telly then I'll go to bed. I can manage all right, Neil.'

Neil closed the front door behind him. Should he go left or right? Left felt better. So many decisions in life. Left or right? Right or wrong? Kill or get killed?

He turned left and took brisk strides along the pavement leading to the shopping centre. Half an hour later and he passed The Water Mark. Strange name for a pub, he thought. It was all lit up and as he passed by the door opened and two women came out accompanied by the sound of music and laughter. He paused. One looked like Bill's "little girl", the convenience store woman, and she had her arm around the other woman. He frowned, then saw them get into a car. He stood back as the car reversed and drove off. He shook his head. The convenience woman might be gay ... But no, hang on, she'd said she had a boyfriend ... bisexual? Stop it, Neil, he rebuked himself. None of your business.

He walked on, gradually feeling calmer.

***

Bill settled back to watch TV, but somehow, he couldn't concentrate. He flipped through the channels before deciding on a recorded soccer match. Even then, half of his mind wondered if Neil was all right. He yawned, he was tired, but it didn't feel right going to bed with Neil still out.

Don't be an idiot, he admonished himself. He's a grown man, ex-army, he can look after himself. You're worrying for nothing.

He put the kettle on. He'd turn on his electric blanket and make a hot drink, then go to bed. Up in his bedroom, he toyed with the idea of turning on the electric blanket in Neil's bed. Then thought better of it. Don't be an old woman, Bill!

He sat in bed drinking his hot chocolate, too tired to watch the TV in his room. As he turned off his bedside light, he heard the front door open. He smiled, sighed and settled down in his bed. Neil was home.

Next morning, he came downstairs to see Neil at the kitchen table tapping his forehead. He stopped, then heard Neil mumbling. Not wanting to interrupt, he hovered by the kitchen door until Neil sensed his presence, for he turned and stood up.

'Oh, good morning, Bill. How are you today?'

'Good thanks, Neil.' Bill paused. 'Um, you okay?'

'You saw me tapping?' Neil frowned.

'Tapping?'

Neil sighed. 'Yeah, it's a new technique I've learned at my group therapy session.'

Bill knew that Neil went to a therapy session every week but he didn't really understand what it was all about.

'Oh?' Bill sat down at the kitchen table.

'It's helped a lot of people. May help you, Bill.'

'Me? I don't have shell shock!' Bill straightened in his chair.

'No, but it's supposed to help with depression and grief and all kinds of things. Dunno if it works ...'

Bemused, Bill nodded. 'I'm not depressed. Just miss Hazel, is all.'

'Anyway. Breakfast?' Neil appeared keen to change the subject.

'Yep!'

***

Brenda hovered by the front door, Edith Milson had arrived and Brenda had shown her around, explained how things worked and now she was waiting for Colin. At last, she heard a car stop outside. She opened the door and peered out. Yes, it was Colin. She picked up her suitcase.

'I'm off now, Mum!' she called out. 'Colin's just outside.'

Edith Milson appeared from the kitchen.

'You have a lovely time, dear. Don't worry about your mother, she'll be fine.'

Brenda's mother hadn't spoken to her since Edith had arrived that morning. 'Thanks, Edith. Ring me if there is a problem.'

Her heart in her mouth, Brenda hurried out to the waiting car, dragging her suitcase behind her.

Colin was in the driver's seat as she opened the passenger door. 'Throw your case in the back, love,' he said.

Brenda heaved in her case, then slid into the passenger seat.

'Hello, sweetie,' Colin said, leaning over to give her a quick peck on the cheek.

Brenda glanced at him. Had he put on weight? It was three months since she'd seen him.

'You're looking well, Colin.'

He smiled at her. 'Good to see you, Bren. Missed you.' He turned up the radio. 'Just got to listen to this match ...'

Brenda nodded and gazed at the passing scene.

***

Mary woke early the next morning. Her head was throbbing and her mouth felt like the bottom of a parrot's cage.

She struggled to sit up then peered at the throw covering her. The previous night's events started to come back. Peter's urn, that little woman, Brenda, was it? The pub? She'd have to apologise when she saw Brenda next.

As she made her way to the kitchen, she noticed her boots neatly placed beside the couch. She drank a glass of water and took two headache tablets.

Where was her car? Oh! The pub. Well, she'd have to either walk there or get a taxi. Walk to clear her head. Shower first …

***

Brenda dozed for a bit. The football match commentary was boring but Colin seemed to be enjoying it. At last, the car drew up outside a row of town houses.

'Wake up Bren! This is it, my pad!' Colin shook her arm.

Brenda dragged herself awake. 'Oh! Lovely, Colin. It seems really nice.'

'Bring your case in, I'll open the front door.'

Colin unlocked the door and took her case as she struggled up the path. 'Shit, what have you got in here? Moving in already, eh? I'll take it upstairs, you have a squizzy at the place. Think you'll like it.'

Brenda walked into the lounge room and through to the kitchen. She could hear Colin lumbering up the stairs with her case. Maybe she'd brought too much with her, but she needed at least four books and a few pairs of shoes for different occasions … It looked nice … She saw a kettle, took it and filled it. A cup of tea would be good.

She heard Colin clattering down the stairs.

'Making a cuppa, are you?'

'Yes.' She turned towards him. It seems a lovely place, Colin.'

'How about a kiss then?' He took her in his arms. 'Mmm,' he murmured. Then he held her away from him. 'Thought we'd have an early night.' He winked. 'We can just get a take-away, save you cooking. A cosy evening together. Been looking forward to you coming, Bren.'

She nodded. 'Yes, it'll be great.' She wondered if she should ring home, see how things were going. But if Edith Milson wasn't coping, there was nothing she could do about it now. And she'd given Edith her mobile number in case of an emergency.

'Kettle's boiled. You sit down, love. I'll bring you a cuppa.'

Brenda smiled. *It's nice to be waited on.*

***

Mary walked to the pub and found her car. She sat in it and wondered what to do. She could drive to the allotment – that Brenda might be there and she could apologise for her behaviour. Anyway, she needed to bring Peter's urn back – couldn't leave it there.

She drove to the allotment. Only a few cars there. Good.

She saw no-one as she walked to her plot – Peter's plot – she couldn't think of it as hers. *Peter! Why did you ask me to scatter your ashes here? Tie me to this ground?* Only for his ashes, she would have let the allotment go, not bothered with it. She was no gardener; she'd listened with a smile when Peter had told her what was growing, how something was coming on, what had been demolished by caterpillars or snails – not really taking in what he was saying, just enjoying the sound of his voice, his enthusiasm ...

She looked at the potatoes Brenda had given her. They were peeping up through the soil. New life. ...

She unlocked the shed and saw the urn there. She'd take it home and smash it – put it in the bin – she didn't want its constant reminder.

Stifling her tears, she clutched the urn, walked back to her car, and threw the urn onto the back seat. As she drove, she noticed a big waste bin outside a shopping centre. She stopped, grabbed the urn, and hurried to the bin. She struggled to lift the lid and managed to open it wide enough to drop the urn inside. There was a shattering noise.

She immediately regretted her action, but there was no way she'd be able to lift the lid and reach inside and retrieve all the pieces.

She made her way back to the car, hardly able to see through the tears clouding her vision.

***

Amanda didn't know if she could be bothered going to her plot today. She'd had a bit too much to drink last night and had woken with a headache. She stood at the kitchen window, a glass of water in her hand and two pain killers. *Why had I ever got the allotment anyway?* She tried to recall her reasons. It was after she'd been made redundant and she'd felt lonely and isolated, with no motivation to get up in the mornings. Her father had taken on an allotment after he retired. It kept him busy and out of her mother's way. At least with an allotment she'd get to know people ... maybe meet a man ... and when the warden's job turned up, she'd jumped at it. The whole allotment needed taking in hand, needed someone like her, with organizational skills, to lick it into shape.

She swallowed the pain killers and grimaced. Hmm, not many eligible men at the allotment, most were elderly, married or widowed. What on earth had she been thinking? She'd have been better off joining a Men's Shed. But then, she barely knew how to use a screwdriver ...

She sighed and turned from the window. Her life was a mess ... no, not a mess, just meaningless ...

Chapter Four
April

The Allotment
"When that Aprille with her showers sweet, the drought of March does pierce to the root."

Chaucer said something like that back in the early days, before allotments. It seems most of the allotmenteers are out, digging, hoeing, weeding, planting ...

***

Neil sat at the breakfast table, twisting a spoon between his fingers.

'You okay, Neil?' Bill asked.

'Yeah, Bill. But I'm thinking it's time I looked for a place of my own.'

Bill's eyes widened. 'What do you mean?'

'Well, I can't stay here forever and I don't want to go back to live with my sister. She has her own problems.'

'Don't want to pry lad, but what happened?'

Neil sighed. 'Well, my marriage broke up ages ago. It's not easy for a woman married to a soldier serving overseas. Deirdre wanted children, but not while I was still in the army. She didn't want to live in an army compound, said it wasn't fair on her and she liked her job. She was fed up with me never being home. Wanted me to leave the army.' He scowled at the spoon. 'I could see her point. But, Bill, the army was my career. What work could I do outside of the it?' He spread his hands, the spoon waving in a question. 'Our house had a big mortgage. We were paying it off from my salary ... well, we sold it and split the proceeds. It was an amicable divorce, I guess, going by what some of the guys in my platoon went through.'

Bill shook his head and mumbled something.

'So, I have some savings, but when I had this, this ... dunno what you'd call it, well, this burnout, PTSD whatever, the army sent me home for treatment. When I came out of hospital, Anna, my sister said to go and live with them for a bit until I got myself sorted.' He grimaced. 'I need to get my act together, try and find somewhere to live. Look for work.'

Bill nodded. 'Not easy to find work after this global financial mess. But lad! I love you being here. I can see it's not the same as having your own place.' He scratched his head. 'You might want to bring friends home, a girl ...' his voice trailed off.

Neil snorted. 'Lost touch with most of my old mates. And a girl ... like I said before, too much baggage, Bill.'

'So, what's the rush?'

'I can't stay here without paying my share.'

Bill brightened. 'Well, let's put our heads together and work out some kind of agreement.'

Neil's lips parted in a rueful smile. 'You figure something out. Perhaps I can give you what I was giving Anna when I stayed with her.' Then he frowned, wondering how Anna would cope without his contributions with Tom still not working. Well, she needn't know that he was paying Bill.

***

Brenda tried to sleep that night but Colin's snoring kept her awake. It was the first time in her life she'd ever slept with another person. It felt strange. She punched her pillow, trying to get comfortable. When the snoring intensified, she gave Colin a shove, wanting to make him turn over.

'Wha ...' he mumbled. The snoring stopped until Brenda had just dozed off, then restarted.

Brenda wondered should she get up and go downstairs, make a cup of tea and read for a bit. But it was a cold night. She decided to stay in the warm and block her ears with the pillows. Eventually she slept.

Next morning, she woke with a start, wondering where she was, then remembered. Colin was still asleep. She crept out of bed and carried her clothes downstairs and put the heater on. She dressed, then rummaged in the cupboards. She found a jar of instant coffee and a cup. She looked inside the cup. It didn't appear very clean. In fact, none of the crockery did. She gave the cup a good scrub then looked for a tea towel. A grubby one hung on a hook under the kitchen sink. She wrinkled her nose and poured boiling water in the cup and swirled it around.

She stood at the kitchen window, looking out at the back garden. It was a small paved area with a few bushes around the sides. Another town house backed onto it.

She wondered how her mother was faring. Should she ring Edith? *Stop it, Brenda!*

She sighed and made the coffee. Only Instant but better than nothing. She sat at the kitchen table then heard the sound of the toilet flushing. A few minutes later Colin came clattering down the stairs, a huge beam on his face.

'Good morning, Bren, love of my life!'

He swooped on her and lifted her from her chair. 'Come back to bed, sweetie! I've got something to show you!' He rolled his eyes suggestively.

She managed a weak smile. 'Um, was thinking about having a look around the place this morning, Colin.'

'Yeah, time for that later! Got to gather the rose buds while you may!'

Reluctantly she followed him up the stairs to the bedroom.

***

Carol Patterson stopped at the allotment car park. Dougie had his seat belt undone and the passenger door open as she pulled the handbrake.

'Dougie,' she started to say, 'you must wait until I stop before you open the car door.' Too late. Dougie was already on the path to their allotment.

'Do you think that new lady, Miss Brenda, will be there?'

'I don't know, Dougie.' Carol struggled to keep up with her son who was racing toward their plot.

'Miss Brenda! Miss Brenda!' he called as they drew near Brenda's plot.

His shoulders sagged. 'Oh,' he muttered. 'She's not here! I wanted to see how her potatoes were going.'

'Look, they're just starting to peep through too,' Carol said, as she came alongside her son.

'Hmm.' Disconsolate, Dougie turned away. 'Okay, Mum.' He heaved a big sigh. 'Let's see how ours are going.'

Carol took his hand. 'They might be just coming through, Dougie. Which means what?'

'Um ...' He frowned then smiled. 'We can earth them up!' He started to run.

'Yes!'

***

The Allotment – Spring is in the air, quite a few people here today. Dougie and his mum, Bill and Neil, that strange man with the pony tail and the messy plot – I'm surprised the warden hasn't been on to him. Everyone seems cheerful, well, except for Neil, who rarely smiles and seems very nervy. Takes all sorts, I suppose ...

***

Brenda and Colin spent the morning at the markets in Solihull.

'It's nice here,' Brenda said, gazing around.

'We could buy a house here, in Solihull,' Colin said. 'It's not far from where I work.' He squeezed her hand. 'What do you think?'

Brenda didn't know what to think. She was worrying about her mother and about Colin. He seemed different from the Colin she'd known back home.

They had lunch. 'How about a quick drink?' Colin asked on their way back

'Not for me, thanks.'

'Okay, but we'll just stop at the pub and see that everything is all right for tonight.'

Brenda stifled a sigh.

'Don't mind, do you love? It's an important match tonight. Got to make sure everything's hunky dorey.'

They stopped at the pub. Brenda didn't understand why, it seemed everything had already been organised.

'Bitter lemon for you?' Colin ordered drinks. After downing several pints of beer, he turned to Brenda. 'Right, love, seems everything's in order, just time to go home for a nap before tonight.' He winked at Brenda, took her hand and pressed it.

At the townhouse she followed him up the stairs.

'Just have to clean my teeth, tidy myself,' she muttered, disengaging herself from Colin's embrace. 'You go ahead.'

Five minutes later, she came out of the bathroom and heard snoring coming from the bedroom. She heaved a sigh of relief and went down to the kitchen to make a cup of tea and start reading a new book she'd found at the markets.

A while later, she was startled awake by Colin.

'I thought you were joining me in bed!'

'Um, you were sound asleep, so I made a cup of tea and started to read my new book and must have dozed off.' Brenda said. 'Would you like a cuppa now?'

He gathered her to him, kissed her, then released her abruptly, as he saw the time.

'Can't stop for a cup of tea, got the match in another half hour. Didn't realise I'd slept so long. Tired after last night.' He held her out and winked at her. 'Right, put on your glad rags, we're off to the local. I'll introduce you to the crowd. Think you'll like them.' He hurried up the stairs and she heard the sound of the shower.

Glad rags? She was dressed in jeans and a shirt and jumper. Well, it was April and still pretty cool. She went up the stairs and into the bedroom. She could hear Colin in the shower. She glanced at herself in the full-length mirror on the wardrobe door. Glad rags? She shook her head. Whatever she did with her hair it didn't seem to matter anyway. The mousy curls just sprang back from the comb. Her mother's words from when she was a child echoed, "Comb your hair, Brenda, you look like you've been pulled through a hedge backwards".

She heaved a sigh as Colin emerged from the bathroom in a cloud of steam with a towel around his waist. 'You look all right, Bren. I won't be a minute getting dressed. Like I said, important match tonight. Think you'll like it. We can eat at the pub.' He leered at her. 'Dunno why I've got this towel around me, you've seen all the tackle before!' He pulled off the towel and thrust his hips towards her, then turned and started to rummage inside the wardrobe.

Appalled, Brenda stared at his bare backside. 'Have I time for a shower?'

'Probably not,' he mumbled, 'you'll be fine, love.'

She started down the stairs. Was this the same Colin she'd been dating for the past two years?

Ten minutes later they were getting out of Colin's car at the pub. 'Come on, Bren, this way.' He steered her towards the entrance. She could hear the noise from outside. Her heart sank. She'd been looking forward to settling down for the evening in front of the TV, maybe with a take-away, a bottle of wine – not that she really drank much – and a nice movie, cuddled up with Colin.

The pub was crowded and loud. 'Over here, Bren …' Colin guided her to a far corner where several women sat around a table.

'Hello ladies! This is Brenda! Love of my life!' Colin's voice was raised to make himself heard above the piped music. He pushed her towards the women. 'What would you like to drink, Bren? Bitter lemon? And ladies? What would you all like?'

'We're right, thanks, Colin,' one of them said.

'Well, I'll let you get to know each other! Getting your drink now, Bren.' He disappeared into the crowd.

'Hello Brenda,' one of the women said. 'I'm Janet.' She introduced the other four women. Brenda tried to remember their names.

Colin reappeared with a glass and a bottle of lemon and lime. 'Here you go, Bren!' He winked at the other women. 'Got to keep the little woman happy, eh?'

Brenda seethed. *Little woman*!

Janet patted the seat beside her. 'Come and sit down, hon, tell us all about yourself. Known Col for long?'

Brenda sat down and poured some of the lemon and lime into the glass. She wished now she'd asked for something stronger. 'Couple of years,' she said.

'Any kids?' It was one of the other women.

'Er, no.'

The woman seemed to lose interest. She turned to talk to the woman beside her.

Brenda took a sip of her drink. She could hear Colin's voice coming from the other side of the bar. The woman next to her said something.

'Sorry, I missed what you said ...'

'Just asking if you worked.'

'Yes, I work at a convenience store, petrol pumps ...' her voice faded. Now that she said it, it sounded so pathetic.

'Oh. Well, you might be able to get work here. I've got a job stacking shelves at the local supermarket. Early mornings. It's handy as I'm home to get the kids off to school.'

Brenda felt she'd been accepted into the group. She was an ordinary person like them. Then she became aware of Colin's braying laugh coming from the other side of the pub. Had he always laughed like that?

The conversation moved from working hours to fitting in with school hours and the cost of school activities.

'At least my mum is minding the kids,' one of the women said.

Dawn, did she say her name was?

'You're lucky,' another of the other women chimed in. 'My mum's working and Darrell's mum's in Scotland, not much use for baby-sitting.'

Brenda's idea of having a family faded. She couldn't see her mother baby-sitting while she and Colin went out. Colin's mother was in Spain with her new bloke. And it appeared Colin liked going to the pub. He might change if they had a child ... The evening dragged on. Colin's braying laugh got worse. At last he came for her.

'Game over!' he crowed. 'Our side won!'

Brenda managed a weak smile. 'Congrats!' She stood and turned to the other women. 'Nice to have met you all. Sorry, I'm a bit tired. Been a long day.' She moved to go.

'We can have one last drink to celebrate our win, what do you say, ladies? And guys?' He turned to the men behind him.

'If you're shouting!' one of them said.

Brenda's heart sank. She couldn't wait to get out of the noisy atmosphere; her head was throbbing.

An hour later the barman called "Time". Colin rose and pulled Brenda towards him. 'Come on sweetie, back to the love nest!' He winked at the others and guided Brenda to the exit.

'Are you all right to drive?' she asked, as he stumbled and caught her arm.

'Course, love!'

At least it wasn't far to the house, Brenda thought as she gripped the sides of her seat.

'Great night, Bren. What did you think? How'd you get on with the girls? Nice bunch, eh?'

She was jolted forward when he stamped on the brake at a red light and didn't reply.

Back at the town house, Colin parked the car outside. 'Won't bother parking in the garage, I've an early start for work tomorrow,' he said. 'That way I won't wake you if you want to sleep in.'

'Thanks, Colin,' she muttered, relieved to be back in one piece. 'That's thoughtful of you.'

***

Bill was up early. He came into the kitchen and surprised Neil who was sitting at the kitchen table staring into space.

'You're early, Bill. I'll start breakfast.'

Bill glanced out the window. 'Shaping up for a nice day ... feel like going to the allotment?'

Neil nodded.

You couldn't call Neil a chatterbox, Bill thought. But then, that suited him. Some of Hazel's friends nattered on about nothing. But Neil seemed very down this morning.

'Got many friends around here?'

Neil blinked. 'Not really. Lost touch with them. Most of my good mates were in the forces with me.' He grimaced. 'Some of them,' he paused and his eyes clouded, 'the best of them, really, are dead.' He picked up the kettle and stared at it before filling it at the tap.

Bill was silent.

***

Mary wondered about Brenda. She'd been so kind to her the other night. She couldn't even remember getting into the house. She hadn't seen her at the allotment when she'd collected Peter's urn. Funny little person that Brenda. Suggesting she make a table lamp out of Peter's urn.

Perhaps she'd ask her to go for a coffee or something. Not that she felt like being sociable and chatting. Perhaps go to the allotment again, she might be there or someone might know where she lived.

She changed her high heels for an old pair of hiking boots when she arrived at the parking area. She'd walked miles in these boots with Peter, the Lake District, Wales ... *Stop it, Mary! You'll only start to cry.* She slammed the car door and started up the path.

She saw two men working on a plot. As she drew near, she saw one was that nice Bill who had helped keep Peter's plot tidy. And the other one was fair-haired. What had Brenda said his name was?

'Hello,' she said.

Bill looked up. 'Oh, Mrs Flynn, Mary. How are you?'

'Good, thank you, Bill.'

'Have you met my friend, Neil? He's been helping me since I broke my wrist.'

Mary smiled at Neil. 'No. Nice to meet you, Neil.' She extended her hand.

Neil wiped his hand on his trousers and held it out. 'It's not very clean.'

Mary gave a slight laugh. 'That's okay, mine will soon be dirty. Um, I was wondering if you knew where I could find Brenda, she's got a plot here somewhere. Um, small, curly hair ...'

'Brenda has the plot just there, right next to mine.' Bill pointed. 'Haven't seen her for a while.'

'I wanted to contact her, she was very kind to me and I wanted to thank her.'

'She works at the convenience store in town. The one with the petrol pumps,' Neil said.

'Oh, right. Thanks, Neil. I'll call round later.' She paused. 'Your plot's great.'

'Thanks to Neil,' Bill replied.

'I'm enjoying it,' Neil added. 'Learning heaps about gardening. Never had a garden.'

Mary saw Bill give Neil a surprised look. 'Well, I'm trying to learn too,' she said, 'following my late husband's diaries.'

'I'm sure Neil would be happy to help you with any heavy stuff, Mary. Wouldn't you, Neil?'

Mary thought Neil didn't look overjoyed.

'Umm, of course.'

'Well, I'll leave you to it and get up to my place. Thanks for telling me where Brenda worked.'

She gave a half wave and walked away.

***

Bill turned to Neil and raised his eyebrows. 'She's a lovely woman, and a stunner, don't you think?'

'Trying to match-make again, Bill?

'Well, you're a fine-looking chap and she must be about your age.' He'd been surprised when Neil had responded to Mary by volunteering information.

Neil nodded. 'Yes, she's beautiful, but Bill, she's a grieving woman and like I said before, I'm a psychological mess. No use to any woman.'

'That will pass.'

'Right. So what are we planting now?'

Bill took the hint. Subject closed. 'Good time to sow parsnips. But they've got to be fresh seeds. Can't use old ones.'

***

Brenda was startled awake by the alarm clock. She heard Colin groan and turn it off. He wasn't particularly quiet, she thought, but she pretended to be asleep in case he changed his mind about going into work early.

When she heard him drive off, she got up and went to the window. The sky was grey and low. A few late daffodils provided a splash of colour. She wondered what to do with the day. First make a cup of tea and go back to bed with her book. Then walk into town, browse around the bookshops. Check out the library, and get some food. Colin hadn't mentioned anything about dinner.

She peered into the fridge. Basically nothing - two frozen dinners in the freezer. In the fridge, half a dozen eggs, some grey and slimy sausages, several bars of chocolate and a carton of beer. She sniffed the sausages then tossed them in the bin. Better get some food in.

It felt so strange to be strolling around the shops with no pressure to rush back to her mother or for work. She bought a new top, had lunch and then bought milk, butter, bread and some vegetables and chops. She'd forgotten she had no car and would have to carry it all back.

As she neared the house, she heard music and looked at her watch. Four o'clock. She hadn't realised she'd been out so long and hadn't checked what time Colin would be home.

The door opened as she struggled up the path with her shopping.

'Buying up the town, eh? Hello love!' Colin bent, kissed her and took the shopping bags. 'Thought you'd run back to Mummy when I got home and no Brenda!'

'It's further to the shops than I thought and I bought food for dinner.' She sounded like she was making excuses for not being at home. And she didn't care for his tone of voice, saying he thought she'd run back to Mummy.

'You're going to cook tonight? Well, let's drink to that!' He dropped the bags on the kitchen table and took a beer out of the fridge. 'Have a beer?'

'No thanks.' She'd like a wine but hadn't thought to buy any. She started to unpack the food and then took out the top she'd bought. 'What do you think?' she asked, holding it up.

He took a cursory glance at it. 'Go and put it on, love. I'll follow you up and watch you.'

'Maybe later.' She folded it and returned it to the bag.

'Looks like you've bought more books.'

She nodded.

'Oh! I should have bought some wine for you.' Colin put his empty beer bottle on the kitchen table. 'I'll pop out to the pub and get you some while you start dinner.'

***

Mary decided to go straight to the convenience store. Anyway, she hadn't felt like doing anything on the plot.

She'd been mildly surprised to discover that Brenda worked at the store. Now, now, she told herself. Don't be judgmental. After all, she'd never had a job. Peter had insisted she be a stay-at-home wife. But she had to admit to boredom at times. Marrying at eighteen had meant she'd never had a career. If she hadn't met Peter, what would she have done? She vaguely remembered something about this Brenda's mother. Could be why Brenda worked at the convenience store.

She might as well fill up with petrol while she was here ...

She paid, then asked, 'Do you have a Brenda working here?'

The man at the desk scowled. 'Yeah, but she's on holiday for a week.' He handed her the docket. 'Most inconvenient,' he said.

'Oh. When will she be back?'

'Next week.' The man looked over her shoulder. 'Next?'

***

Brenda took her books and top upstairs then came down and started to prepare dinner. She checked the time again and frowned. It was now six-thirty. Colin had been gone ages.

She peeled potatoes and wondered should she start cooking. Or read for a bit. She'd just settled down with her book when she heard the sound of his car. She jumped up and lit the gas under the potatoes and waited.

'Hello love!' He burst in the door. She could smell drink on his breath. 'Sorry I took so long, met one of the team at the pub.' He plonked a bottle of red wine on the kitchen table. 'Got you a nice red.'

She nodded. 'Thanks.'

'How's dinner?' He must have noticed her dark look for he pulled a face. 'You all right?'

'Yes, fine,' Brenda muttered.

'No, you're not! You're upset with me! Is it because I was too long?' He hugged her to him.

Brenda shook herself free. 'It's okay, I'm getting the dinner now.'

'Right. I'll pour you a glass of wine, you'll feel better after a drink.' He found two wine glasses and opened the bottle. 'It'll breathe in the glass,' he joked. 'Cheers, love! Lovely to have you here.' He clinked her glass and handed it to her.

Brenda took a sip and nodded. 'It's nice. Thanks, Colin.' She turned back to the stove.

'I'll lay the table.' Colin took a swig from his wine glass then went to the kitchen drawers, took out cutlery and spread knives and forks on the kitchen table. 'Big day at work,' he said and proceeded to tell Brenda in minute detail all the ins and outs of his day.

She barely listened, concentrating on cooking. Eventually she set plates of food on the table.

'Looks yummy!' Colin exclaimed. 'So nice to have a home-cooked meal. Thanks love.' He picked up his knife and fork and smiled at her.

Brenda nodded. She picked at her chops. Somehow, she'd lost her appetite.

Colin ate with relish. Clearing his plate, he sat back and sighed. 'That was lovely, pet. Now, I'll wash up in a minute. Let's just sit down for a bit to let the food digest.' He stood up, belched, then took her hand and led her to the lounge room, setting her down on the couch. 'Let's cuddle up and watch the telly.' He turned on the TV and found a sports channel. 'This is a good match, you'll like this, love.'

Brenda sighed and tried to concentrate, but after a few minutes, Colin had fallen asleep.

Slowly she extricated herself from his arms and went to the kitchen. She filled the sink with hot water and started to wash the dishes.

***

Carol parked outside Dougie's new school.

'I can go in by myself, Mum,' he said as he undid his seat belt. 'Don't come in with me. The other mothers don't.'

For the first time Carol said. 'Okay then, Dougie. Take care.'

Dougie blinked and seemed unsure. He stood straighter and picked up his school bag. "bye, Mum.'

Her heart was in her mouth as she watched him walk in the school gates. She worried that the other children would mock and humiliate him.

The school principal had assured her that inclusion in a mainstream school would benefit Dougie more than a special school. 'And it's good for our ...' she'd hesitated - Carol thought she was trying to find another word for "normal" – then the principal had coughed and continued, 'pupils who don't have special needs.'

'I'm just a bit worried,' she'd said.

'Well, I think coming for this last week of term before the Easter break will be good for Douglas,' the headmistress said. 'We don't do much the last week of term and it will give Douglas the opportunity to settle in. And he'll be ready to go to secondary school in September.' She'd smiled and continued, 'and by then he will have made friends who will be going on to the same school.'

It was Dougie's third day at this primary school and the first day she hadn't taken him in to his class room.

He disappeared into the playground. With a heavy heart, Carol started the engine and drove home. She had a new manuscript to edit that would keep her busy until it was time to collect Dougie.

She made a cup of coffee and sat in front of her computer. She wondered how Dougie was going. She pictured him walking into his classroom, saying "Hi" to everyone, a big grin on his face.

Would they humour him, but mock him behind his back? Kids were like that. She sighed as she turned on her computer and loaded the latest book to edit.

"He was dazzled by his reflection in his armour" she read. Hmm. A passive sentence, not good. She changed it to "His reflection in his armour dazzled him." But then she sat and thought. Perhaps she should read a bit more to determine what the writer was trying to say.

She looked at the clock. Ages before she could pick up Dougie.

***

Neil had been weeding all morning and his back ached. He straightened and scanned the other allotments. No sign of Bill, who seemed to be content wandering around chatting to the other allotmenteers. Neil smiled to himself, pleased that Bill seemed happier of late.

Then he saw Mary Flynn coming down the path towards the carpark. He turned and concentrated on his weeding.

'Hello! It's Neil, isn't it?'

He took a deep breath. The last thing he wanted was to engage in conversation with anyone.

'Um, yes.' He turned towards her.

'I haven't been able to contact Brenda Evans. Apparently, she's got a week off work.'

'Oh?'

'Thought you might know where she lives.'

'No.' Neil bent down and dug out a dandelion root.

'I just want to thank her for ...' Her voice trailed away.

'Sorry. I don't know anything about her.' He concentrated on his weeding.

'Just thought you might know. Apparently, you saved her life.'

Neil shrugged and made no comment.

'Thanks, anyway.' She moved away. Out of the corner of his eye, Neil watched her leave.

***

Brenda was bored. Was this what married life would be like? Colin went off to work every morning leaving her to amuse herself. After she'd cleaned the house and had breakfast she walked to the shopping centre, browsed the library, bought food for dinner then walked back to the row of terraced houses.

She wondered was her mother all right; was Edith coping; what was happening on the allotment.

On the fourth day of her stay, she rang home.

'The Evans residence.'

Brenda smiled. Edith was so formal!

'That you, Edith?'

'Oh, Brenda! Yes, it is I, Edith. How are you dear? Are you enjoying your little break?'

'Yes, thank you, Edith. How's Mum? Everything all right?'

'Yes, dear. The taxi you booked came yesterday right on time and we went to the physiotherapist. Your friend Bill was there. Such a nice man!'

Brenda could picture Edith getting all fluttery around Bill. 'Yes,' she said, 'He's very nice.'

'Your mother did all her exercises and then Bill said his friend Neil would give us a lift back home, instead of getting a taxi.'

'That was kind of him ...' Brenda rolled her eyes; she'd booked the taxi to take her mother to the physio but had forgotten to book one to take them home.

Edith nattered on until Brenda interrupted. 'That's great, Edith, well I'd better let you go now. See you at the weekend.'

'Yes, dear.'

Brenda found herself wishing she could go home right this minute. The weather had been lovely and she regretted not being able to get up to the allotment.

***

Bill liked chatting to anyone who happened to be working at the allotment. As he ambled back to his plot, he saw Neil weeding the radishes.

'You're going great, lad!' he called as he drew near.

Neil raised his head and nodded.

'Have you seen little Brenda's plot?' He gestured to the plot adjoining his.

'Not really.'

'Her potatoes need earthing up.' He looked meaningfully at Neil.

'Got the message Bill. Do it next after the radishes.'

'I'll be able to get back to weeding soon, lad.' Bill flexed his right hand. 'Still a bit stiff.'

'You have to keep going with squeezing the little ball the physio gave you, Bill.'

'I will, I will.' Bill turned at the sound of someone passing his plot.

'Oh, there's Harry. I'll pop up to his plot and see how he's going.'

***

Carol couldn't concentrate on the book she had started editing. She took a deep breath, shut down her PC and stood.

Five minutes later and she was in her car and on the way to her allotment.

She felt a bit guilty at being there without Dougie, but she needed some fresh air. Walking up to her plot she passed Bill's allotment. Only the helper there. *What was his name? Neil?*

He nodded as she drew near.

'Hello. Neil, is it?'

'Yes.'

Carol paused at the small gate, unsure what to say. 'Are those radishes you're weeding?'

'Yes.'

'Right.' She kept walking. Neil didn't seem very chatty.

She reached her own plot to see Bill walking down the path towards her.

'Hello, Carol,' he called. 'Where's Dougie?'

Her face lit up. 'He's in school. Went in by himself today.'

'Wow. That's a big step.' He smiled and walked on.

'Yes.' And it was a big step, she acknowledged to herself.

She looked at her plot. *Lots to do.* She unlocked her shed, found her gardening gloves, took the hoe and started on the peas.

***

Brenda woke early on the last day of her visit. She lay and listened to the dawn chorus. Colin had mercifully stopped snoring.

She slipped out of bed, found her clothes and crept downstairs to the kitchen. When she heard Colin stirring, she hurriedly dressed and started to prepare breakfast.

'Morning, love! Mmm! That smells good. I'm going to miss you, Brendie.' He sat with his elbows on the kitchen table as she poured him a coffee.

She mumbled a reply.

'So, what do you think? Ready to move in here with me?'

Brenda flipped the eggs in the frying pan. 'I'll have to think about getting a job and sort out mum first.'

'That won't take you long.' He shook sauce over his egg, buttered some toast then dipped it in the sauce.

Brenda sat opposite him and tried not to watch him eating.

With his plate empty, he wiped his mouth with the back of his hand and drank the rest of his coffee. 'That was lovely, Bren.' He glanced at the clock. 'I guess we'd better make an early start if I'm to be back in time for the match on TV tonight.'

'I'm all packed, just have to clean my teeth.' Brenda got up from the table and filled the sink with hot water. 'I'll wash up first.'

'I'll bring the car round.'

Brenda stood with her hands in the soapy water, staring out the kitchen window. *Do I really want to spend the rest of my life with Colin? Being a household drudge; sitting in a pub while he plays darts?* She sighed and finished washing up.

'Ready, Bren? Roads'll be busy.'

***

The Allotment

Only Carol seems to take much notice of the Easter festival – the old Druid time of Oestrus - goddess of spring or renewal and that's why her feast is attached to the vernal equinox. Pagans used the first full moon after the equinox for their worship. The Christian Church associated the equinox with Christ's resurrection, hence the Church decreed that this would now be Easter.

"Easter is the only time when it's perfectly safe to put all your eggs in one basket" - Evan Esar.

***

Carol hid small Easter Eggs around her allotment while Dougie was occupied with Brenda. He seemed to love stopping and chatting with her.

She went down the paths towards Brenda's plot, smiling when she saw them deep in conversation. *Dougie made friends everywhere he went.* His week at the primary school had gone well. His class teacher had been pleased. 'He'll settle in well next term,' she'd said. 'The teacher's aide loves him.'

Carol felt cheered by this comment. As she approached Brenda's plot, Dougie saw her. 'Mum,' he called. 'Brenda has lettuce coming up! She said we can take some of the seedlings.'

'Thanks, Brenda. That would be lovely.'

'Dougie, if you go into my shed, you'll see a few empty plastic plant tubs. Bring one out and we can put some seedlings into it.'

Carol smiled at Brenda. 'Thank you, Brenda. Dougie seems to love being with you.'

'He's adorable,' Brenda replied, watching Dougie rummaging in the shed.

Carol studied Brenda. 'You know, you'd make a great teacher's aide.'

'Really?' Brenda seemed surprised.

'Yes.' Carol wondered how that comment had popped out. 'Well, I've just hidden little Easter eggs around my plot for Dougie to find. I know he's too old for the Easter Bunny but I think he plays along to keep me happy. I came to get him.'

'Could I come and watch?' Brenda's eyes shone.

'Of course! I'm sure Dougie would love you to.'

***

Brenda thought about Carol's comment. A teacher's aide ... She'd always wanted to be a teacher ...

Back home she went straight to her computer.

'What are you doing, Brenda?' Her mother's petulant voice.

'Coming Mum. Just checking something.'

Half an hour later Brenda burst into the living room where her mother was sitting in front of the television.

'Hmph! Since you came back from that Colin, you've totally ignored your mother ... I could die from hunger for all you care. And there's a parcel for you. In the hall.'

Brenda stopped short and beamed. 'I've made a decision. I'm going to train to be a teacher's aide. I can study on-line. I think I know someone who can help me get work experience.'

'And what does that no-good Colin think of that?' Her mother thumped her walking stick on the ground.

'Oh!' Brenda frowned and thought. 'Well, I haven't told him yet.'

The more Brenda thought about Colin, the more she realised she really, really did not want to live with him.

But how to tell him without hurting him? She went to the hall and found the parcel. A large box. She turned it over. Sender: Colin Barnes. Her heart sank as she opened it. An enormous Easter Egg and a card: *'To my Love, Happy Easter.'*

That was sweet of him. He was a good person – he didn't deserve to be hurt.

***

Neil stopped in the carpark near the physiotherapist. 'You okay Bill?'

Bill was studying the trees surrounding the parking lot. Pale green shoots adorned the bare branches.

'Spring has sprung!' he said, then turned his attention to Neil. 'Yes, I'm fine, Neil, you take a break. Look, there's your little friend, Brenda, with her mother. You could take her for a coffee.'

Neil grimaced. But at least Brenda had a boyfriend, he could relax with her. Speak of the devil, here she came.

'Hi Bill, Neil. Good to see you both again. How's the physio going, Bill?'

'Great, thanks, Brenda. See.' He wiggled his fingers at her.

'That's excellent, well done. you must have been doing the exercises.'

'Yep! Neil keeps my nose to the grindstone.'

Neil stared at the ground.

'How was your holiday, Brenda?' Bill continued.

'Good, thanks.'

From the tone of her voice, Neil thought that Brenda didn't seem all that enthusiastic about her holiday experience.

'Well, I'd better do a bit of shopping,' Brenda said.

'Neil was hoping you'd have a coffee with him,' Bill smiled at Brenda.

'Oh! Well, all right, that would be nice. Thanks, Neil.'

Neil gave Bill a look which said "I'll get you for this", but Bill simply smiled sweetly and made his way to the physiotherapist.

***

Brenda walked beside him to the coffee shop. 'How have things been, Neil?'

'Fine, thanks.'

They settled down in the corner of the café. 'My turn,' said Brenda going to the counter.

'So, how was your break?' Neil asked, when she returned.

Brenda rolled her eyes and stared at him.

'To be honest, not that good. Between you and me, I realised that Colin isn't the man for me. You know Mary Flynn? She has an allotment on the other side from me. Well, she remarked one day that if I really loved Colin, I'd up and go to him. Made me think.' She paused and studied Neil, who was looking around the café as if he didn't want to hear.

'Sorry, it seems you don't really want to hear this, do you Neil?'

'Here's our coffee,' he said.

'The thing is I've decided to train as a teacher's aide.'

'Oh?' His eyes widened.

Brenda started to tell him all about it. 'I can study part-time while I'm working at the store, and then once I've passed the basic exams, I can get work at a school and keep studying. Carol, you know, the lady with the Down Syndrome boy, Dougie, said I could probably get a placement at Dougie's school.'

'That's great.'

Brenda finished her coffee and stood. 'Better fly – lots to do. Bye, Neil.'

***

Neil sat finishing his coffee, as Brenda almost skipped out of the café. She was really pretty when she was animated, he thought. In a way he envied her, having found a new purpose in life.

His brows drew together as he thought about his life. He needed some kind of motivation. But what? He sighed and rose from the table. Better go and wait for Bill.

He was worried about Bill. He'd been a bit strange lately. He'd forgotten his wife's name a few times when talking about her. 'Heather always said ...' he'd started to say one day and then paused, his eyebrows drawn together. Then he resumed, 'I mean Hazel always said ...' and then he'd stopped and stared at Neil. 'Something ...'

He'd ask Anna next time he saw her. He sighed. *Better go and get Bill.*

***

Amanda frowned at her watch. Five to three. *The new plot holder said he'd be here at three.* She hated unpunctuality.

'Ms Harris?' A voice behind her said.

She whirled round. 'Mr Jenkins?'

He nodded. 'I parked around the corner as I wasn't sure if I would be able to park here.'

'Well, I'll be able to give you a key today. We can just go over the formalities and then I can take you to your plot. It's right at the far corner of the allotment.'

She was impressed by this Mr Jenkins. Not only was he good looking – he did have a small beard which she wasn't so keen on – but he was very polite, deferential even, and he stood ramrod straight. She almost expected him to salute! *Silly me,* she thought. Her heart quickened, then she told herself to calm down. He probably had a bus load of children and even grandchildren – he must be sixty at least.

She led the way to his plot. 'The previous holder left the key to his shed with me.' She held it out to him. 'You'll be able to familiarise yourself with everything. If you have any questions, don't hesitate to ask.' She smiled and turned away. 'I'd better get back to the gate in case anyone is waiting for me. It's a busy time.'

'Thank you, Ms Harris.'

She could feel his eyes on her as she walked away.

***

Mary picked up her phone. Her heart sank. A message from her sister, Veronica, inviting her to dinner the following week. She meant well, but Mary wished Vronnie would leave her alone with her grief. She always invited a man to make up the table, and always a single man. Couldn't Vronnie understand that she just wanted to mourn in peace?

It was seven months, three weeks and two days since Peter had died.

She fetched a glass and poured whiskey into it. *Just the one.*

***

The Allotment

Lots of allotmenteers here lately. Most of them erecting sticks for runner beans. Haven't seen Mary Flynn lately, or little Brenda. But wait, here IS Brenda ...

***

Brenda wondered if her plot would be too much for her once she started her teacher's aide distance learning class. She had no-one to talk to about it. She hadn't told her mother the details of her plans – she could guess her reaction. If she asked Bill, he would probably suggest Neil help her and she felt she couldn't ask him.

She parked outside the main gate and as she went in, noticed the warden working on her plot.

'Hello, Amanda,' she called. 'Your plot's looking good.'

Amanda straightened, holding on to her back as she stood. 'Not getting any younger,' she said with a grimace.

'I wanted to ask you a question.'

'Of course. Please do.' Amanda focused her gaze on Brenda.

'Well, I've decided to train as a teacher's aide and I work at a convenience store and care for my mother. I'm worried that I won't have time to work my plot.'

Amanda put her hands on her hips. 'And?'

'Well, I was wondering if I would be able to pay someone to help on my plot. I couldn't see anything in the rules that I signed which forbade that.'

'Do you have to work full-time?' Amanda's gaze was steely.

Brenda stopped short. 'Oh! I hadn't considered that. I expect I could get the store owner to let me work part-time, two or three days a week …'

'However,' continued Amanda, 'as far as I am aware the rules don't specifically state that you cannot pay someone to help. You are not allowed to sell your produce, but you are allowed to have family or friends help on the plot, provided you are here at least fifty percent of the time.'

Brenda beamed. 'Amanda, I think your suggestion that I only work part-time while I do the course is the way to go. Thank you!'

She hurried to her plot, filled with enthusiasm. *Why hadn't I thought of reducing my days at the store? Of course, Mr Dunning wouldn't be pleased, but it is my life, after all …*

***

Amanda watched Brenda march off to her plot. She shook her head. *These young ones have no idea. You would have thought Brenda would have seen the obvious solution.*

She turned back to her efforts at putting bamboo canes into the ground to support runner beans.

She sighed. *But everyone will have runner beans coming up at the same time! You couldn't give them away! Maybe I should plant something else ...*

***

Neil hesitated when he saw Brenda outside the physiotherapist. She seemed to be looking for someone. He made an attempt to melt into the background.

'Neil!'

She'd spotted him and was hurrying towards him.

'Neil, I, I was wondering if you'd come for a coffee.' She paused and seemed doubtful. 'I'd like your advice.'

He cringed inwardly.

'You see, you're a man ...'

Neil took a step back. 'I'm not qualified to give advice.'

'I just want your opinion. Please?'

She seemed so anxious. He hoped it wasn't boyfriend problems. He sighed. 'Okay, let's go for a coffee.'

She took his arm. 'You see, Neil. Well, like I told you, I spent a week with Colin, my boyfriend that is, and I realised I can't bear the thought of spending the rest of my life with him. And now he's sent me this lovely big Easter Egg and a card, and I don't know how to tell him.'

His heart sank as they approached the café. 'I'm not the person to ask.'

Brenda turned to him, her face a mixture of worry and sorrow. 'I'm sorry, Neil. I didn't know who else to talk to.' She took her arm away. 'It's all right. I'll not bother you anymore.'

'No. Come on. I'm sorry, I didn't mean it like that.' *What the hell do I mean?* 'Come on. Let's get a coffee and you tell me.'

He guided her into the café. 'Look, there's our seat.' He tried to smile.

'Thanks, Neil.' She sniffed. 'Sorry to be such a pain.'

'Flat white?'

She nodded.

He came and sat opposite her. 'So, tell me.'

'Well, like I said, I realized I don't really love Colin. But I don't know how to tell him.' Brenda's eyes filled with tears.

He hoped she wouldn't start blubbing.

'I thought you might be able to suggest a way.'

Neil shook his head. 'Probably best just to come out and say it.'

Brenda stared. 'Just like that?'

Neil shifted in his seat. Their coffee arrived, saving him from having to reply. 'Like I said, I'm not really the person to ask.'

Brenda stirred her coffee.

'Best to be honest,' he said. 'Anyway, won't you be so busy doing your teacher training you won't have time for a relationship?'

Brenda raised her eyes. 'You're right, Neil! Thank you.' Her eyes shone. 'I'll tell him I'll be studying for the next year. I knew you were the person to ask!'

'But.' He stirred his coffee.

'But what?' Her smile faded.

'You can't keep stringing him along for a year.'

She looked down at her coffee and frowned. 'No. You're right.'

She looked up. 'And it is best to be honest. Thank you, Neil.'

***

Brenda collected her mother from the physiotherapist. 'You're doing great, Mum. They were telling me while I was waiting for you that you've come on in leaps and bounds!'

Her mother sniffed. 'It's far from leaping and bounding, I'm feeling.'

'Yes, but remember this time two months ago when you could hardly leave your bed, and now here you are, up in the morning, eating in the kitchen, doing a few things around the house ...'

'Only because I'm forced to – what with you gallivanting off to Birmingham, leaving me to the mercies of that Edith Milson ...' She stomped out to the car.

'Edith Milson loves coming over to you, Mum. You're doing her a favour.'

'Hah! The last thing I want is to be doing Edith Milson a favour. She was a hopeless bridesmaid, dropped my bouquet, stood on my train. I don't know why she keeps coming around annoying me.'

Brenda ignored her mother. 'I think she's lonely, Mum. She hasn't any family and lives on her own.'

'Well, who would want to be bothered living with her anyway?'

Brenda took her mother's arm. 'Come on, Mum. I must get to work and then tell Mr. Dunnin I'm only going to work two days a week while I'm studying.'

Her mother glared. 'Studying? What are you studying?'

'I told you! I'm going to train as a teacher's aide.'

Her mother scoffed. 'You! A teacher's aide? What do you know about teaching?'

Brenda took a deep breath. 'Nothing. That's why I'm going to do a course.'

Her mother sniffed and muttered something about it all being a waste of time, Brenda was useless at everything. Then she stiffened. 'And what if he says no?'

'He won't,' Brenda ploughed on. 'He knows he gets good value from me. I'm sure he pays me less than the minimum wage, he'll keep me on my terms.'

'Brenda! Let's go home, I'm tired from all this nonsense. I'm not going back to that physiotherapist woman.'

'As you wish, Mum.'

Her mother drew back and frowned.

'Get in the car, Mum.' Brenda tapped her watch. 'I have to be at work in another hour.'

***

Carol grew increasingly nervous as the first day of the summer school term approached.

Dougie couldn't wait. 'Is it tomorrow, Mum?'

'No, Dougie. Look at the calendar. Show me today.' She pointed to a calendar hung on the wall, a square for each day.

He hesitated and then mumbled, 'It's Friday.'

'Yes. Now show me on the calendar.'

His hand hovered above the dates, then pointed to a square.

'Yes! Well done. So today is Friday. Now show me where I have written "Douglas back to school."'

His finger went along the calendar to the following Tuesday.

'Yes. Now count how many more days.'

He muttered to himself and then beamed. 'Four days!'

She put up her hand. 'High Five!'

'No, Mum! High Four!'
Carol smiled as Dougie burst out laughing.

***

Mary parked at the allotment. She still hadn't seen that little Brenda person. She really wanted to apologise to her.

She walked up to her plot. Well, Peter's plot actually. There seemed to be great activity, people putting in sticks. According to Peter's diaries now was the time to plant runner beans.

It all seemed too much. Why would she go to the effort of planting beans – she didn't cook anymore, so why bother? She approached Brenda's plot. Oh, there she was – little Brenda. *Why do I call her little Brenda?* Then she realised – Brenda was a small, bubbly woman with a mess of curly hair. She reminded her of one of the dolls she'd had as a child ... No, not the Barbie ones – one of those cuddly dolls – you put a bottle of water in its mouth and it wet its nappy. She burst out laughing at the memory.

Brenda turned at the sound of her laughter.

'Oh! Hello, Mary, how are you?'

Mary walked over to her. 'Good, thanks, Brenda. Just want to apologise for my behaviour the other night and thank you for getting me home safely.'

Brenda shrugged. 'No need, happy to help. How're you going? What are you intending to plant today?'

Mary heaved a sigh. 'Dunno. Peter's diary said he planted runner beans this month ...'

Brenda glanced around at the other allotments. 'Looks like everyone has the same idea. I was going to do exactly that.'

'I don't cook much these days, I'm wondering should I bother with beans?'

'You must!' Brenda exclaimed. 'Green beans are good for you and I'm sure your late husband would be pleased.'

'Maybe,' she muttered. 'Did you have a nice time on your break?'

Brenda blinked. 'How did you know I was away?'

'Oh, I went round to the convenience store to say sorry for being such a pain and the man at the counter said you were on holiday.'

'Hmm. Well, I went to stay with my boyfriend in Birmingham for a week.'

'Oh? So, you made it then? Escaped from your mother?'

Brenda stared at her feet. 'Yes. But actually, I realised that I don't want to marry him. What you said about if I really loved him, I'd just go to him. Made me think. And I don't.'

'Oh!' Mary didn't know what to say. 'Maybe I shouldn't have said that.'

'No, you were right.'

'I'd better get going.' She made her way up the path to her plot.

***

Brenda turned back to her bean sticks and started tying them together. She'd been trying to find the courage to write to Colin. Possible words kept going around in her head. Then she heard shouting. She turned to see Dougie.

'Brenda! He came running towards her and then stopped. 'What are you doing?'

'Making a frame for runner beans.'

He started to laugh as his mother appeared.

'Hi Brenda, you're getting ready to plant runner beans too?' Carol asked.

'Mum, Mum,' interrupted Dougie. 'She's doing it all wrong!'

'Hush, Dougie, people have different ways of doing things.'

Brenda studied her wobbly frame and smiled. 'Dougie is probably right. Perhaps you could spare him for a bit to help me?'

Dougie jumped up and down. 'Please, Mum.'

Carol nodded. 'Okay.' She turned to Brenda. 'How are you going with the teacher's aide program?'

'I'm starting next week. Distance learning. I must find a school to take me on as a trainee.'

'What about Dougie's school? I'm sure they'd love to have you. Why don't you go and see them? It's the Primary School in Beech Road.'

Dougie heard the name of his school and turned around from the ball of twine he was trying to untangle. 'My school!' His chest rose with importance. 'I'm in proper school now, Brenda.'

'That's brilliant, Dougie. Now how about I help you with that ball of twine?'

'Bye, Mum. See you later.'

Brenda grinned at Carol. 'I think you've been dismissed!'

***

Neil picked up the mail and came into the kitchen. He thought he'd heard Bill mumbling.

'Did you say something, Bill?'

'No, talking to myself. It's our wedding anniversary today.'

Neil glanced at the calendar. April 25th. 'Oh.'

'I always bought her flowers on our anniversary and took her out to dinner.' Bill blew his nose. 'Where is she now, Neil?'

Neil thought about the urn on one of Bill's bedside tables. 'Um, in a better place, Bill.'

'I suppose so.' He sighed and got up from the kitchen table.

'Er, Bill?'

The old man looked up.

'Did Hazel ever say where she wanted her ashes to be spread?'

Bill appeared confused. 'No. Somehow, I never believed she'd leave me. Why do you ask?'

'Well, I was thinking that if there was somewhere special that you both loved, that could be the place.'

Bill sat back at the table and appeared to be thinking. 'We went on our honeymoon to North Wales. Stayed at Llandudno. Ever been there, lad?'

Neil shook his head.

Bill frowned. 'So, you're suggesting I scatter Heather's ashes there?'

'No, I was just wondering.' *Bill called Hazel Heather again.*

'Hmm.' Bill seemed to lapse into his thoughts.

'Feel like going to the allotment, Bill?'

'Nah. Feel a bit down today. You go if you want.'

'Not the same without you to give me instructions.'

Bill stretched and sighed. 'Okay, then. Fresh air might do me good. Another cup of tea before we go?'

Neil smiled. 'Good idea. Here's your mail.'

Bill glanced at it. 'Royal Horticultural Society Garden Magazine. Have a look at it, might give you some ideas.'

Neil flipped through it and then an advertisement caught his eye. Horticultural courses ...

He'd started to enjoy working on the allotment, and he'd been drinking less since being with Bill. *That could be the direction I need to go.* He thought about Brenda and how excited she seemed about her course.

***

Brenda sat down at her computer and started to type:

Dear Colin,

I've started a course as a teacher's aide. I'm hoping to start training soon at a local school. So I'll be pretty busy for the next year.

She bit the corner of her thumb nail and read what she'd just written, then thought about Neil's comment not to string Colin along. She stood and paced around her bedroom. Squeezed into one corner was a small desk with her computer and printer. She'd moved into this room after her grandmother had died. Nothing had changed in it since then. Maybe she could make new curtains – even change the wallpaper. Freshen up the room.

She sighed, then sat back at the computer, read what she'd written and started to type.

I think it best that we go our separate ways. I hope we can still be friends.

Best wishes,

Brenda

She wondered if she should email it or print and post it. She sighed. Perhaps she'd think about it for a day or two. No! Seize the day, Brenda! She pressed the send button.

Chapter Five
May

The Allotment

The 1st of May. In past times, people celebrated romance on this day, when lovers gave each other crowns of spring flowers, usually lily-of-the-valley, or muguet as it's known in France.

The custom is said to have begun in 1560, when knight Louis Girard presented King Charles IX with a bunch of lily-of-the-valley flowers as a token of luck and prosperity for the coming year. The King thought it a good idea and began presenting lily-of-the-valley flowers to the ladies of his court each year on the same day.

***

Brenda sat at her computer, ready to start the evening's lecture, when she saw she had a message. Her heart sank as she clicked on it – it was from Colin.

Hi Bren,

Pleased you've started your course. There would be lots of openings in Solihull for a teacher's aide, so I'm happy to wait until you're qualified. Don't worry about me. I'll find things to keep me occupied until you're ready to move.

Lovely weather here. Off to the cricket now.

Love you,

Col.

It was the last thing she wanted to hear. Maybe she'd just let things slide. Hopefully, Colin would give up eventually ...

***

Mary reached the plot and saw the white bells of the lily-of-the-valley dancing in the breeze. Peter had planted them around the rose bush. One of the last tasks he'd undertaken on the plot had been to prune her rose bush. When a thorn had pierced his thumb, he'd smiled at her and quoted Abraham Lincoln:

"We can complain because rose bushes have thorns or rejoice because thorn bushes have roses."

She picked a lily-of-the-valley and smelled the sweet perfume. Sadness overwhelmed her as she remembered Peter bringing her a bunch on May Day every year. *So many memories here.*

She walked along the path towards the shed, noticing the grass on it was getting long and untidy. She recalled seeing a small push mower in one corner of the shed that Peter used for cutting the grass paths. She pulled it out and dragged it along between the garden beds, struggling to push it.

'Need a hand?' It was Bill.

'Didn't realise it was such hard work,' Mary gasped.

Bill came over to her. 'You've got the blades set too low for a first cut of the season, I'll adjust them for you.' He appeared to think. 'Or maybe I could get young Neil to cut and trim the paths for you.'

'No, no, I must learn how to do it myself, thank you, Bill.'

'Good lad, our Neil.' He surveyed Mary from under his brows. 'Divorced you know.'

'Oh. Well thanks, Bill.'

He turned the mower over. 'Have to get a few tools. I'm on my way to check up on Tommy Brown,' he said. 'I saw him pass by earlier. I'll fix your mower when I get back.'

Mary watched him go then abandoned the mowing.

***

Neil waited until Bill came back from wandering around the allotment where he stopped to chat with anyone he saw.

'I've got some news, Bill.'

'Oh? Good news, I hope?'

'I've decided to do a computer course in horticulture.'

'How does that work then? Digging in your computer?' Bill laughed at his joke.

Neil smiled. 'I can do an on-line course for twelve months and then I can apply to the Royal Horticultural Society to do a Diploma. Of course, I may not be accepted, but who knows? There are other openings.'

Bill stopped in his tracks and slapped his thigh. 'Well, that's great news, lad!'

'You've been instrumental in interesting me in horticulture, Bill. Only for you, I would never have thought of it as a new career.'

Bill beamed, then his face fell. 'You won't be moving out, will you?'

'No, no. I'll be studying on-line in the evenings for a good while.'

'Then you'll be teaching me, lad.'

'Not much I can teach you, Bill.'

'Can I tell everyone, Neil? It's such good news.'

Neil shrugged. 'Don't think anyone will be interested, really.'

'I'm going straight over to little Brenda. She'll be thrilled. Oh, by the way. Could you pop up to Mary Flynn, her lawn mower blades need raising. The tools are in the shed.'

Neil shook his head as Bill headed across the path to Brenda's plot, then found the tools he needed and made his way to Mary Flynn.

She was standing by the lawn mower, looking lost.

'Hello, Mary.'

She turned. 'Oh, Neil. Really, I can mow the paths.'

'Of course. I'm just going to adjust the blades for you. Won't take a jiffy.'

He felt her watching him. 'There you go.' He righted the mower and pushed it along the path.

'Thank you, Neil.'

'Any time.' He picked up his tools, made a slight farewell gesture and walked away

***

Bill approached Brenda who was hoeing her potatoes.

She smiled when she saw him. 'Am I doing it right, Bill?'

'Course you are, love. Now, I've got some good news!'

'Oh?' She straightened and leaned on her hoe.

'Yes! Neil is going to study horticulture.'

'Really?' She beamed. 'That is good news.'

Bill winked and lowered his voice. 'I think you inspired him, you know.'

'I did?'

'Yes, doing your teacher's course.'

Brenda frowned. 'How did you know about that?'

Bill laughed. 'Everyone on the allotment knows.' He bent down and whispered in her ear. 'I think Dougie spread the word.'

'Oh!'

'All good.' He looked around, 'Carol and Dougie here?'

'Haven't seen them.'

'Well, I'd better go and tell that nice Mrs Flynn about Neil.' He hastened up the path.

***

Brenda watched him go, then turned towards Bill's plot. Neil was crouched picking weeds from what seemed to be tiny onions.

She strolled towards him.

'Good news, Neil.'

He straightened and grimaced. 'No secrets at the allotment, eh?'

Brenda considered. 'It's nice in a way. Everyone seems to be concerned for each other. Bit like a family really.' She paused. 'Not that I'd know much about how families behave.'

He stared at her.

'Anyway. It's good news.' She considered. 'Maybe I should have thought of studying horticulture instead of teacher's aide.'

'You'll be perfect as a teacher's aide.' She thought his gaze seemed intense and felt the colour rising in her cheeks.

'Thanks Neil. Well, I'd better get back to my spuds.' She made to go, then turned back. 'By the way, I told Colin that I was starting a course and best we finish ...'

'Oh? So, everything's settled then?'

She looked down at her feet. 'I sent him an email, didn't actually speak to him,' she muttered.

He nodded. 'I see.'

'Thought it might be easier.'

'Hmm.'

'Back to it.' She hurried back to her plot, feeling somehow inadequate.

***

Bill saw Mary pushing her mower. 'Goodness,' he said. 'You're doing well.'

She stopped. 'Neil came up and fixed the blades.'

'Already? Goodness, he's a fast worker.' He winked at her, then thought she might have been offended by his innuendo. 'Just came to tell you, he's going to do a horticultural course.'

'That's good.'

'Well, I'll leave you to it.' He hurried off. Maybe he'd go and see the new bloke at the end of the allotment.

***

Amanda decided to check up on her latest allotment holder, Donald Jenkins. As she approached his plot, she scowled at the sound of music coming from his shed. Loud music could be annoying for people who enjoyed the peace of their garden.

Outside his shed she stopped and cleared her throat. 'Er, Mr Jenkins.' She could see him inside.

He turned around. 'Oh, hello, Ms Harris. I didn't hear you coming.'

'Just checking how you're going. And by the way, we have a policy about loud music.' Then her attention was caught by the music. 'Oh, that sounds like the Sunday concert!'

'Yes, it is.' He paused and stared at her. 'Do you like classical music?'

'Absolutely! I usually listen to the recording on a Sunday evening. I try to visit the allotments in the afternoon if the weather is fine. However, back to our policy. The playing of loud music is discouraged, but in your case, where there is no-one else present, well, I suppose I could turn a deaf ear, so to speak.' She smiled at him.

'Of course! I quite understand, very sorry indeed. Hate to start off on the wrong foot. I'll turn it off now.'

He went back into his shed and the music stopped.

'Now, Mr Jenkins, tell me, are you settling in all right? Any issues?'

'No, I don't think so,' he replied. 'Everything seems to be ship-shape and Bristol fashion.'

Amanda vaguely thought that was a nautical expression. 'You're lucky,' she said, 'Ronnie Davison left everything in good order. He was sorry to go, but his company moved him just when everything was producing.'

'Yes, I can see.' Donald surveyed his plot. 'Lots of beans and lettuce, not to mention beetroot. I'll be taking much of the stuff to my sister. She's a widow with children,' he explained.

Amanda nodded. 'Very good. Well, I'll leave you to it.' She turned around. 'Here's Bill Thompson coming to visit you. Lovely man, recently widowed. Right, I'll be off. Let me know if you have any problems.'

With a wave of her hand, she set off down the path, greeting Bill as she passed him.

***

Bill nodded a greeting as Amanda passed, then approached Donald and extended his hand. 'Hello, I'm Bill Thompson. I haven't met you before.'

Donald took the proffered hand. 'Donald Jenkins,' he said. 'Fine woman.' He indicated the retreating figure of Amanda Harris.

Bill studied the warden as she made her way across the allotment. 'Mmm,' he said, then watched Donald Jenkins, who appeared to be awestruck. 'Yes. A good woman,' he eventually agreed.

Donald sighed. 'I put my transistor on, but Miss Harris has just informed me it's not approved of on this allotment.'

'I don't mind a bit of music myself,' Bill said, 'but I prefer to listen to the birds. Anyway, just thought I'd introduce myself. Your plot is at the far end of the allotment, bit out of the way.' He surveyed the site. 'Looks in good order.'

'Yes, indeed, I'm lucky.'

Bill nodded.

'I'm new to gardening,' Donald confided. 'I've got a lot to learn. I always wanted a garden but I was in the Navy. Not easy to garden on board ship.' He smiled.

'Wife in every port, eh?' Bill winked.

Donald drew himself up. 'The *Royal* Navy. Retired.'

'Ah!' Bill didn't know quite what to say.

Donald must have seen his discomfort, for he shuffled his feet and muttered, 'Apparently it's the time to sow carrots for a winter harvest.'

Bill scratched his chin. 'That's right,' he said. 'I must remind Neil.'

'Neil?'

Bill proceeded to tell Don about Neil, then he stopped. 'But I'm delaying you.'

Donald smiled politely. 'Not at all. It seems you're fortunate to have Neil.'

'Yes, indeed. Well, I'd better let you get back to your carrots, Don.' Bill raised his arm in a half salute and sauntered off down the path.

***

Brenda was eager to see what had come up on her plot since she'd been there three days ago. As she went in her gate, she spotted something poking up through the soil at the far end. Was it asparagus? Wow! She looked around at the other plots nearby, keen to ask someone if she was right.

She saw Neil working at Bill's. She ran over to him. 'Neil! Come here. Do you think this is asparagus?' She caught his sleeve and dragged him through the gate and into her garden.

Neil rubbed his forehead, leaving a dirty mark. 'Dunno,' he said. 'Could be. Better ask Bill. Look, here he comes.'

'Bill! Quick, come and see this. Is it asparagus?'

Bill beamed. 'Yes! Arthur had a lovely asparagus bed. I reckon you'll be eating it in a few days. Have to keep cutting it, else the spears grow up and go to seed.'

'Imagine!' Brenda was elated. She smiled at the two men. 'Allotments are great, aren't they?'

'Yep!' said Bill. Neil nodded.

'Asparagus makes your wee smell,' Bill remarked.

Brenda and Neil looked startled.

'Just saying.' Bill seemed delighted with their reaction. 'Spuds need earthing up again, Brenda.' He nodded towards her potato patch.

'Right, Bill.'

Chapter Six
June

The Allotment

"I like unearnest people, and easily suit my mood to theirs. In fact, I like to grouse with a grouser. I don't like to spoil things by appearing too conscientious to a grouser or too slack to a non-grouser, just as l don't like to be too sincere in the presence of an insincere person, and, I may add, just as often lie to liars." – John Stewart Collis – *The Worm Forgives The Plough*

"Ne'er cast a clout 'til May be out." The older people on the allotment seem to follow this advice, sweating in their winter clothes for a few more days.

It's the Summer Solstice – longest day of the year. It's still light at ten o'clock and the place is buzzing. I think there might be a party happening.

***

Amanda couldn't help herself. She loved to organize. Some people thought she was bossy, but she didn't think so. People needed guidance. She'd pinned a notice up in the exchange shed. "Come and celebrate the Summer Solstice. 21st June 6pm. Meet at the shed. Bring nibblies and drinks to share."

What if no-one comes? Don't be silly! She went through these nervous panics every year since she'd been warden. *Doesn't mat-*

ter. She'd made some cheese biscuits and a strawberry flan, cut up into bite sized pieces. If no-one came, well, the biscuits could keep and the flan she'd eat over the next few days.

She put up a picnic table, added a few chairs and nervously waited.

By six o'clock several people had arrived. She saw Bill and his helper, Neil, Carol Patterson and Dougie, Ron Brooks and Donald Jenkins. She smiled when Mary Flynn arrived.

Brenda came hurrying in with a basket of food. Amanda overheard Mary talking to her. 'I wasn't going to come, Brenda, but then I told myself Peter would have wanted me to.'

Brenda smiled and nodded.

Donald Jenkins came over. 'Thank you for organizing this, Miss Harris. It is Miss?'

'Yes.' She breathed in and drew herself up. Donald Jenkins was very reserved, kept himself to himself, didn't really mix with the others. Only had his allotment a few months. But always polite. 'Miss,' she repeated. 'It's nice you came, Mr Jenkins.'

'Oh, please call me Donald.' He hesitated. 'I'm not much of a cook, so I brought some chocolate biscuits. I hope that's all right?' He looked anxious.

'Perfect,' she replied. *He'd said he was not much of a cook! Does that mean he doesn't have a wife?* Her pulse quickened. 'If it's like last year there will be heaps of food. Now, have you met all the others?'

'Well, I think I've met Bill.'

Amanda laughed. 'Bill's great, he loves wandering around, chatting to everyone. Especially since he broke his arm and can't do much. Here he comes now.'

Bill approached them, 'Hello Don, great you made it, come and have a drink. Someone brought home made elderberry wine. It's a pretty good drop.'

Donald turned to Amanda. 'Perhaps I can bring you a glass, Miss Harris?'

Amanda felt her face redden. 'That would be lovely, Donald, and it's Amanda.'

Bill winked at her as Donald disappeared into the group. 'Think you've made a conquest there, Amanda!'

'Don't be silly, Bill, you've had too many glasses of elderberry wine!'

Bill tapped the side of his nose and grinned as he walked away.

Donald came back with two glasses of wine.

Amanda suddenly felt a warm glow of happiness.

Someone had brought a guitar; others came with picnic stools and, in no time, there was a happy gathering singing old English folk songs around the laden picnic table.

***

Brenda stood to one side of the group. She'd never been good at this kind of thing. She sipped her wine and nibbled on a cheesy biscuit.

'Good crowd,' said a voice in her ear.

'Oh, Neil! You startled me.'

'Sorry,' he said. 'I'm not very good at these gatherings, saw you hiding over here behind an ornamental ...' He paused and examined the small tree in a pot. 'Lime tree and thought I'd join you.'

'I'm the same,' she sighed. 'But it's nice, isn't it? They all seem to know each other. I'm the newbie.'

'Yes,' he agreed. 'How's your course going?'

'I was about to ask you the same thing! Well, I'm really enjoying it, and I love being with the children and helping them. What about you?'

'Same. I've learned a lot from Bill, but the course goes to a much deeper level.'

'Like bastard trenching?' Brenda joked.

'A bit.' He smiled.

'I read up on bastard trenching when I first got my plot, but it sounded like a lot of work.'

'Yes, there are different views on digging.'

'Really? Such as?'

'I found an old book on Bill's shelves. "The Worm Forgives The Plough". It's fascinating.'

Neil started to tell her, then stopped. 'I'm sure I'm boring you.'

'No, it's really interesting. Keep going.' She looked around. 'There's a couple of stools no-one's using. Let's bring them over here and you can tell me more. I'd love to read that book if Bill would lend it to me.'

They perched on the stools.

***

Neil had spotted Brenda on her own at the side of the group. He'd noticed Mary Flynn surrounded by several men and smiled to himself. He didn't enjoy this kind of thing, wouldn't have come only for Bill.

He'd taken a paper plate and a glass of wine and gone over to Brenda, with the thought that no-one would bother him if they saw him talking to her.

Now, he was pleasantly surprised to find he was enjoying talking with her. She appeared to be listening intently.

'I'm talking too much, 'he said.

She blinked. 'No, I'm fascinated. Have you learned anything about planting by the phases of the moon?'

He laughed. 'Not yet.'

'I remember my father talking about it, but I was only little and didn't really understand.'

They chatted on, until interrupted by Bill.

'There you are, Neil. I think the party's breaking up. Just going to help Amanda tidy up if you want to help.'

'Of course,' Neil jumped up and took Brenda's plate and empty glass.

***

The Allotment - Marcus Tullius Cicero said 'If you have a garden and a library, you have everything you need.'

I wonder if the Warden got the book, *The One Straw Revolution* that Pony-tail man mentioned. She seems a bit pre-occupied lately.

***

Bill had been mulling over Neil's comment about scattering Hazel's ashes. He lay on his reclining chair thinking about their honeymoon at Llandudno – the small guest house where they'd stayed. Bed, breakfast and evening meal. Hazel had been so embarrassed the first night when it seemed the other diners had been made aware of their newly-wed status. She could hardly eat, she was so nervous. One of the men had winked at Bill as they left the table. 'Sleep well!' he'd said with a leer. Hazel had gone beetroot red. He'd nodded at the man and had taken Hazel's hand. 'I'm sure we will, good evening to you all.' He remembered that magical first night and then was overcome with loneliness. Until Hazel had to go into hospital, they'd never spent a night apart. Over forty years!

Neil was right. He should deal with Hazel's ashes. Hazel's parents had been killed in the blitz when she'd been young and she'd been brought up in a foster home. She'd looked forward to having a family. At Hazel's suggestion they'd made their wills just after they were married. For when we have children, she'd said. She'd been so practical.

When she'd died, he had to take the medical certificate showing cause of death to the Registry Office. They'd been very kind at the Registry Office, explaining that he'd need to come back with a copy of her birth and marriage certificates. A death certificate was required before he could plan her funeral. ... *Who would do that for me when I die?*

There'd been no reason to do this probate thing. Everything had been in joint names. He should probably make a new will. And who would take care of everything when he died? Maybe he'd talk to Neil about it.

What would happen to Hazel's ashes if he died before spreading them? Probably someone would come in, clear the house and maybe just toss Hazel's ashes aside. He couldn't bear the thought. And what about his own ashes? Who would look after them? He needed to take care of Hazel's ashes as soon as possible. And maybe he'd put it in his will to do the same with his. His thoughts went back to Llandudno ... All the Welsh signs! They'd had no idea what they had meant ... Spent ages trying to pronounce the names on the signposts. Bwlch was one. Maybe he should go back to Bwlch.

He squared his shoulders.

'Neil?' he called.

There was the scraping sound of a chair being pushed back from upstairs.

'You called, Bill?' Neil's voice came from the upstairs landing.

'Just thinking about Hazel's ashes, Neil. When can we go to Llandudno?

Neil came down the stairs. 'I guess it would be best to do it before the school holidays start in another two weeks.'

Bill nodded. 'It's a long drive. Or we could get the train. Do you think we should stay overnight?'

'We'd be more flexible if we drove, Bill. And it's a good idea to stay overnight. Would you like me to find a B & B? Or will we just play it by ear?'

'Play it by ear. We might find the guest house where we spent our honeymoon. I think I can remember the place.'

'Okay. When? Next weekend? I have my course during the week, but the weekend would be fine.'

Bill nodded. 'Thank you, lad. Cup of tea?'

'I'll put the kettle on, Bill.'

'Lovely. Oh, and Neil, do you think your sister would come and help me with Hazel's clothes?'

Neil blinked. 'I'm sure she would, Bill. I'll ask her.'

Bill turned away and wiped his eyes. 'Thanks, lad.'

***

Brenda had the jitters. Her first parent-teacher meeting was this evening. It was the last week of summer term. The end of the school year.

'It's okay, Brenda, most of them will want to talk to me about their child's academic progress,' Pamela, the teacher Brenda mostly worked with, assured her.

Brenda wasn't so sure. She arrived early and had hardly eaten the dinner she'd cooked for their evening meal.

Her mother had sniffed. 'Parent-teacher evenings, for goodness sake! There was none of that when you were at school, Brenda!'

Well, actually, there had been. But you never bothered to come. Only Dad had made the effort.

'Well, that's the way it is now, Mum,' she'd replied. 'Times have changed.'

Her mother had started to make a derogatory remark, but Brenda forestalled her. 'Gotta go, Mum.' She'd hurried out of the house.

Now she sat beside the teacher, listening to her comments as parents arrived to talk about their children.

A man came and sat before the teacher. 'I'm Jayne's father,' he said.

Brenda started. Jayne was one of her favourite pupils she didn't really qualify for special needs tuition but she definitely had issues.

Brenda leaned closer as Jayne's father started to talk. She'd been surprised when she saw him - mostly it was mothers who came to these meetings.

Then he mentioned her name.

'Um, I was wondering if I could meet Miss Sevens,' he was saying.

'Miss Sevens? Oh, you mean Miss Evans! Brenda. Of course! She's right here.'

Brenda drew back.

'I'll hand you over to Brenda now, while I talk to the next parent.'

Brenda gulped.

'Hello, Miss Evans,' he was saying. 'Jayne seems to really love you.'

'Oh!' Brenda didn't know what to say.

He grinned. 'Sorry, but Jayne never stops talking about Miss Sevens.'

Brenda blinked. 'Well, I guess it does sound a bit like Sevens ...'

'Anyway, according to the internet, we have to ask our child what questions they would like us to ask at these meetings.'

'Oh ...'

He looked straight at her and smiled. 'Well, Jayne said I MUST ask you to come to her birthday party next week!'

Brenda stared at him.

Then Jayne's father lowered his gaze. 'It's a big imposition, I know, Miss Sevens, but she really, REALLY wants you to come.'

'Oh!'

Jayne's father appeared dubious. 'Maybe it's against the rules?'

She found her voice. 'I don't think so ...'

He smiled. 'Then you'll come?'

Brenda was speechless.

'Please? Jayne adores you. You're all she can talk about.'

Brenda looked around anxiously. Her teacher was frowning at her, obviously it was time for the next parent.

'Okay,' she said.

Jayne's father beamed. 'Great! Here's my card.' He stood and took a card from his wallet and handed it to her. 'I'd better go, I can see I'm delaying everything. Please, please ring me.'

Brenda's heart skipped a beat as she took the card.

***

Neil carried Bill's small suitcase and Hazel's urn down to the car. 'Ready, Bill?' he called. He tucked the urn into the back seat beside his backpack and put the seat belt around it.

'Coming, lad. Just doing a final wee.'

Neil smiled to himself. Poor old Bill and his prostate. Then he chided himself. He'd be old one day and maybe have prostate problems.

He heard Bill calling, 'Did you put a flask of tea in the picnic hamper, lad?'

'Yes, Bill. Egg sandwiches, chocolate biscuits, milk and the flask of tea.'

Bill appeared. 'You ready, then? I can lock up?'

Neil nodded. 'All set for Llandudno. Want me to drive?'

'Yes please, lad. My hand is still a bit weak.'

Neil suspected that Bill's hand was fine, but that he'd lost confidence in his driving ability.

They reached Llandudno in the afternoon.

'Want to see if you can find the guest house where you spent your honeymoon, Bill, or will we just see if any that seem nice have vacancies?'

Bill yawned. 'Bit tired, Neil. How about you find a place for tonight and we can look tomorrow.'

Neil stopped at the first house with a B & B sign showing "Vacancy", in a row of tall terraced buildings. 'What about this one, Bill?' He turned to Bill who seemed to have nodded off.

'Looks all right, lad.' Bill shook himself and peered out the car window.

'I'll check if they have two rooms available.'

A few minutes later he came back to the car. 'All good, Bill. We can park around the back.'

***

Brenda wondered if she should ask Mr Dunning at the convenience store if he could give her a few days a week during the school holidays. She'd stopped working there once she'd started on the job training, but as a casual at the school, she was only paid for the actual days she worked. She didn't really need the money – she'd always been careful and, with having to look after her mother, she'd never had a holiday – apart from the week with Colin – so she had quite a bit of savings. Maybe she'd do nothing. Spend the time at the allotment and do some study on her course …

***

Mary dragged herself out of bed. The day stretched ahead of her, seemingly endless. She had no interest in doing anything. Maybe she should get a dog. They'd decided not to have any animals as they travelled a lot – wouldn't be fair – Peter'd said.

At least a dog would make her get up and take it for walks. Still in her dressing gown, she made coffee and sat at the kitchen table. The sound of mail flopping onto the front door mat interrupted her thoughts. *Better see what bills to pay. That had been Peter's domain. Now I have to cope with all that too.*

No bills, only a gardening catalogue addressed to Peter. Idly she tore off the wrapping and flipped through the pages. Seemed like now was the time to order bulbs to plant for spring.

The colourful pages caught her interest. Pictures of tulip fields brought back memories of the time she and Peter had gone to that place in the Netherlands with all the tulips. What was it called?

She propped her head on her fist, trying to remember. *Keukenhof, that was it.*

Her coffee had gone cold. She tossed it and started to make a fresh cup, then sat with her chin in her cupped hands, staring at the pictures of tulips. Peter had loved Keukenhof, his enthusiasm had even infected her.

As the coffee machine hissed, she had a sudden idea. Turn her allotment into a mini Keukenhof! Plant it out with bulbs as a memorial to Peter! And if she did that, well, then she'd have no need to feel guilty about not eating the vegetables she tried to grow – not that she'd had much success with them, only the runner beans had thrived. And surely it would be less work? Wasn't it the case that bulbs kept on growing year after year? Look at the daffs in the woods.

She sat sipping her coffee and leafing through the catalogue. Apparently, you ordered bulbs now ready to plant in autumn for a spring show. She rubbed her chin. *Who could I ask how to go about it?* One of the things she'd learnt at the plot was that ground had to be prepared prior to planting, and it seemed different plants needed different conditions.

Neil! Of course, he'd be the person to ask. Doing that horticultural course. She started to read more about how many of each type of bulb to plant for a good display. Perhaps she should go to the library and get some books to give her more ideas.

Feeling slightly more optimistic, she dressed, found Peter's library card and went out.

***

Brenda kept getting messages from Colin, asking how was the course, was she on summer holidays and why didn't she come down to Solihull. Maybe they could go away for a few days …

She wrote back that she still had to study, even if she wasn't working at the school.

After a few more texts she decided to only reply to every second one, then make it every third and perhaps Colin would get the message eventually.

'Going up to the allotment, Mum,' she called and hurried out before her mother could find an excuse to delay her.

She'd just started to plant out winter cabbage and broccoli, when a voice called out hello.

'Oh, Mary, how are you?'

'Good. I was hoping to see Neil today.'

'Haven't seen him or Bill for a few days. 'Brenda frowned. 'Hope they're all right. They usually come at least every other day.'

'I wanted some advice about growing spring bulbs; thought Neil would be able to help me.'

'I'm sure he would. Have you tried the library?'

Mary nodded and sighed. 'Got a few books, but it all sounds terribly complicated.'

'Yeah, I was scared when I first started here. But after a bit it kind of comes together.' Brenda grinned. 'Basically, just dig, rake, dig, rake, sprinkle blood and bone everywhere, plant and then weed and weed and weed.'

'Right.' Mary hesitated. 'Well, better let you get on with whatever you're planting.'

'Cauliflower.'

Mary screwed up her nose.

***

Neil took their luggage up to the rooms. 'Seems nice,' he remarked, setting down Bill's case. He'd given Bill the room overlooking the ocean. 'It's only four o'clock, Bill. I was thinking of having a stroll around town. Would you like to come?'

'No, lad. I'm feeling a bit tired. You go. Maybe I'll have a lie down.'

Neil noticed the tea-making equipment on a shelf next to the television. 'Like me to make you a cuppa, Bill?'

Bill smiled, then yawned. 'That would be great, Neil.'

Neil filled the kettle and plugged it in. 'I'll just put my stuff in my room across the corridor, then I'll come back. Toilet's just next door, if you need it.'

'Good idea. I'll go now before I lie down.'

Neil unlocked the door of his room. Looked fine. He left his backpack inside and returned to Bill's room to make his cup of tea. He'd just squeezed the tea bag and added milk when Bill walked in.

'Thanks, lad. I'll put it on the bedside table. Would you turn on the telly for me?'

Neil obliged. 'Sure you're okay, Bill? I won't be long, just take a stroll around, see if there's a nice place to eat tonight.'

Bill smiled. 'You're a good lad, Neil.'

Neil fetched a jacket from his room. It might be breezy out. He wanted to check out possible places where Bill could scatter Hazel's ashes. On his walk, he passed a promenade which advertised boat trips. He had an idea ...

***

Bill drank his tea then lay back on the bed. The television was showing some old soapie. He got up, turned it off and went out to the toilet again, remembering to leave the door of his room open. *Don't want to get locked out.*

He came back, went to the window and stared out at the beach. Mostly pebbles, he remembered. The day was overcast but there were still a few holiday makers. It was years since he'd been here. He and Hazel had made a small ritual of returning on each ten-year mark of their wedding anniversary. But on their fortieth Hazel had been in hospital getting another round of chemotherapy. He thought that not much had changed in Llandudno since their thirtieth anniversary. He sighed and turned away from the window, maybe he'd lie down for a spell. Wait for Neil to come back. What a champion Neil was! How lucky it was that Mrs Bridges had brought him over to help when he broke his arm. He lay on the bed. He felt so tired ...

***

Next morning he woke with a start when he heard knocking on his bedroom door and Neil calling.

'You okay, Bill?'

Bill stumbled out of bed. 'Yes, all good, Neil, just woke up.'

'Sorry, I disturbed you, it's nearly eight o'clock. Thought we might go down for breakfast.'

Bill yawned and scratched himself. 'Give me ten minutes, lad.'

He fell back on the bed, trying to orientate himself. He wondered if he had time for a cup of tea, his mouth was parched. The electric clock on the bedside table showed 7:44. No, better get dressed and go down for breakfast. From what he could remember about B & B places they were quite strict about breakfast times. Anyway, he needed to go to the toilet.

Several minutes later he was knocking on Neil's door. 'Ready, Neil.'

The door opened and Neil appeared. 'Sleep well, Bill?'

'Yes, I did,' Bill replied. 'After that lovely dinner.'

They'd gone to a small restaurant that Neil had found.

'Must have been the garlic,' Neil smiled.

***

Neil indicated a table set for two. 'I think this is ours.'

'Right, Bill. Now, about today.' But he was interrupted by a girl asking them if they'd like tea or coffee and a full English breakfast.

'Yes, please, and a cup of tea,' Bill replied. 'The sea air has given me an appetite.' He grinned.

'Same for me, but coffee, please,' Neil said.

When the girl disappeared, Neil turned to Bill. 'So, Bill, yesterday I found a boat that would take us out to sea to scatter Hazel's ashes. Unless you'd like to go on the beach and do it, but I checked the wind direction and I'm afraid the ashes might get blown back into your face rather than out to sea.'

Bill grimaced, and toyed with his napkin. 'What do you think, lad?'

Neil took a sip of the coffee that had just arrived. 'Perhaps the boat would be more personal. No onlookers wondering what you're doing.'

Bill nodded. 'Would you organise it, Neil?'

'Will do.'

Bill's eyes misted over. 'You're a good lad, Neil.'

Neil smiled. 'Here's our breakfast, Bill. Enjoy.'

***

Bill ate his breakfast, pondering Neil's suggestions. How could he ever repay Neil? He'd be lost without him. He really hoped Neil would stay with him after his course finished.

The two men ate in silence.

'Right, Bill.' Neil drained his coffee cup and placed it in the saucer. 'Do you want to stay here another night and think about Hazel's ashes?'

Bill shook his head. 'If you can book the boat for today, that will be good. Then we can head home tomorrow.'

Neil nodded. 'Okay. I'll ring the man with the boat. He's keeping eleven o'clock free for us. I just have to confirm before nine.' He glanced at his watch. 'It's half-eight. I'll ring him now.' He stood and raised his hand to Bill. 'See you down here at ten-thirty, Bill.'

Bill heaved a sigh. 'Right, Neil. Thanks. Think I'll have another cup of tea.'

***

Neil helped Bill into the boat. He thought Bill seemed a bit shaky today. He introduced Bill to the boatman, who nodded.

'Perfect weather, Bill.'

Bill stared at the sea. 'Um yes. I'm not very good on the water.'

The boatman smiled. 'Very calm today. I'll just motor out a bit. I have a nice place in mind for you, Bill.'

Neil took Hazel's urn from the bag he'd brought with him.

Not far from the shore, the boatman stopped the engine.

'Reckon this is a good spot,' he said. 'No breeze.'

Bill nodded.

'Ready Bill?' Neil had been researching appropriate words he could say while Bill was scattering Hazel's ashes, but he'd found nothing suitable.

Bill took a deep breath and tilted the urn.

The words of a song drifted into Neil's thoughts. He started to sing softly:

"We'll meet again, don't know where, don't know when,

But I know we'll meet again some sunny day.

Keep smiling through,

Just like you always do,

Till the blue skies drive the dark clouds far away."

Bill turned to him; his eyes full of tears. 'Vera Lynn! Hazel loved that song!'

He slowly tipped the urn over the side of the boat, letting the ashes drift away on the current.

'We'll meet again, Hazel,' he murmured. 'Soon, Hazel, soon.'

Chapter Seven
July

The Allotment

It's the 15th of July, St. Swithin's day. I wonder if any of the allotmenteers remember the old saying:

"St Swithin's Day, if it doth rain

Full forty days, it will remain

St Swithin's Day, if it be fair

For forty days, t'will rain no maire"

Well, it looks like being a lovely day, sun just rising. So, no rain for forty days! And school holidays next week! No one on the allotment yet. But according to the sundial on Paddy Murphy's plot it's only five o'clock in the morning. Bit early …

***

Brenda took out the card Jayne's father had given her. "Damien Burrow she read for the umpteenth time. IT Consultant and his phone number. Should she ring him? She knew Jayne would love her to come to her birthday party, she'd been talking about it for days before school broke up, and had kept asking Miss to come.

She took a deep breath and dialled the number on the card. It answered after a few rings, just as she was about to hang up.

'Damien Burrows, how may I help you?'

'Oh, Mr Burrows, this is Brenda Evans, Jayne's Special Ed assistant teacher.'

There was a pause. 'Miss **Evans**? Oh, I thought your name was Sevens ... Jayne calls you Miss Sevens.' He laughed. 'Sorry, I'm teasing you. I'm so pleased you rang. Jayne has been pestering me ever since the meeting. Can you come? Please say yes.'

Brenda hesitated. 'Yes, of course!' She tried to keep her tone efficient and light.

'Thank you so much. My address is on my card, but I can pick you up, if that's more convenient.'

'No, no.' Brenda read the address on the card. 'It's not too far, I can easily drive.'

'Right. Next Saturday afternoon. Three o'clock.' She heard the relief in his voice. 'Look forward to seeing you.'

Brenda collapsed onto a chair.

'Who was that, Brenda?' Her mother called.

'Just the parent of one of the pupils at school.'

'Hmm! You're not paid to talk to parents during school holidays!'

Brenda resolved not to mention the following Saturday.

***

Brenda needed to get a birthday present for Jayne. She had no idea what to get an eight-year-old girl, and began to regret agreeing to go to the party. Anyway, she was no good at this kind of social event.

She ended up getting a picture puzzle book the girl in the shop had recommended for an eight-year-old. 'Goodness,' she said to the girl, 'when I was about that age, I was given a book with pictures of girls and clothes. You cut them out and the clothes had tags that you folded over the girls ...'

The shop assistant gave her a strange look. 'Hmm, well things are a bit different now ...'

Suitably chastised, Brenda paid and left.

Saturday arrived. Brenda drove up and down the Burrow's street before finding a parking space amongst all the BMWs, Mercedes and four-wheel drive cars parked along the row of expensive-looking homes.

Her heart in her mouth, she walked up the path to the house and rang the bell.

Damien opened the door. 'Oh! Miss Sevens!' he exclaimed. 'I'm so pleased you came. Jayne has been bobbing up and down every time the doorbell rings, hoping it's you. Come in, come in.'

As she went in the door, Jayne came hurtling towards her. 'Miss Sevens! You came!' she squealed.

Brenda was enveloped in a hug.

'Right, Jayne, give Miss ...' he hesitated then grinned. 'Um Miss Sevens, time to get in the door.' He winked at Brenda and smiled.

Brenda couldn't help smiling back.

The party over, she watched as various mothers or fathers came to collect their offspring. She noticed the time, six o'clock. Her mother would be fuming.

'Miss Sevens, um Brenda. Thank you so much for coming today, you made Jayne's day!'

Brenda picked up her bag. 'Would you like me to stay and help you clear up?'

'No, no, all good.'

'Miss Sevens, thank you for coming today!' Jayne had wrapped herself around Brenda's legs.

'Miss Sevens has to go home, so say good bye now.' Damien turned to Brenda. 'Busy weekend?'

'Yes,' she replied. 'I have an allotment and I'm planning on going there early tomorrow morning before it gets too hot.'

Jayne's eyes opened wide. 'What's a 'lotment, Miss Sevens? Can we come?'

Brenda smiled. 'It's lots of little gardens where people can grow food.'

'Can we come?' She turned to her father. 'Please, Daddy? Please?'

Damien raised his eyebrows at Brenda.

'Well,' she hesitated, 'There's not much to see. Just gardens.'

'Please, Miss Sevens. I want to see your garden.'

Brenda looked at Damien. 'I'll be there about eight o'clock.'

'I don't think Jayne will give me a minute's peace until I agree.' He regarded his daughter. 'Right, miss, if you really want to see Miss Sevens' garden, then you'd better help me tidy up and get ready for bed. We'll have to get up early in the morning to be at the allotment by eight.'

'Do you know where they are?' Brenda asked.

He shook his head.

'Keep going past the Beech Road Primary school and you'll eventually get there.'

She slung her bag over her shoulder. 'Better go. Bye bye, Jayne. Happy Birthday again.' She bent down and hugged the little girl.

Driving home she felt happy until she parked her car in the garage and went into the house.

'What on earth kept you?' her mother demanded. 'I've been waiting ages for my tea!'

Brenda smiled. 'I'll get it now.'

***

Brenda arrived at her allotment just after eight o'clock the next morning to find Damien and Jayne already there.

'Miss Sevens, we've been waiting AGES for you!' Jayne called out.

'Oh, I'm sorry I kept you waiting.' She took a garden trug from the back of her car.

'What have you got there, Miss Sevens?'

'These are little spring cabbages that I'm going to plant today.'

'Can I help you?'

'Of course.'

Brenda smiled at Damien, who grinned, nodded hello and took the trug from her.

Jayne skipped along the path. 'Let me guess which is your 'lotment, Miss Sevens.'

Brenda smiled.

Jayne stopped at every plot along the main path, announcing, 'It's this one, Miss Sevens!'

Brenda shook her head at each one. 'Now Jayne, we have to turn right along this path and it's number twenty-seven.'

Jayne stopped at the little gate with the number 27 on it. 'This one!'

Brenda unlocked the gate and opened it.

'What can I do, Miss Sevens?' Damien grinned.

'Here's a tub. You can pick all the caterpillars off the broccoli.' She pointed to a row of green leaves.

'Ah!' He took the tub and went over to the row of vegetables.

'Oh! Can I help Dad, Miss Sevens?'

'Of course,' Brenda said, slightly relieved that she could plant out the tiny cabbage seedlings herself.

She had just finished when she heard voices.

'It's Dougie!' Jayne squealed, 'Dougie, I'm helping Miss Sevens!'

Carol came over to the fence. 'Hello Brenda, I see you have helpers.'

Brenda felt the colour rise in her cheeks. 'This is Jayne, she's in one of my classes, and this is her father, Damien.'

She was interrupted by Jayne who was jumping up and down and asking Dougie if she could come and see his 'lotment.

'Now, Jayne, everyone is really busy and we should probably be going home, now that you've seen Miss Seven's allotment.' Damien interrupted his daughter.

Carol smiled. 'It's good to see them interested in gardening. That's partly why I took on this plot. Dougie's counsellor said it would help him.' She looked at Dougie who had drawn himself up and was standing tall.

'I'm called Douglas now,' he informed Jayne. 'Because I'm going to Secondary School next term.'

Jayne's mouth fell open. 'Oh,' she breathed.

'But you can come and see our allotment, can't she, Mum.'

'Of course.'

Brenda and Damien watched them go.

'Well, Miss Sevens, I should probably follow them, but I'd much rather stay here and talk to you.'

Brenda felt her cheeks grow warm. She rubbed her nose, leaving a muddy smear. 'Um. Please call me Brenda.'

'I much prefer Sevens.'

Is he flirting with me? Brenda didn't know what to think.

'Here are all the caterpillars I've collected.' He held the tub out for her inspection. 'Oh! Some have escaped. What do you do with them?'

'Plot number thirty-six has a few hens. I usually tip caterpillars and any scraps into their run.'

He looked around.

'Oh, thirty-six is on the other side of the allotment.'

'Maybe I'll just tip the tub into your compost bin. Is that all right?'

Brenda nodded.

'While Jayne is busy, I'd really like to have a little talk with you, Sevens. Can we sit somewhere?'

Brenda indicated a plank resting on two oil drums. 'It's a bit wonky.'

'I just want to tell you a bit about my situation,' Damien said, perching on the end of the plank.

'Hmm.' Brenda lowered herself gingerly on the other end.

Damien took off his glasses, rubbed his eyes, and took a deep breath. 'Jayne's mother and I are separated. Bethany is a model. I met her in New York when I was working there a few years ago. She's American.' He paused and ran his fingers through his hair. 'We fell in love and married in the space of three months. Bethany didn't want children, but I thought she'd change her mind once she held her baby in her arms.' He raised his head and contemplated the allotments. 'Well, she got pregnant and we moved back to England when my firm relocated me. Bethany didn't like it here. She missed the bright lights and her career. So, when Jayne was six months old, Beth went back to New York and resumed modelling. You may have seen her in magazines.'

Brenda shook her head; she didn't read those magazines. Now she wondered why Damien was telling her all this.

'You're probably wondering why I'm telling you all this,' he continued. 'But I wanted to give you some background to account for Jayne's behaviour. Bethany and I are still friends, it was an amicable separation, thank goodness. But Jayne really misses not having her mother at home. Bethany flies over a few times a year to see Jayne, spoils and indulges her for a week and then leaves.

Jayne gets very upset – she sees her friends with mothers around all the time and I think she feels rejected. I'm only guessing that. But you can see she often gets hyped up.'

Brenda frowned. 'Um, I don't really know much about children, I've only just started my teacher's aide course ...'

Damien waved his hands. 'My mother comes down and stays during school holidays. I'm lucky that I work from home most of the time but I have to focus on my work and it's difficult with Jayne. You know how demanding she is. But what I'm trying to say is that Jayne adores you. Miss Sevens is her main topic of conversation. Miss Sevens had a blue shirt on today, Daddy. Do you think I could get a blue shirt? Or Miss Sevens said I did well today. Nonstop.'

'Oh, my goodness!' Brenda grimaced. 'Poor you. She'll probably get over it when she no longer has me helping her in school.'

'The thing is, she's done so well this term with you.'

Brenda didn't know what to say, she looked around hoping for inspiration.

'I just want to thank you and tell you how much I appreciate what you do for her.'

Brenda nodded. 'She's a delightful child.'

As Damien made a move to stand, conscious of the unstable bench, Brenda rose at the same time.

'I'd better not take up anymore of your time,' he said. 'Where can I find this Dougie's plot?'

'I'll show you.' She started towards her little gate.

Damien paused. 'Just a minute, Sevens, I don't know if you work during the school holidays?' He raised his eyebrows.

'No, not at the moment.'

'I was wondering if you would consider spending a day or two a week with Jayne, to give my mother a break. Of course, I would pay you ...'

'Oh! Well, um ...'

'Anyway, think it over and give me a ring if you'd like to. You've got my card?'

'Yes.'

'Thank you, Sevens.' He smiled and waited by her gate for her to lead the way.

Chapter Eight
August

T**he Allotment**

The harvest season used to begin on the 1st of August and was called Lammas, meaning 'loaf Mass'. Farmers made loaves of bread from the new wheat crop and gave them to their local church. Doesn't happen these days, probably due to Henry VIII breaking away from the Catholic Church.

"People don't notice whether it's winter or summer when they're happy." ~Anton Chekhov, 1898

***

Bill welcomed Anna Bridges, who had come to do her weekly clean. 'Come in, Mrs Bridges.'

Anna had wanted to cancel her visits when Neil first moved in, but Bill had said no.

'But Neil keeps it all spotless,' she'd protested, when she'd told Bill she felt bad coming when there was nothing to clean.

'Yes, but it still needs a woman's touch,' Bill had said.

Now, he led her into the kitchen. 'Before you start, Mrs Bridges, I wanted to talk to you about Hazel's things.'

'Yes, Neil mentioned it.'

'I just don't know what to do with her clothes,' Bill muttered.

She put her bag on the table. 'What would you like me to do?'

'Thought you might know,' he replied.

'Usually, people send the clothes to charity shops.'

Bill flinched.

'Why don't we have a look,' Anna said gently.

Bill nodded and led the way upstairs. He sat on the bed in his room and gestured towards a chest of drawers and a wardrobe.

'Hazel always kept lavender bags in the drawers,' he said. 'I planted lavender on the allotment, I used to cut it for her to make the bags.'

Anna came over to him. 'Bill. Why don't you go down and make us a cup of tea, and I'll see what's here and maybe make a few suggestions?'

He nodded and blew his nose. 'Right,' he mumbled. He stood and made for the bedroom door.

Downstairs he filled the kettle and got out the tea cups. He could hear Mrs Bridges opening and closing drawers. He sighed.

When she appeared, she smiled. 'The thing is, Bill, Hazel had some lovely clothes, things that will make some other women really happy to wear.'

He frowned, and indicated the tea cups.

'From what I knew of Hazel, I think she'd be thrilled to think that someone might get pleasure from her clothes.'

Bill nodded. 'Yes, she was a very generous person.' He sighed. 'Right then, Mrs Bridges, I think I'll get Neil to take us to the allotment and perhaps you can go through Hazel's things and take whatever you think, and maybe, what's left, um...' He couldn't continue.

She came over and put an arm around his shoulders. 'It's all right, Bill. I understand. Yes. Good idea.' She turned and called out. 'Neil! Can you come down?'

Neil appeared and leaned over the balustrade. 'What?'

'Bill wants to go to the allotment while I sort out a few things here. That okay?'

'Yeah, sure. Just wait while I shut down my computer.'

Five minutes later Bill and Neil were in the car on their way to the allotment.

***

Neil opened the gate to Bill's plot. 'Look at the garlic, Bill. It's dying back. Time to harvest it.'

Bill surveyed the blue balls of garlic flowers. 'Leave it to you, lad. I know nothing about garlic.'

'And according to my notes it's a good time to plant oriental greens like pak choi.'

'Know nothing about them things neither,' Bill responded. 'Foreign stuff. Think I'll have a wander around and see who's here.'

'Good idea, Bill.'

Neil smiled to himself as Bill headed off up the main path. He opened the shed and got out the garden fork, ready to lift the garlic.

'Hello, Neil?'

He groaned inwardly. 'Hello Brenda.' He came out of the shed and put on a busy air.

'I know you're busy, but I just wanted to ask your advice about something.'

His heart sank, but he knew that Brenda would give him no peace until she had told him all her woes.

'So, is it um,' he wracked his brains for the guy's name. 'Colin?'

'No, no. The thing is, one of the children in my class, Jayne; well, her father has asked me to work two days a week looking after her during the school holidays and I don't know what to do.'

'Is he paying you?'

'Yes, of course.'

'So, what's the problem?'

'Well, I don't know ...' Brenda shuffled from foot to foot. 'When you say it like that it sounds silly.'

'Silly?'

'I thought, well, maybe he had an interest ... oh! Never mind, I think I was panicking about nothing. All good.' She turned and smiled. 'Sorry Neil, but you're right. Thanks!'

Neil shook his head as he watched her walk back to her own plot.

***

Brenda rang Damien's number. 'It's Brenda,' she said. 'Brenda Evans.'

'Oh! Miss Sevens! I hope you're ringing with good news?'

'Um,' she hesitated. 'I've been thinking about your suggestion, and if you still want me to come and care for Jayne two days a week, well I'd like to.'

'That's fantastic! Mum's been coming down on a Monday, spending the week with Jayne and going home on Friday afternoon. But I know she's finding it a strain. She'd be happy to do three days if you can manage the other two.'

'Yes. Whichever days suit your mum.'

'How about you come Thursdays and Fridays?'

'Yes, that would be fine.'

'Great. Could you come this Thursday? Bit short notice.'

'No, that's okay. What do I need to bring?'

There was a pause, then Damien said, 'Today is Wednesday. Would you be able to pop over this afternoon and Mum can show you around?'

Brenda's heart thumped. 'Yes, okay, what time?'

'About two?'

'Right. See you then.'

***

Bill studied Neil over breakfast. 'I need to go into town today,' he said.

'Right, want me to drive you?'

'If you don't mind.'

'Somewhere in particular?'

Bill hesitated. 'A solicitor. I've made an appointment. Ten o'clock.'

Neil nodded. 'No problem,' he mumbled through a mouthful of toast.

That's what he liked about Neil, Bill thought. He wasn't nosy.

***

Brenda parked outside Damien's house. She'd taken extra care with her appearance.

'You're all tarted up to go to the allotment,' her mother had sniffed.

'I'm not going to the allotment.'

'Oh, so where are you going, then?'

'To see about a part-time job – just for the school holidays.'

'Hmph.'

Now, Brenda took a deep breath and rang the bell.

There was a scurrying inside and the door opened.

'Come in Miss Sevens,' Damien smiled, holding the door wide.

'Who is it?' a little voice said, then a scream of joy. 'Miss Sevens! You came to see me!'

Brenda bent and gave Jayne a hug.

'Look, Granny, this is Miss Sevens! I told you all about her.'

An elderly, elegantly-dressed woman came forward holding out her hand. 'Marjory Burrows,' she smiled. 'How nice to meet the mythical Miss Sevens at last.'

'Mythical?'

'Well, I've heard such amazing, wonderful things about you, that I was sure you couldn't be real.'

Brenda laughed. She liked this woman.

Damien closed the front door. 'I'll leave Mum to show you around and explain things to you, Sevens.'

His mother made a face of disapproval. 'Really, Damien, I think Miss Sevens would prefer not to be addressed by her last name!'

Damien laughed. 'Actually, it's Miss **Evans**,' he whispered. 'Brenda Evans.'

Jayne caught Brenda's hand and pulled at her. 'Come and see my bedroom, Miss Sevens.'

'Just a minute, Jayne. I need to talk to your grandmother first.'

'I'll leave you and Mum to it,' Damien said. 'Better get back to work.'

***

Bill got out of the car at the solicitor's office. 'I'll be about an hour, Neil, if you want to have a stroll around.'

'Okay, I'll potter over to the library.' Neil checked his watch. 'I'll be back at the car in good time.'

An hour later Bill returned to find Neil waiting in the car.

'All good,' he said. 'I need to come back in a week's time.'

Neil started the engine. 'No worries, Bill. I found a good gardening book in the library.'

Bill smiled. 'That's great, lad. I'll have a read of it when we get home.'

***

Amanda was absorbed in preparing a new strawberry bed when she heard the allotment gate opening. She looked up to see Donald Jenkins walking towards her.

'Good morning, Amanda. What's that you're doing?'

'Preparing a strawberry bed.' She wished she'd worn something more glamourous than her old gardening overalls. She straightened, talking care not to rub her back, and took off her gloves.

He nodded. 'I'm glad to have caught you.' He gave a nervous cough. 'There's concert on in the Town Hall this Saturday afternoon,' he hesitated, smoothing his beard. 'I was wondering if you'd like to come?'

Her heart fluttered; she thought he sounded tense. 'Yes, I'd love to.'

He gave a relieved sigh. 'I'm not certain what they'll be playing...'

She smiled, 'I'm sure it will be most enjoyable.'

Donald fiddled with his car keys. 'Could I pick you up?'

'That would be lovely, thank you. Or I can meet you there? What time?'

'Two-thirty. But please let me pick you up. It might be raining.'

'Just a moment, I've got a pen in my shed, I'll write down my address.'

He took the paper and studied it. 'I'll see you at two o'clock. That should be plenty of time. Looking forward to it. I'll get the tickets.' He turned, waved, and went back to his car.

Amanda watched his retreating figure. *Had he only come to the allotment today with the hope of seeing me?*

***

Brenda followed Damien's mother into the kitchen – all stone benchtops and gleaming appliances. A far cry from her mother's kitchen.

'Please call me Marjory.'

'And I'm Brenda.'

'Would you like a cup of tea? We can have a little chat.'

'Granny!' Jayne was jumping up and down. 'I want to show Miss Sevens my bedroom! And my nurse's station.'

'Jayne!' Brenda put out her hand. 'I must talk to your grandmother for a while. Now, how about you go to your bedroom and get your patients ready, and I'll be matron and come and inspect them a bit later.'

Jayne nodded. 'Yes, Miss Sevens,' she breathed. She turned to go. 'But don't be too long,' she said over her shoulder.

'Well, you certainly have the knack of dealing with her,' Marjory Burrows remarked. 'I must say she's a handful. I so appreciate you coming to give me a break.' She indicated an elegant, stainless-steel and cushioned chair.

'A pleasure,' Brenda smiled. 'Jayne can be a bit over powering but she's a delightful little girl.'

'Yes. I'm afraid her mother does her no favours when she comes over.' Marjory sat opposite Brenda and rested her arms on the table.

Brenda didn't comment.

'I expect Damien has told you the background?'

Brenda nodded.

'Well. Now I've met you, is there anything you want to know?'

Brenda frowned. 'Damien didn't tell me exactly what I'm supposed to do.'

'Oh! Well, basically, it's just to keep Jayne amused. Damien gives her breakfast and then I spend time with her, maybe go for a walk to the playground, give her lunch, read to her. I usually get dinner for us ...' Her voice tailed off. 'Jayne's not an easy girl to manage. Damien was a great child. He seemed to entertain himself, I never needed to do much with him ...' Her eyes clouded. 'But I'm so pleased you agreed to come for a couple of days. It's really getting too much for me.'

Brenda smiled. 'Well, I'm here now. Damien said you would be going home today so why don't you head off early and I can look after Jayne for the rest of this afternoon.' She checked the time. 'Only another hour or so. I'm happy to stay here.'

Marjory seemed relieved. 'Really? That would be great, I can miss the traffic. Thank you. I'll just say goodbye to Damien.'

'But, please show me Jayne's bedroom first!'

***

Mary hurried to the front door when the bell rang.

'Consignment for Mary Flynn,' the courier said.

Mary's heart sank at the sight of the boxes arrayed on her doorstep.

She signed the acknowledgement of receipt.

She hadn't realised she'd ordered so many bulbs. She picked up the boxes and carried them to the garage. *Shit! How on earth am I going to plant all these bulbs?*

***

Neil looked up from lifting the onions. A neat row lay spread on the ground to dry.

'Oh, hello, Mary.'

'Um, Neil, I wonder can I ask your help?'

He stood and raised his eyebrows.

'You see, I've bought all these bulbs to plant to make a memorial garden ...'

'Uh huh.'

'I think I need help.'

Neil nodded. 'Okay. Let me know when you're ready.' He turned back to the onions.

***

Brenda drove home, thinking about the afternoon. She'd heard Damien come out of his study and say goodbye to his mother. Then he'd come up to Jayne's bedroom and knocked on the door.

'Who is it?' Jayne had asked.

Brenda said in a loud voice, 'I think it might be the doctor, come to check on your really sick patient, Jayne.'

'It's Doctor Foster, come from Gloucester.' Damien had replied in a sombre tone of voice.

Jayne squealed and opened the door. 'Come in, doctor.' But then she'd giggled so much that she could hardly keep her balance. She threw herself on her bed. 'Oh, Daddy, Miss Sevens is so much fun!'

Now, thinking about the look Damien had given her, her heart started to flutter.

She parked her car in the garage and went indoors.

Her mother raised her eyes. 'Took you long enough. Did you get the job?'

'Yes, Mum. Thursdays and Fridays. Start tomorrow at eight o'clock.' She hung up her car keys and went into the kitchen. 'I'd better start dinner.'

'So how much will you get paid?'

Brenda paused. 'We didn't discuss pay.'

Her mother made a snorting sound. 'Seems a bit fishy to me! You'll probably end up working like a slave for nothing.'

Brenda sighed. 'Story of my life,' she muttered.

***

Neil stopped the car outside the solicitor's office and helped Bill out.

'Should only be ten minutes, Neil.'

'Okay, Take your time, Bill. I'll wait here, I've brought some course notes to study.'

Twenty minutes later, Bill returned and waved an envelope at Neil. 'Now, Neil,' he said, 'This is my will. I'm going to put it in the drawer of the sideboard where I keep all my important papers.'

Neil blinked. 'Right.' He knew that drawer. It contained a jumble of old bills and notices. 'It'll certainly be safe there.'

'And the solicitor pinned her card on the envelope, so when my number's up, you'll know who to contact.'

Neil let in the clutch. 'Right. Bill, it's good to be prepared, but I hope it won't be needed for many more years.'

'I'll tell Mrs Bridges as well next time she comes.'

Neil cast a sidelong look at Bill.

'Well, in case you've gone on a course or something.' Bill patted Neil's knee and stared straight ahead.

***

Brenda sighed with relief when four o'clock on Friday came and Damien came out of his study. Jayne was certainly a handful. She could quite understand how a week with her granddaughter would have exhausted Marjory.

Damien smiled at his daughter. 'Jayne, would you go to your room for a few minutes, please, while I talk to Miss Sevens?'

Jayne pouted. 'Oh, but Daddy I want to stay with Miss Sevens ...'

Her father stared at her. 'Now, Jayne, I don't think Miss Sevens will want to come back next week if she knows you don't do as you're told.'

Jayne's lower lip jutted out, then she flounced out of the room, muttering to herself.

Damien raised his eyebrows at her retreating back, then turned to Brenda. 'Thank you so much, Sevens. Jayne seems to have had a wonderful time these last two days.' He handed her an envelope. 'We didn't discuss money, but I'm hoping this will be enough to make you return next Thursday.'

Brenda didn't know what to do. She stared at the envelope *Should I open it now?* She tried to stay cool and composed.

'Thank you, Damien. I'm sure it will be fine.'

'Busy weekend ahead?'

'Probably go up to the allotment tomorrow, it's been so dry I must do some watering.'

'Could we come and help?'

'Oh! Well, it's quite a lot of work, we don't have garden hoses, so it means taking the water from my rainwater barrel and filling the watering can ...'

'Then the answer is yes?'

Brenda nodded. 'Well, if you're sure ...'

Jayne's voice came from her bedroom. 'Can I come down now?'

'Yes, come and say goodbye and thank you to Miss Sevens.'

Jayne came flying down the stairs and hurled herself at Brenda. 'You are coming back next week aren't you, Miss Sevens?'

'Yes, of course.' Brenda bent and gave her a hug. 'But only if you're really good next week, when Granny is here.'

***

Amanda's stomach fluttered with nerves when Saturday afternoon came around. She couldn't eat lunch, just had a small glass of wine to settle herself and then reviewed her wardrobe. The weather appeared fine and sunny, but it might be chilly in the Town Hall. The branches on the trees in the garden opposite, barely moved, but a breeze might whip up later. She dithered so much that by two o'clock she still wasn't dressed.

Hastily, she put on a flowery summer dress and threw a light cardigan around her shoulders. As she slipped on a pair of sandals, she heard a car outside.

Exactly two o'clock! Naval precision! Steady on old girl. Deep breaths! She opened the front door to find Donald standing there about to ring the doorbell.

He smiled. 'Thank you for being so punctual Amanda!' He blinked, gave a little bow and continued. 'And if you don't mind me saying so, you look lovely!'

Amanda locked the front door behind her and glowed as he took her arm, escorted her down the path and held open the car door.

'It's Mozart and Bartok today,' he said. 'I hope you'll enjoy it.'

'I'm sure I will. I love Mozart, haven't listened to much Bartok so it will be a new experience for me.' Amanda replied.

He smiled as he got into the car. 'It's so nice to find a kindred spirit,' he said. 'Thank you for coming today.'

***

Neil noticed Mary carrying a box up to her plot.

'Hello, Neil,' she called.

He stood. 'Need a hand, Mary?'

She put the box on the ground. 'Yes please, Neil. I wanted to ask your advice about planting all these bulbs. You see I made a plan. Can I show you?'

'Okay.' He put down his hoe as she came over, pulling out a sheet of paper.

'See, this is my rough plan.' She pointed a red-painted fingernail at the diagram. 'I thought I'd plant hyacinths along here where I've coloured blue, daffodils just here where I've coloured yellow, snowdrops just there and ...'

He was distracted by the blood-red of her nail varnish. 'Looks fine. How can I help?'

'Well, if you could help me with the boxes ... what do you think? Is my plan okay?'

He shrugged. 'Seems okay to me, but I'm not a garden designer.'

'Oh. I thought you'd know.'

'Have you any more boxes?'

'Yes, back in the car.'

'Right. I'll help you. I can leave Bill's weeding for now.' He knew he sounded surly, but who cared?

She gave a sigh. 'Thanks, Neil.'

***

Amanda enjoyed the concert. 'That was lovely, thank you so much for taking me, Donald,' she said as he parked outside her house. 'Now, would you like to come in for a coffee?'

'That would be very nice, thank you.' He jumped out and opened the passenger door. 'Madam!' he said with a flourish.

Amanda beamed. She climbed out and led the way to her front door. Cato greeted her, mewing and rubbing himself around her legs.

'Oh! You have a cat!'

'Yes, meet Cato.'

'Er... unfortunately, I'm allergic to cats ...' Donald's eyes were already watering, then he sneezed.

'Oh!' Amanda pushed her cat away. 'Oh, I'm so sorry!'

'Excuse me!' He sneezed again. 'Never mind, Amanda. So stupid of me ... I'd better go! Thank you for the lovely afternoon.' He turned, waved and went back to his car.

Amanda looked down at Cato. 'Oh, dear, love me, love my cat. What will I do, Cato?'

Chapter Nine
September

The Allotment

"If of thy mortal goods thou art bereft,
And from thy slender store two loaves alone to thee are left,
Sell one, and from the dole,
Buy hyacinths to feed the soul" – Sadi.
I think that dole in this case means change.
Now I see that Peter's widow, Mary has planted lots of bulbs. But she doesn't seem happy about it. I wonder if she really fits in to my Allotment?

***

Bill wandered around the allotments looking for someone with whom to chat. He liked to leave Neil on his own to work on the plot; he was sure it helped with the shell shock. He spotted Mary Flynn standing by her shed, looking helpless.

'You okay, Mary?'

'Oh!' She turned around at his voice. 'I was just thinking about all the work I have to do here. It's too much, Bill!' Her eyes filled with tears. 'I've bought all these bulbs and apparently the daffodils, crocus and hyacinths all have to be in before the end of September. I'll never manage it, Bill!'

'It's a lot of work, all right,' Bill said, catching sight of the boxes of bulbs in her shed. 'Tell you what, I'm sure Neil will be delighted to help. Not much to do now on my plot.'

She frowned at him dubiously. 'No, no, it's too much to ask.'

Bill smiled. 'He'll be delighted, I'm sure ...'

***

Neil's brows drew together when Bill told him about Mary's deadline for the bulbs.

'Daffs, crocus and hyacinths have to be in by the end of this month,' Bill informed him. 'It's too much for her, I said you'd help her.'

'Of course, I'll help her, Bill. Can't have her breaking a nail.'

Bill looked puzzled.

'Sorry, Bill. Bit grumpy this morning.'

***

Brenda was pleased to have Damien's help with the watering. There wasn't much water left in the rain barrel connected to her little garden shed; there had been no rain for weeks.

He and Jayne were at the allotment car park when she arrived.

'What kept you, Miss Sevens?' Jayne demanded as Brenda parked.

'I had a few things to do,' Brenda replied. She showed Damien the water barrel and gave him the watering can. 'Those seedlings need watering,' she said, pointing to a row of tiny shoots.

Jayne was distracted. 'Where's Dougie?' she demanded.

'He and his mother aren't here every day.'

'Oh. But I wanted to see him!'

'They might come later,' Brenda said.

'Right,' said Damien. 'Now, Miss Sevens, what can Jayne do to help?'

'Would you like to find caterpillars, Jayne?' Brenda asked.

'Okay. Maybe Dougie will come then.'

'Maybe.' Jayne didn't sound very happy, Brenda thought.

***

Carol felt anxiety gnawing at the pit of her stomach. Dougie was starting the new school year next month at the local secondary school. His time at the primary school had been a term to familiarise him with a mainstream school. He'd loved it, especially when Brenda Evans started working there.

A few of his old classmates would be going to the new school which might help, but he'd miss Brenda. Perhaps she could suggest to Brenda that she change schools. But maybe that wasn't allowed while still undergoing training?

She'd bought Dougie's new school uniform a few weeks before. He'd tried it on, looking at himself in the long mirror in her bedroom.

'I can't wait to start school next week, Mum. Will Brenda be there?'

She smiled at him. She'd told him several times that Brenda wouldn't be there but other lovely people like Brenda would.

'I'm so proud of you, Dougie.' She hugged him.

'Mum, I'm getting too big for hugs.' He disengaged himself from her arms but must have noticed her face for he continued, 'it's okay at home, but not outside.' Then he smiled at her and returned her hug.

'Better take off your uniform now, Dougie, or it'll be worn out before you even start school.'

She saw his look of consternation and watched as he carefully removed the uniform and hung it in his wardrobe.

'Um, Dougie, now you are getting too big for hugs, you must remember to shut the bathroom door when you go to the toilet.'

His eyes widened. 'Why?'

'It's what grown-ups do.'

He considered this. 'Right. Can we go to the allotment now, Mum?'

She sighed. 'Sorry love, but I must work today.'

He nodded. 'Okay, I'll maybe read some of my old school books.'

She resisted the urge to hug him again and went to her bedroom where she'd installed a small workstation. She turned on her computer. While she waited for it to power up, she sat thinking about the progress Dougie had made over the years. If only you could see your son now, Angus, she thought. She'd never forget the sight of her husband's face after Douglas's birth when they received the news that their baby had Down Syndrome. Angus was super competitive – he was the Physical Education teacher at the school where she taught English. It was where they had met. He had to excel at everything. He'd never came to terms with having a son who would not meet his exacting standards. And Dougie was a colicky baby. Sleepless nights didn't help. Their marriage lasted a year after that. She took a deep breath. Better get working. Angus paid child support for Dougie, but it was still hard to make ends meet. It helped that she grew most of their vegetables at the allotment.

She grew ever more nervous as the September term approached. Dougie had been trying his new uniform on nearly every day. She'd tried to distract him by going to the allotment.

She wished she could afford to go for a short holiday, camping or something. Maybe next year ...

'Dougie, dear. Your new uniform will be worn out if you try it on any more,' she called.

'Just polishing my new shoes, Mum.'

'Don't get polish on your uniform!'

There was silence. Apprehensive, she got up from her desk and went downstairs. Dougie looked up at her, an expression of fear on his face.

'Just a bit of black polish on the pants, Mum.'

She took a deep breath. 'It's okay, Dougie. Why don't you take off the pants and give them to me and we can finish polishing your shoes later.'

He gulped. 'Right, Mum. Sorry.'

***

Amanda kept thinking about Donald and Cato. Just her luck that a man she found attractive – and who appeared to find her attractive – had an allergy to cats. And what made it worse was that he enjoyed the same kind of music as she did, and they had a lot in common. She stared out the window, it was getting dark earlier and earlier. She poured herself a glass of wine, sat on her reclining chair and tried to relax. Cato jumped on her lap.

'You're a blight on my love life, Cato,' she murmured, stroking him.

Her phone rang. She pushed the cat off her lap and went to the phone. 'Hello?'

'Oh, Amanda, it's Donald.'

Her heart jumped. 'Oh, hello, Donald.'

'Just wanted to say sorry about last weekend, and your cat.'

'Quite understandable,' she replied.

'The thing is …' he hesitated. 'Well, the thing is, I went to my doctor and got these tablets, antihistamines, which should help with my allergy …'

'Oh, that sounds good,' Amanda smiled. *Fancy him doing that for me!*

'Anyway, I was wondering if you'd like to have a drink and a bite with me one evening?'

'That sounds lovely!' Amanda's smile broadened.

'Next Saturday? How about I pick you up?'

'That would be nice.'

'Six o'clock? Do you know The Water Mark? According to my sister, they do nice meals there.'

'Lovely. Look forward to it.'

'See you then. Bye for now.'

Amanda thought she'd burst with excitement. 'Come here Cato. It's going to be all right after all.'

The cat jumped on her lap and purred.

***

The Allotment - Harvest festivals everywhere. A lot of the allotmenteers are picking giant marrows and pumpkins; must be competitions coming up. Some of them are gathering Michaelmas Daisies to decorate the churches.

***

Amanda patted her hair, admiring the highlights her hairdresser had suggested. She checked the time. Five fifty-five. Donald had said he'd come for her at six o'clock. She hovered by the front door and then heard a car stop outside.

Her doorbell rang.

'Hello, Donald!' she exclaimed as she opened the door.

'Madam,' he said and gazed at her. 'If you don't mind me saying so, you look wonderful!'

'Thank you, Donald.' She tried to appear nonchalant.

'Your carriage awaits.'

She picked up her handbag, locked the front door and followed him out to his car.

'I think I told you that I'm staying with my sister at the moment,' Donald said as he drove to The Water Mark.

'Yes. You mentioned it.'

'I've retired from the Navy and I needed a bit of time to look around and decide where to live, before rushing into buying a house.'

Privately, Amanda thought it unlikely that Donald would ever rush into anything. 'Good idea,' she said.

'Well, my sister is keen to meet you and asked me to invite you over one afternoon.'

'Oh!'

He glanced sideways at her. 'That's if you'd like to ...'

'Yes, I'd very much like to meet your sister.'

Donald gave a sigh. *Of relief?*

***

Brenda's stomach churned – her first day back at the primary school after the summer break. She breathed in the familiar distinctive smell of school, and hoped she'd have some nice kids to help, kids like Dougie. She wondered how he was getting on at his new secondary school. She imagined how nervous Carol must be.

Her fears about her new pupils were allayed; apart from one boy who was a bit of a bully, most of the others were lovely and it was comforting to know she'd have Jayne back this year.

'Hello Miss Sevens!' Jayne bounced into the class room.

Brenda gave her a hug. 'Now Jayne, remember what I told you? You must let the other children get a look in!' She tapped the side of her nose.

Jayne giggled and tapped the side of her nose. 'Over and out, Miss Sevens!'

***

Amanda wondered if things were getting serious with Donald. He'd spoken a lot about his sister, Judy, a widow with three children. One at university and the other two at school.

She'd gone to visit Judy, and the visit had gone well. At least, Amanda thought so. And it must have, she reassured herself, as Donald had rung her the next day, suggesting a film she might like to see.

She poured herself a glass of wine, put her feet up and picked up her latest library book. Cato jumped onto her lap and purred.

'Things are looking good, Cato!'

***

The Allotment

The 29th of September – Michaelmas Day – Allotment rents to be paid, it's traditionally the last day of the harvest season.

***

Mary opened her mail. A renewal notice from the Council. Time to pay the allotment rent for the next year. She heaved a sigh. Was it already over a year since she'd renewed the rent on Peter's allotment? He'd still been alive then. He'd died the last day of October. She really did not want to renew her plot. It took so much effort to get there and then try and find the energy and the will to do anything. That nice Bill had suggested his helper could work on it, but she didn't like to ask him. Neil, poor sod. He had his own problems by the look of him. And then her sister Veronica kept bugging her. "Time to start dating, Mary," was her constant refrain. "Come to dinner, Mary." And she would turn up to find yet another "eligible" bachelor invited just to meet her.

Mary sighed. Then she had an idea.

***

Neil worried about Bill. He didn't seem himself lately. A bit confused. That morning at breakfast, he'd got out his packets of seeds and started shuffling them.

'Right, Bill. What's the plan for today? It's the end of September. What can we plant?' Neil's mind went over the possibilities that he'd learned from his course.

Bill frowned as he moved the seed packets from left to right, up and down. 'Dunno, lad. Broad beans? Heather loved broad beans. Not so keen myself, but she loved them.' He paused. 'Broccoli? Beetroot?'

'Let me see.' Neil took the packets of seeds and sorted through them. 'I'll look it up on the internet, Bill.'

'Internet?' Bill's brows drew together.

'Yes, everything's on there. Or maybe you have some gardening books?'

Bill brightened. 'Yes. Books! On the shelf over there.' He gestured towards a bookcase.

Neil pulled out a book. '*The Gardener's Year*, let's see what they say for September, eh, Bill.'

Bill rotated the seed packets. 'September? Already?' He took a deep breath. 'Heather died in September. Or was it December?'

'Heather?'

'My wife.'

'Oh, Hazel.'

'That's what I said. Hazel.'

'Oh. Of course, sorry Bill. Anyway, it's the end of September. We need to think of Autumn sowing.'

'Yes.'

The clatter of the letter box roused Bill.

'I'll get the milk and the mail,' Neil said, rising from the table.

Bill nodded. 'We'll go to the allotment today, Neil?'

'Of course.'

***

Mary knew that Bill went to his allotment most days. She passed his plot. *Great! Neil was there on his own.*

'Hello Neil.' She walked towards where he was picking the last of the runner beans.

He lifted his head. 'Hmm.'

'Neil, I want to ask you a favour.' She saw a hunted look in his eyes. She hurried on before she lost her nerve. 'Apparently you're single.'

He scowled.

'Bill told me. Anyway. The thing is, my sister keeps trying to fix me up with men. I mean, she thinks I should start dating again ...' She twisted her wedding ring. 'And I don't want to. She doesn't understand.'

Neil stared at her.

'So, I was wondering, thought that perhaps I could tell her that you and I were dating.'

He shook his head as if he hadn't heard right.

'Don't say no! Please. All I'm asking is that when she invites me to another dinner party, I can ask if I can bring my new man friend.' She saw the look of panic in his eyes. 'Or I can just say I'm busy going out on a date ...'

She put her hand on his arm. 'You won't have to commit to anything.'

He stared at her hand, his frown deepening.

'The next time she asks, I can say I'm meeting you. We can go for a drink. No strings.'

'Well, hello, Mrs Flynn.' Bill's voice broke the tension. 'Oh, sorry, was I interrupting something?'

Mary snatched her hand away. 'No, Bill. I just invited Neil to go for a drink with me some evening.'

Bill's face lit up. 'That's great, Neil!' He turned to Mary. 'Top lad, our Neil.'

Mary tried to ignore Neil's scowl. 'Right,' she said, 'I'd better get up to my plot. Nice talking to you, Neil!'

***

Neil watched Mary walk along the path.

'Good work, lad!' Bill crowed. 'How did you pull that one off?'

Neil grunted. 'I didn't! She just came and asked me.'

'See? I've been telling everyone what a lovely bloke you are! You've got me to thank for that, Nigel.'

Neil groaned. He wanted to say, it's Neil, not Nigel, but instead he said, 'I don't want to go for a drink with her, Bill. She's just using me as an excuse not to go out with other men.'

'Don't be soft, lad. She fancies you all right.'

'And she's high maintenance.'

'What do you mean, "high maintenance"?'

'Just think about it.' He finished picking the beans. 'Lots of beans here, Bill. Do you know how to freeze them?'

Bill shook his head. 'Hazel used to freeze them but I've got no idea.'

Neil breathed a sigh of relief; he'd got Bill off the subject of Mary Flynn. *Okay, she was gorgeous, he had to admit, but the last thing he needed was to get tangled up with a grieving widow, who must spend a lot of time at the hairdressers and nail salon!*

***

Brenda received her allotment renewal notice that morning. She thought back to a year ago; she'd been still working at the convenience store with no idea how much her life would change. She smiled to herself. And all from an armed holdup. She'd seen in the local paper the results of the inquest on the gunman. Apparently, he'd accidently shot himself when Neil had jumped him. Poor Neil. He probably felt responsible for the man's death. She made a mental note to reassure him next time she saw him.

***

Neil surveyed the garlic cloves he'd planted. Bill had been bemused when Neil had mentioned now was the time to plant garlic.

'Not a garlic man, myself, Neil.'

'Really?' Neil had grinned. 'Bill, you've been eating my cooking for months now, and it's had lots of garlic in it. Adds flavour and it's good for you too.'

Bill had been surprised. 'You didn't tell me. But you're a good cook, Neil. Have to say.'

Neil smiled to himself at the memory of Bill's reaction. He looked at Bill's retreating figure making its way up the allotment.

'Hello, Neil.' A voice interrupted his thoughts. He turned.

'Oh, hello, Mary.'

'Um, Neil. You remember you agreed to have a drink with me, so I could tell my sister I was dating?'

'Mmm.' He didn't think he'd actually agreed.

'Well, she's having a Fireworks party next month ...'

He stiffened. 'No!' His eyes narrowed. 'Sorry, I can't make it.'

'Oh.' Mary drew back. 'Well, maybe we could have a drink before that night then I can tell her that you can't make the party? That might get her off my back.'

He could think of no excuse. 'Right.'

'So how about this weekend? Say Saturday night at The Water Mark? Seven o'clock?'

Neil frowned at the ground. 'Um. Okay.'

'Thanks, Neil. Remember, no strings. This is just a business deal.' She walked up the grassy path towards her plot.'

He watched her retreating figure. *How have I got into this? And if it was a business deal, what do I get out of it?*

***

Mary wondered about Neil. Most of the men her sister had introduced her to had been extremely keen to take her out, but Neil displayed no enthusiasm, in fact, quite the reverse. The next time Bill appeared at her plot to check on her progress, she'd ask him.

***

Bill wandered around the allotment looking for someone with whom to chat. Since he'd broken his wrist and arm, he'd not done much on his plot. Anyway, it was good for Neil to get hands on experience while he was doing his horticultural course – at least that's what he told himself. Maybe old age and laziness, or was he just plain tired?

Ah! He spotted Mary Flynn coming out of her shed.

'Hello, Mary! How are you?'

'Hi Bill. Well, I'm just wondering what I should be doing next.' She sighed. 'I was all enthusiastic at the thought of planting spring bulbs – making this a kind of "Keukenhof" in Peter's memory, but now I'm wondering if it was such a good idea.'

'Cookenhoff?'

Mary smiled. 'Yes, it's a huge place in the Netherlands with amazing displays of tulips and daffodils and other spring bulbs.'

'Ah,' Bill nodded. 'I'm sure Peter knew what he was doing when he wanted his ashes scattered here. I reckon he'd like your idea.'

'Do you think so?' Mary scanned her plot. 'I've been digging and raking and spreading yukky blood and bone. My bulbs arrived last month, together with instructions.'

'Instructions?'

'Yes, I think I told you ... Apparently each bulb has to be planted twice the size of its bulb deep.'

'Well, I just stuck my daffodil bulbs in and hoped for the best.' Bill smiled.

'I've spent hundreds of pounds on these bulbs.' Mary frowned. 'I have to do it right.'

'Of course. And now it's autumn. According to Neil, it's time to plant garlic.'

'Garlic?' Mary screwed up her nose.

Bill laughed. 'I know. Apparently, Neil's been cooking with lots of garlic without my knowledge. But I must say he's a great cook.'

'Hmm.' Mary stared at Bill. 'Actually, I wanted to ask you about Neil ...'

Bill blinked.

'The thing is, I asked him to have a drink with me next Saturday and he seemed very reluctant ...' her voice trailed away. 'I mean ...'

Bill's brows drew together. 'And?'

'Well, I thought he'd like to have an evening out with me. But now I'm wondering is he ... I mean, is he ...' she paused, her eyebrows raised.

'Oh, you mean, is he ...' Bill didn't know how to continue, then he brightened. 'The thing is he was in the army for years and now he has shell shock – no, some other name. PS something.'

Mary stared at him. 'Do you mean PTSD?'

'Yes!' Bill exclaimed, 'that's the word.' His face fell. 'But I probably shouldn't be telling you that. It's his private life.'

'Hmm, well that explains a lot. Thanks for telling me, Bill.'

Bill nodded, anxious to change the subject. 'You can plant out cabbage ready for spring now.'

Mary made a face. 'Cabbage? I don't really cook much these days, Bill, and I've never been a fan of cabbage.'

'My Hazel used to put a few rashers of bacon in with the cabbage when she cooked it. Delicious!' Bill smacked his lips. 'I must tell Neil that trick.' He sighed. 'Right Mary, I'd better not keep you, I can see you have lots to do here.'

Chapter Ten
October

The Allotment
"Autumn - Season of mists and mellow fruitfulness,
Close bosom-friend of the maturing sun." John Keats

***

Brenda took the envelope that Jayne thrust at her.

'Daddy said to give you this, Miss Sevens,' Jayne said.

'Thank you, Jayne.' Brenda's heart skipped a beat. She'd seen Damien a few times since the summer school holidays – he'd come to the allotment with Jayne – just to see her, she hoped, not because Jayne pleaded with him. She stuffed the envelope in her pocket. No time to open it now.

During her lunch break she took the envelope out and opened it.

Dear Sevens

I think it's half-term in a couple of weeks. Would you be able to do the honours and mind Jayne? Maybe the whole week if possible. Usual financial arrangement.

I hope you can!

Damien

She wrote on the bottom of the letter, *'Yes, of course!'* put it back in the envelope, found a stapler, secured the envelope, then crossed out her name and replaced it with Mr D. Burrows.

At the end of the school day, she found Jayne and gave her the envelope. 'Please give it to Daddy,' she said and watched as Jayne ran out the school gates to meet her father.

***

Neil regretted having agreed to Mary's invitation for a drink. He'd cooked his and Bill's dinner and eaten. Then he excused himself to Bill.

'Sorry Bill. I've got to get ready to meet Mary Flynn.'

Bill smiled. 'That's the way, lad! Gather ye rosebuds where ye may!' He frowned. 'Who said that?'

'Robert Herrick, apparently.'

'Never heard of him.'

'Indeed.' Neil took their empty plates and started to rinse them before putting them in the dish-washer. He was grumpy with himself for agreeing to this "rendezvous".

He showered and changed into something his sister called "smart casual".

'You're looking great, Neil.' Bill said as Neil clattered down the stairs. He winked at Neil. 'Don't forget the rosebuds, Neil.'

'I won't, Bill. Now are you okay for tonight? I won't be long, anyway. It's just to give Mary a reason to stop her sister trying to palm her off on different men.'

'I'll be fine, Neil. Don't you worry about me.'

***

Mary was early at The Water Mark. She walked over to an empty table in the far corner of the bar. She took off her coat and draped it over the seat next to her, then sat down and moved her handbag to the seat on the other side of her. She fidgeted with her rings. A man came over and asked her what she would like to drink.

'It's okay, I'm waiting for someone,' she replied.

'Lucky guy,' he muttered and wandered off.

Then she spotted Neil. She saw him scanning the room.

He noticed her and hurried over. 'Sorry, Mary, am I late?'

She smiled. 'No, I was nervous.' She hesitated. 'I came early, this is my first time out with a man other than my husband, since I was eighteen.'

'Oh.' He frowned. 'Er, what would you like to drink?'

'Brandy, please.'

She watched as he went to the bar. It was the first time she'd seen him smartly dressed.

He placed her glass in front of her.

'Thanks, Neil.'

'Cheers.' He lifted his glass of beer.

'Cheers.' She drained her glass.

He indicated her drink. 'Another?'

She nodded and studied him as he stood at the bar.

***

Neil returned to their table and placed the brandy in front of her.

'So how have you been, Mary?' He asked as he sat down.

She took a sip of her drink. 'All right, I guess. Thanks to you most of my bulbs have been planted, but apparently I must wait until November to plant the tulips, so I'm at a bit of a loose end at the moment.'

Neil looked around the crowded room, trying to think of something to say.

'I see that little Brenda,' Mary continued, 'She's a different person since she started her teacher's aide studies and the new job and even you seem much happier since you started your course ...'

He thought that possibly the source of Brenda's happiness was the attentions of that bloke, Damien, who always seemed to be hanging around her plot. He dragged his attention back to his companion. 'Well, I'm enjoying my course, I must say.'

Mary sighed. 'I wish I could find something interesting to do.'

They sat in silence until Neil said, 'Well, what did you do before you were married?'

She stared at him. 'Nothing. I'd just left school and had planned on going to Art college when I met Peter and, well, the rest is history.'

'Well, maybe you could find an art class.'

She rubbed her chin, a slight frown on her face. 'That's a thought.'

'Hello, Mary!' A voice said.

Neil looked up to see a vivacious red-head surveying him.

'Oh, Vronnie! This is Neil ... um Neil ...' She looked at Neil helplessly.

He realised she didn't know his last name. 'Neil Blakey,' he said as he stood and held out his hand.'

'Oh, Neil, this is my sister, Veronica,' Mary said.

'Nice to meet you, Neil. We're at a table just around the corner. I spotted Mary when I went to the bar. Why don't you join us?'

Neil gave Mary a hard look.

'Maybe later, Vronnie.'

Veronica nodded. 'Right oh.' And she made her way back to her table.

'Sorry about that. I forgot that Veronica often comes here on a Friday evening.'

Neil's brows drew together. He wondered if Mary had really forgotten or had planned it.

He turned his wrist to expose his watch.

Mary bit her lip. 'Are you bored, Neil?'

'I was just checking the time. I told Bill I wouldn't be long.'

Mary tossed her head and finished her brandy, then placed the empty glass down on the table with a small thud.

'Another brandy, Mary?'

'Yes, please.'

He returned from the bar and carefully set the glass in front of her. She stared at him. 'Nothing for you, Neil?'

'No. I'd better get back to Bill, I'm a bit worried about him.'

Mary picked up her glass. 'Right.' She slid a bank note across the table to him. 'It was my treat, Neil. You were not supposed to pay.' She stood. 'I'll join my sister. Thanks for the evening, Neil.'

He stared at the banknote, leaned over, put an arm around her shoulders and kissed her cheek.

'In case Veronica is watching,' he murmured. Then he picked up the banknote and stuffed it into her handbag.

***

Brenda looked forward to half-term. Being a teacher's aide, she realised, although rewarding, was also very demanding.

She'd enjoyed the time she'd spent with Jayne over the summer holidays. The more she saw Damien, the more she liked him and she was nearly certain he felt the same way about her. Whenever she thought he seemed to be on the brink of saying something, Jayne would interrupt.

She checked her calendar again. Half-term was the last week of October. She started to plan what to do with Jayne for the week, and what meals to prepare for Jayne and Damien's lunch. He'd usually come down to the kitchen about twelve-thirty to get a snack.

They got on so well, she thought, and Damien was always so grateful for how she managed Jayne.

On her way home she'd noticed some boys collecting conkers from a big horse chestnut tree. That might be something she could do with Jayne! She'd been storing up suitable activities.

***

Neil parked the car in the garage, walked down the path through the garden to the back door. The curtains were drawn in the lounge room but he could see the outline of the TV. He opened the back door into the kitchen.

'I'm back, Bill!' he called, going to the lounge.

Bill looked up. 'You're early! Come and tell me how it went, lad.'

'Cup of tea?' Neil didn't feel like talking about the evening.

'Yes, please. Come and tell me.'

Neil went back to the kitchen and put the kettle on.

Bill turned off the television and followed him.

'Not much to tell, Bill. We had a drink and a bit of a chat, then Mary's sister was there with her husband and friends and asked us to join them.'

'And did you?'

Neil busied himself with tea cups. 'Kettle's boiled, Bill.'

'And did you? Join them, I mean?'

'No... Mary did, but I was a bit tired so I left.' Neil focused on making the tea.

'I hope you didn't leave early because of me, Neil?'

'No, of course not, Bill. But it's been a busy week, and I didn't feel like staying and chatting to people I don't know.'

'Hmm.'

He saw Bill giving him a hard look.

'So, a second date not arranged, Neil?'

'No.'

Bill didn't pursue the matter.

***

Amanda glowed. Even her friends had remarked on it.

'What's the secret, Amanda?' one of them had asked at their monthly get-together lunch the day before.

'What do you mean?'

'Well, you seem like you've been reborn, bouncy and sparkly. Even your hair looks different.'

Amanda patted her hair. 'I'm going to a different hairdresser,' she smiled. 'Got highlights in it.'

'Found religion, have you?' another enquired with a snigger.

'Maybe ...' Amanda had decided not to mention Donald. *Early days*.

'Or have you found a man?'

'Give me a break!' Amanda rolled her eyes. 'Now, tell me what each of you have been up to? Your creative writing group, Jocelyn?'

While Jocelyn filled them in with the latest on how to write a best-selling novel, Amanda's thoughts drifted to Donald. She so enjoyed his company. And this evening he was taking her to see a film; he'd carefully studied the review and thought she'd enjoy it.

'What do you think, Amanda?'

She mentally shook herself. 'Um, sorry I didn't quite catch what you were saying. I think I might be going a bit deaf ...' she laughed.

'One of the trials of old age,' another said.

***

Carol waited outside the school on the Friday before half-term. *Dougie needs a break, He tries so desperately hard to keep up with the other students in his class. At least he seems to be getting on well socially; he said he's made friends with another Downs student, Clare.*

She saw him coming out, holding hands with a girl. As they approached the school gates, they paused and embraced. Carol's heart stood still. Dougie stopped and watched for a few seconds as the girl waved and walked towards a woman. He hurried through the gates.

'Mum!' he called out. 'Clare has invited me to her birthday party next week!' He thrust a pink envelope at her as he jumped into the passenger seat.

'Oh! That's nice.'

'Open it, open it!'

'Wait Dougie, I must drive off and leave room for other parents to park. Do up your seat belt and then you open it and read it to me.'

He did as she asked and stumbled over the words on the card.

'Dear Douglas, you are invited to my fourteenth birthday party next Wednesday at three ...' He paused. 'Um, three ...'

She glanced sideways at the card. 'PM, Dougie. That means three o'clock in the afternoon.'

'Three o'clock in the afternoon,' he continued. 'Um, RSVP. What word is that, Mum?'

'It's French for "please would you reply."'

'So, can I go, Mum? Please?'

'Of course, dear! Where is it?'

'Her address is here, Mum. I think it's near us, I'm not sure. Thirty-nine Harcourt Drive.'

'Right, so you must write back and say you will be pleased to accept.'

'Will you help me, Mum?'

'Of course, dear.'

Oh, my God, was all Carol could think. My baby is dating! Then she gave herself a mental shake. *It's just a birthday party, Carol! But he'd kissed the girl!*

'What do you think she would like for a birthday present, Dougie?'

He considered. 'A bracelet?'

'That's a good idea.'

***

Brenda enjoyed looking after Jayne during the half-term break. She and Jayne were making biscuits for Damien's afternoon tea, when the doorbell rang. Before Brenda could say anything, Jayne leaped up, raced to the front door and opened it.

'It's Mummy!' Brenda heard her scream. 'Daddy, it's Mummy!'

Damien came rushing down the stairs and Brenda followed him from the kitchen, dusting the flour from her apron. Jayne had her arms wrapped around the knees of a tall, blond woman.

'Whoa! Darling! Let me get in the door!'

Jayne released her grip on her mother.

Brenda hung back, watching Damien. The look on his face said it all.

'Beth! Wasn't expecting you! Why didn't you let us know?' He put an arm around her and kissed her.

'Thought I'd surprise you both.' Then she noticed Brenda. 'Who's this?'

'Oh, this is Brenda Evans, she's Jayne's school aide and is helping with Jayne during the holidays, just to give Mum a break.'

Brenda's guts twisted. *Just to give mum a break!* She saw Damien's expression. *He still loved his ex-wife!* She felt sick. She went back to the kitchen, pulled off her apron, threw it on the kitchen table and picked up her bag. Taking a deep breath she walked towards the front door.

'I'm so pleased your mummy has come, you won't need me this week after all,' she said brightly to Jayne, then gave Damien a tight smile as she passed through the open front door.

'Wait, Sevens.' Damien put out a hand to stop her. 'Hold on, Sevens! Brenda!'

But she marched on. Tears came to her eyes as she got into her little car. She started driving mindlessly, then blinked as she realised she was heading towards the allotment.

Breathing rapidly, she pulled up at the parking area. *No other cars! Great.*

She walked up to her plot and collapsed onto the makeshift seat outside her shed.

***

Neil looked in the fridge, then the pantry. Shit! He'd meant to go to the allotment and get some vegetables for their dinner.

'I'm popping up to the allotment for some veg, Bill, before it gets dark,' he called out.

'Okay, lad,' came the reply. 'Just watching a bit of TV.'

Neil noticed Brenda's little grey hatchback in the car park as he pulled up. On his way to Bill's allotment, he heard muffled sobs coming from her plot.

He paused and saw her outside her shed sitting on the plank that served as a seat. Taking care not to make a noise, he opened her gate and went towards her.

'What's wrong, Brenda?' he asked quietly.

She jumped. 'Nothing, nothing!' She blew her nose and twisted her sodden handkerchief into a ball.

He felt in his pocket then cautiously lowered himself onto the unsteady plank and held out his hand. 'Clean hanky. Not ironed but clean.'

'Thanks.' She took it and wiped her eyes.

Staring straight ahead, he repeated, 'What's wrong, Brenda.'

She gulped. 'Jayne's mother arrived this afternoon. Unexpectedly. A surprise visit ...'

'Oh?'

'And I saw his face! Damien's face when he saw her! He still loves her, Neil!' She burst into fresh sobs. 'I'm *just* his daughter's special needs teacher.'

Neil put an arm around her shoulders and drew her to him.

'That's rotten; the bastard!'

Suddenly defensive, Brenda mumbled, 'It's not his fault, maybe I read too much into his attentions.'

'He did seem very attentive,' Neil murmured. 'From what I saw the few times he was here at your plot.'

'He just wanted someone to look after Jayne.'

'Jayne loves you, Brenda.'

'I know!'

'He took advantage of you, the swine!'

Brenda straightened in his arms. 'No, he paid me to mind Jayne. It's all my fault. I read more into it than I should have.'

Neil kept holding her.

'I'm just a domestic drudge! That's all Colin wanted – someone to cook and clean and take to bed.'

Neil drew back a little. 'Did you, er did Damien …'

'No, no, nothing like that! He never even kissed me!' She blew her nose. 'Sorry, Neil. Um, what are you doing here? It's getting dark.'

'I forgot to get vegetables for dinner tonight. Just popped up to get some carrots and broccoli.'

'I've delayed you.'

'Well, I guess Bill will be wondering where I am. That's unless he's fallen asleep in front of the telly.'

'How is he? I haven't seen him much lately.'

'He's okay, just very tired.' Then he had an idea. 'Why don't you call in and see him. I think it would cheer him up. You could come now. He'd be thrilled.' *And it will take her mind off Damien..*

'I look a mess, maybe another time.' Brenda sniffed and made to wriggle free from his arms. The unbalanced plank tipped with their weight and with a crash, he toppled onto the ground still clutching Brenda in his arms.

Brenda let out a shriek of laughter. 'Oh, my God! Sorry, Neil. I must do something about that seat.'

Neil froze. The crash had startled him. Then Brenda's hysterical laugh brought him back to earth. He tried to breathe, and realised he was still holding Brenda tightly. 'Sorry, Brenda,' he murmured into her hair. He made an attempt to relax, then he drew her to him and lightly kissed her cheek. 'You're a beautiful woman, Brenda,' he whispered. 'Damien isn't even half good enough for you.'

'Oh!' Brenda touched her cheek where he'd kissed it.

He released her and got up, putting out a hand to help her. 'Come on, lock your gate while I get those carrots and you can follow me in your car to Bill's. No arguments, Bill would love to see you.' His tone was brusque.

'I'm a mess,' Brenda examined her dirt-stained clothes. 'And so are you! All muddy.'

'All the more reason to come and tidy yourself before you go home.'

He walked around to Bill's plot, pulled two carrots and took a deep breath. The crash of Brenda's makeshift seat had sent him into a spin, but her hysterical laughter had brought him back. Perhaps he was starting to recover after all ...

***

Carol drove to Clare's house, Dougie in the passenger seat, clutching Clare's present. He'd helped to wrap the simple bead bracelet they'd chosen.

When she parked outside the house, Dougie turned to her. 'No need to come in with me, Mum.'

'I'll just pop in and say, hello,' she said. 'It would be rude not to, and anyway I need to know when I can come and get you.'

'All right, but you're not to stay. Okay?'

She nodded as Dougie pressed the front door bell.

A tall fair-haired man opened the door. 'Welcome!' he said. 'Who shall I say it is?'

'Douglas Patterson,' Carol said. 'I'm Carol, Dougie's mum.'

'Come in, come in!' He held out his hand. 'I'm Clare's dad, Norman. Nice to meet you. Clare is always talking about Douglas.'

Just then Clare appeared, a huge smile on her face. 'Hello Douglas!'

'Happy birthday, Clare, look, I've got a present for you.' He thrust the package at her.

'Thank you, Douglas. Can I open it now, Dad?'

'Why don't we wait until later and Mum can watch you open it,' her father replied, then met Carol's eyes. 'Come and meet my wife, Jill, and Clare's brother and sister.'

Carol smiled. 'Thank you, that would be nice. Can I do anything to help?'

He smiled. 'No, it's all ready.' He rolled his eyes, 'Clare has had us all rushing around since six o'clock this morning. Oh, here's Jill,' he said as a harassed looking woman came into the hall. 'Jill, this is Carol, Douglas's mum.'

'Lovely to meet you,' Jill said, leading the way into a large room where several young teenagers stood awkwardly around.

'This is Douglas,' Clare announced, pushing him forward. 'My boyfriend.'

Carol's heart skipped a beat. Boyfriend!

There were mumbled greetings.

Dougie gave her a worried look over his shoulder.

Norman must have noticed, because he patted Dougie's arm. 'Come and help me to set up some games, Douglas.'

Carol breathed a sigh of relief.

'Well, let's leave Norm to start some games,' Jill said. 'Have you time for a glass of wine? I need one!'

Carol smiled. 'Thanks.' She thought she was going to like Clare's parents.

'Douglas seems a very nice boy, but I feel Clare is a bit young to have a boyfriend.'

Carol grimaced, 'Agreed. Douglas is still very immature.'

'Clare's older sister had a boyfriend two years ago when she was fourteen, but it was a very innocent affair, it all fizzled out after a few weeks, and now she and two of her girlfriends seem to hang out with a crowd. White?' She held out a glass and a bottle. 'Take a seat. It's a bit of a mess, but I need a breather while Norm holds the fort.'

Carol sat and took a sip of wine.

'I'm so glad you came this afternoon.' Jill took a gulp of her drink. 'Clare doesn't stop talking about Douglas, so it's nice to meet him at last, and you. Maybe you could all come round for a barbecue some afternoon.'

Carol studied her glass. 'That would be nice. But it's only Douglas and me. I'm divorced. Douglas is my only child.'

'Oh! It must be hard for you.'

Carol toyed with the idea of telling Jill about Angus, when the kitchen door opened and Clare burst in.

'Mum, I came to get kitchen towels, some lemonade got knocked over.'

Jill sighed. 'Okay, sweetie.' She finished her wine and stood up.

'I'd better go and leave you to it,' Carol said, placing her empty glass near the kitchen sink. 'What time shall I come for Dougie?'

'About six?'

Carol drove home preoccupied with thoughts of Clare and Dougie and the ups and downs of puberty.

***

Brenda was reluctant to go to Bill's house. She took a quick glance at herself in her car mirror. Her eyes were red-rimmed and there was a dusting of flour on her nose. She rubbed at it, then took a comb from her bag and dragged it through her hair. It made no difference, and now she had a red nose.

Once at Bill's she followed Neil into the house.

'Bill! Look who's come to see you,' Neil called, opening the door to the lounge room.

'Wha?' Bill appeared to shake himself awake.

'Brenda's come to see you.'

'Oh Brenda! Come in, come in.' Bill blinked and made to get up, but Neil put out a restraining hand and indicated a chair to Brenda.

The room was stifling; Brenda unbuttoned her coat and smiled at Bill.

'Take a seat, Brenda, while I put the kettle on. Hold on, Brenda, let me take your coat.'

Bill became animated. 'Tell me what's been happening, how's your plot, and your mother?'

As Brenda chatted, she thought Neil was right, Bill seemed more cheerful having someone different with whom to talk.

Neil came in with a tea tray and put it on a small table. 'I was thinking,' he said and looked at Brenda. 'How about we go and see a film this evening? That's if it's okay with Bill.'

'You and Brenda go,' Bill said and winked. 'I'm a bit tired.'

Brenda smiled. She was pretty sure that Neil's invitation had only been meant for her. Being so kind, he probably thought it would cheer her up.

'What's on?' was all she could think to say.

'Dunno. We can take pot luck.'

Why not? She thought. 'Hmm. But I must go home and make Mum's dinner first.'

Neil nodded and smiled. 'I can pick you up if Bill doesn't mind me taking his car.'

Bill smiled. 'Fine by me.'

Brenda rose. 'I'd better go, lovely to see you, Bill.'

'Come anytime, Brenda love. You're a tonic!'

Neil followed her to the front door. 'I'll call for you about seven? I know where you live, I gave your mother and her friend a lift back from the physiotherapist while you were away.'

'Thanks, bye for now.' She drove home feeling slightly more cheerful, until she got indoors and saw her mother's face.

'You're late! I thought you finished at five.'

'I didn't notice the time.' She wished her mother would shut up. 'I'll get the dinner on now.'

Her mother stared at her. 'Have you been crying?' She demanded.

'No, I think I'm starting a cold. I'll make a hot lemon drink.'

'Hmph. I suppose you caught it from that girl you've been minding.'

The phone rang as Brenda stood at the kitchen sink, washing potatoes.

She dried her hands and snatched the phone. She'd pressed "answer" at the same time as she noticed the caller: Damien.

'Hello?'

'Sevens, it's Damien. Why did you rush off this afternoon? I wanted you to meet Jayne's mother.'

Brenda swallowed. 'Oh, I did meet her, but I thought you'd all like some time together without me hanging around.'

'Jayne was upset. She's been telling Bethany all about you and what you've been doing.'

'I'm sorry to hear she's upset.'

'Anyway, you'll come back tomorrow?' He sounded hopeful.

'Um, no. I think it's best Jayne gets some quality time with her mother.'

'Please?'

Brenda took a deep breath. 'It will be good for Jayne to spend time with her mother, Damien.'

'So, you won't?'

'No. Look I'm a bit busy at the moment. I'm getting ready to go out. Bye for now.' She hung up.

'Who was that?' Her mother came sailing into the kitchen.

'Just an acquaintance.'

***

Brenda had no appetite for her dinner, but her mother ate with relish.

'Nice dinner you cooked,' her mother said. 'For a change.'

'Glad you enjoyed it, Mum.' She stood and picked up the plates. 'I'm going out this evening, but I'll be back in time to make your Horlicks.'

Mrs Evans's brows drew together. 'Going out! What do you mean, going out? Leaving me all alone.'

Brenda sighed. 'I won't be late.'

Her mother sniffed. 'You're so hard, Brenda.'

'Yes, Mum, I know.' Brenda exhaled. 'Anyway, like I said, I won't be late.'

'So where are you going?'

'A friend is taking me to see a film.'

'Not that man with the little girl?'

'No. Another friend.'

Her mother sniffed. 'So, what do **they** want?'

'Want?'

'Well, no-one would take **you** to see a film unless they had some kind of motive.'

Neil just wants to cheer me up. But she didn't say so to her mother.

'Dunno, Mum. Just want company perhaps.'

***

Amanda's spirits rose. She put on a dress she'd bought only that morning and looked at herself in the mirror. The girls were right, she had blossomed since Donald had come on the scene. She didn't care what the film was about, just being with Donald was enough.

***

Neil managed to find Brenda's house. *It all looks different in the dark.* When he reached the house, he saw Brenda waiting by the front door.

'Thought you might have had trouble with the numbers,' she said as she walked down the path to the car.

'I did,' he said. 'Thanks for lurking there, I nearly missed you.'

He jumped out and held the passenger door for her.

'I found a film I think you might like,' he said. He didn't mention that he'd been anxious in case the only films were violent with loud sound effects.

'Thanks, Neil. It's so good of you to cheer me up.'

'It's good for me to socialize,' was all he said as he parked.

They walked to the entrance of the cinema.

Suddenly Brenda grabbed his arm. 'Wait, Neil,' she hissed.

'What? What?'

'Look! By the ticket office! It's the warden, Amanda and, and … you know, the man Bill calls "The Admiral"'

He frowned. 'You mean Donald Jenkins?'

'Yes! Hush! Don't let them see us!'

'Why not?'

'It'll be all over the Allotment tomorrow!'

He laughed. 'Don't be silly,' he said, 'Who cares?'

Brenda stared at him. 'Don't you care?'

He smiled down at her. 'I'm proud to be seen with you, Brenda.'

'Oh!'

She squeezed his arm. 'You're a good person, Neil.'

He laughed. 'We should form a mutual admiration society! Come on now. The Warden and the Admiral have gone in.'

'That sounds like a children's poem.' Her eyes narrowed as she tried to remember. Then she laughed, 'The Walrus and the Carpenter?'

Neil grinned and recited, "The time has come, the Walrus said, To talk of many things: Of shoes — and ships — and sealing-wax — Of cabbages — and kings —And why the sea is boiling hot — And whether pigs have wings."

Brenda burst out laughing. 'You're so funny, Neil, that's exactly it!'

'Popcorn?' he asked, moving towards the ticket office.

'Not for me, thanks.' She shook her head.

'Good, I can't stand the smell of it.'

Neil bought their tickets and led Brenda into the darkened theatre. 'There looks good,' he whispered, pointing to two vacant seats.

***

Brenda followed Neil, then she stopped. 'Goodness, there's the Walrus and the Carpenter,' she said in a low voice, indicating Amanda and Donald, who were seated several rows in front.

'Shhh,' Neil said, with a finger to his lips.

She started to giggle.

'Stop!' Neil leaned towards her and planted his lips on hers.

'Oh!' she gasped when he moved away.

'That was just to shut you up,' he murmured. 'No ulterior motive. It was either that or a slap.'

Brenda felt suddenly breathless.

'Come on,' Neil whispered. 'There are seats just here.'

They made their way along the row, passing people who raised their knees to let them through.

***

Amanda was nervous when Donald stopped outside her house after the cinema. 'Like to come in for a nightcap?' she asked.

'Thank you, Amanda, that would be lovely.' He hastily took a packet from his pocket, drew out a tablet and swallowed it, then hurried around to the passenger seat and opened the door. 'Madam,' he said with his usual flourish.

'Thank you, Donald.'

She led the way up the garden path to the front door and opened it.

Cato was there to greet her.

'Hello, pussy,' Donald murmured.

'His name is Cato.'

'Ah.'

The cat came and wound itself around Donald's legs.

'He likes you,' Amanda said, her heart in her mouth.

'Hello, kitty,' Donald said a bit uncertainly.

'Come in out of the cold.' Amanda held the door wide.

Her house was warm and cosy. She turned on a leadlight table lamp. She thought its warm reds and yellows added to the ambience. 'Sit down, Donald. What would you like to drink? Wine, or something stronger?'

He sat on the long leather lounge she indicated and leaned back onto the cushions. 'What are you having?'

'A white wine, I think.'

'Then I'll have the same. Thank you.' He half rose, 'Can I help?'

'No, no, nothing to do.'

She went to the kitchen, turning on some background music as she went.

'Here we go.' She placed two glasses on a coffee table and sat beside him. 'Cheers!' They clinked glasses and drank.

She suddenly felt self-conscious, wondering what to talk about.

Donald cleared his throat. 'There's something I wanted to ask you.'

'Oh?' Her heart started to race.

'As you know, I'm staying at my sister's house at the moment, while I investigate a place to buy. I've not been very pro-active in the matter so far, but now I've decided the time has come.' He gave a small cough. 'I wanted to ask if you would come with me to view houses ... um, I'd like your opinion.' He stroked his beard nervously.

'Well, I ...' Amanda didn't know what to think. 'Wouldn't your sister like to help you?'

He cleared his throat again and took another sip of his wine. 'I respect your judgement, Amanda.'

'It's nice of you to say that, Donald, and well, yes, I'd like to come with you.'

He seemed to relax. 'There are two places I would like to look at on Saturday. Could I pick you up about nine-thirty?'

She nodded, as he put his empty glass on the coffee table and made to get up. 'Another wine, Donald?'

'No, no, thank you. I have to drive. It's been lovely. Thank you, Amanda.'

She stood. 'See you on Saturday, then.' She went to the door with him and watched him drive off. *So much for the glam underwear I'd put on in case he stayed.*

***

Brenda followed Neil out of the cinema. 'I really enjoyed that film,' she said. 'It's ages since I went to a movie.'

'We must do it more often then,' Neil said.

Brenda turned to him. 'Really? You're not just saying that to cheer me up?'

Neil laughed. 'No, I enjoyed it too.'

'We might be able to persuade Bill to come the next time,' Brenda said.

'Perhaps,' was all Neil said. 'Now, remind me of the best way to get to your house.'

Brenda concentrated on the road. Neil stopped at her gate and before he had cut the engine, Brenda opened the passenger door and jumped out. 'Thank you again, Neil.'

'My pleasure, Brenda.'

She wondered about inviting him in, but the thought of her mother glowering in the background put her off. Unsure what to say, she shut the passenger door, waved and walked up the garden path to her front door.

She turned, saw Neil waiting until she was safely inside and then drive off.

What a strange day. So much had happened. She hung her coat on the hallstand and went into the kitchen.

'About time too!' shouted her mother.

Brenda poked her head around the lounge room door. 'Yes, the film was lovely, thank you for asking,' she said. 'I'll make your Horlicks now.'

***

Bill looked at his watch. Neil should be back soon. He hoped they'd enjoyed the film. He heard the back door open and close.

'That you, Neil?' he called.

'Yes, Bill.' Neil's face appeared around the lounge room door. 'You okay? Like a cup of tea?'

'Yes please.'

Bill waited until Neil returned with two cups of tea. 'So how was your evening?'

'Good, thanks, Bill.'

'Nice film?'

'Yes.' Neil started telling him about the dog and the penguins, until Bill interrupted.

'And little Brenda? Did she enjoy it?'

'She said she did.'

'So, you asked her out again?'

Neil shrugged. 'No. She seemed a bit down today so I thought a film would cheer her up.'

'Ah!' Bill nodded sagely. 'That was nice. And did it?'

'Did it what?' Neil had picked up the daily newspaper and started to read it.

'Cheer her up.'

'Dunno. Didn't ask her.'

Bill shook his head.

***

Neil didn't want to discuss Brenda with Bill. She was lovely. Warm and friendly and she made him laugh. And he felt comfortable with her. Now she was in love with that plonker, Damien. Still, he didn't know the full story and it wasn't likely Brenda would tell him. Not that he cared he told himself. He tried to read but couldn't concentrate. He sighed and lowered the paper.

'Bed time, Bill?'

Bill nodded. 'Nothing I want to watch on the telly and I'm feeling a bit tired.'

'Want to pop up to the allotment tomorrow?'

Bill shook his head. 'Forecast is for rain tomorrow. Anyway, don't you have to study?'

'I'm up to date with my lectures but there's a big exam coming up. I should probably do a bit more study tonight.' He stretched. 'But I don't feel like it.'

'Do you think you could get the DVD of that movie you saw tonight, Neil? It sounds nice.'

Neil smiled. 'I'll try.'

***

Carol had arranged to meet Clare's mother for coffee. She'd been doing some research on Down Syndrome and puberty. Somehow, she'd avoided thinking about it. Maybe if Dougie had been a girl, it would have been easier; she knew nothing about adolescent boys. Of course, she knew their voices would change but apart from that …

She saw Jill already sitting at a table in the café, a coffee in front of her. 'Am I late?'

'No. I was early.'

Carol ordered and sat down. She fiddled nervously with her rings. 'Jill, I've been reading up on puberty and Downs. I'm afraid I've been a bit slack with Douglas. The thing is, I don't know how or what to talk to Dougie about what he's going through…' her voice tailed off.

Jill smiled. 'I'm sure Norm would be happy to have a chat with Douglas about things.'

Relief flooded Carol. 'Really? That's so kind of you both. I know a boy's voice gets deeper, but apart from that, well …' she spread her hands. Then looked up as her coffee arrived and she nodded her thanks to the girl.

'It must be hard for you – coping all by yourself,' Jill said.

'Well, Dougie makes it worthwhile.' She took a sip of her coffee. 'Clare is gorgeous.'

'Yes, she is. We love her to bits. As do her older brother and sister.' Jill smiled. 'Now, if you're not doing anything this weekend, why don't you and Douglas come over for a barbie on Saturday?'

Carol smiled. 'Love to! What can I bring?'

***

Brenda's stomach was in a knot the first day back at work after the half-term break. She knew Jayne would be in her first class of the day.

As soon as Jayne saw her, she came up to her desk 'Miss Sevens,' she pouted. 'I so wanted you to meet my Mummy! And you ran away!'

'No, Jayne, I didn't,' Brenda smiled. 'I met her when you opened the front door.'

Jayne considered. 'Yes, but then you didn't stay.'

Brenda tried to laugh. 'But your Mummy wanted you to herself, Jayne. Not with me hanging around.'

'Maybe.' Jayne appeared to think. 'But, anyway, Mummy has gone back to Merica now.'

'Right. Well, how about we concentrate on your school work, Jayne? After all, it will soon be time for you to go to secondary school, like Douglas.'

Jayne frowned. 'Okay, Miss Sevens. But Dad said you might still come at Christmas.'

Brenda's heart leaped. Settle down, Brenda, she told herself. Christmas is still two months away. Then she remembered Damien's look when he saw his ex-wife...

Chapter Eleven
November

The Allotment

"The gloomy months of November, when the people of England hang and drown themselves." Joseph Addison

***

Mary scanned the notice board at the local Library. She thought about their evening. Neil hadn't picked up the banknote ... and his comments. *An art class ...*

She'd enjoyed drawing a plan of her plot and colouring the areas for the different bulbs. But there were no classes advertised. She went over to the librarian and enquired.

The librarian smiled. 'Well, you could try the local art college, but probably not much happening now until after Christmas. There may be some on-line courses, or perhaps private tuition. Look, why don't you check out the magazine section over there.' She pointed to the back of the library. 'There are quite a few art magazines, and I think there may be ads for classes in some of them.'

'Thank you!' Mary's spirits rose. 'Can I borrow some?'

'Of course! Not the most recent ones, but the older ones you may certainly borrow.'

An hour later, Mary left with three magazines and some art books.

***

Neil steeled himself to face Guy Fawkes' night.

Remember, remember the 5th November,

Gunpowder, Treason and Plot

He hated the spasmodic blasts of fireworks, which sent him into meltdown. At least he'd got out of Mary's invitation to her sister's Guy Fawkes' party. He wondered how she was going there.

'Might do a bit of study and then have an early night, Bill,' he said, as he cleared up after their evening meal.

'Right, lad. I'll watch the telly and have an early night too.'

'I'll turn on your electric blanket, Bill. Cup of tea?'

'Thanks, Nigel.'

Neil worried about Bill. He seemed less and less interested in going to the allotment. Content to stay at home with his feet up and a blanket over his legs, and sometimes that confusion with his and Hazel's names.

'Are you cold, Bill?'

'No, no, but it's a bit chilly.'

Neil went over and lifted up the blanket covering Bill's legs, meaning to tuck it around him. Then he frowned. 'Bill!'

'What? What?'

'Your legs! They're so swollen! Why didn't you tell me? You must see the doctor at once!' He peered closer. 'And what's this? It looks like the skin is broken!'

'No, no, lad.' Bill shuffled in his chair, 'just a bit of swelling!'

'Bill, I'm going to make an appointment with your doctor first thing in the morning.'

'Please, lad, I hate doctors! They'll only send me for tests and stuff.'

Neil crouched down beside the old man. 'Bill,' he said gently, taking his hand. 'Please. I'm worried. Let me ring the doctor. It's probably something minor that can easily be fixed.'

Bill heaved a sigh. 'Okay, okay, don't pester me, lad. Whatever you say.'

***

Bill thought he'd successfully managed to hide his swollen feet and ankles and that ulcer until Neil had tried to rearrange the blanket. Now Neil would be nagging him to see the doctor. But he only wanted out! He wanted to join Hazel! Tears welled in his eyes.

***

Neil was angry with himself. How had he missed Bill's swollen legs? Yes Bill had been sneaky – using a blanket to cover the evidence!

He made an appointment with the doctor for the following day.

Bill had groaned and grumbled but Neil insisted. 'Come on, Bill. It's nothing to be alarmed about!'

'You don't understand, lad! Hazel didn't want to go to the doctor either, but I made her!'

'Exactly! Bill, perhaps if she'd gone earlier, she might still be here.'

That had silenced Bill until he exclaimed, 'But that's the point, Neil! I don't want to be here! I want to be with Hazel.'

Neil studied Bill. 'I need you, Bill.'

'What do you mean?'

Neil lowered his gaze. 'Bill, you've been so good to me. If anything happens to you, how do you think I'd feel and where would I go?'

Bill sighed. 'Stop Neil. Stop putting the guilt trip on me. That's what they call it now, isn't it?'

Neil smiled. 'You're too sharp, Bill.'

'No, lad. It's time for me to go.'

'Nonsense, I need you, Bill. And that ulcer could turn into gangrene. You might have to have your leg amputated!'

'Stop trying to frighten me, Neil!'

Neil smiled. 'Okay, but I think you need to do as you're told.'

Bill laughed suddenly. 'You're a tonic, Neil.'

***

Mary poured herself a glass of wine. She sat in her reclining chair, then picked up one of the art magazines and started to read. All these hints, and the new painting mediums! Mixed media! So much had happened in the art world since she'd left school. *Why didn't I continue with my painting?* Once she'd met Peter, he had become the focal point of her life. She didn't regret it. No! No! He had been her life. But the time had come to start again.

Peter's allotment needed minimum care now that she'd established her memorial garden. Her back muscles twinged as she remembered all the hours she'd spent, with Neil's help, planting the daffodils and hyacinths. November was the time to plant tulips ... She refilled her glass and sat, thinking. Then had an idea...

***

Neil brought Bill's car around to the front of the house. 'Are you ready, Bill?'

Bill came out of the house, grumbling about how ridiculous it was to be going to the doctor.

'Bill, you haven't got your overcoat on!' Neil got out of the car and went back inside the house.

'You'll catch your death,' he said. 'Come on, put it on.' He held out the coat.

'You're turning into a right old woman,' Bill muttered.

Neil laughed. 'Wouldn't need to if you did as you were told, Bill.'

At the surgery, Bill turned to Neil. 'Will you come in with me, lad?' he quavered. 'It's Dr Davis. She was Hazel's doctor.'

'Of course, Bill.'

'Hello Bill.' The doctor looked up from her computer screen. 'Haven't seen you since your lovely wife passed away. Now, what's the problem?'

'Nothing. All good,' Bill said. 'Don't know why Neil, here, is fussing. Nothing wrong with me, just a little spot on my leg,'

She raised her eyebrows at Neil.

'He's got an ulcer on his leg,' Neil replied.

Dr Davis gave Bill a look. 'Now, Bill, I need to see that leg of yours.'

Bill sighed and rolled up his trouser leg.

'Hmm. Right. Well, we'll need to treat that.' She looked at Neil. 'Are you Bill's son?'

'No, er, I, well, I'm ...'

Bill interrupted. 'Neil is staying with me at the moment. Great bloke.'

'Well, I'm going to put Bill on a course of antibiotics and show you how to dress the ulcer to keep it clean and dry, er, Neil.'

He nodded.

'And while you're here, Bill, I'll just check your heart and lungs.'

'No need, Dr. I'm fit as a fiddle. Isn't that right, Neil?'

Neil was silent.

After the doctor had listened to Bill's heart and chest, she frowned. 'I'd like you to go for more tests, Bill.'

'No, no,' Bill exclaimed, 'No tests. I'm fine.'

Dr Davis frowned. 'I wouldn't be doing my job if I didn't refer you for more tests, Bill.'

Neil watched Bill, who had stood and started to pull on his jacket. He intervened. 'I'll make sure Bill goes for the tests, Doctor,' he said.

Dr Davis turned to her computer and in a few minutes the printer whirled and spat out two pages of referrals.

'Here you go, Neil.' She handed them to him.

'Thanks, doctor.'

Neil ushered Bill out of the surgery.

'You've got to go for these tests, Bill!'

'Did you see how she looked at you, Neil? Reckon she fancies you. Nice young girl like that!'

Neil sighed. 'Stop trying to change the subject, Bill! I'm going to make appointments for these tests.'

'Don't waste your time, lad. I'm not going.'

'We'll see ...'

Once out of the surgery and in the carpark, Neil waved a prescription. 'You get in the car, Bill. I'll get these tablets and the cream for your leg.'

'Anyway, what are these tablets for?' he asked Neil on his return from the chemist.

'Diuretics, Bill.'

'What do they do?'

'They'll make you pee more to get rid of the fluid, Bill.'

'That's all I need, lad! You might as well move the TV into the toilet. I already spend hours there!'

Neil laughed. 'You'll feel much better once the fluid has gone and your ulcer has healed.'

'Hmph.'

***

Brenda thought she'd pop in and see Bill on her way home from school. It had been raining all day, and she felt a bit low. The children had been difficult; it could be the weather and not being able to go outside at play time. She didn't feel like facing her mother.

She parked her car, hurried up the path and pressed the doorbell. A few minutes later Neil opened the door.

'Brenda!' he exclaimed.

She could hear Bill's voice in the background.

'Come in Brenda, Bill will be so pleased to see you. He's been a bit down today. Here, give me your coat.'

Brenda shook the rain from her curls.

Neil smiled. 'You remind me of that dog with the penguins!'

'Thanks, Neil, that's the kind of compliment I appreciate.' But she smiled.

'I can hear Brenda's voice!' Bill shouted. 'Come in Brenda! Neil, put the kettle on.'

'Hello, Bill, just thought I'd pop in and see how you're going.'

'Good, Brenda, Neil forced me to go to the doctor and get tablets and cream for my leg.' He pulled up his trouser leg and gingerly peeled back the dressing. 'See, it's much better now.'

Brenda peered at it.

'That's great, Bill. Good on Neil for making you go to the doctor.'

'He's getting too bossy for his own good. Told him he's turning into an old woman.' Bill replaced the dressing and rolled his trouser leg back down.

Brenda looked at Neil as he came into the room with cups of tea. She couldn't imagine anyone less like an old woman.

Bill gave Neil a sly look as he took his cup. 'Neil was just saying, how much he enjoyed the cinema the other night and thought you'd like to go again soon.' He smiled innocently.

Brenda raised an eyebrow at Neil. 'Really? That would be nice.'

Neil grinned. 'Whatever evening suits you, Brenda. I'll give you my phone number and you can let me know.'

She stared at Bill and then at Neil. *Was something going on?*

'Tell me how your plot is going, Brenda. I haven't been up for ages,' Bill said.

'Neither have I, it's been too cold and wet,' she replied. She changed the subject and went on to talk about her school work.

Half an hour later, she stood. 'Lovely to see you, Bill. I'd better get going now.'

'Come again soon, Brenda.'

'Don't get up,' she said as Bill made to stand. 'Neil can see me out.'

At the front door, Neil held her coat.

'Are you sure about going to the cinema,' she said in a low voice. 'Or was Bill just stirring.'

Neil grinned. 'Both.' He handed her a note. 'My phone number. Please ring and let me know if there is a film you'd like to see.'

She suddenly felt cheered. 'Will do.'

***

Mary found an art shop in town. She was bewildered by all the paints, brushes and art materials. After wandering around for a while, she went to the counter and attracted the notice of one of the assistants.

'Excuse me, but it's years since I bought any paints. I think perhaps I should go to an art class before I spend any money ...'

'That's probably a good idea, you need to know if you want to go acrylic, oils or water colour.'

'So, can you recommend an art class?'

The assistant pointed to a notice board 'Lots of classes and teachers,' she said, and turned to a waiting customer.

Mary looked at the board. She hadn't noticed it before. *So much for notice!* One card seemed to stand out. She made a note of the phone number and resolved to ring it when she returned home.

'Thank you!' she said to the assistant, who was busy serving someone and merely nodded in Mary's direction.

Back home Mary rang the number she'd noted. A strange recorded message answered her call, giving details of classes. Mary resolved to attend at least two a week. *What have I got to lose?*

***

Brenda steeled herself to ring Neil's number. It took some courage, but she needed to talk to someone about whether she should go and look after Jayne in the Christmas holidays. She knew no-one else who would understand. She dialled his number.

'Hello?'

'Um, Neil, you asked me to ring you.'

'Indeed,' he said. 'Did you find a film you'd like to see?'

'Not really. Seem to be all war or violence.' She suddenly re-membered Bill had mentioned Neil had been in the army and had PTSD. 'Um ... I prefer something cheerful.'

'Are you just saying that in case I go bonkers watching a war film?'

'No. I...'

'It's okay, Brenda. I'm getting better. I guess Bill has told every-one I have PTSD.'

She sighed. 'No secrets on the allotment where Bill is con-cerned. I wonder does he know about the Warden and the Ad-miral?'

'No, that's our little secret.'

Her spirits lifted. 'Thing is, Neil. I'd like your opinion on some-thing.'

She heard him sigh, then say: 'You must have heard the saying that if someone saves your life, they are responsible for you for the rest of your life.'

She giggled. 'I won't hold you to it.'

'Right. How about we meet at The Water Mark for a chat? Actually, there is something I'd like to tell you.'

'Oh? Well, okay then.'

'Tomorrow at about seven? Will that be enough time to give your mother her evening meal?'

'Yes! Right. Tomorrow. Great. Thanks, Neil, see you then.'

'Who have you been talking to, Brenda?' Her mother shouted from the lounge.

'Just a friend, Mum.'

'What friend? You don't have any friends now that no-good Colin has gone.'

Brenda shrugged. She wondered what Neil had to tell her.

***

Amanda waited at the front door for Donald. He was always so punctual. She heard a car stop and then footsteps coming up her path. She counted to ten after her doorbell rang. *Mustn't seem too eager!*

She opened the door. 'Donald! I'm ready, just have to put my coat on. Come in.'

He came in and held her coat for her.

'Thank you, Donald. Now, where are we going today?'

He told her the address. 'It's a three-bedroom house. Small garden but garage space for two cars ...'

She nodded. 'Sounds nice. You don't need a large garden when you have an allotment.'

He nodded. 'That's true. It's close to the shops and not far from my sister.'

Amanda enjoyed viewing houses. After coming out of the first one, Donald looked at her anxiously. 'What do you think?'

'Well, the house itself is nice, but the aspect is wrong.'

'What do you mean?'

'The main rooms face north. Only the garage will get the sun. The agent had all the lights and the heating on. But it would be cold and gloomy all winter.'

Donald nodded. 'I didn't think of that. Let's see the next one.'

But the next one Amanda found was even worse. 'There's no storage, none of the bedrooms have built-ins and by the time you put a wardrobe in, there will be barely enough room for a bed.'

'Hmm. Now I think about it, you're right, Amanda. I knew it would be a good thing to ask you to come with me. Right. How about going to The Water Mark for lunch? And next weekend maybe we could look at more houses?'

'Lovely!'

***

Carol could sense Dougie's nervousness as they drove to Clare's house for the barbecue.

'Are you sure I look all right, Mum?' he asked for the fourth time.

'You look very handsome,' she replied.

'You like Clare, don't you, Mum?'

'I think she's lovely.'

Clare opened the front door as they walked up the path. 'Hello, Douglas,' she said, giving him a hug and a kiss. She turned to Carol, 'Hello, Mrs Patterson, how nice you could come.'

Carol smiled to herself. Clare's manners were impeccable! 'Hello, Clare, now why don't you call me Carol?'

'Thank you, Carol. Come on in. Dad's outside getting the barbecue going. He said to send Douglas out to help him. And I'm to look after you.'

Jill came out of the kitchen. 'Come in, Carol. Hi, Douglas. Would you go and help Norm with the barbecue? He seems to be having problems getting it going.' She gave Carol a wink. 'And Clare will look after you while I just sort out a few things.'

Douglas straightened his shoulders. 'No worries, Jill.'

Carol held out a bottle of wine. 'Perhaps you could take care of this for me, Clare.'

Clare looked at her mother. 'In the fridge, Mum?'

'That's right, darling. White wine needs chilling.' Jill smiled at Carol. 'Clare is helping to prepare a salad. She's a very good cook.'

Clare smiled.

Carol followed Jill and Clare into the kitchen. Through the window she could see Norm and Dougie in earnest conversation at the barbecue. Norm appeared to be asking Dougie's advice about something. She took a deep breath.

***

Brenda arrived at The Water Mark at the same time as Neil. He smiled and held the pub door open for her.

'What would you like to drink, Brenda?'

'Bitter lemon, please.'

'Nothing stronger?'

'No, I have to drive home.'

He nodded. 'I should have picked you up. Sorry. Didn't think.'

'That's okay.'

'Next time, I will. There's a couple of seats by the fire.'

She sat and warmed herself by the log fire as she watched Neil go to the bar. *Next time?* He returned and smiled at her as he set her bitter lemon in front of her.

'Right. You go first. You wanted to run something past me.'

'Well ... you see, Jayne ... you remember Jayne, Damien's daughter?' He nodded. 'Well, she gave me a note from Damien, asking if I would look after her for a couple of days during the Christmas holidays, to give his mother a break ...'

'And?'

'Well, I don't know what to do ... should I?'

'Does the thought of seeing Damien make your heart sing?'

She looked at him in amazement. 'Make my heart sing?'

He studied his pint of beer. 'Well, you know what I mean ...'

'I don't know ...' She frowned and looked at him. 'Let me think about that. Okay. Your turn. You wanted to tell me something.'

Neil shuffled on the hard stuffed cushion. 'Well. The thing is, I've been offered a position at Wisley, that's a Royal Horticultural

Society garden, which would mean I could learn how to do graft-ing and a lot of other things that need practical experience.'

'That's brilliant, Neil! Congratulations!' She clapped her hands and grinned. Then she grimaced as she saw his face. 'But you have doubts, Neil? I guess it's Bill?'

'Yes.' He sighed. 'I can't leave him. He needs me and he's been so good to me.'

'Yes. Can you defer?'

He frowned. 'Possibly.'

Brenda sighed. 'Hard choice.'

He drank some of his beer. 'I guess I've made my decision. I won't leave Bill.'

Brenda leaned forward and put her hand on his knee. 'It's the right decision, Neil.' She suddenly thought her gesture was a mistake. *A bit intimate?* She took her hand away.

'Yes,' he nodded, then looked up at her. 'I guess I just wanted to brag about getting the offer.' He smiled deprecatingly. 'Bit boastful really.'

'And rightly so. That's an awesome achievement, Neil! You've done so well!'

'You won't mention it to Bill?'

'Of course not! Although he'd be so proud of you.'

'Yes, it's a catch twenty-two situation.'

'Neil?'

'Yes?' He turned to her.

'Thanks for telling me.'

He smiled. 'I don't know anyone else to tell.'

'Your sister?'

He grinned. 'Didn't even cross my mind to tell Anna. I don't think she'd understand. She's not a gardener. Now, back to you.'

'Me?'

'Yes, you've had five minutes to assess your feelings."

She breathed deeply. 'I don't know. I think perhaps I read too much into the whole situation.'

Neil nodded. 'Possibly. But I've seen Damien lurking around the parking area a couple of Saturdays when I've been at the allotment.'

Her head jerked up. 'Really?'

'Hmm.' He studied his drink. 'Maybe I shouldn't have told you that.'

She swirled her glass and took a sip, then she looked up with a smile. 'Well, they say, knowledge is power ...'

He sighed and rolled his eyes. 'And I have to be responsible for you for the rest of my life ...'

She laughed. 'Another beer?'

Chapter Twelve
December

The Allotment

"The Lord of Misrule - December 17th. This is the first day of the Roman festival Saturnalia - a period of great feasting and festivity, with a lot of drinking and eating. Slaves would become masters for the festival, and everything was turned upside down. This part of the Roman festival survived into the 17th Century."

Well, I don't think it survived here in rural England! But we have the Winter Solstice instead. A druid festival that the Christian church tried to make into Christ's birthday!

***

Amanda started to arrange the Winter Solstice get together at the allotment. Every year since she'd been Warden, she'd organised a special event for the 21st of December. It seemed most people enjoyed it. This year she enlisted Donald's help.

'What do you usually do?' he asked.

'Well, there are a couple of braziers to warm us, then we roast chestnuts and people bring stuff, mince pies and so on.'

'You're amazing, Amanda!' He looked at her admiringly.

'Thanks, Donald. If it's like previous Christmases then everyone chips in. I just put a flyer on the notice board.'

Donald shook his head. 'I think my sister has mistletoe growing on a tree in her back garden.' He grimaced. 'It's about the only thing growing in her garden!'

'Lovely! Well, bring plenty, Donald.' She looked at him meaningfully.

He shuffled his feet. 'Will do! Um... my sister was wondering if you'd like to have Christmas dinner with us ... that's unless you've made prior arrangements?'

Amanda's heart raced. She stared at Donald. 'No prior arrangements, so I'd love to have Christmas with your family. Thank you, Donald.'

He smiled at her. 'That's excellent. I'll tell Judy. She'll be delighted.'

***

Neil told Bill about the party. 'Sounds good, Bill.'

Bill sighed. 'Hazel and I used to go. Hazel made mince pies and it was nice.' He frowned. 'But I don't feel up to it this year, Neil.'

Neil studied him. 'Please, Bill. I'd like to go, and I won't go without you.'

Bill sighed. 'You're doing the emotional blackmail thing again, Neil.'

'I know, but I'll only go if you go, Bill.'

'Okay. Then, I'll go. But only for half an hour.'

'Deal!'

***

Mary saw the flyer on the notice board at the allotment. She hadn't been to her plot for ages, but thought she'd better check on it before Christmas.

The last thing she wanted was to hang around the allotment engaging in idle chatter. But then she thought about Neil. He would surely be there with Bill. And she might need Neil in the future. Veronica had tried to find out more about the good-looking man she'd had drinks with at The Water Mark. Kept on asking if he'd come to dinner one evening. Perhaps she'd go to the Solstice Party after all.

***

Carol knew Amanda would be organizing a Winter Solstice evening. She went up to the allotment to check the notice board and told Dougie when she got home. 'Do you think Clare would like to come, Dougie?'

His eyes lit up. 'Yes, Mum! I think she'd love it! I'll ask her tomorrow at school.'

Dougie had told her that he'd helped Norm get the barbecue going. 'Norm is nice, Mum. We had a good talk, man, to man, Norm said.'

She hid a smile. But how could she ever thank Norm? Dougie had been very quiet and thoughtful after the barbecue. 'Norm said you were a wonderful mother, Mum,' he told her. 'And he told me a lot of stuff that only men know.' He'd nodded knowledgeably.

'That's good, Dougie.'

He'd been silent for a while, then said, 'What happened to my dad, Mum? You said he died. What happened to him?'

The moment she'd been dreading had come.

'Well, when I said your father had died, I was speaking metaphorically, Dougie.'

His brow wrinkled. 'Metaphor ... what do you mean, Mum?'

She sat down on a kitchen stool and put her head in her hands.

'Well, he didn't actually die, but as far as we're concerned, he's dead.'

Dougie was about to open the fridge door, but he stopped and turned to her. 'What do you mean?'

'He decided he didn't love me anymore and wanted to make a new life with someone else.'

'So, he didn't know about me?'

Shit! Carol didn't know what to say. Should she lie? Lie to save his feelings?

'Well, he kind of knew about you, but he wasn't ready to be a father.'

'Not like Norm?'

'Indeed. Not like Norm.'

'I wish Norm was my father.'

She paused. 'But then Clare would be your sister.'

He thought for a moment. 'And she wouldn't be able to be my girlfriend?'

'Exactly!'

He smiled, came over and gave her a hug. 'You're the best mum ever. Is there any ice-cream?'

***

Brenda thought about the school holidays on her way home from work. Maybe she would take up Damien's offer. She didn't enjoy Christmas – all that false bonhomie. They always invited Edith

Milson, and her mother would spend Christmas day moaning and groaning. She wondered how on earth Edith put up with it.

Looking after Jayne would be a change. It would only be for a few days before school resumed. Apparently Damien had been hanging around the allotment ... was it to try and see her? Her pulse quickened.

Perhaps she should pop up next Saturday morning, see if anything new had grown. The brussels sprouts she'd planted some months ago might be ready for Christmas dinner ...

She hadn't seen Bill for a few days. Maybe she'd call round and see if he and Neil would be going to the Solstice party. Her thoughts were all over the place.

When Neil opened the front door, he seemed surprised, 'Lovely to see you, Brenda. Bill has been wondering why you haven't called by lately.'

'Busy time, Neil.'

She heard Bill's voice calling out, 'I can hear Brenda! Come in Brenda!'

He was sitting in his usual arm chair with his feet on a stool.

'How are you, Bill? How's the ulcer?'

'Good, good. Now come and sit down and tell me all the news. Neil, put the kettle on, there's a good lad.'

Neil grinned. 'Yes, boss.'

She sat opposite Bill. 'Been busy, Bill. All the kids are hyper with Christmas coming.'

'I suppose they're making Christmas presents for their parents.' He paused, 'I remember we used to make paper spills and ashtrays from cocoa tin lids when I was a lad at school.'

'Paper spills?' Brenda stared at him.

He brought his attention back to her. 'Yes, long thin strips of cardboard that your dad could put in the fire and use to light his cigarette or his pipe.'

Brenda shook her head. 'Goodness, how times have changed. Now, Bill. I wanted to ask you something. A favour.' She'd suddenly had a bright idea.

'Oh? Thanks, Neil,' he said as Neil came in with the tea tray.

'Yes. I was wondering if you and Neil would like to come and have Christmas lunch or dinner or whatever with us.'

Bill brightened. 'Lovely, Brenda! What do you say Neil?'

Neil grinned. 'How is that a favour, Brenda?'

She smiled. 'Well, usually it's just me, Mum and Edith Milson. I think you've met Edith.' She raised her eyebrows. 'I thought if you and Bill came, Mum might be in a better humour and not grumble as much.'

'Well, what can we say, Bill?' Neil grinned, 'except that we'd be delighted. My sister usually invites me, but I think she'd be thrilled that I'm otherwise engaged this year!'

'That's great! And I didn't know if the Walrus, I mean, the Warden,' she spluttered, 'is having a Solstice party this year. Someone said she organises one every December.'

'Yes, indeed,' Bill leaned forward eagerly. 'Neil and I are going, how about you, Brenda?'

She looked at Neil and smiled. 'Of course, Bill!'

Neil went to the front door with her. 'Thanks for asking us on Christmas Day, Brenda. It's cheered Bill up no end!'

She smiled. 'Purely altruistic, Neil!'

'Oh, dear, and I'd hoped you asked because you wanted my company!'

'That too.' She smiled and hurried out to her car.

***

Amanda was nervous – as she always was before these Solstice parties.

'What can I do to help?' Donald asked her several times.

'Nothing really, unless you can bring some mistletoe ... um, didn't you say your sister had a tree in her back garden with mistletoe?'

'I think it's mistletoe,' Donald frowned.

'And if you could get some charcoal for the brazier and chestnuts ...' She turned away, consulting a list she had in her hand. 'Do you think your sister would like to come?' She turned to him.

'My sister? You mean Judy?'

'Well, do you have any other sisters?'

'Um, no.'

'Then ask her.' Thinking she might have been a bit abrupt, she smiled at him. 'Sorry Donald, I'm a bit stressed at the moment, but it would be nice if Judy could come.' Taking a chance, she leaned over and kissed his cheek.

'Oh!' he said, as the colour rose in his face. 'Well, I'll certainly ask her.' He paused. 'Right, so charcoal and chestnuts ... I'll get onto those at once.'

She thought he was going to salute her as he turned on his heel. 'Lovely! Thank you, my dear.'

***

Neil started to regret Bill accepting to have Christmas dinner with Brenda. 'We'll have to get presents for them,' he said to Bill.

'Oh! I hadn't thought of that. Bugger. What do you think, lad?'

'Dunno. How about a pot with hyacinths in it for what's her name. Edna? No, Edith. Brenda's mother is a problem. She'd find fault with anything we buy for her. And Brenda? A book token? I think she likes reading.'

Bill nodded. 'Perhaps get the same for Edith and Mrs Evans, then there's no favouritism!'

'Good thinking, Bill. And they won't be able to argue! Okay. I'll find two nice pots and do the necessary. And a book token for Brenda.'

'Good lad.'

***

Brenda drove to the allotment on Saturday morning. No other cars were there. She shivered as she got out of the car and went up to her plot. Her spirits lifted when she saw her brussels sprout plants with nice fat, firm sprouts. She resolved to come up on Christmas Eve and pick them.

Hearing a noise behind her, she turned, hoping it was Damien.

'Oh! Hello, Neil.'

'You sound disappointed, Brenda. Were you expecting Damien?'

'Of course not!' But she felt herself flush. 'He wouldn't be able to get in without a key to the allotments.'

'True.'

She saw him eyeing her sprouts. 'Looking good.' He nodded towards the plants.

She smiled. 'Christmas dinner.'

'Yummy ...'

But she noticed his mouth had turned down at the sides. Perhaps he didn't like brussels sprouts.

***

The Allotment – The 21st of December - the Winter Solstice, the shortest day of the year, heralding a new beginning. The Christians tried to convert the Druids and made Christmas Day around the same date. As she usually does, the warden has organised a party to celebrate the end of the year and the start of a new one.

***

Amanda smiled at Donald. 'Looks good, doesn't it?'

'You've done a wonderful job,' he replied. The two braziers were blazing, lanterns were strung around the shed and on poles. 'So sorry Judy couldn't make it.'

'And your music is perfect, Donald. Thank you.' She looked around at the two speakers Donald had installed. Soft music played in the background. 'Where's the mistletoe, Donald?'

He produced a sprig and held it over her. 'Um, Amanda ...'

Just when she thought Donald was going to kiss her, a voice interrupted them.

'Hello, Amanda! You've done a wonderful job here!'

Bugger! It was that little Brenda. 'Yes,' muttered Amanda, turning away from Donald.

'Am I late, Amanda?' Brenda asked.

'No, no! It's just getting going,' Amanda replied, fuming inwardly.

'It's so festive! I've brought some tiny mince pies.' Brenda held out a container.

'Hello, hello, Amanda!' Bill came towards her, followed by Neil. Amanda sighed. *At least people are coming ...*

***

Carol parked her car. Douglas was in the back and Clare in the front passenger seat.

Douglas jumped out and opened the door for Clare. Carol hid a smile at the gallant behaviour of her son.

'Mum gave me some Yuletide biscuits,' Clare said. 'I've got them here.'

'Lovely,' Carol said. 'I made bite-sized sausage rolls. Douglas, can you bring them, please?'

She'd started calling him by his full name lately, instead of Dougie. Dougie sounded so babyish ...

'Right, Mum. This way, Clare.'

Carol watched him take Clare's hand and lead her up the path to the Warden's plot. She wished she had a man like Clare's father, Norm, to help her ...

***

Neil studied Bill, who seemed to be enjoying himself; chatting to people he hadn't seen in ages. He looked around and saw Brenda standing to one side. He moved towards her. 'Hi Brenda, how's things?'

'Good, thanks, Neil. Amanda has done us proud, don't you think?'

'Indeed. Can I get you a glass of something?'

She smiled and held up a bottle of bitter lemon. 'Got my poison here.'

'Ah! Okay.' He indicated Bill. 'Bill didn't want to come, but I persuaded him. Thought he needed to get out more.'

Brenda nodded and smiled at him. 'You're a good man, Neil.'

'Don't be silly, Brenda,' he replied, feeling embarrassed.

'I think the Carpenter is about to propose to the Walrus,' she giggled, indicating Amanda and Donald. 'He looks like he's going to explode!'

'Shh!' he whispered. 'I've seen him with a piece of mistletoe in his hand all evening! Holding it behind his back. I think he's trying to get the Walrus ... sorry ... the Warden into a dark corner and steal a kiss.'

Brenda laughed. 'You're a tonic, Neil!'

'Funny, but Bill said that recently.' He stared at her. 'Maybe I should grab the Carpenter's mistletoe.'

Brenda laughed. 'He'd probably clock you one!'

He thought she didn't get his meaning.

***

Mary hadn't wanted to go to the Solstice party, but she'd hoped to see Neil there. Veronica kept bugging her about coming for Christmas Day and bringing "her new man". She heard the music and talking as she walked from the carpark. The enticing smell of something roasting on the braziers wafted over. She wrapped her snood around her head and neck. It was freezing. *Lucky I put on my thick socks and sheepskin boots!*

'Hello, Mary,' several voices said as she approached. Soon a group of people surrounded her. She smiled and nodded as she scanned the crowd. Then she spotted him – standing outside the main group talking to that little Brenda. She sidled away and made her way towards him.

'Hello, Neil, Brenda,' she said when she was near.

'Hi, Mary,' Brenda said. 'Haven't seen you for ages, how are you?'

'Good, thanks, Brenda. Um, I just wanted a quick word with Neil.'

Brenda looked a bit startled. 'Oh, of course. I was just about to go and talk to Carol.' She gave a small wave of her gloved hand and walked away.

***

Neil was irritated when Mary came over and scuttled Brenda. He stared at Mary. 'How can I help you?'

Mary tried to laugh. 'Well, just wondering what you were doing on Christmas Day? My sister has invited us to spend the day with them.'

'Oh?' Neil frowned. 'That's kind of her, but Bill and I have already accepted an invitation to spend Christmas day with friends.'

'Oh! I guess I left it a bit late to ask you.'

'Bill is really looking forward to it.' He wasn't going to tell her who had invited them. He stared at her. She hadn't even thought of Bill and what he would do all on his own if he'd accepted her invitation.

'That's good. Um, how is he?'

'As you can see, he's enjoying himself this evening. I had to force him to come out.' Neil surveyed the crowd around the braziers where he could see Bill laughing. 'I'd better go and see if he's ready to go home. He only wanted to stay half an hour.' Neil moved away.

'Okay. Happy Solstice, Neil.'

'Thanks, Mary. Same to you.'

***

Mary mentally kicked herself. It had been silly of her to leave it so late to invite Neil, and stupid of her not to have thought of Bill. She didn't think Bill would fit in with Vronnie's crowd somehow. She was about to edge away from the crowd and go home when a man she hadn't met before came over to her.

'Glass of punch?'

She stared at him. 'Oh, thanks.' She didn't know him, but he must be an allotmenteer, she thought.

'I'm Jack. Have a roast chestnut. Careful, they're hot.' He held out a paper plate.

'Thanks, but not at the moment.' She took the glass of punch and moved away.

***

Brenda made her way back to the braziers, where Bill noticed her.

'Hello, Brenda!' he called. 'Looking forward to Christmas Day!' He turned to someone beside him. 'Going to Brenda's for Christmas Day,' he confided. 'Can't wait.'

She heard someone reply. She'd felt happy when Neil had come over and started talking to her, and mentioning mistletoe. But then Mary Flynn had arrived and spoilt the moment. She shrugged. *Expect nothing and you won't be disappointed.* She moved towards Carol who was standing on the edge of the group.

***

Carol watched her son and Clare. *They're so sweet.* She sighed.

'Hello, Carol!'

Carol turned to see Brenda approaching her.

'A lot has happened since the Summer Solstice, Carol,' Brenda remarked.

'Yes, indeed. Have you met Dougie's girl-friend, Clare?'

'Yes. She seems delightful.'

'To be honest, I'm a bit worried,' Carol confided. 'I think Dougie's too young to have a relationship.'

Brenda appeared to consider. 'It's good for him to have friends of the opposite sex.'

'I guess so.'

'I really don't think you need to worry, Carol. Dougie is more aware than you think.'

'I don't want him hurt.'

'Ah, Carol, that's just part of growing up – learning to deal with emotional hurt.'

Carol stared at her. 'Perhaps,' she managed to mutter. *Easy for her to say that! She doesn't have a child.*

***

Brenda walked away. Perhaps she should take her own advice and deal with emotional hurt. She decided it was time to go home, so walked over to Amanda.

'Lovely party, Amanda,' she said. 'Sorry but I've got to rush away. Thanks for organizing everything.'

Amanda smiled graciously.

Brenda saw Donald hovering in the background and went over to him. 'Thanks, Donald, I know you've done so much to help Amanda organise the party. But I have to go now.'

Out of the corner of her eye she saw Neil making his way towards her.

'You're not going, are you Brenda?' he called.

'Yes, must get back to Mum.'

He seemed disappointed. *At least I hope so...*

'Well, we'll see you in a few days, Brenda. Bill is so looking forward to it.'

'That's good to hear,' she replied. *But what about you, Neil? Are you looking forward to coming?'*

***

Amanda gave a sigh of relief as most of the allotmenteers and their friends and family left. They'd all chipped in and helped clear up. Now she and Donald were the only ones left.

'It was a great success, Amanda,' Donald remarked as he set about dismantling his music speakers. 'Lots of people said how much they enjoyed it.'

'Yes, indeed, and a lot of that was due to you, Donald.'

He put down a speaker and came over to her. 'Um, Amanda,' he said. 'I've been waiting all evening to steal a kiss under the mistletoe ...'

He seemed shy.

'And now, I seem to have lost the sprig I've been carrying ...'

Her heart leaped as she leaned towards him. 'We don't need mistletoe,' she breathed, drawing him towards her.

***

Brenda still hadn't replied to Damien. She left the Solstice party and walked back to her car. She was so tired! It had been a busy term at school. Only four days to Christmas and she had to organize the meal. She was pleased that Neil and Bill were coming. Hopefully their presence would prevent her mother from complaining too much.

As she drove home, she thought about Damien and came to a decision.

***

Neil suddenly remembered he was supposed to buy Christmas presents for Brenda's mother and her friend. And a book token for Brenda.

'Going shopping, Bill,' he called next morning, 'Do you need anything?'

'Don't think so, lad.'

'How much should I spend for the book token for Brenda?' He stopped at the front door.

'Dunno, lad. Whatever you think.'

Neil browsed the shopping mall. He had no problem getting pretty pots for Brenda's mother and her friend. He'd just have to call at the garden centre to get potting mix and the bulbs, but somehow, he couldn't bring himself to buy a book token. He wandered around the bookshop. He found himself in the children's section and staring him in the face was an anthology of nonsense poems. He picked it up and it fell open at the poem "The Walrus and The Carpenter". He turned the pages and saw "The Owl and the Pussy Cat". He took a deep breath. It struck him that Brenda would love it, and he could picture her reading it to the children at her school. He bought it, asking for it to be gift wrapped.

Now for the garden centre.

***

Brenda raced around the shopping centre buying a small turkey and other essential things for Christmas Day. Five people! Would there be enough sprouts from her allotment? Should she buy a few more? Crackers! She'd forgotten crackers … By the time she got home, she was exhausted. Her phone rang.

'Hello?'

'Hello Sevens, it's Damien.'

'Oh, hi, Damien.'

'Just wondering what you're doing for Christmas … thought you might like to pop around for a drink …'

'Oh! Well, actually I have a lot going on over Christmas but thanks for asking.'

'No worries. Um, Jayne will be so disappointed.'

'So sorry, Damien.'

'Right. Okay then. Well, you have a happy Christmas, Sevens.'

'Thanks, Damien. You too.' She ended the call, her heart thumping in her chest.

***

Amanda was thrilled that Donald's sister had invited her for Christmas lunch. Then the thought occurred to her … what should she take? Would his nephews be there? Bugger, bugger, bugger!

She rang him.

'Donald, I need to get a present for your sister! What should I bring?'

'Goodness, I didn't even think of that,' he replied. 'I don't think she will expect anything …'

'I've got to bring something!'

Donald sounded worried. 'No, no, she won't expect anything!'

'I'll think of something! It's all right, Donald.'

***

The Allotment - Christmas Day
  "At Christmas I no more desire a rose,
  Than wish a snow in May's new-fangled mirth;
  But like of each thing that in season grows." Shakespeare

***

Here's Paddy Murphy – he comes every Christmas Day, sits and stares into space for an hour, then leaves. I didn't expect anyone else here today. But hello! It's that little Brenda! She's probably forgotten to pick the brussels sprouts. Yes! There she goes, her fingers and nose red with the cold. Silly woman.

***

Brenda had spent Christmas Eve preparing for the following day. Now she had everything ready, turkey in the oven since early morning, Dining room table covered with a freshly ironed linen table cloth with matching napkins, and set with her mother's best crystal glasses that only saw daylight once a year; silver cutlery all polished, a bowl of holly as the center piece and a cracker at every setting. She only had to prepare the vegetables, then she'd just have time for a shower and change. She took the vegetables from the fridge. Bugger! She knew she'd forget something! The sprouts! She pulled on her coat, wrapped a scarf around her neck, and called out, 'Just going to the allotment, Mum! I forgot the sprouts.'

She drove up to the allotment, not expecting to see anyone on Christmas morning. Most people would either have children opening Christmas presents, or be going to church, but as she parked, she saw an old man going through the gate. She stared. It looked like Paddy Murphy! She didn't really know him, only heard about him from Bill, and had seen him a few times.

'Um, hello. It's Mr Murphy, isn't it?'

He turned around. 'Yes.' His voice almost a growl.

'I'm Brenda.' She suddenly thought he would have no idea who she was. 'I have the plot next to Bill Thompson.'

He drew himself up. 'Ah! Bill.'

She gave him a hard look. 'What are you doing here today, Mr Murphy?' She glanced towards the carpark, hers was the only car there.

He frowned. 'No business of yours.'

She took a deep breath. 'Bill is coming to my place for Christmas dinner. I know he'd love you to come and keep him company. He misses his wife.' She didn't know what made her say that. 'Would you mind coming and keeping him company?'

His face darkened. 'Being the good Samaritan, are you?'

She studied him. 'No, just trying to help Bill. It's a hard time for him.'

'Hard time for everyone. What're you doing here anyway?' He scowled.

'Forgot the sprouts.' She made to go. 'Well, my car is just there,' she nodded towards the car park. 'Not locked. Jump in out of the cold. I won't be long.'

She didn't expect to see him in the passenger seat when she got back with a bowl of sprouts. She nodded at him 'Bill will be delighted.'

'Hmph.' He didn't raise his eyes. 'I won't hang around, just say hello to Bill.'

'I think I may have got too much food, so you'll be doing me a favour if you'll stay.'

He didn't reply and was silent for the rest of the way.

Brenda's heart sank when she parked and saw Bill and Neil walking up the path to the front door, Neil carrying a large bag. They turned when they heard her behind them.

'Hello, love,' Bill exclaimed. 'Are we too early?'

'No, no, Bill, I had to pop up to the allotment to get fresh-ly-picked sprouts!' She saw Neil trying to hide a smile. 'And look who I found! Your friend, Mr Murphy!'

Bill beamed. 'Paddy! You're coming too, what a lovely surprise! How are you?' He held out his hand.

'Can't grumble. Not staying. Just say hello.'

Brenda had the door open and before he could object, she ushered Paddy inside, followed by Bill. Neil put his bag under the coat stand then took the men's coats. Her mother came sailing out from the lounge room.

'Mum, this is Mr Murphy, and you know Bill and Neil.'

Her mother inclined her head graciously. 'Pleased to meet you, Mr Murphy.' She nodded at Bill and Neil. 'Do come in. Close the front door, Brenda. You're letting all the cold air in.' She turned and led the way into the lounge.

Neil turned to Brenda. 'Found another waif and stray, Brenda?' he whispered. 'Sorry we're so early, Bill couldn't wait!'

She handed him the bowl of sprouts. 'I'm all behind, not even changed, and I must lay another place at the table, and here's Edith now ...'

He took the bowl. 'Go and get changed and see to the table. I'll look after these.' He gently pushed her towards the stairs. 'Hello,

Miss Milson, please come in. Let me put this dish in the kitchen and I'll take your coat.'

As Brenda ran up the stairs, she saw Edith blush and unbutton her coat.

***

Neil couldn't help smiling at the sight of Brenda, all flustered, her nose red from the cold and with what looked like a very reluctant Paddy Murphy trailing behind her. He put the sprouts in the kitchen sink and took a bottle of brandy from his coat pocket. 'Come into the warm, Miss Milson,' he said, opening the lounge door.

He made the introductions, then heard Brenda coming down the stairs as he hung up her coat.

'I think Paddy and Bill could do with a nip,' he whispered.

'Oh! I don't have any spirits!'

'I brought some brandy for the pudding; thought you might not have any.' His eyes crinkled in a smile. 'Now, show me where the glasses are, then I'll help you in the kitchen.'

She gave a jerky smile. 'Thanks, Neil. I'm a bit bothered at the moment.'

'You look lovely when you're bothered,' he grinned.

'I didn't have time for a shower,' she said, her cheeks growing red.

'And even more lovely when slightly grimy and ....' He sniffed. 'A bit smelly.'

She started to laugh. 'Glasses on the sideboard in the dining room.'

***

Amanda had taken extra care with her appearance. She heard a car stop outside. Donald had insisted on coming to fetch her.

'Oh, you do look lovely,' he exclaimed as he came in. 'As usual, may I say.' He leaned over and kissed her cheek.

'Thank you, Donald. Come in. I'm ready. Just have to get the presents.'

He cleared his throat. 'I wanted to give you mine now.'

'Oh!' She was surprised. 'Well, take off your coat, while I get yours.'

He followed her through to the lounge, where she picked up a bag, felt inside and drew out a gift box.

He held out a small package. 'Happy Christmas, dear Amanda.'

Her heart thudded, as she took it and sat with a sigh on the lounge. 'Thank you, Donald.'

He sat beside her and watched anxiously as she carefully undid the wrapping. 'Oh, they're beautiful!' she breathed, lifting out a pair of ornate gold earrings. 'Thank you, Donald.' She leaned towards him and kissed him. 'I'll put them in now.' She removed the little Christmas bell earrings she was wearing and replaced them with Donald's. 'How do they look?' She asked, moving her head from side to side.

He took a deep breath. 'Lovely. Like you, Amanda.'

'Now my turn,' she smiled, holding out the gift box.

Donald opened it to reveal a pair of gold cuff-links. He took one out. 'Oh! My ...' He held it up and frowned. 'I need my glasses; it seems there is something engraved on it.'

'Yes. Your initials.'

'They're lovely. Um, I've never had a present like this before.' He stared at her. 'Can you help me with them?' He held out one wrist.

'Of course.' Her heart beat faster.

She rested his hand in her lap while she undid his cuff link and replaced it with hers. Then held out her hand for his other one.

'They're beautiful, Amanda.' He turned his arms to display them. 'Thank you. My turn to give you a kiss.' He took her in his arms.

Ten minutes later and Donald said in a husky voice, 'I'd like to stay here, my dear, but I think we should make a move. My sister will be waiting for us.'

Amanda stood, straightened her skirt and patted her hair. 'I'll just tidy myself.'

'Wait a minute, I nearly forgot. I have another present.'

'Oh?'

'Yes, for Cato.' He went into the hall and took a package from his coat pocket.

She laughed when she unwrapped it and took out a pretty bowl with "Cato" on the side. 'You're so kind, Donald.'

***

Carol ran a comb through her hair and called out, 'Are you ready, Dougie?'

'Yes, Mum. Just checking Clare's present.'

Carol groaned, she was about to remark that the wrapping paper would be all crumpled if he undid it yet another time, when she heard him muttering. He came into her room. 'Um, I've torn the wrapping paper. Have we any more?'

'Yes, but this is the last time we wrap it, Douglas. It's a beautiful necklace and I'm sure Clare will love it.'

'Do you think she'll have a present for me, Mum?'

'Maybe not, Douglas. The fact that we've been invited for Christmas might be a present in itself.' She wanted to prepare him for disappointment.

He nodded. 'I guess.'

'Put your jacket on, or we'll be late.' She picked up the bag she'd prepared with wine, chocolates and crackers. She'd also bought a classy set of barbecue tools, having noticed that Norm's were old and falling apart.

***

Mary poured herself a brandy and drank it in one gulp. She wasn't looking forward to this day. Her second Christmas without Peter. *Vronnie would probably have invited a token man for me. At least we've given up the present giving business years before.* Now she picked up her bag with the wine and chocolates and made her way to the garage.

***

Bill leaned back in his chair with a sigh. He wiped his mouth with his napkin. 'That was a wonderful meal,' he said, looking around at them all with silly hats on, well, everyone except Brenda's mother.

'I take off my hat to you, Brenda, you've done us proud.' He waved his paper hat in the air, then raised his glass of wine. 'Here's to our lovely hosts, Brenda and Mrs Evans.'

They raised their glasses.

'Our pleasure, right, Mum?' Brenda said, glancing at her mother, who appeared slightly mollified by being included in the toast.

'I've eaten too much,' Bill remarked, holding his napkin to his mouth to hide a belch.

'Well, why don't you all go into the lounge and wait for the Queen's speech while you let the food settle,' Brenda said. 'I'll tidy up a bit and make some coffee.'

Edith wobbled to her feet. 'I'll help you dear, you must be tied, I mean, tried, um ...'

'I'm not tired at all, Edith, thank you. Perhaps you could help Mum and the boys to the lounge.'

Edith blinked a few times. 'Right, Benda.'

Paddy Murphy stood up and clutched the back of his chair. 'I might wait a bit before I go home,' he muttered.

Bill smiled to himself, Paddy had relaxed after a couple of tots of brandy and even smiled at one stage. He looked over at Brenda. Then he noticed Neil also staring at Brenda.

'Where's the mistletoe?' He asked, thinking he'd hold it over Neil and Brenda.

'Come on, Bill,' Neil said, helping him up. 'You're too old for mistletoe. Tea or coffee? I'll help Brenda.'

***

Neil took Paddy's arm. 'Feel like a ciggy?' he whispered. He'd noticed the nicotine stains on Paddy's fingers. 'I'm going out the back for one.'

Paddy stared at him then nodded.

Neil followed Brenda into the kitchen. 'Back door out here?' he asked.

Surprised, she nodded.

'Just taking Paddy out for a smoke.'

'Okay.'

He saw her frown. 'Don't frown, Brenda. You'll get wrinkles. Paddy's gasping for one.'

She smiled. 'It's Christmas Day. Of course, you can both go for a smoke!'

He felt like kissing her. Instead, he led Paddy outside and offered him a cigarette.

'Thanks.' Paddy took one and leaned over as Neil struck a match and held it in his cupped hand.

Paddy inhaled deeply and glanced at Neil. 'Reminds me of Kathleen, that Brenda,' he said.

'Oh?'

Paddy kept smoking. They were both silent until Paddy ground out his butt and looked around for somewhere to put it.

'Here.' Neil held out his hand. 'We have time for another.'

Paddy reached into his jacket. Neil thought he was groping for his own smokes, but Paddy pulled out his wallet and opened it. 'My Kathleen,' he muttered.

In the dim light Neil peered at a creased black and white photo of a curly-haired woman smiling into the camera. He caught his breath. 'Yes. I see what you mean.'

Paddy closed the wallet and tucked it back in his inside pocket.

Neil took two cigarettes from his packet and handed one to Paddy.

***

Brenda went to the kitchen and filled the kettle. She'd started to stack the dishwasher when Neil returned with Paddy Murphy in tow.

'This way, Paddy,' he said, guiding him to the lounge.

Neil turned to Brenda. 'If you have a tray, I can collect things,' he told her.

'Oh, thanks so much, Neil. You've been great. What a good idea to give Bill and Paddy that brandy.'

'I gave your mum and Edith some as well,' he grinned. 'Put some ginger ale in with theirs.'

Brenda laughed. 'I thought Mum seemed in an unusually good mood! You really have taken this saviour business seriously, haven't you?'

'Mmmh,' he said as he took the tray she offered. 'Actually, I'm enjoying it. I love seeing you get overcome with excessive gratitude.'

Her heart seemed to speed up. *Must have had too much wine.*

***

Neil glanced at Brenda who was sitting on the arm of her mother's lounge chair. He thought she looked tired. Bill's chin was sunk on his chest and Paddy Murphy's eyes were closed. He seemed to have nodded off. Neil looked at his watch. 'It's nearly seven o'clock,' he said. 'I think it's time we left and let Brenda and Mrs Evans have a rest.'

Bill's head jerked up. 'Whas that, lad?'

'Time to go, Bill.'

'Oh! Right.'

Paddy Murphy gave a grunt and opened his eyes.

'We can give Paddy a lift home, and also Edith,' Neil said smiling at Edith.

'Oh, I only live around the corner. I can walk,' Edith simpered.

'It's dark. No, we'll drop you home.'

Neil saw Brenda go over to Paddy who was hanging back behind the others. 'Thank you for coming,' he heard her say and then she gave Paddy a hug. Paddy blinked and patted her back.

Numerous hugs, thank yous, farewells and happy Christmases later, Paddy, Bill and Edith were settled in Bill's car, being waved off by Brenda.

They dispatched Edith at her house, then Paddy Murphy gave Neil directions. 'It's fairly close to the allotment,' he said. 'Handy for me. Here we are.'

Neil stopped the engine and made to get out.

'I can manage. Thanks for the lift.' Paddy walked to the gate of a little cottage without a backwards glance.

Neil wondered what was his story.

***

Bill settled in his armchair in front of the TV. 'What a grand day out!' he remarked. 'She's a top little girl, that Brenda, don't you reckon, Neil?'

'Indeed, she is,' Neil sighed. After a pause, he said, 'What do you know of Paddy Murphy, Bill. He seems an unhappy kind of bloke.'

'Known him for years, poor sod. His wife and young daughter were killed when the car he was driving skidded on ice. Nasty accident. Christmas Day; they were going to Mass.' He sighed. 'Must be over thirty years ago now. That was in the days before seat belts. Dunno how he kept going afterwards. I think he blamed himself. Having the allotment helped him.'

'Brenda said he was at the allotment when she saw him today, and invited him to have Christmas lunch,' Neil said.

'I'm amazed he agreed to come.' Bill shook his head.

'She's pretty special,' Neil murmured. 'Paddy showed me an old photo of someone he called Kathleen. I suppose that would have been his wife?'

'Could have been.'

'Apparently Brenda reminded him of Kathleen.'

Bill considered. 'Maybe. Only met her a few times. Long time ago now.' He saw Neil's look. 'I guess Paddy's little girl would be about the same age now as our Brenda. That's if she'd lived.'

'Very sad,' Neil murmured.

'I think poor old Paddy had a good day.' Bill yawned. 'I'm plumb tuckered out, lad. Think it won't be long before I go to bed.'

***

Neil nodded at Bill. 'Good idea.' He went up to the bedrooms and turned on the electric blankets. Poor old Paddy. And it was probably the fact that Brenda reminded him of his wife that had made him accept her invitation to join them for Christmas.

Knowing Brenda, he thought she'd be taking Paddy under her wing. He couldn't stop thinking about her. Had he fallen in love with her? It didn't feel the same as when he fell in love with Deirdre. Anyway, there was no point in thinking about it. He had nothing to offer any woman, let alone someone like Brenda. He wondered what that Colin was like, she'd seemed keen on him until she went to stay with him. And that Damien. Did she still fancy him? He went downstairs and found Bill sound asleep and snoring.

***

Carol sipped her wine. 'Thank you, Jill. I think that's the best Christmas Douglas and I have ever had.'

Jill looked at her curiously. 'Really?'

'Sounds strange, but somehow it's not the same when it's just the two of you.' She thought about the fun and laughter they'd had today, with the paper hats and silly jokes. It was good to see Dougie accepted and enjoying himself.

'Do you not have any family?' Jill came and sat opposite her in the lounge. Norm, Clare and Douglas were playing pool in another room. Clare's older brother and sister had gone to see friends.

'My parent's divorced when I was twelve. Dad remarried and moved to Australia.' She stared at her glass. 'Mum never got over it ...' She couldn't finish the sentence.

'You've had a tough life,' Jill said softly. She refilled Carol's glass.

Carol nodded and shrugged. 'Perhaps. But I'm pretty happy and contented now.' *At least that's what I tell myself.*

***

Amanda smiled at Donald. 'It's getting late, I should probably leave soon.'

'I hope you've had a good time, Amanda.'

'It's been wonderful, best Christmas ever, Donald.'

His eyes lit up. 'I hope we can have many more,' he paused. 'Er, together.'

He gave her a meaningful look.

'I'll just go and thank Judy.' She stood and made her way to the kitchen, where Judy was tidying away the crystal glasses.

'Judy! I would have helped you, why didn't you call me?'

Judy smiled. 'You know how it is when someone puts things away for you and you can never find them again!' she paused. 'I wanted to say how happy I am that Donald has found you, Amanda.'

'Oh!' Amanda didn't know how to reply. 'He's a lovely man. I'm very fond of him.'

Judy examined a crystal wine glass she had in her hand, then met Amanda's gaze. 'I think he's more than fond of you, Amanda.'

'I've brought the car round, Amanda,' Donald's voice interrupted them.

'Thank you again, Judy. Perhaps we could get together for a coffee sometime?'

'Lovely. Look forward to it.'

Amanda saw Donald at the door, a fatuous beam on his face.

***

Mary took a peek at her watch. She thought the day would never end and she could go home and have a few drinks. She'd had a bit to drink already, but had carefully monitored her consumption.

'Perhaps I can drop you home,' a voice said in her ear.

It was Vronnie's spare man, Liam, who'd been sitting close to her most of the evening.

'I have my car,' she said.

'Now, Mary.' Veronica interrupted. 'I hope you're not thinking of running off so early. We're just about to play cards. I've paired you with Liam.'

'Oh, I've got a bit of a headache, Vronnie. Not up to playing cards.' She gave Liam a rueful smile. 'You would lose every hand if you had me as a partner.'

'I don't think so ...' he winked at her.

Vronnie pulled a face. 'Oh, Mary, if you go, someone will have to sit out.'

'Sorry, Vronnie.' She picked up her bag. 'Great party, thanks so much, and lovely to meet you, Liam.' She flashed her most inviting smile at him. She walked into the middle of the room and waved at the other guests. 'Bye everyone. Happy Christmas and prosperous

New Year!' Taking pity on Liam, she gave him a quick kiss. 'Catch up again, Liam,' she whispered. His eyes lit up. *Bitch*, she said to herself.

***

The Allotment St Stephen's day. They call it Boxing Day now. Supposedly because landlords gave the servants the day off after working all Christmas Day or perhaps the alms boxes being opened on that day. Whatever. St. Stephen was the first Christian martyr, apparently stoned to death. It's all silent here.

***

Brenda dragged herself out of bed. *Boxing Day.* She pulled back the curtains to reveal a grey morning dawn and gave herself a mental shake. Yesterday had gone well. Everyone seemed to have enjoyed the day. She suddenly thought of Colin. She hadn't heard from him in ages. Not since his last, somewhat sarcastic message:

Looks like you've found someone else, he'd written. *Well, I'll do the same. Bye Brenda. Have a happy life.*

She thought that was the last thing he wanted her to have – a happy life. Anyway, she was happy. Well, kind of. She hadn't replied to Damien, maybe she should ... see if she still found him attractive. Then she thought about Neil. He really had been her saviour. Always there when she needed him. She sighed. But he seemed to have no interest in her.

She pulled on her dressing gown and went downstairs and opened the fridge. The hulk of the turkey carcass challenged her. She could make something out of the remains and the other leftovers. She slammed the fridge door shut and filled the kettle. Coffee first, then she'd think about other things.

She heard her mother stirring, then the toilet flush. She ground coffee.

***

Bill woke with a slight headache. *Might have had a bit too much to drink yesterday.* He heard Neil moving around downstairs. *A cup of tea would be nice,* he thought as he heard Neil coming up the stairs.

'You awake, Bill? I've brought you a cup of tea.'

'You're a saviour, lad! Was just thinking I could do with a cuppa. Think I had too much to drink yesterday.'

'Don't think so, Bill. Just the unaccustomed socializing. Gone to your head. All that chatting up of Mrs Evans!'

Bill grimaced. 'She's a piece of work all right! Reckon our Brenda must take after her dad 'cos she's not a bit like her mother.'

Neil appeared to consider this. 'If so, then he must have been a lovely man.'

Bill stared at him. 'Brenda would be just the woman for you, Neil.'

'Don't be silly, Bill. I've got nothing to offer a woman, especially someone as lovely as Brenda.'

'You're the silly one, Neil. I reckon she fancies you all right.'

Neil burst out laughing. 'Bill, you say that about every woman we meet, nurses at the hospital, your physiotherapist, that Mary Flynn. Dr Davis ... Next, you'll be saying Edith Milson fancies me ...' He paused and appeared to think. 'Actually, Bill, I think it's you she fancies! Saw her giving you honeyed looks.'

'Honeyed looks! What the hell is a honeyed look?'

Neil raised his eyebrows. 'You know exactly what I mean, Bill!'

Bill gave Neil a smug smile and stroked his chin. 'Maybe, lad, maybe!'

***

Amanda yawned as Cato rubbed his face against her chin. 'Okay, Cato! I know you want to be fed. In your swish new dish that Donald gave you.'

She stretched luxuriously. *Yesterday had been wonderful! How lucky I am!*

Donald had brought her home last night and had seemed reluctant to leave, but she had insisted. She thought about their farewell on her front door step. She'd considered inviting him in for a nightcap, but then thought better of it; it had been a lovely day, and she needed her beauty sleep, and anyway, one had to play a little bit hard to get! She smiled to herself as her phone rang. She could guess who! She let it ring for a few seconds and then picked up. It was so amazing to be loved!

***

Mary groaned as the pale dawn light filtered through her bedroom window. She'd forgotten to pull the curtains the night before. She half opened her eyes to peer at the bedside clock. *Nine o'clock! My second Christmas without Peter!*

She groped for her dressing gown and made her way downstairs. Coffee and a painkiller. Her head thumped. She hated Christmas now. Used to love it when Peter was alive. He always had something organised for them. One year skiing in Austria, another a bothy in the Scottish Highlands. Cosying up in front of a peat fire ... She remembered the year he took her to Australia for Christmas. She'd laughed at the Australian idea of Christmas. A barbecue on the beach! And a Father Christmas sweating profusely in his red garb. She smiled at the memory.

Her phone rang. She glanced at it. No one she knew. She ignored it, but a message came through. "Hi Mary, it's Liam. Um, we met last night. I got your number from your sister."

Mary felt a twinge of irritation. 'Fuck Vronnie!'

The message continued. "Just wondered if you'd like to come for lunch ..."

She considered her options. A long, lonely day by herself, drinking too much or ...

She picked up. 'Hi Liam. Sounds good. Where can we meet?'

'I could pick you up if you give me your address.' She heard the pleasure in his voice.

What the hell! She told him her address.

'Noon suit you?'

She agreed.

***

Neil thought he'd better call over to see his sister. Wish her Happy Christmas. Well, Happy New Year, too late for Christmas. He'd bought a box of chocolates for Anna and a bottle of whiskey for Tom – not that he deserved it, but just to express the Christmas spirit.

He rang the doorbell and stood waiting.

'Neil! Come in! Why didn't you go round the back and just come in?' She took his arm. 'Haven't seen you in ages.'

'Yeah, been busy with Bill.'

'Happy Christmas, love!' She planted a kiss on his cheek. 'What have you been doing?' She led him into the kitchen. 'Look who's here, Tom.'

His brother-in-law barely looked up from the paper he was reading and grunted.

'Won't stay. Just wanted to see how you were,' Neil said. Tom's reception wasn't exactly welcoming. He put his parcels on the kitchen table.

'How was your Christmas?' Anna asked.

'Good thanks. Bill and I were asked to one of his allotment friends for Christmas lunch.'

'So you said.'

He thought Anna seemed a bit down. 'How was your day?'

'Good. The boys were here, but they've gone out with friends now. You've missed them.'

He nodded. He liked his nephews. 'Haven't seen them in a while. Well, I'd better get back to Bill.'

'How is he?' His sister asked.

'He's had a few health problems but seems much better lately.'

The formalities over, Neil edged towards the door. 'Better go. See you, Tom.'

His brother-in-law grunted.

Anna took his arm as he went out the front door. 'Tom's a bit down,' she whispered. 'The new job's not working out.'

'Sorry to hear that. Must be hard for you, sis.'

She sighed. 'At least you seem brighter.'

'Yes.' And realised it was true.

***

Brenda made a decision. She took a deep breath and rang Damien.

'Sevens!'

He sounded pleased. 'Hi, Damien. I thought I could spend a couple of days minding Jayne over the holidays to give your mother a break. That's if you'd still like me to.' But the words, *This is Jayne's teachers' aide* still echoed in her head.

'Excellent! Thanks so much, Sevens. Can't wait to see you. Which days will suit you?'

She told him. Then he asked did she have a good Christmas ... Wonderful, she replied but didn't ask him how his was. She hung up. It would get her out of the house for a couple of days. There was nothing much to do on the allotment, plus the money would be useful. She smiled to herself.

***

Carol woke to the smell of coffee being brewed. Startled, she leapt out of bed, pulling her dressing gown on as she ran downstairs to the kitchen. Dougie was standing by the coffee maker. He looked up, a big grin on his face.

'Good morning, Mother dear. Just thought I'd bring you a cup of coffee in bed.'

'Oh! That's lovely of you, Dougie.' She collapsed onto a kitchen chair, anxiously watching him.

'Clare gives her mum a cup of coffee some mornings,' he said, carefully pouring the hot coffee into a cup. He smiled as he pushed the cup towards her.

'Wow! That's lovely, Dougie. Thank you so much.'

He stood, proud of his first attempt at making coffee. 'Drink up, Mum.'

'It's a bit hot.' She smiled at him.

'Did you have a good time yesterday, Mum?'

'Yes,' she said. 'They're a lovely family.'

'Clare's pretty special, don't you think?'

'She certainly is.'

'Could we get married?'

Carol frowned. 'Well, I think you're too young at the moment to be thinking about weddings. You've both got a lot of growing up to do before then.'

'Clare said her mum and dad thought so too.'

Carol heaved a silent sigh of relief.

***

Bill settled back in the lounge room. Neil had gone to see visit his sister, Mrs Bridges. He thought back to the previous Christmas – his first without Hazel. It had been terrible. But he'd enjoyed yesterday. He looked at Hazel's photograph.

'I know you would have been pleased, Hazel. I really only went for Neil's sake. And we met Paddy Murphy there. That little Brenda invited him. I'm amazed he came. You'd like Brenda, Hazel.' He sighed. 'I won't be long, Hazel, dearest and we can be together again.'

He closed his eyes. Yesterday had tired him out. He'd have a nap while he waited for Neil to come home.

***

Carol's phone rang that evening. She picked it up without thinking.

'Carol?' A man's voice.

'Um, who is it?' She thought she recognized her ex-husband, but he hadn't rung her for years, so she hesitated.

'Angus.'

'Oh.' She waited, unwilling to make the first move.

'How are you?'

'Good, thanks,' she said cautiously.

'And Douglas?'

'He's great, thanks.' *What was all this leading to?*

'The thing is,' he said, 'I'd like to see Douglas.'

Her brows drew together. 'Why now?' her tone flat.

'Well, I've been doing a lot of thinking. I've been diagnosed with an incurable cancer. A year, maybe two ... and I see now I did the wrong thing, abandoning you and Douglas.'

'Oh?' She wasn't going to make it easy for him. It hadn't been easy for her.

'And, well, I'd like to meet Douglas, try and make amends.'

Against her will she began to feel sorry for him, but she was silent. What could she say?

'So, I wonder would that be possible?'

She didn't know whether to laugh or cry. 'He's going well. In secondary school. Got a girlfriend.' Her voice tight.

'A girlfriend? But isn't he, I mean ...'

She gripped the phone. 'You mean what, Angus?'

'I'm sorry, Carol.'

She thought he sounded close to tears. 'Yes, well, you've missed out on knowing an amazing boy.'

'I'd really like to meet him.'

She could hardly hear him.

'Do you think he'd like to meet me?'

Her thoughts flew all over the place. 'I'll think about it. I don't want Dougie upset.'

'No, no, of course not. Look – I had a chemo treatment today. I'm a bit out of it. How about I ring you tomorrow evening?'

'Okay.'

'Thanks, Carol.'

She hung up, her head spinning.

'You all right, Mum?' Dougie came into the room. 'Thought I heard you talking.'

She made a sudden decision. 'Your father just rang me.'

'What?' His head jerked up.

'He wants to meet you. Say sorry because he went away when you were a baby.'

Dougie collapsed onto the settee. 'My father? My dad?'

She nodded.

'Why?' She saw the worried look on his face.

She studied her hands. 'Apparently he's not well and he's been thinking about you.'

'What do you think, Mum? Do you want to see him?'

She sighed. 'It's not about me, Dougie. It's about you.'

His frown deepened. 'What do you think, Mum?'

She sat beside him and put an arm around him. 'I think it would be good, Dougie.'

He smiled. 'Can Clare come too?'

'Um, not the first time, love.'

He beamed. 'I hope he's like Norm.' He jumped up. 'I must ring Clare and tell her.'

She sighed and wished she had someone with whom to share this news. Then went to the kitchen and poured herself a glass of wine.

***

Brenda shoved the turkey carcass into a big pot, threw in herbs, an onion and a carrot, added water and put it on the stove to simmer. Then she wandered around the house, not feeling up to doing much. She'd stayed up late the night before, clearing up the place after the festivities.

She picked up the book Bill and Neil had given her, well, Neil really. She made a cup of coffee and sat and turned the pages of the book, smiling as she read each nonsense verse.

Neil was lovely. So kind and thoughtful. Look how good he was with Bill. Even Paddy Murphy had thawed and seemed more friendly with Neil. She'd miss him if he ever decided to go to Wisley. Yesterday had been the best Christmas she could remember. Even when her father and Granny had been alive Christmas Day hadn't been as good.

Her thoughts turned to Damien. She'd totally misread the situation. Perhaps she'd been searching for someone to replace Colin. And realistically, Damien had never intimated any special feelings towards her. Then she'd gone and made a fool of herself in front of Neil. She cringed inwardly. That episode of the upset seat and both of them lying in the mud! And he'd been so kind, taking her to see Bill and tidy herself up before she went home and then taking her to see a film ...

She heard her mother calling. Sighing, she put the book down and went up to her mother's bedroom.

'What is it, Mum?'

'What's that smell?'

Brenda's brow creased. 'Oh! That's the turkey carcass. I'm making a stew for dinner tonight.'

Her mother wrinkled her nose. 'Isn't there anything else we can have?'

Brenda shrugged. 'Cold ham and mashed potato and left-over Christmas pudding?'

Her mother turned away. 'You're a hopeless housekeeper, Brenda. No wonder no one wants to marry you!'

Brenda stuck out her tongue behind her mother's back. 'Going to the allotment, Mum.' She had to get out of the house.

***

Carol hovered around her phone the following evening, waiting for Angus's call. She'd been awake half the night, agonising over the situation.

At last it rang. She snatched it up.

'Carol?'

'Yes. Angus?'

'Yes. Er, have you decided?' His voice sounded very faint and shaky.

'Douglas has decided he would like to meet you.' She tried to keep her voice low and steady.

'Great! When? Where? How soon?'

She considered. 'Over the school holidays is good. So, this week?'

She heard him sigh with what she thought was relief.

'Where?'

She named a garden centre nearby.

'Really? A garden centre?'

'Douglas loves gardening. We have an allotment. Just thought it would be a kind of neutral place. I can hover behind you, in case it's too much for him.'

'Right.' He paused. 'Tuesday okay with you?'

'Yes. Eleven o'clock suit?'

'Right. Thanks Carol. I really appreciate this.'

'You must thank Douglas, not me.'

'Anyway … well, I'll see you both on Tuesday.'

'There's a coffee shop … we'll be there.'

'Thanks, Carol.'

She ended the call.

***

Mary woke and blinked. Her head pounded. She frowned. Her bedroom had changed. She screwed up her eyes. Where was she? She could smell coffee being brewed. She froze as she remembered the previous day. Liam had picked her up and they'd gone out for lunch. She vaguely recalled going to a pub and having too much to drink. Now she looked around the shadowy room with only the outline of the window visible. She cringed inwardly at the thought that she must have agreed to go home with him and … what had happened next?

She buried her face in the pillow. *Peter, oh, Peter! I'm sorry, I don't know what happened!* She felt around for her clothes, but then realised she was still dressed. She had no idea where she was, how far from her house, and where was her phone?

Her eyes gradually became accustomed to the gloom. Where was she? Panic filled her.

The bedroom door opened slowly. 'Are you awake?' whispered a voice. 'I've brought you coffee … and a couple of aspirin, in case you needed them.'

She lifted herself up onto her elbow. 'Liam?'

'Yes. You were pretty out of it last night, so I brought you back to my place, and well, put you to bed.'

He must have noticed her questioning look, for he continued, 'Nothing happened, Mary. I slept on the couch in the lounge room.'

She sank back into the bed and mumbled, 'Sorry.'

He put the coffee cup on the bedside table and held out the aspirin and a glass of water.

'Thanks.' She gulped the aspirin and lay down again, staring at the ceiling. 'I'm sorry, um ...'

'Liam.'

'Yes, Liam, I'm sorry. You see my husband, Peter, was the love of my life.'

He was silent for a few minutes, then sighed. 'It's okay, Mary. I understand. Why don't we just stay friends for a while.' He grinned. 'It might keep your sister off your back!'

Mary managed a smile. 'Thank you, Liam.'

'Look. Drink your coffee and rest for a while. When you're ready I can drive you home.'

'Thanks.' She sniffed, feeling teary all of a sudden.

***

Brenda drove up to the allotment and parked. There was nothing really to do, she just wanted to get away from her mother.

This is ridiculous. Running away from my own mother!

She walked up to her plot. She righted the old oil drums which had held the plank making the temporary seat and picked up the plank. She plonked it down and sat on it, then folded her arms and scowled.

'What's with the angry look?'

She raised her head at the sound of Neil's voice.

'Didn't hear you coming. Was just thinking.' She patted the plank beside her. 'Have a seat.'

Neil laughed. 'Is it safe?'

She smiled. 'Dunno. Try it and see.' She shuffled along to make room.

'Okay. But don't get up until I say so.' He lowered himself beside her. 'So, what's with the grumpy face? Not like you, Brenda.'

'I know.' She let out a breath. 'Just my mum getting on my nerves.'

He nodded. 'You're amazing, the way you put up with her.'

'It's just that I can't seem to do anything to please her.'

'I don't think she actually wants to be pleased, otherwise she'd have nothing to complain about.'

Brenda turned to him. 'I hadn't thought of it like that. Anyway, what are you doing up here?'

'Bill sent me out to check that everything was all right at his plot as he hasn't been for a few days.'

She grinned. 'Typical Bill. How is he really? I know he seemed okay yesterday, but his ulcer and swollen legs don't look good?'

'Much improved, and, as you could see, he's in great spirits.'

'Mmmh.'

They sat in silence for a few minutes until Neil said, 'I'd better go and check his plot. Do you think we could both stand up at the same time?'

Brenda caught his arm. 'Ready, steady. Go!' Laughing, they both stood.

***

Carol studied herself in the mirror. She wanted to appear her best for the meeting with Angus.

Dougie came out of his bedroom. 'Do I look all right, Mum?'

She turned around. 'Of course you do, love.'

'Do I call him Dad? Or Angus? Father?' He scuffed his feet nervously.

She considered. 'Maybe ask him ...'

He nodded. 'Good idea. Like um, "Hello, what shall I call you?"'

'Doesn't sound right, Dougie. Let's play it by ear and not worry at this stage.'

She took her winter coat from the wardrobe. 'Get your scarf and gloves, it's cold out.'

In the car she tried to stay calm. It would be over thirteen years since she'd last seen Angus. He'd be just over forty now. Too young to have terminal cancer.

She parked at the garden centre and they walked past the array of ceramic pots and bird baths towards the café, Dougie hopping and skipping beside her. 'How will you know him, Mum?'

She pushed open the door to be greeted by a fug of warm air. As they entered a man rose from a seat at a nearby table.

She was momentarily stunned when she realised the gaunt, bald figure was Angus. She walked towards him.

'Hello, Angus.'

He nodded, 'Carol.'

'This is your son. Douglas.'

Douglas held out his hand. 'How do you do?' he asked politely.

Carol's heart swelled with pride.

Angus stared at Dougie. 'Um, how do you do, Douglas?' They shook hands.

'Won't you sit down?' Angus indicated the bench seats. 'What would you like?' He made to get up.

Carol put her hand out to stop him. 'Dougie can go.'

Dougie considered. 'Can I have a chocolate milk-shake, please?' He turned to Carol. 'Is that okay, Mum?'

'Sure, darling, why don't you go to the counter and order for us. A flat white for me. How about you, Angus?'

He pointed to the cup in front of him. 'I'm okay, thanks.' He felt in his pocket for money. 'Here, Douglas.' He held out a handful of coins. 'Will that be enough?'

Douglas gave his mother a worried glance. 'Should be fine, Douglas,' she said.

Angus watched Douglas going to the counter. 'He's not how I imagined,' he murmured.

'Oh? What did you imagine?' She wanted to say, *a drooling idiot?* But stopped herself when she saw Angus's face.

'I'm sorry, Carol. It was heartless and cruel to leave you to bring him up on your own.' He took out a handkerchief and wiped his eyes. 'Sorry, the medication I'm on seems to make me a bit emotional.'

'Tell me what's been happening over the years, Angus. Did you remarry?'

He nodded. 'Yes, but it didn't work out. She wanted children, and to be honest I couldn't face having another child that might be ... might be ...' his voice tailed off. 'What about you?'

She pulled a face. 'Not many men want to take on a child with issues. And anyway, I've been too busy with Douglas and working.'

'Still teaching English?'

'No. Couldn't take a regular job. I do book editing. It meant I could work from home while Douglas was young, and choose my own hours.' She sighed. 'The only drawback is that you don't meet people. But I have an allotment, one of Douglas's therapists suggested it. And it provides much of our food. Douglas loves going there.'

He was silent.

She regarded him. 'Douglas wanted to know what he should call you.'

'Oh, I didn't think. What do you suggest?'

'Don't know. Here he is now.'

'The lady will bring it over,' Douglas said, taking a seat on the bench next to his mother. He stared at his father. He held out his hand. 'Here's the change.'

Angus seemed uncertain. 'Keep it, Douglas.'

'Thanks, um, Dad.'

'Your mum tells me you've got a girlfriend, Douglas. Tell me about her.'

Dougie's eyes lit up. 'Yes. She's called Clare. She's beautiful, isn't she, Mum?'

Carol smiled. 'Yes.'

'And she lives with her mum and dad, they're called Jill and Norm, and her big brother and sister. They're called John and Isobel. Oh, here's my milkshake and your coffee, Mum.' He smiled at the waitress. 'Thank you.'

He chatted away and Carol watched Angus listening carefully to every word. She looked around as more people came into the café. 'I think we should move outside,' she said. 'Make room for others, as the place is filling up.'

Angus followed her gaze. 'Of course. Good idea. Um, Douglas, I understand you like gardening. Perhaps you can show me around and tell me about the plants. I'm afraid I know nothing about gardening.'

Douglas beamed. 'My pleasure, Dad.'

As Angus stood and buttoned his overcoat, Carol noticed how thin he was. A far cry from the muscular physical education in-structor she'd married. He took a woolly hat from a pocket, wound a scarf around his neck and grasped a walking stick from the back of his chair.

'Lead on, McDuff,' he said.

Dougie turned around, a frown on his face. 'My name is Douglas, not McDuff.'

'Sorry, Douglas, just a turn of phrase.'

'Okay, Dad. Whatever.' He led the way out of the café.

***

Neil went to Bill's plot. Nothing to do there, he was sure Bill had sent him just to get him out of the house. The days between Christmas and the New Year seemed boring somehow. He looked back at Brenda who appeared to be studying her brussels sprouts. The more he saw of her, the more he was attracted to her. He sighed. She hadn't mentioned that Damien lately. He unlocked the shed door, had a quick glance around and went back outside. He felt at a loose end. He'd enjoyed his horticulture course and regretted not being able to take up the offer to work at Wisley. But he owed it to Bill to stay with him.

He looked over again at Brenda, where he could see her mooching about, not really focused on anything. He locked up and made his way back to the car.

***

Brenda watched Neil walk over to Bill's plot. He was so good, she thought. Just imagine, he'd given up the chance of working at Wisley in order to care for Bill. Not many men would do that. She knew about his PTSD issues – Bill seemed to have told everyone on the allotment about Neil's problems – but when she thought back to the first time she'd met Neil, when he'd dug over her garden beds, she could see there had been a great improvement in him. He seemed more settled, more at ease and communicative.

She checked the sprouts. Still a few coming on. She sat back on her makeshift bench and took note of Neil locking up and leaving. She heaved a sigh. Her feet were getting cold, but she didn't feel like going home. After a few minutes she saw Paddy Murphy coming in the main gate, plodding slowly up the central path.

'Hello, Mr Murphy!' she called as he drew near. His head went up. Then he spotted her.

He inclined his head and she thought he'd just continue up to his plot, but then he deviated and came towards her. 'Brenda, isn't it?'

'Yes, Mr Murphy.'

He walked over and came in her gate. 'Just wanted to say thank you for inviting me for Christmas Day.'

'Oh!' she said and patted the plank beside her. 'Have a seat. It's a bit unstable, but as long as we both move together, it's okay.'

He frowned but carefully lowered himself onto the seat.

'Bill was delighted you came,' she said.

'Hmph.'

'I don't think he's that well.'

'Indeed.'

'He's lucky to have Neil staying with him.'

'Yes. Seems a nice fellow.'

'You live on your own, Mr Murphy?'

'Call me Paddy.'

'Paddy.'

'Yes. On my own.'

She wondered what had happened in his life to make him so sad. They sat in companionable silence for a while, until Paddy said, 'well, I'd better get up to my plot.' He made to rise but Brenda grabbed his arm. 'We both have to stand at the same time,' she said. 'Otherwise, the seat collapses. Okay, ready, steady, go!' She dragged him up.

He made a noise that she interpreted as a laugh. A strange gurgling sound that it seemed he hadn't made in years.

***

Bill relaxed after he'd sent Neil to check on the allotment. He smiled to himself and looked at the photo of Hazel. *Not long now my darling.* He stretched out on his reclining chair, tucking the blanket around his legs. He closed his eyes and then they shot open as a pain gripped his chest. He grimaced, then, as the pain subsided, he smiled. 'I'm on my way, Hazel. I haven't told Neil about these chest pains. He'd only cart me off to the doctors. And everything is in order, Hazel. You'd be proud of me.' He thought she smiled back at him.

***

Mary quite liked Liam. He was quiet and gentle – characteristics that she'd appreciated in Peter. This was their second time out together. She'd told him all about Peter's allotment, and now she thought about it, it seemed she'd done all the talking, and mainly about Peter. Oh well. At least he would have got the message that she wasn't ready for a new relationship.

He was coming around today and they were going to the allotment. He'd asked to see it after she'd told him about all the bulbs she'd planted.

***

Brenda took a deep breath as she pressed the doorbell at Damien's. A flurry of noise, the door flew open and Jayne flung herself at Brenda. 'Miss Sevens! You came!'

'Jayne! At least let Miss Sevens get in the door!'

Brenda looked up to see Damien smiling at her. 'Hi Damien! How are things?'

'Good, thanks, Sevens.'

She bent down to give Jayne a hug, trying to hide her face which she could feel flushing.

Damien closed the door behind her. 'Thanks so much for coming, Sevens. My mother hasn't been well and I have some important work to finish before the new year.'

'That's okay, Damien. It makes a change from being stuck indoors in this weather.' *Stuck with a grumpy old mother.*

'Right, I'll leave you and Jayne to do whatever it is you've planned to do today.'

'Can we do baking, Miss Sevens? Pleeeze?' Jayne tugged Brenda towards the kitchen.

Brenda nodded as she watched Damien disappear up the stairs to his office.

***

Amanda checked the time. Donald was coming over and they were going to drive around and look at a few houses that were for sale.

'We won't be able to view them until after the New Year, but I thought we could drive past and you can see what you think,' he'd said.

She took one last look in the mirror then went to her bedroom window. She saw his car pull up outside her gate and hurried down the stairs as the doorbell rang.

'Hello Donald! Come in.'

He gave her a kiss on the cheek. 'Do you know that one of the things I love about you is that you're always punctual,' he said.

'One of the things?' She raised her eyebrows.

She thought she saw the colour rising in his cheeks – that was the trouble with a beard, it was hard to see if a man was blushing.

'One of many things.' He turned towards the hallstand. 'Er, this coat?' He took it and held it out for her.

'Thank you, Donald.'

'Um, Amanda.'

She looked up from buttoning her coat.

'You may have been wondering why I have been asking you to view these houses with me.'

'Well, it's always good to have a second opinion.'

'The thing is, Amanda, I think it would be a good idea if we moved in somewhere together.'

'Oh?' She waited expectantly.

'What I'm trying to say, is that I have deep feelings for you and I think we get on very well together.We like the same music and well ...'

'What are you trying to say, Donald?'

He took her hand. 'I'd like us to get married.'

She smiled. 'I think I'd like that too.'

He let out a sigh of relief and took her in his arms. 'You'll make me a very happy man,' he mumbled into her hair.

***

Carol let Angus and Dougie walk ahead of her.

'Do you like sport?' She heard Angus ask.

There was a pause then Douglas said, 'Well, I like it, but I'm no good at it.'

'I see. So, what do you like doing?'

'I like going to the allotment and seeing what's growing in people's gardens and I like being with Clare; we play games on her computer.'

'Oh, right.'

Douglas chattered on.

Carol noticed Angus's pace slowing. She came along-side of them and said, 'Douglas, why don't you have a look around and see if you can find something nice that we can take to Clare's on New Year's Eve?'

'Good idea, Mum!' He turned to his father. 'Won't be long, Dad.'

'Come and sit down here.' Carol took Angus's arm and led him to a nearby bench.

'Thanks, Carol. I tire easily these days.'

'I've heard chemo does that.'

'Carol, I feel so bad that I left you when Douglas was just a baby. It was very wrong of me.'

She patted his knee. 'It's okay. Sometimes it's been hard going, but on balance I've been privileged to have Dougie in my life.'

'He's a credit to you.'

'Where are you living now, Angus?'

He sighed. 'I'm renting a flat close to the hospital. I stayed with Mum and Dad for a while when I was first diagnosed, but they live too far from the hospital so the flat seemed a better option.'

'How are your mum and dad?'

'Mum's kept busy looking after Dad, he's got dementia.'

'Oh, that's sad.' She'd got on well with Angus's parents. 'They always send a card and a present for Dougie on his birthday.'

'That makes me feel even worse. I never sent him anything.'

She made an effort to change the subject. 'So, who is looking after you now?'

He gave short laugh. 'No-one, dear Carol. I live by myself.'

She turned to him. 'That's pretty rough.'

He shrugged. 'Shit happens. I cope.'

She thought about her small two-bedroomed town house. There was no room for another person. Then she gave herself a mental shake. *I'm not responsible for him. And anyway, I live too far from the hospital.*

'I think I'll have to go, Carol. I'm very cold. Can you tell Douglas goodbye for me?'

'I can see him over there.' She pointed to a display of potted poinsettias. 'I'll get him.'

Douglas came running over to his father. 'Bye, Dad. I hope you can come and see us again soon.'

Angus was on his feet. 'I certainly will, Douglas. It's been lovely to catch up at last.'

'I'm just choosing a plant for Jill. See you, Dad.' He turned and hurried back to the poinsettias.

'Thanks, Carol.' Angus bent and gave her a peck on the cheek. 'Appreciate all you've done.'

She noticed tears in his eyes as he walked towards the exit.

***

Brenda didn't feel like going home after leaving Damien's. It was dark already at four o'clock. Maybe she'd call in and see Bill for a few minutes.

Bill opened the door. 'Brenda! How nice to see you. I was just thinking about the lovely Christmas Day we had. Come on in. Let me take your coat.'

'I've been at Damien's all day. Minding Jayne,' she said.

'Oh, right. How was it?' He took her coat and hung it on the oak hall-stand.

'Good. Where's Neil?'

''He's at one of his group sessions.'

'Oh?' She raised her eyebrows.

'Yes, you know it's for veterans who have this PS thingy. They get together and talk about how they're coping and do this stuff.' He tapped his forehead.

'Oh.'

'Come on into the warm. I'll put the kettle on.'

'No need, Bill. I only called by to see how you were.'

'Neil shouldn't be long.'

There was such a nice comfortable atmosphere at Bill's, Brenda thought as she started to tell him about her day with Jayne, but he interrupted her.

Leaning towards her, he whispered, 'Just want to tell you something, while Neil's not here.'

'Oh?'

'Top bloke, our Neil.' He seemed to expect an answer.

'Yes, lovely man.'

'He fancies you, Brenda, but he doesn't think he's good enough for you.'

She blinked. 'Really? What on earth makes him think that?'

'Well, he says he has too much luggage and nothing to offer you.'

She frowned. 'Luggage? Are you sure?'

'Yes, love. I've seen him watching you. He's mad about you.'

Just then she heard the sound of the front door opening and closing.

'Is Brenda here? That's her car outside.' Neil came into the lounge and stopped when he saw their heads together.

'What are you two whispering about?'

'Brenda was just telling me about her day. That Jayne sounds a handful all right,' Bill said innocently. He turned to Brenda. 'You must be tired now after a day looking after her.'

'Yes, she's hyperactive and a bit over the top. I feel for her grandmother who usually cares for her in the holidays.'

'Where's her mum, then?'

Brenda started to explain the situation as Neil went out to the hall to hang up his overcoat.

'Sounds like a strange set up,' Bill muttered.

Brenda made to get up. 'Better make a move now, Bill. Lovely to see you.'

'Come any time, Brenda. Always a tonic to see you.'

In the hall she turned to Neil, as he held out her coat. 'Um, Neil, I realized today that what I felt for Damien was just a silly crush. Probably on the rebound after Colin. It was all in my head. The days when he came to the allotment were just to please Jayne.'

Neil smiled. 'As long as you haven't been hurt.'

She blinked. 'Hurt? No, wounded pride maybe, but not hurt.'

'I'm pleased,' he murmured as he helped her on with her coat.

***

Neil went back into the lounge room after Brenda had left.

'Lovely girl that Brenda,' Bill said. 'Reckon she fancies you all right, lad. She doesn't come here to see a boring old fart like me. It's you she comes to see.'

Neil scoffed. 'Oh, Bill, don't be silly.' But he smiled to himself all the same.

'You like her, don't you, lad?'

Neil nodded. 'Who wouldn't like her?'

'Reckon you should snap her up before that Damien bloke does.'

'Hmm. Maybe.' He gave a rueful smile. 'I'm not sure how to "snap" her up, Bill.'

'Well, you ask her out again. Take her to the pictures, or for dinner or something. I dunno. In my day we'd walk out with a girl on a Sunday afternoon. And after a good few Sundays, she'd invite you to have tea with her parents. That kind of put a seal on things.'

Neil laughed. 'I've already had a meal with her mother. And Christmas Day to boot. Does that count?'

''course it does! It was you she wanted! I was only invited to provide a foil.'

'Well, you could have foiled me, Bill!' He laughed at his own joke. 'I'd better get the dinner on.'

'Hold on, lad. Just had a thought. Why don't we invite Brenda and her mum for New Year's Eve?'

Neil froze as Bill continued, 'We could have something simple. No need to make anything fancy. What do you think?' He looked up at Neil. 'You've got Brenda's phone number. Ring her and ask her. Well, she wouldn't be home yet, but a bit later. Have a chat.'

Neil stared at Bill. 'What are you plotting, Bill?'

'Why nothing lad! Just thought it'd be nice to return their hospitality.'

Neil sighed. He'd been planning on New Year's Eve being an early night with ear plugs to stop the noise of the fireworks and midnight horns.

***

Brenda went home thinking about Bill's words. *Was he right? Does Neil really fancy me? And why would he think he isn't good enough for me?* No. Bill had it all wrong.

'Where've you been?' Her mother's querulous voice hit her as she came in the back door. 'I thought you'd be finished at that man's place long before now.'

'I called in to see Bill,' Brenda replied, as she went in to the lounge room.

'Hmph and never mind about your poor old mother! Bill is more important!'

'Well, he's kind and thoughtful.'

'And I'm not?' She scowled.

Brenda was silent. 'I'll get the dinner on, Mum.'

'What are we having, Brenda? I hope it's something I can digest.'

'Not decided yet, Mum. What do you feel like?'

'Do I have a choice?'

'Of course. Left-over turkey or pork chops.'

'I'd like a little bit of roast lamb, but of course, you'd never think to ask me!'

'Mum. The shops are closed.'

'Pork chops then. I'm sick of left-over turkey.'

Brenda hung up her coat and made her way to the kitchen. At least tomorrow she'd be out of the house, even if it was only to look after Jayne.

***

Neil felt unsettled by Bill's suggestion of inviting Brenda and her mother over for New Year's Eve. He had the feeling that Bill's health was failing, even though Bill kept insisting he was fine. He wanted to do everything he could to please Bill, but New Year's Eve? Fireworks! He was afraid he'd make a fool of himself.

He paced around his room, then went out for a smoke. Might be a good idea to contact someone in his support group, talk it over with them. He stubbed out his cigarette and went inside.

***

Carol drove home in a thoughtful mood, Douglas beside her in the front passenger seat, balancing a pot of poinsettias on his lap.

'When can we see Dad again, Mum?'

'Don't know dear,' she answered.

'Can you ask him?'

'He has to go to hospital for treatments.'

'Yes, but will you ask him? And why does he have to get treatments?'

'He's not well.' She jerked her thoughts back to the present. *Was this such a good idea after all? Dougie meeting his father? What if he becomes attached to him and then when Angus dies? Dougie will be devastated.*

'Do I look like him?'

'A bit.'

'Hmm. Clare doesn't look like Jill, does she? Or like her sister.'

'No. Everyone's different, Douglas, love.' She made an effort to change the subject. 'I like your choice of plant for Jill. I think she'll love it.'

'Hmm, I can't wait for New Year's Eve, Mum. Do you think there'll be fireworks?'

'I think we'll be able to see the ones in the park from Clare's house.'

'How many more days Mum?'

'Two.'

***

Amanda sat beside Donald as he drove around checking out the houses for sale.

After the third house, Donald said, 'Not much point in just driving by potential houses, is there? How about we go and see Judy and tell her the good news?'

Amanda smiled. 'Great idea!'

Donald gave a little cough. 'One little thing, my dear.'

Her heart skipped a beat. *Is he going to tell me that he's got a mad wife hidden in his sister's attic?*

'About an engagement ring. My mother gave me her engagement ring just before she died. It was her mother's. My grandmother's. I'd very much like you to have it. But perhaps it's too old fashioned. I'll show you when we get to Judy's.'

'I'd be honoured to wear it, Donald.'

'You're a beautiful woman, Amanda,' he turned his head and smiled at her.

'Watch the road!' she exclaimed as he narrowly missed a bus.

'Sorry, sorry,' he muttered. 'I'm a bit over excited.'

She pressed his knee. 'Me too.'

***

Mary gave Liam directions to the allotment.

'No one else here,' she said as Liam parked. 'That's good, probably because of the hard frost last night.'

She led the way to her plot, Liam looking around at the other gardens.

'I didn't realise it was so big. How many plots are here?' he asked.

'I think maybe fifty … apparently there are some allotments with over a hundred plots. This one is a nice size as there seems to be a great community spirit.'

They approached her allotment. 'It looks so bare,' she said, 'because I've planted all these bulbs and they don't come out until Spring.'

'What's that?' He pointed at one bed.

She walked over for a closer look. One little white flower peeped through the frosty ground. 'Ooh, I don't believe it! They're snowdrops, how lovely.' She beamed at him. 'It makes it all worthwhile. Thank you for bringing me today, Liam. I wouldn't have come otherwise.'

He smiled. 'My pleasure. I knew nothing about allotments so it's an eye-opener.'

She took his arm. 'Let's have a look at some of the other plots.' Her thoughts were all over the place. She couldn't wait to get home and start painting. She visualised a single snowdrop in a stylistic background.

***

Bill heard Neil in his bedroom, talking on his phone. He felt a bit guilty at suggesting they invite Brenda and her mother for New Year's Eve. The fireworks at midnight could send Neil into a tail spin. He knew it would be bothering him. But he had to bring that pair together before he joined Hazel. It had taken a lot of effort on his part to hide his increasing chest pains from Neil.

Once he was gone Brenda would have no reason to come over and Neil would probably end up getting a job at one of those fancy horticultural places. Someone new would take over his allotment, and hopefully it would bring them joy, like it had for him. But he had to work fast at playing cupid. *Queer old cupid I am*! He drifted off to sleep and didn't hear Neil come down the stairs.

The sound of the kettle whistling woke him. 'You making tea, lad?' Bill shouted.

'Yes. Just brewing it,' Neil said, coming into the lounge room. 'Well, it's all settled, Bill. I rang Brenda and she said they couldn't come on New Year's Eve as it would be too late for her mother to stay up until Midnight, but they could come on New Year's Day, if that would be okay.'

'That's a much better idea! Midnight would be too late for me too! I can picture Mrs Evans and myself snoring our heads off, while you and Brenda canoodle on the settee!'

Neil laughed. 'Some hope of that.'

Bill winked and tapped the side of his nose.

***

Carol couldn't stop thinking about Angus; living on his own, going through chemotherapy and all the surgery and treatments with no-one at home to care for him.

She rang Jill. 'Feel like a break, Jill?'

'Always,' came the reply.

'Well, how about coming over for a chat and bringing Clare?'

'Give me ten minutes!'

'Dougie,' she called to him. 'Jill's bringing Clare over to see us for an hour or so. Can you make sure your room is tidy?'

He raced out of his bedroom. 'Really? I'd better change out of these old jeans.'

'Your jeans are fine. Just find a DVD that you think Clare would like and you can watch it together.'

With Dougie and Clare settled in front of the TV, Jill and Carol went into the kitchen. It was Jill's first time in the apartment.

'This is a lovely little place,' she remarked.

'Little is the operative word, but it's all I can afford. It's enough for myself and Dougie. Wine?'

'Yes, please, but tell me all about Douglas's father,' Jill said. 'Douglas rang Clare and told her that his dad was very ill ...'

'Yes.' Carol told Jill about Angus's treatment and living on his own. 'I feel so bad that he has no-one to care for him.'

'Hmm.' Jill studied her. 'How far is the hospital from here?'

'Oh, about one and a half hour's drive, I think.' She stood and paced around the small kitchen. 'Angus is so sorry now about how he left me when Douglas was a baby. What should I do, Jill?'

'Do? Well, there isn't much you can do, is there? I mean, I guess he couldn't come here – for one thing, I don't think there's room, and it's simply too far from the hospital.'

Carol sat back at the table. 'That's what I've been telling myself.'

Jill put her hand on one of Carol's. 'He's not your responsibility, Carol,' she said softly.

'I know. But I still feel sorry for him.' She looked down at Carol's hand. 'I guess I still love him, Jill.'

Jill squeezed Carol's hand. 'I understand.'

***

Brenda couldn't stop smiling when Neil rang to invite them for New Year's Eve. But she knew her mother wouldn't last until after midnight, and would be like a weasel the next day. So, when she suggested lunch on New Year's Day, Neil seemed keen.

Her smiled faded when the thought occurred to her that perhaps Bill had put Neil up to it. She wouldn't put it past the old man.

Anyway, it would be a break from staying at home listening to her mother grumbling about the rubbishy programs on the television.

One more day with Jayne would get her out of the house and then school would start the first week of January. She couldn't wait!

***

Chapter Thirteen
January – another year

The Allotment

New Year's Day. Doesn't mean much to me. The Winter Solstice is really the start of the new year. But these modern times! No one here. Not surprised, heavy frost last night.

"January grey is here,

Like a sexton by her grave..."

Percy Bysshe Shelley, Dirge for the Year 1821

***

Bill enjoyed New Year's Day. Brenda had rung back and asked if they could bring Edith Milson. 'Of course,' he'd said. Neil had laughed. 'Two women competing for your favours, Bill.'

Bill had appreciated the joke. But it had all gone well. He'd tried to get Neil and Brenda some time alone together but it had been difficult. Brenda's mother was such a killjoy, wondering what Brenda was doing when she'd gone out to the kitchen to help Neil.

***

Neil was on edge, waiting for that stray firework which would give him a flashback and send him under a table or something equally ridiculous.

Brenda came out to the kitchen carrying a tray of plates and leftovers. 'Lovely meal, Neil. Thanks so much.'

'A pleasure, Brenda.' He took the tray from her. 'New year resolutions?'

She laughed. 'Gave up on them, years ago. How about you?'

He studied her. 'Secret!'

She smiled. 'Not fair!'

He turned away from her and bent over the kitchen sink where he started to scrub a cooking pan. 'Got some news,' he muttered.

She moved closer. 'Did you say you had news?'

'Yes.' He turned to face her. 'I've been offered a job.'

'That's wonderful, Neil!'

'Yes. Assistant Gardener at the local Council.'

'Brilliant!' Her eyes shone as she ran over and gave him a hug. 'Well done! And you'll still be here to care for Bill!'

He nodded, and smiled, his wet hands held out from his sides.

'What does Bill think?'

He bent back over the sink, 'Haven't told him yet.'

'Why not?'

'Wanted to see if you think it's a good idea before I tell him.'

'I think it would be great, you'll still be here in the evenings to look after him. I'm sure he'll be delighted for you!'

'Thanks, Brenda. It's a start. There are lots of jobs in the horticulture field but not around here at the moment.'

He dried his hands and turned to her. She was close, smiling up at him, he moved towards her, about to kiss her when the sound of her mother's voice made her jump away.

'Brenda! It's time to leave.'

'Coming, Mum. Just helping Neil clear up,' she shouted back.

He shook his head.

***

Brenda was annoyed with her mother; she was sure Neil had been about to kiss her.

'Thanks for the lovely day, Neil. Sorry we have to leave now. Mum has her routine and it's time for her afternoon nap.'

'I understand. Bill has a nap in the afternoons too.'

'When do you start the new job?'

'I'll check with Bill first that he's happy about it. Means I won't be able to drive him to the allotment during the week, but not much is happening there at the moment with this cold, wet weather. But if he's happy, then I start the week after next.'

'Brenda!' Her mother's voice was even louder.

Brenda rolled her eyes at Neil. 'Coming!'

***

Amanda couldn't wait for the next get together with her friends. They'd booked a table at a trendy restaurant for a New Year's Day lunch.

She purposely timed her arrival to be a few minutes late.

'Hello, ladies! Happy New Year!' She smiled at the four women already seated at the table. She slipped off her coat, hung it on a nearby coat stand and took the remaining seat.

'Happy New Year, Amanda,' they responded, as they watched her sit down at the table.

'What's that on your ring finger?' Jocelyn exclaimed.

Amanda held out her left hand and wiggled her fingers. The diamonds surrounding the sapphire stone sparkled. 'An engagement ring,' she said nonchalantly.

'What?' There was a chorus of disbelief.

'Yes, I've just got engaged to a wonderful man. Donald, Royal Navy, retired.'

'Where did you meet him? How long have you known him?' The questions came thick and fast.

'He's got a plot on my allotment, had it for nearly a year.'

'Why haven't you let us in on this before, Amanda?'

'Nothing to tell, it was just a simple friendship until just before Christmas. Came out of the blue, really.'

'When's the happy day, Amanda?'

'Not decided yet. We've been looking at houses, so probably once we find a place to live, we'll name the day.'

'Hmm, so this is the result of a new hairstyle ...'

'I think I'll have to get a plot on your allotment, if that's where the eligible men are to be found,' said Jocelyn. 'Right, let's order and you can spill the beans, Amanda. Tell us all about this handsome sailor of yours.'

****

Carol didn't know whether to ring Angus and wish him a Happy New Year. It might be his last, and the year probably wouldn't be very happy with all the pain and discomfort associated with chemotherapy and radiation. In the end she rang him to simply ask how he was.

'Okay, thanks, Carol. It was so lovely to see you last week, and to meet Douglas. Thank you again for agreeing to it.'

'No problem.'

'How did your friend like the poinsettia?'

'She loved it.' She tried to think of something else to say. 'Um, when is your next chemo?'

'Thursday.'

She could think of nothing else to add. And apparently neither could Angus. 'Right. Well, keep in touch. Douglas is anxious to meet with you again.'

'Really?' She heard the pleasure in his voice.

'Yes, he couldn't wait to tell Clare all about you.'

'Thanks. Carol, maybe weekend after next? I guess he's back at school this week.'

'Yes. Okay, I'll be in touch to make arrangements. Bye for now.'

She ended the call, feeling she'd done her duty.

***

Bill enjoyed the New Year's Day lunch.

'Well done, lad,' he said when their guests had left. 'That was excellent! Think I'll have a little snooze now.'

'That's good, glad you enjoyed it, Bill.' Neil paused. 'Um, Bill, just wanted to tell you I've been offered a job.'

'Oh?' Bill sat upright in his reclining chair.

'Yes. Assistant gardener with the council.'

Bill flopped back in his chair. 'That's great news, Neil!' He beamed.

'Just wanted to make sure you're happy with it. Means I won't be able to drive you to the allotment or to your medical appointments.' Neil frowned at his hands.

'That's no problem, lad! I don't want to go to the doctor anyway, and the allotment? Well, it's January and not much is happening there at the moment! Good on you, lad, that's great news.' He smiled. 'Did you tell our Brenda?'

'Er, yes. I wanted to see if she thought it was a good idea before I asked you.'

Bill beamed. 'And she said yes?'

Neil nodded.

'Great girl, our Brenda.'

****

Brenda cheered up when school restarted. At last, she was out of the house. It had been hard over Christmas; her mother constantly carping. With the cold, damp weather the only bright spots had been Christmas and New Year's Day with Bill and Neil.

Jayne came running towards her the first day of term. 'Miss Sevens! You didn't come to us for Christmas and New Year's Day!'

'I know, Jayne,' she said, trying to peel the girl off her. 'But you must have had a lovely Christmas with Granny and your dad.'

Jayne screwed up her face. 'It was okay, I guess, but not the same without you, Miss Sevens. Dad missed you too!'

Brenda's heart twisted. 'I'm sure your dad wouldn't have missed me!'

Jayne put her head on one side. 'I think he might have.'

'Run along to your class now, Jayne.'

Brenda watched Jayne skip along to her form room.

****

Neil started his new job. The Head Gardener set him to pruning hedges around a park.

'Nice work,' the Head Gardener commented when he caught up with Neil in the afternoon.

'Thanks,' Neil felt a glow of pride at the praise.

'Was a bit wary about you in the beginning,' the head gardener said. 'Thought you might be one of these NHS people who think they know it all just because they have a certificate.

'I'm keen to learn different ways,' Neil said.

The Head Gardener nodded his head. 'That's the spirit.' He moved on.

Neil's first thought was that he'd love to share this with Brenda. *You're a hopeless case, Neil!*

***

Mary began her art class. She'd made a few attempts at painting a lone snowdrop against a dark earth background but somehow it hadn't worked. She took her canvas in to class. The teacher had been pleasantly critical.

'You're trying to run before you can walk,' she'd said. Then turned to face her. 'But at least you're making an effort. That's good.' She smiled and went to the next student.

***

The Allotment 6th January. The twelve days of Christmas have ended for another year, not that it affects the allotment. Everyone is supposed to take down their decorations before today, but I've heard some lazy people keep theirs up all year!

***

Brenda finished work early on Wednesdays, so decided to call into Bill's on her way home.

He seemed delighted to see her. 'Come in, Brenda, love,' he smiled as he opened the door. 'Been wondering how you're going now you're back at school.'

'Good, thanks, Bill.' She hung her coat on the hall stand.

'Come into the lounge, it's nice and warm there,' he said.

'I was wondering how you're coping without Neil.'

'Well, I miss him, that's for sure, but I'm so pleased he's got that job. He needed to get out and meet people and put what he's been learning into practice.'

She nodded. 'Do you need anything from the shops, Bill? I can go now.'

'No, love, Neil did a big shop at the weekend, and I think he's got everything organised.' He shuffled in his reclining chair. 'Tell you what, Brenda, a cuppa would be nice.'

She jumped up. 'I'll put the kettle on.'

He beamed. 'I'm getting lazy in my old age!'

The kitchen back door opened as Brenda filled the kettle and Neil came in.

'What a lovely surprise! Hello Brenda.' He grinned. 'Making me a cup of tea, are you?' he said as he bent down to take off his boots.

'Just called in to see Bill.' She plugged in the kettle. 'Nice to see you, Neil.'

They stood looking at each other for a few seconds, then Bill's voice came from the lounge room.

'Is that Neil come home? Thought I heard voices.'

Brenda went to the kitchen door and yelled, 'Yes, Bill, he's here now.' She turned to Neil. 'How's the job going?'

'Good. It's nice to be out in the open and working, although not so pleasant in this wet weather. I've been in the plant shed all day, potting up seedlings. It's quite therapeutic. How's school?'

'Definitely not therapeutic!' She laughed as she poured boiling water into the teapot.

'Um, you have to work with Jayne again?'

She nodded, 'Yes, she's as frenetic as ever.'

'See anything of her father?'

'I saw him the other day when he came to pick Jayne up from school.'

He raised his eyebrows.

Brenda laughed. 'No heart stopping moments, Neil!'

She thought he seemed relieved.

'You two still canoodling out there, Brenda? The tea will be stewed,' Bill shouted.

She felt her cheeks redden as she poured the tea. 'Coming Bill.'

Neil's hand brushed hers as he took two cups from her. It made her heart thump.

***

Mary was pleased with her snowdrop painting. Her art teacher had shown her different methods for a background. At home she'd experimented with mixed media. The time had flown by. She realised she hadn't thought about Peter all the time she'd been painting. She looked forward to going to the allotment to see what other bulbs had emerged.

***

Carol arranged to meet Angus again at the garden centre.

'I know it's a long drive for you, so you're welcome to spend the night at my place,' she told him. 'I spoke to Douglas and he said you can sleep in his bed and he'll sleep on the couch.' She laughed. 'He seemed quite excited at the thought. He wants to bring Clare to meet you if that's okay.'

'I'd like that. Thanks, Carol.' She thought he sounded pleased. When she rang Jill to ask if Clare could come over and meet

Angus, Jill immediately invited them over to their place and stay for dinner.

'Thanks, Jill. That would be great. I'm already having second thoughts about Angus coming here for the night. I don't know what to talk to him about.'

'I guess it's difficult after so long, what did you say? Thirteen years?'

'Yes.' She sighed, 'But I think it's important for Douglas to know his father. He's very excited.'

Jill laughed. 'I think Clare is a bit bemused. She was asking me why Douglas hasn't seen his father for such a long time. I didn't know what to say, so I quickly changed the subject.'

'Yes, it's a difficult question to answer. I'll try and think of a good reason and get back to you! Thanks, Jill.'

It was a tricky one, Carol thought. Douglas had accepted that his father wasn't dead after all, simply pleased to meet him.

***

Bill felt frustrated. His efforts at bringing Neil and Brenda together had come to nothing.

He lay on his reclining chair watching the midday news on the television. Now that both Neil and Brenda were working, he had no opportunity to pursue his match-making activities. He pursed his lips, annoyed. The weather was miserable. He looked at his photo of Hazel and wished he could join her.

'Soon, Hazel, love,' he murmured, 'but I have to get Neil and Brenda together. It's obvious they're made for each other.' He closed his eyes. The television bored him.

***

Neil had spent the whole day bending over a work bench potting up seedlings and his back ached. The benches were too low for someone as tall as he.

He saw the house in darkness as he walked down the garden path from the garage to the kitchen door. Only the flickering light of the television in the lounge was visible; the curtains not drawn. He grimaced, Bill was usually in the kitchen when he came in from work, the kettle on ready to make a pot of tea.

He opened the back door, hurriedly pulling off his boots. 'Bill?' he called. No reply. Not waiting to put on his slippers, he ran to the lounge and turned on the light. Bill appeared to be fast asleep, his chin on his chest.

Relief flooded him. When Bill didn't stir, he went over and took his hand. It was cold and limp. Then realisation dawned. Bill had died.

He was overcome with a wave of emotion – his eyes filled with tears. He'd seen plenty of dead bodies, most of them with horrific wounds. He took a few deep breaths then, after a few moments, he pulled himself together and tried to think what he had to do. His mind blanked. How would he tell Brenda? She'd be devastated. He should ring Bill's doctor. He reached for his phone and scrolled through the list of contacts. A voice answered.

'Hi Neil! I've just walked in the door.'

'Brenda.' Somehow, he'd rung her number instead of the doctor's.

'What's wrong, Neil?'

'It's Bill.'

'Bill?'

'He's dead, Brenda.' His voice was flat. 'I thought I was ringing the doctor. I didn't mean to ring you.'

There was a pause. 'I'm on my way over.'

He heard her calling out to her mother, then the call ended. He rang the doctor then sat with his head in his hands until he heard the front door bell. He jumped up and opened the door. Brenda put out a hand to him, then walked past him into the lounge room.

She stared at Bill's body for a few moments. 'Did he die in his sleep?' she murmured and turned to him. 'Doesn't look like he was in pain.'

'I should never have taken this job and left him all alone to die,' he muttered.

'Did you ring the doctor?'

'Yes, someone is coming as soon as possible.' He sat back on the settee and Brenda sat beside him. She suddenly started to cry, great ugly sobs. Neil put his arms around her and held her close.

There was a knock on the front door and it opened. A voice called, 'Hello? Doctor Davis here. Can I come in?' A woman's voice.

Neil stood, 'Yes, in here.' He was relieved that she was Bill's regular doctor.

Dr Davis came in bringing a blast of cold air with her.

Neil watched as the doctor pulled the blanket from Bill's legs and examined him. 'By all appearances he died in his sleep – heart just stopped,' she said. 'When did you last bring him in to see me?'

'Before Christmas. I took him in to get the ulcer on his leg checked.'

'That's right.' She lifted one of Bill's feet and pushed up the trouser leg. 'I remember now. And he was supposed to go for tests. I was concerned about his heart.'

'Other leg,' Neil said. 'Well, he refused to go for those tests.'

She sighed, examined the other leg and nodded. 'Healed nicely. Well, it looks as if Mr Thompson died peacefully in his sleep.' She glanced at Neil. 'You're his family?'

'No, but I,' Neil didn't know how to describe his situation. 'Well, I lodge here and Bill is, I mean, was, my friend. He doesn't have any family. At least, not that he's mentioned. Um, I'm Neil Blakey. This is Brenda Evans.'

The doctor nodded. 'That's right, I remember now, you brought Bill in to see me.' She frowned. 'About what time did you find him?'

'Just before I rang the surgery, I've been at work all day and just come in.' He looked at his watch. 'Maybe half past four.'

'Do you know if he ate lunch?'

Neil frowned. 'I usually leave something prepared for him, like soup that he just has to heat up.' He stood. 'I'll check.'

He went out to the kitchen. The saucepan of soup he'd left was on the stove, untouched.

'No. He didn't eat lunch,' he said as he went back into the lounge. 'But it looks as if he had a cup of tea at his usual time around ten o'clock, as there's a mug in the kitchen sink.'

'Then he probably died between ten and lunch time.'

Brenda blew her nose and wiped her eyes. 'What do we do now?' she quavered.

'Probably easiest is to ring a funeral home. They'll organise things for you.' She pulled a pad and a pen from her brief case. 'Because I saw him only a couple of weeks ago, I can write the death certificate now.' She sat in front of the coffee table.

She held the completed form out to Neil. 'Sorry for your loss.' She returned the pad to her case, snapped it shut and stood.

He took the form and went to the front door with her. 'Thank you, Doctor.' He closed the door behind her.

'Did Bill mention any funeral plans, Neil?' Brenda asked.

'He made a will several months ago, but he didn't say anything about funeral arrangements.'

'What about when his wife died?'

Neil frowned. 'I'll ring Anna. She might remember.'

***

Brenda stayed silent as Neil contacted the undertaker – his sister had supplied the details.

'They'll come soon,' he said.

'I'll stay with you until then.'

'Your mother will be hopping if you don't go home.'

Brenda shrugged. She found a sheet in the linen cupboard and draped it over Bill's body. 'Rest in peace, Bill,' she muttered.

Neil drifted around clenching and unclenching his hands. 'I think I need a strong drink.'

Brenda went to the kitchen. 'I'll put the kettle on. Do you know where Bill kept his will?'

'In one of the drawers in the sideboard. He told me to go and see the solicitor who made out his will when his time came.'

She found a bottle of brandy in the pantry. 'Here you go, Neil.' She handed him a glass. 'I'll just have a cup of tea.'

They sat in silence until the doorbell rang.

'Undertakers,' Neil muttered, jumping up to open the door.

Half an hour later Bill's body was on a stretcher and being wheeled out to the waiting van.

'Bill may have left instructions for his funeral in his will,' Brenda said.

'Hmm.' He went to the drawer and rummaged around the collection of old letters and invoices.

'Here it is.' He held out an envelope. 'It's got the solicitor's card attached to it.' He slid the card from the paper clip. 'I'll ring first thing in the morning.' He put the envelope back in the drawer.

'What about your job?'

'I'll go into work and ring from there, solicitors won't be open until nine. I can explain to the head gardener.' He glanced at his watch. 'It's late. You'd better go home, Brenda.'

'I don't like leaving you on your own.'

He smiled. 'You're the best, Brenda.' He gave her a hug. 'But you look exhausted. I'm fine. You go home and get some sleep. I'll let you know what happens.' He took her hand and led her to the front door. He paused and looked at her. Taking a deep breath he took her in his arms and kissed her.

***

Neil poured himself another brandy and slumped onto the settee. Bill's empty reclining chair seemed to reproach him. His phone rang. His sister.

'Neil? Has the undertaker been?'

'Yes.'

'Then come over here for tonight.'

'I'm okay, Sis. Anyway, I've had a couple of brandies. Can't drive.'

'I'll come and get you.'

He couldn't face the thought of meeting Tom. He'd probably make a few snide remarks.

As if she read his thoughts, she said, 'Tom's in bed, asleep.'

'Thanks, Sis, you're a star, but there's a few things I have to do here, and I've got to leave early for work tomorrow morning.'

'Okay, then, take care.'

He was suddenly overwhelmed with exhaustion. He went up to his room, undressed and fell into bed.

***

Carol rang Angus the morning of their next meeting. 'It's pouring rain here,' she said. 'Probably not a good idea to meet at the Garden Centre, unless we just have a coffee there and then come back to my place. It's only five minutes' drive.'

'Good idea,' he said. 'I wasn't looking forward to wandering around looking at plants in the rain.'

'I won't bring Douglas. He's cleaning his room, making it all nice for you.'

'That's kind of him. Oh, Carol, how can I make it up to him?'

'You already have – just by coming into his life.'

There was silence and then she heard him blowing his nose.

'Thanks, Carol. Anything I should bring? Pillow? Blankets?'

'No, all good. Douglas has a brand-new sleeping bag that he got for Christmas. He's bursting to use it. Actually, yes, bring a pillow.'

***

Neil made an appointment to see Bill's solicitor for later in the afternoon after he'd finished work.

He changed out of his work clothes and took the envelope containing Bill's will from the drawer.

He hadn't long to wait to see the solicitor.

'Mr Blakey?' She held out her hand. 'Delia Humphries. Come this way.'

He followed her into her office and sat on the chair she indicated.

'I assume you're aware of the contents of Mr Thompson's will?' She sat behind her desk, pushed her glasses up her nose and picked up a slim folder.

'I have it here,' he said, laying the envelope on the desk between them. 'Haven't looked at it. Bill's private business.'

She smiled. 'I've just been refreshing my memory. Lovely man, Mr Thompson.'

'Yes.'

'Well, you do know that Mr Thompson left you everything? Apart from a few bequests.'

Neil frowned. 'What do you mean?'

'He's left you all his worldly goods, house, contents, car etc.'

His frown turned into a scowl. 'I can't possibly accept that.'

She burst out laughing. 'Mr Thompson said you'd probably say that. If you read the copy you have, you'll see that he says you brought joy into his life and made it bearable after the loss of his wife. He was so grateful for the way you cared for him.'

'It was a pleasure. He helped me in more ways than I helped him.'

'Well, the fact is, these are his last wishes.'

He raised his eyes to meet her gaze.

'He also asked that you would have him cremated, and scatter his ashes in Llandudno, on the ocean, the same as you and he did for his late wife.'

Neil shook his head in disbelief. Then he stood and paced around the small gloomy office. He barely noticed the shelves stacked with legal books.

Delia Humphries watched him, then said, 'Would you like a cup of coffee, Mr Blakey?'

He shook his head and returned to his seat.

'Can I get out of it? Get out of this bequest, I mean.'

'Well, I suppose you could sell everything and give the proceeds to charity but Mr Thompson was adamant that he wanted you to have everything. I think it would be disrespectful not to follow his wishes.'

'It's been a shock,' he muttered. 'So, what do I do now?'

'As the executor, you can leave everything to me. There may be death duties to pay.'

She picked up a pen. 'I need a few details from you. Have you organised a funeral director?'

He nodded.

'They will clarify all the details. You have to take the death certificate to the Registrar of Births, Deaths and Marriages and register the death within five days of the death. Only then can you have the funeral.' She opened a drawer in her desk and took out a booklet.

'This explains everything you have to do in the event of a death in the UK.' She slid the booklet across the desk to him, rose from her chair and walked around her desk.

Neil stood.

'I'm sorry for your loss, Mr Blakey, but Mr Thompson had a great deal of pleasure making this will. He chuckled several times and said he'd like to be a fly on the wall and see your face when you found out.'

She picked up his copy of the will and took his arm. 'He thought the world of you. Told me you were like a son to him.' She led him out of the office. 'We'll be in touch.' She handed him the envelope.

Neil managed to mutter his thanks and left, pausing outside the office to blow his nose and wipe his eyes.

***

Carol's stomach churned on the drive back from Jill's. Angus sat beside her with Douglas in the back. She couldn't stop thinking that inviting Angus to stay the night had been a stupid thing to do.

'You'll be sleeping in my bed tonight, Dad.' Dougie tapped Angus on the shoulder.

'Yes, that's very good of you, Douglas. I hope you'll be comfortable sleeping on the settee.'

'I got a sleeping bag for Christmas. Mum and I are going to go camping in the summer holidays and I want to get used to sleeping on the ground.'

'Perhaps the settee will be more comfortable,' Angus turned his head to Dougie.

'Maybe you could come camping with us, Dad.'

Carol swallowed hard and stared straight ahead, thankful she was driving.

'Maybe I could. I'd like that, Douglas.'

Later that night, after Douglas had given in and gone to sleep on the settee, Carol said goodnight to Angus. 'Hope you sleep well, Angus. Call me if you need anything.'

'Thank you, Carol. I'll be fine.' He went into Dougie's room and closed the door.

She lay in her bed, unable to sleep, her brain jumping from Dougie to Angus to Jill and Norm and back to Angus. She tossed and turned, debating whether to get up and make a hot drink, then heard scuffling noises from Douglas's room and the door opening.

She slid out of bed, grabbed her dressing gown and opened the door. She saw the shadowy figure of Angus going down the stairs. Silently she followed him.

'Are you okay, Angus,' she whispered, trying not to wake her sleeping son.

'Oh! Carol! You startled me. I was looking for my overcoat to put on the bed. Sorry but I was very cold.'

'Oh! I don't have any spare blankets. This place is so small, I only keep the minimum.'

Angus was shivering. 'It's okay, I'll just put my overcoat on the bed.'

'Wait!' She went up to his room and took the doona from the bed.

'Come into my room and sleep in my bed,' she whispered from the stairs. 'I'll put Douglas's doona over you. With two doonas you should be much warmer.'

'Are you sure?' He seemed surprised.

She nodded, and led the way. 'Here you go. Get in that side and I'll cover you up.'

He did as she said and then she slid in beside him. 'Lucky I kept the queen-sized bed,' she murmured.

She lay rigid, trying not to touch him, then she moved towards him and wrapped her arms around him. When she heard his breathing change to a slow rhythm, she was able to relax and fall asleep.

***

The Allotment - "It is deep January. The sky is hard. The stalks are firmly rooted in ice." – Wallace Stevens

I heard poor Bill had passed. There's an atmosphere of gloom over the whole place. But it's January and a gloomy month anyway.

***

Neil rang Brenda. 'Bill's funeral is next month, 5th of February,' he told her. 'Apparently a lot of people die after Christmas and New Year, and there's a waiting list – it's hard to organise funerals ...' his voice trailed off.

'Oh, Neil! It must be so hard for you – so much to organise. Can I help?'

'You already have,' he replied. 'Just being there for me.'

'Oh!' He heard the surprise in her voice. He couldn't believe he'd actually said that, but it was true. He suddenly realised that he wanted her in his life – wanted to be with her.

'That's a nice thing to say, Neil.'

'Well, right, we'll talk soon.' He waited, not knowing what to say next.

'Okay, Neil.'

'Bye then.'

'Bye.'

***

Brenda ended the call. *That was a lovely thing that Neil said, about being there for him ...*

'Brenda! Who was that you were talking to?' Her mother's voice broke through her thoughts.

'It was Neil, Mum. Just ringing to let me know that Bill's funeral is next month.'

'Humph! Well, I won't be going. Not in this awful weather. Terrible month for a funeral. Not that I cared much for the man anyway. Thought he was quite a vulgar person. But mustn't speak ill of the dead.'

Brenda shrugged. 'Of course, Mum. Not good for you to go out in the cold and wet.' *Just as well.*

'And that Neil! He'll be all over you now. I saw him looking at you on New Year's Day. Trying to get around you. And now that man has passed away, he'll have nowhere to go, and I bet you anything he'll be like that Colin, making up to you and next thing he'll be wanting to come and live here!' Her mother paused for breath. 'Well, I can tell you, he's got another think coming!'

Brenda stood still. *Had Neil been looking at me? Trying to get round me?* She hadn't told her mother about Neil inheriting Bill's house. It would only have led to a lecture about rogues and thieves influencing old people to change their wills. Neil wasn't like that. *Had he been "looking" at me on New Year's Day?*

She pinned up a notice about Bill's funeral in the shed at the allotment. She hoped people would see it. Bill had been very popular. She wandered around the allotment looking at various plots. It was February now. Not much happening. She caught sight of Paddy Murphy and hailed him.

He looked up as she approached and nodded.

'Hello, Paddy. I've just pinned up a notice about Bill's funeral. It's on Tuesday at eleven o'clock. Will you come? I could pick you up. I'd be pleased to have your company.'

Neil had told her about Paddy's car accident. Apparently, he hadn't driven since.

He nodded. 'I live near here. I'll be waiting by the allotment shed.'

Chapter Fourteen
February

The Allotment.

"February is a suitable month for dying. Everything around is dead, the trees black and frozen so that the appearance of green shoots two months hence seems preposterous, the ground hard and cold, the snow dirty, the winter hateful, hanging on too long."- Anna Quindlen, "One True Thing."

***

Neil walked behind the coffin. From the corner of his eye, he spotted Brenda in one of the front seats in the crematorium, Paddy Murphy beside her. She'd said she was going to bring him. He slid into the seat next to her. She took his hand and squeezed it. *Bill would be pleased.* He still hadn't come to terms with the will. He now owned the house, everything in it and Bill's car. There had been so much paperwork to fill out, but the solicitor had been very helpful.

At last it was all over. So many people from the allotment had come. He saw the Warden and the Admiral – he still couldn't think of Donald Jenkins as anything other than the Admiral – Mary Flynn, Carol and Douglas, his sister, Anna, even Edith Milson – and many others whom he didn't know. He'd been asked to give a eulogy. Anna had encouraged him and Brenda had helped him write it. He'd choked up as he read it out.

He wondered if he should have organised some kind of funeral meal afterwards but Brenda hadn't been in favour of it. He was glad now; he didn't feel up to chatting and being sociable.

What would he have done without Brenda through this difficult time? He took her hand as they walked out to their cars. Bill's car …

'Thank you, Brenda.'

'For what?'

'For being here. For being with me.' He turned to her, his hand about to lift her chin and kiss her when a voice interrupted them.

'Oh, Brenda! That was such a lovely funeral! And Neil, your eulogy was wonderful!'

It was Edith.

'Thank you, Edith. Can I give you a lift home?'

'Thank you, Neil. That would be most kind. Bill was a lovely man. So many mourners.' She sniffed and dabbed at her nose with a lace handkerchief.

He looked at Brenda. She smiled, took his hand and gave it a gentle squeeze.

He opened the passenger door for Edith, got in his car, took Edith home, then drove back to Bill's house.

***

The Allotment – Full circle. It was last year when I started this journal. It's Easter now and things have changed – like the seasons. Lots of the allotmenteers saw little Brenda's note in the community shed and went to Bill's funeral. Now there's a woman working his plot. I heard her telling Brenda she was from Sudan and would be growing vegetables that she couldn't buy here.

The warden has given up her ground, she's moved to Donald Jenkins's plot and another allotmenteer has taken over her plot and the warden duties.

Peter's widow seems happier. Her bulbs are a great success, I was a bit dubious at first, but now the daffodils are a golden carpet and the tulips are a rainbow of colour. Lots of visitors have come just to see them.

And little Brenda and Bill's helper, Neil, seem to have joined forces. Neil is often working on her plot with her. They seem happy, always laughing. I noticed them holding hands at times.

Dougie has grown, he works on Carol's plot and sometimes a girl joins him. Clare, he calls her. I see a man sometimes with them. He looks very ill. Reminds me of Mary Flynn's husband, Peter, before he died.

The seasons change – life goes on.

About the Author

Lyn Behan grew up in the English West Country. She spent her working life as a systems analyst and computer programmer in Europe and Australia.

She now lives on the south coast of NSW with a variety of chooks and dogs.

If you enjoyed this book, please give a review at your point of sale. You may also enjoy her other books:

The Men and the Medium - When radio inventor and spiritualist medium, Leslie Carter, meets the beautiful psychic medium, Lily Bancroft, he knows she's his soulmate and he could love only her. But Lily is focused on becoming a healer and spiritualist medium. Through two world wars and three marriages, she struggles to fulfil her dreams. Leslie stands by her as each of her marriages fail. Will his love ever be returned? Based on a true story.

Seeking Samuel Goldberg –In 1965, on the day of her beloved grandfather's funeral, Liesel discovers that she has Jewish heritage – a family secret held since the days of Nazi Germany – and learns of her grandfather's unfulfilled quest to find family members missing since the outbreak of World War Two. After an unfortunate love affair, Liesel takes on the task of locating her father's cousins, using the few clues her grandfather left. Her travels from Sydney to England and Germany bring her more that she could ever have expected.

Stolen Love, Fractured Lives – An incurable hereditary disease haunts the lives of three generations of women and the men who love them. Add a stolen baby to the mix to make a tangled web of lies and deceptions.

The Unpredictable Past – When a mysterious man, Will, moves into the house opposite hers, Elizabeth's quiet village life is turned upside down. Their friendship develops when Will helps with researching the involvement of one of her ancestors, Edward, in the last revolution in England. This friendship sets the neighbours gossiping and infuriates Elisabeth's daughter, who is convinced Will is a con man preying on her mother, thus raising doubts in Elizabeth's mind. Elizabeth and Will delve more into the past and attempt to solve the mystery surrounding the death of Edward's son, Edmund. How can Elizabeth find out the truth about Will? Is he who he seems?

Acknowledgements

Thank you to my wonderfully patient beta readers: Trish Behan, Shirley Gould, Sylvia Mason, Jennifer Smith, Barbara Spence and Dell Brand.

Resources

One True Thing – Anna Quindlen
My Life on a Hillside Allotment – Terry Walton
The Allotment – David Crouch & Colin Ward
A Million Bullets – James Fergusson